A DANGEROUS ENCOUNTER

There was a shout, then the screams of outraged horses as the driver of the chariot hauled his animals back. Anqet ducked to the ground beneath pawing hooves. The horses reared and stamped, showering stones and dust over her.

From behind the bronze-plated chariot came a stream of oaths. Someone pounced on Anqet from the vehicle, hauling her to her feet and shaking her roughly.

A string of obscenities rained upon her. The retort she thought up never passed her lips, for when she raised her eyes to those of the charioteer, she forgot her words.

Eyes of deep green, the color of the leaves of a water lily. Eyes weren't supposed to be green. Eyes were brown, or black, and they didn't blaze with the molten fury of the Lake of Fire in the *Book of the Dead*. Anqet stared into those pools of malachite until, at a call behind her, they shifted to look over her head.

"Count Seth! My lord, are you injured?"

"No, Dega. See to the horses while I deal with this, this . . ."

Anqet stared up at the count while he spoke. He was beautiful. Exotic and beautiful, and wildly furious.

"You're fortunate my team wasn't hurt or I'd take their cost out on your hide."

Anqet's temper flared. She forgot that she was supposed to be a humble commoner. Her chin came up, her voice raised in command.

"Release me at once."

HEART OF THE FALCON

ACKNOWLEDGEMENTS

It is difficult to acknowledge everyone who contributed or influenced the writing of this book, for they include the many people who in some way helped me decide to write. The most important of these is my spouse and best friend, Wess Robinson. It was he who first urged me to write and wouldn't let me quit when I got discouraged. The encouragement and support of my family has made me realize how lucky I have been to be surrounded by people who love to read—my beloved mother, Ann Heavener, Brian O'Doherty, Ann O'Doherty (critic and editor), and Nancy and Russ Woods.

Hand-in-hand with all this personal support came the professional expertise of a wonderful agent, Cherry Weiner. I would like to thank several talented editors, including the one who first bought this manuscript, Leslie Cheeseman, as well as Becky Cabaza and Jackie Dowdell. Each has made the publishing process both a pleasure and an invaluable educational experience.

A final thanks goes to those teachers and professors of anthropology and archaeology whose training enabled me to bring to the reader a glimpse of everyday life in ancient Egypt. To communicate the essential humanity of these forebears has been a lifelong goal.

Suzanne Robinson

Heart of the Falcon

Suzanne Robinson

BANTAM BOOKS
New York • Toronto • London • Sydney • Auckland

To Wess

HEART OF THE FALCON
A Bantam Book

PUBLISHING HISTORY
Bantam paperback edition / May 1990
Bantam reissue edition / January 1997

ISBN 978-0-553-38131-3

Published simultaneously in the United States and Canada

Bantam Books are published by Bantam Books, a division of Bantam Doubleday Dell Publishing Group, Inc. Its trademark, consisting of the words "Bantam Books" and the portrayal of a rooster, is Registered in U.S. Patent and Trademark Office and in other countries. Marca Registrada. Bantam Books, 1540 Broadway, New York, New York 10036.

PRINTED IN THE UNITED STATES OF AMERICA

146659772

1

Year Six of the Reign of the Pharoah Tutankhamun

It was the fourth month of the season of Shemou, the season called Drought; the time of harvest. Anqet sat in her father's workroom beside the scribe Nebre and let her eyes run down a column of figures. Nebre's voice droned in her ears like the ceaseless creak of a water lift, but Anqet paid no heed. Memories of the hours spent in the room with her father crept upon her. They had shared so much: mornings filled with the simple yet pleasurable tasks of record keeping, the challenge of obtaining the best exchanges for the year's harvest of wheat, moments of laughter and joy. She could almost hear his deep, quiet voice—even now, though he was with her mother in a modest tomb set in the cliffs at the edge of the desert, overlooking the estate he loved.

Anqet's father had named their home Nefer after the amulet that brings happiness and good luck. When she had asked why, he had smiled and glanced at her mother.

A cough brought Anqet back to the present. Nebre was looking at her. His wrinkled brown hands with their prominent veins toyed with the reed brush he had been using to tally the week's threshing. Anqet smiled at the worried expression on the steward's face.

"I'm sorry, Nebre. What were you saying?"

"Mistress, perhaps you are weary?"

"No," she said. "The work helps. I need to be busy." Anqet played with the knot in the linen scarf that crossed her shoulders and tied at her breast. "I was remembering."

1

"Yes, mistress. I too remember. Your father was a kind man. His journey to the arms of Osiris will be a swift and easy one." Nebre looked directly into Anqet's eyes. "But I think you worry about the visit of your Uncle Hauron too. He is a stranger."

Anqet's reply was interrupted by the entrance of a plump woman with graying hair and the manner of a harassed mother quail. "Thinks he can come here with his dogs and his chariots, stinking of foreign scent," the woman said.

"He?" asked Anqet. "Bastis, it isn't Hauron, is it?" She wasn't ready to see this mysterious uncle.

"No, lady, that Lord Oubainer is here again. Wouldn't go away. I told him you were busy, but he says he'll wait. If he waits long, I'll have to purify the reception room of his smell."

In spite of her relief that the visitor wasn't Hauron, dismay crowded on exasperation as Anqet listened to her old nurse. Not Oubainer again. In the four months since her father's death, the man had offered marriage three times.

"Bastis, please," Anqet said. "Get rid of him."

The nurse folded her arms across her chest and scowled. "He heard that you refused that nice boy Menana last week."

"I've refused others."

Bastis nodded. "That's the trouble. You promised your father you'd marry."

The nurse pursed her lips. Anqet prepared for another lecture, rolling her eyes toward Nebre in mute appeal. Nebre was the only one who could temper his wife's tirades. Nebre opened his mouth, but he was too late.

"That's the trouble," Bastis said. "You refused Menana. You refused old Lord User-het. You refuse everyone. Oubainer thinks you mean to impress him with your desirability."

Anqet gave another exasperated sigh.

"You'll do more than sigh if you don't settle on a

husband, my girl," Bastis said. "You're seventeen and
blessed by Hathor with beauty. You've got a productive
estate and no parents. If you don't choose before your
uncle gets here, you may not get a chance. Hauron will
pick a husband for you."

"That's enough," Anqet said. "We've sailed this route
before. I'm not leaving Nefer, and all those men want me
to give up my home. I want someone who understands
how important Nefer is to me. Other women run estates
alone." She stood up and shook out the white folds of
the gown that fell to her ankles above small sandaled
feet.

"Widows and mature women guide their own holdings, not little girls."

Anqet sighed. "Go tell Oubainer I'll be with him
soon. I want to comb my hair."

"Little Heron," Nebre said. "Willfulness is a fault that
will get you into trouble."

Anqet met the glance of the old man. She grinned.
He had repeated her father's habitual warning. She gave
her customary reply.

"I'm not willful. I just know what I want."

She hurried out of the room and down the hall to her
chamber. It was a room of modest proportions, barely
large enough to contain her low bed, the sheer-curtained
canopy that formed a small room around it, her cosmetic
table, and a few chests that held her clothing. Anqet loved
the room, for her mother had hired a gifted painter from
the city of Memphis to decorate it with scenes of the
gardens and fields of Nefer. Each morning, sunlight illuminated the rich greens and earth-browns of the wall
panels. The artist had captured the living hues of the
fields that stretched from the house to the banks of the
Nile.

Anqet settled before her cosmetic table and lifted a
mirror of polished bronze to her face. Large black eyes,
darker than the Black Land—the fertile soil of Inundation—
glowed at her. Anqet scowled at her reflection. She always
thought of her eyes with dissatisfaction because their

ebony was marred by flecks of golden brown. They reminded her of the enormous eyes of the monkeylike creature of the night she'd seen at the market in Memphis.

Making a face at herself, Anqet took a brush and dabbed at the dark lines that highlighted each eye. She regarded her handiwork but quickly lost interest in the fragile jawline and wide, full mouth. She ran a comb through her hair. Shimmering black like the Nile on a moonlit night, it fell in a curtain almost to her shoulders. Anqet tossed the comb down. She wasn't putting on a wig or jewelry for the likes of Oubainer.

Her guest was waiting for her in the columned reception hall. Anqet choked as a whiff of powerful scented oil reached her. She peeked around the edge of the door at Lord Oubainer. Owner of one of the largest holdings in the Memphite nome, Oubainer was fortunate in his riches, for he had little else to recommend him. He was of middle height (Anqet was taller) and sagged at the waist like a half-filled sack of barley. He had stringy, sparse hair covered by a fat wig and a short beard at the tip of his chin that curled in little fashionable ringlets as though it were a nest of miniature snakes.

Anqet wouldn't be concerned with his less-than-handsome exterior if it weren't for the fact that, like his dress, Oubainer's personality was overdone. The man was full of tiresome enthusiasms, the most prominent of which was his social position. Oubainer had a country estate, a townhouse, and princely connections—and he made sure that all knew that he possessed these things.

Anqet muttered to herself: "Smelly old baboon."

She shoved away from the door and stepped into the reception hall. Oubainer occupied her father's favorite high-backed chair of ebony. The chair had slender legs fashioned in the shape of lion paws, and it creaked with the strain of his weight. Anqet hastened to make her presence known so that the man would get up. He struggled to his feet, sloshing wine from the goblet he held onto the woven mat that covered the floor. Some of the wine trickled down the pleats of his kilt.

Anqet waited for him to recover his composure. Sometimes she felt sorry for Oubainer. It must be disheartening to try so hard to be elegant and fail so completely.

Oubainer brushed droplets from his chin and raised his goblet to her in a toast to her immortal soul.

"To thy ka, beautiful Anqet."

"You honor me, Lord Oubainer," Anqet said. "I was going over my accounts with Nebre. Your visit is unexpected."

"Ah, lady, it saddens me to hear the things you are forced to endure."

"Endure?"

Oubainer sidled up to her. A wave of perfume made her hold her breath.

"Yes. I have come to offer you relief from the burdens you bear with such courage. I know how great is your worth as a bride. I was foolish not to realize it before, and I'm willing to offer much more."

"Oubainer, I have refused the honor of becoming your wife, now that your first lady has gone to the netherworld. I haven't changed my mind."

"But you haven't heard my offer." He held up his hand before Anqet could interrupt. "I realize that you fear becoming the wife of a man with no position in the Two Lands. I do have quite a few concubines. And, after all, you are young and lovely, and deserve a position of importance. I assure you that in my house you will have that position. You'll have your own servants, your own rooms separate from the harem, as many clothes and jewels as you wish, and you won't even have to help run the household. You will live in comfort and leisure." Oubainer said this last with a flourish of his bejeweled hands, as though bestowing a godly favor.

Anqet shook her head. The life Oubainer described might suit his idea of what a woman desired, but it filled her with disgust. She couldn't think of anything more deadening to the spirit than hour after hour, day after day, spent in trivial occupations and self-indulgence.

Oubainer continued with a smirk. "And I will allow you to keep this house."

"Allow?" Anqet's patience began to evaporate.

"My only requirement of you is that you give me a son."

"Oh."

Oubainer nodded, his oiled face registering solemn regret. "You see, my wife gave me three daughters, but no sons." The man put his hand on Anqet's bare arm. "My dear, I must have a son to provide for my ka in the afterlife. Surely that is obvious."

"I understand your concerns, but I don't wish to be the one to provide you with a son."

Anqet pulled her arm from Oubainer's grasp and walked to a bronze stand that held the wine ewer. She poured herself a drink in an eggshell-thin pottery goblet. She gasped as she felt Oubainer come up behind her and pull her into a clumsy embrace. She twisted to face him. With her free hand, she pushed at his sagging chest.

Oubainer thrust his face at her and mumbled, "You're so lovely. I can make you happy. I may not have the form of a young man, but I know what pleases a woman. Let me teach you."

Anqet dropped her goblet. Wine splashed across the mat and onto Oubainer's toes. But he didn't notice, for his hands were busy running down her throat to her breast. Anqet growled, balled her fist, and shot it deep into the man's stomach.

"*Uf!*" Oubainer backed away from her and gripped his middle.

"Fruit, my lord?"

Bastis had appeared with a tray of candied fruits. She thrust it at the man.

His lordship puffed and heaved for a few moments before snarling at Bastis. The nurse bent low with humility and spilled the sticky contents of the tray onto his wine-drenched feet.

By this time Anqet had recovered from her outrage

and stood trying not to howl with laughter. She went to
the chair where Oubainer's enameled fly whisk lay. She
handed the object to her visitor.

"Please forgive me, my lord," she said innocently. "I
was quite startled." Anqet took Oubainer's arm and led
him to the sunlit portico at the front of the house. "You're
discomforted. Perhaps it is best if you seek the advice of
your physician."

"But you haven't agreed yet," Oubainer said. He
stepped into his waiting chariot.

"And I won't. Again, thank you for the honor and the
offer."

Anqet stepped away from the chariot. Oubainer's
servants took their positions behind him. Left with no
choice, the man took up the reins.

You're a stubborn girl," he said. His eyes traveled
from her head to her feet, taking in the full breasts and
small waist. "But you're worth the trouble it will take to
amend your manners. I will speak to your uncle when he
arrives. May thy ka find contentment, lovely Anqet."

She watched Oubainer disappear down the avenue of
sycamores that lined the approach to Nefer. His threat to
speak with her uncle Hauron brought back the grief and
anxiety she had controlled all morning. Seeking peace for
her troubled ka, Anqet turned back to the house and let
her glance take in the beauty of the only home she had
ever known.

Built of white-plastered mud brick, Nefer was surrounded by a high enclosure wall. Gardens rich in sycamore, acacia, and tamarisk trees stretched to either side of
the main house. The front loggia of the house rose two
stories and was supported by fluted wooden columns with
capitals designed in the shape of a lotus bud. The whole
structure gleamed white, except for the borders of red and
blue at the top of the house. Inside, the reception chambers, master's suite, guest rooms, and servants quarters
boasted murals showing scenes of wildlife and the cool
refuge of the gardens.

Anqet started toward the house but hesitated. Bastis

would be waiting for her. She turned aside and took the path to the artificial pond at the back of the house. The smell of fresh water drew her to the edge of the papyrus-fringed pool. Lotus blossoms floated on its surface, and fish swam in its depths. Anqet nodded at the slave who swung the counterweighted water bucket to irrigate beds of oleander and jasmine.

She found a shaded spot under a sycamore and propped her back against its trunk. No one would disturb her here. She closed her eyes and let her mind flow back to her past, to the home her father had left her and how to keep it. All her life Anqet had lived at Nefer under the loving protection of her parents, Rahotep and Taia. It seemed an enchanted life, now that she looked back on it. The family rarely left their modest estate south of Memphis, preferring the peaceful, unpretentious life of the countryside to the cosmopolitan bustle of the great city of the god Ptah to the north.

Unlike many girls, she learned to read and write the sacred hieroglyphs, to go hunting and fowling, and to manage a large household and its dependents. She could supervise a banquet for the landowning friends of her parents and yet was equally at home in the marshes on a papyrus-reed skiff using her throwing sticks to bring down wild ducks for the household larder. And through all the years of her childhood beat the cyclical pattern of life on the Nile: Inundation, the time of life-giving flood that brought a new coat of silt for the land; Emergence, when the fields emerged from the water ready for planting; and Drought, the season of harvest.

Yes, her life at Nefer was good, but she knew now that there was some mystery about it. For she and her parents lived far away from her father's family and never saw them. Unlike her friends, whose families were large and closely dependent upon one another, her own seemed a single water lily in a pond with no buds or branches. That isolation had been brought home to her when the first letter from Hauron arrived.

She was eight years old when Rahotep brought the

folded and sealed bundle to her mother. Lying with her head cradled in Taia's lap, Anqet listened while the two adults spoke.

"She sleeps?" Rahotep asked.

"Yes."

"This is from Hauron."

Anqet heard the crack of the seal on the letter. Rahotep and Taia were quiet.

"He wants to see me," Rahotep said. "It's hard to believe, after all this time. He says he's forgiven us."

"He has forgiven us!"

"Shhh."

"My love," Taia said, "it was Hauron who took offense. You both courted me. I chose you, and he acted as if I had questioned his virility."

"He was hurt. And anyway, Hauron was always difficult. He turned night into day and day into night at the slightest provocation. I could never be sure of him."

Taia laughed. "Then I don't see how you can be sure of his intentions now. It was he who asked us to leave the Delta. I remember that evening. He was full of three jugs of beer, staggered into our chamber and ordered us off his land, the land of your own father and mother."

"I know," Rahotep said. "Drink turns Hauron into a scorpion, but he says in the letter that he regrets his cruelty, and after all, we're well off here at Nefer. Taia, I must see him."

"Of course. I won't try to stop you. It's only that..."

"Say what you mean."

"I can't, because I'm not sure. Hauron always made me uncomfortable, and at the last, I was afraid of him."

Anqet shook her head clear of the memory of that night. Neither parent would ever answer the questions she later asked about that whispered conversation. They allowed it to fade from her mind, replacing it with dolls and lessons and outings. Life resumed its peaceful cycle, and Anqet forgot to ask what happened when her father made his trip to the Delta to see his brother.

Not even the great events taking place in Thebes had disturbed the tranquillity of Nefer. Far to the south, when Anqet was eleven, Pharoah joined the gods. There was rejoicing throughout the land. Rahotep said it was because the heretical pharoah had cast down the old gods in favor of Aten, the sun god, and persecuted the ancient ones who had protected the Two Lands since the beginning of time.

Now the young king Tutankhamun had brought back the old ways. No longer did the priests of Ptah, Osiris, and Amun-Ra go in fear of their lives. The humble man was free to worship whatever god he chose. The Living Horus, Tutankhamun, protected the Two Lands. After years of neglect, Egypt's empire had a pharoah who stood against the incursions of northern barbarians and who prayed to the chief god, Amun-Ra, his father. But these great events touched Anqet not at all. Her world was Nefer.

A deep breath of air scented with water called Anqet back to the garden. Order and regularity. She loved the order and regularity of her life at Nefer. Crops were sown, tended, and reaped. Linens were made; gardens were cultivated—all according to ancient practice. She could depend upon the unchangeable character of these activities. They gave structure to life, just as hieroglyphs could give structure to thoughts.

This beloved, structured world had changed three years ago when Mother conceived the child for whom they had all prayed to the gods. For a long time Anqet had wanted brothers and sisters like those of her friends. Big families were exciting; there was always someone to talk to, someone to do chores with, someone to fight with. Yet not until Anqet was on her way to becoming a young woman were the family's prayers answered.

Then one day she returned to the house from a ride in the desert to find the female servants wailing and Nebre waiting at the door, his wrinkled face pale. Ignoring her anxious questions, he led her to her father's chambers.

Rahotep was on his balcony staring down at the gardens below. Anqet called to him. He turned, and she saw tears streaming from his eyes. He held out a hand. When she came to him, he gathered her in his arms.

"Little Heron," he said in a broken voice, "your mother is dead. She miscarried the child and—there was bleeding. So much blood, so much."

Rahotep's arms trembled, and Anqet felt his body shake as she braced herself to accept his weight. Rahotep leaned on her, and they wept.

After Taia was gone, Rahotep's life-force had faded. Where once he was as steady as the prevailing north wind, now he fluttered and faltered like the sail on a becalmed vessel. Anqet tried to comfort him, to take her mother's place in some small way. Gradually Rahotep responded, taking pleasure in her company. But six months ago he began to grow weak, although he was only thirty-four. He wasted away before Anqet's eyes. A permanent cough took hold of his body, and he suffered from fevers.

When he could no longer leave his bed, Rahotep sent for several of his friends, including a priest of the god Ptah, and put his seal and name to his will. Anqet was to have Nefer and rule it in his place. At the same time, he sent for his brother. Anqet couldn't see that Hauron was needed. He had never bothered to visit in all the years she'd been alive. There wasn't anything he could do, and she secretly harbored a resentment of him from her childhood. He'd been unkind to her father and mother.

"Be patient, Little Heron," Rahotep told her. "I wish to bid farewell to him, no more. He will come and be gone quickly."

Hauron sent word that he was coming. His letter reached Nefer three days before Rahotep died and sparked a bout of worry that took badly needed strength from him.

Anqet sat beside her father after reading Hauron's letter. Rahotep was in one of his fevers. Anqet dabbed at his brow with a wet cloth.

"I don't know. I don't know," Rahotep said. "Read the last few sentences again."

"'I grieve for you, my brother. I will come as swiftly

as the Nile can carry me, and I will atone for my neglect. Have no fear for your daughter. May Osiris welcome you.'"

Rahotep moved his head restlessly. "I don't like this atonement. I shouldn't have written. Shouldn't have. But he was so contrite."

"What's wrong?"

"I don't know. Nothing perhaps." Rahotep was stopped by a fit of coughing. When he resumed, his voice was thin and weak. "Your mother didn't trust Hauron. It may be that her ba spirit warns me. You don't know Hauron. Strange notions come to roost in his heart. I fear for you."

"Fear?" Anqet put a wet cloth to her father's brow and shook her head.

"I should have foreseen."

Anqet had to lean down to catch her father's words.

"Marriage. That will be protection."

"I don't understand," Anqet said.

"For protection. Marry, Little Heron. In the Two Lands young girls are under the protection of the men of their family. No judge of pharaoh would leave you by yourself if Hauron were to challenge your right to govern Nefer."

"Don't worry so, Father."

Rahotep caught Anqet's hand and lifted his head, his eyes burning with the intensity of his fever. "There is need for worry. I should have remembered what Hauron is like. I should have prepared, chosen for you. Too late." Rahotep gasped, then coughed, long, throat-tearing seizures that ended only when he lost consciousness.

Anqet's eyes filled with tears as she remembered the way her father had suffered from fear for her yet longed to find his beloved Taia. In the end, she had promised to marry so that Rahotep could let go of life peacefully. She drew her knees up, rested her arms on them, and lowered her head. An ache rose in her throat, and her body shook with sobs. She had loved her father, and he had left her—almost gladly—for the shadowy world where her mother dwelt. She was alone.

*   *   *

On the eighth day following the visit of Lord Oubainer, Anqet was out in the fields watching the last of the wheat harvest being winnowed. Lines of tenant farmers stretched before her, heads covered against the dust. She watched, mesmerized by the rhythm of the workers as they bent, scooped a load of heavy grain and light chaff into wooden troughs, and tossed it in the air where the two components separated in the wind. It had been a good harvest. None of her people would go hungry. The house of Rahotep fed its own, down to the last and lowest slave. Only in a lame year did her people suffer. Then, if the flood came late, or too little, all suffered.

"Mistress, mistress!"

The son of the cook trotted up to her. He was covered with sweat and breathed heavily. Anqet caught his arm and laughed.

"What's wrong, Isesi? Did Bastis catch you stealing pomegranates again?"

Isesi grinned at her. "No, mistress. I was waiting for you to help me like you promised." The boy's grin disappeared as he remembered his mission. "Bastis says you must come. Lord Hauron's yacht is downriver. She says you must come immediately."

She ran all the way back to the house, Isesi at her heels. Bastis waited for her in the bathing chamber adjoining her room. The nurse pulled her out of her old coarse linen shift and herded her toward the stone-lined cubicle where a maid waited to pour water over her. Anqet gasped at the shock of the water on her warm skin.

"A fine mess you'd be in if I hadn't sent someone to look out for that boat and give warning. Look at you. Hair all wild, dusty and sweaty. Your mother would have taken a fit if she'd seen you. What if her ba spirit is flying around here right now?"

Anqet patted herself dry. She barely heard Bastis's ranting. She wondered what this uncle would be like. Would he understand that she wanted to remain at Nefer? Underlying her curiosity was a vague sense of dread.

Rahotep had died tormented by concern for her, and that concern had to do with Hauron.

She stood still while a maid dropped a pleated sheath of fine linen, sleeveless and formfitting, over her body. It wasn't as sheer as the see-through creations worn at court, but its delicate weave clung to her breasts and hips. Bastis fastened a broad collar about Anqet's neck. Fashioned of gold inlaid with dark blue lapis lazuli and turquoise, it covered her shoulders and chest almost to her breasts.

She fastened matching bracelets on each wrist and took up her mirror. Deftly she applied touches of eyepaint of green powdered malachite and lines of black with powdered galena so that her eyes took on an almond shape. Meantime, Bastis bound her wet hair and settled a wig on her head. Its black tresses fell well past her shoulders. Anqet took up an obsidian jar containing jasmine perfume and dabbed some at her temples, throat, and wrists. Last, she slipped into delicate leather sandals.

"How much longer do I have?" she asked as Bastis returned from the reception hall.

"He's on his way. I'm going to the kitchens. Nebre is waiting for you." Bastis looked her up and down. "For once you look like a lady."

Anqet tossed a black lock over her shoulder. "I am a lady."

"Only when you have to be," Bastis said. She hurried away with Anqet's laughter rippling after her.

Anqet joined Nebre on the portico. The steward craned his neck and stared down the sycamore avenue. Rounding the corner formed by the avenue and the path to the back fields was a long procession headed by a chariot that glinted bronze in the sun's rays. Anqet squinted. Surely all of those people couldn't be in Hauron's party. Three less elaborate chariots followed the one occupied by her uncle, and behind them trotted pair after pair of kilted and robed retainers. Hauron hadn't come with just a yacht, but with a fleet that bore servants, chariots, and horses.

Anqet bit her reddened lips. Had the man brought his whole household? Did he intend to move to Nefer?

The chariot came to a halt before the steps of the portico. A man wearing a shortsleeved robe and heavy gold jewelry threw the reins to a groom and stepped to the ground. He set one foot on the steps, looked up at Anqet, and stopped. As his people fell into line behind him in silent attention, Hauron continued to stare—his mouth open, his eyes narrowed as they took in the sight before him. A gust of wind molded Anqet's sheath to her hips and legs. Hauron swallowed.

"Taia?" he whispered.

She shook her head.

"Of course not," he said. "Anqet, brother's daughter, I give you greeting."

Hauron stooped and touched his cheek to Anqet's. Startled, she bore the familiarity for a moment before disengaging herself. Except for Oubainer, who hardly counted, the only man who had ever held her was her father. Together, Anqet and her uncle turned and walked into the house while Nebre took charge of Hauron's servants. As they moved toward the coolness of the reception room, Hauron began to apologize for his absence from her father's deathbed.

"You know that we fought long ago? But that no longer matters." Hauron drew in a long breath and let it out. "Though it grieves me, I know that it was the will of the gods that Rahotep died before I could reach him. It took much longer than I thought to arrange everything."

Anqet furrowed her brow. She paused in the doorway. "What arrangements are you speaking of, Uncle? Those for your visit?"

"No, such details are safely left to underlings." Hauron turned back and smiled down at her. "No. I meant the arrangements for your quarters at my house and the hiring of a staff to run an estate this large. I couldn't leave Nefer in the hands of just anyone. Surely you realize that you must come to live in my household."

Anqet's heart thudded in her breast. She opened her

mouth to object, to correct the misunderstanding. Her eyes caught movement on the portico outside. Nebre stared at her over the shoulder of one of Hauron's guards. Anqet suddenly noticed how many of her uncle's entourage were soldiers. Any well-to-do citizen traveled with some protection, but Hauron had brought at least fifteen henchmen, each armed with bow or spear. It occurred to her that Hauron traveled with a great many warriors for a visit to a dying brother.

Don't be such a donkey. The man is cautious, that's all. And you should be cautious too. He thinks he's going to order your life for you.

Under the pretense of giving instructions to a serving girl, she studied her guest. Hauron was a larger, older duplicate of her father. Where Rahotep had been slender, Hauron was thickset. Although he was tall, his musculature was of the sort that ran to fat without constant exercise. His brows arched high on his forehead as though he were continually surprised, but his face was square like her father's. Hauron possessed Rahotep's thin wide mouth. Lines of temper, or perhaps severity, marred the skin on either side of his lips, and he carried the air of one who expected obedience.

Anqet turned back to her uncle. Again she found him staring at her. Puzzled, she met his intense look. Hauron's face was flushed. His jaw tightened, and he appeared determined to strangle the beaded belt at his waist.

"Are you ill, Uncle?"

Hauron wet his lips. "Weary perhaps."

"I have refreshment waiting. If you will honor my house?" She gestured toward the reception room where ale and food awaited.

Hauron indicated that Anqet should precede him. He bowed as she passed and caught a whiff of jasmine and freshly laundered linen. He barely managed to keep his hand from reaching for the girl as she went by.

She was even more beautiful than her mother had been. He hadn't been prepared for it. He had not thought

Isis would bestow her favor upon another as she had upon Taia. Those breasts. Each was a full, ripe lotus bud. He felt a tingling heat in his loins as he watched Anqet bend over a side table heaped with food. Her robe clung to her hip and leg, exposing the lines of her body.

It wasn't fair to be so cursed twice in his life, cursed with a demon's obsession for a woman unavailable to him. At least this one wouldn't humiliate him by refusing to—

Hauron's thoughts scattered as he watched Anqet move. He drew nearer, his eyes fixed again on the swelling abundance of his niece's breasts. He took a goblet of ale from the girl but stayed next to her while she filled a plate with food for him. He edged closer as Anqet stood with her back to him. When she would have turned with the plate in her hand, he caught the dish from her and managed to move at the right moment so that she backed into him. He felt her softness meet his hips and opened his eyes wide. What was he doing? Did she suspect what he felt?

"Forgive me, my child. I am clumsy with fatigue."

Hauron smiled beneficently at the girl's flushed response. He took a chair opposite hers and waited for a servant to place a table before him.

He waited also for his desire to cool. It did not. He had known it wouldn't. Hauron's smile became a fixed, immobile thing. He stared at the food before him without seeing it. He would instruct his scribe to hurry the arrangements for the transfer of responsibility for the estate. He wanted to get away as soon as possible. Already he endured the tortured memory of a desire unfulfilled. If he didn't leave soon, he would die of this torment.

Only after Anqet left him did he realize that he was taking the source of his obsession with him.

2

Anqet stood at the prow of Hauron's yacht, her back to her uncle and his crew She held her shoulders straight and her head erect and clasped her hands together to still their trembling. With her father's death she had thought the worst that could befall her had happened. She'd been wrong. Wrong, and stupid.

Hauron had ruthlessly taken control of her home, her servants, and herself, and there was nothing Anqet could do about it. Rage welled up in her as she remembered Hauron's words when she defied his orders to leave Nefer to live with him. At first he'd been patient. He attributed her defiance to grief over Rahotep's death. When she refused to agree with him, Hauron dropped his solicitous facade.

The scene was etched in her memory as if it were a sacred carving hewn on the wall of a temple. Hauron had sent for her the morning after his arrival as though he were the master of Nefer and she the guest. He received her on the veranda that looked out on the garden.

"We have nothing to say to each other, Uncle. I'm staying here. I love Nefer, and I have a responsibility to my people."

She tried to turn away, but a callused hand caught her bare arm in a grip that bruised. He smelled of beer. His face, an echo of the proud visage of her father, was distorted with rage.

"I'm tired of arguing with you. No, don't try to get away. You'll only hurt yourself." Hauron smiled when her arm fell limp. "I don't have the time or the patience to humor your odd whims. I'm your only male relation. That means I stand in your father's place. You know this to be true. You owe me obedience as you would owe it to him, and your life and your possessions are mine to dispose of until you marry."

Anqet spat her words out. "Then I'll marry."

Hauron shook his head.

"I don't think so. Not until I give the matter the study it deserves. You're coming home with me. One of my scribes will remain to administer Nefer in my name."

Anqet wrenched free and faced him.

"You can't keep me if I don't want to stay," she said.

"Oh?"

The soft, pitiless monosyllable made her lift wary eyes to her adversary. Hauron moved toward her. His voice was low, but there was no mistaking the danger in it.

"I will dismiss your precious Nebre and Bastis. I'll dismiss the household staff, the tenants, the grooms, the cooks. I will sell off the slaves to the nearest overseer. And if you are still not repentant, I'll sell your lands and destroy this house."

If Nefer were destroyed, who would see to her parent's tomb and provide the necessary prayers and offerings that protected their souls?

"And if I go?"

"Everyone may remain, under my control."

And so she had left. Anqet closed her eyes and listened to the water lapping against the sides of the boat as the current took her north, into the Delta. Hauron had allowed Bastis to accompany her but no one else.

This was the evening of the second day of the voyage. During most of the trip, she had stayed as far away from her uncle as possible, speaking to him only when she couldn't avoid it. She ignored the curious and covertly admiring glances of Hauron's men and kept to herself, either in the cabin set amidships or at the prow behind the ship's lookout. Bastis stayed with her, a silent, belligerent chaperone.

For his part, Hauron watched her constantly during the day. He spent his days prowling about her with a cup of wine in his hand and his nights avoiding her in favor of his beer jug.

Anqet opened her eyes. To her left, the solar disk sank toward the horizon. The sun-god Ra had almost completed his daily journey, and light would soon give way to the darkness of the evil god Seth. Hauron barked an order. The yacht, a shallow-bottomed river craft, would be beached for the night. Few traveled the river in darkness, for the chance of running aground in the uneven depths of the Nile was too great.

"Little Heron."

Anqet jumped. She hadn't heard her companion approach. Bastis snarled at a crewman who passed them on his way to the stern. The man hurried away from them. Taking advantage of their isolation, Bastis whispered to Anqet.

"There is trouble."

Anqet's lips stretched into a wry grin. "I know."

"No you don't, child." The woman placed a hand on Anqet's arm. "You're so busy hating him that you don't see. But I do. I've seen him looking at you. I've seen him touch you, pretending clumsiness. Anqet, that dung-eater is dangerous."

"You don't think I know that?"

Bastis groaned and shuffled nearer. She pulled Anqet down until her lips were near her charge's ear.

"Foolish girl. Hauron wants you. He burns with lust. Mark me. He forced you to come with him for that reason, not because he thinks your proper place is with him or because it's his duty. I'm sure of it."

Anqet's eyes widened. She looked down at Bastis and shook her head, but she knew that her old nurse spoke the truth. In a heart's beat, her father's anxiety became clear to her. Remembering his concern that she marry for protection, she groaned aloud. Bastis grunted in reply and headed toward the cabin. Anqet followed, taking care to avoid her uncle as he sat on his stool in the pavilion of brightly colored hangings that stood in front of the door.

Before she crossed the threshold, Hauron called to her. She turned but remained in the doorway. She could see that he was already into his second jug of beer, but he had a great tolerance for the stuff. It must flow in his veins.

"Niece, we will be spending the evening ashore." He lifted a cup to his lips before speaking again. "I have lands near this village and would speak with my overseer of the fields. Prepare yourself. We leave immediately."

Behind her she heard Bastis curse. Anqet nodded to Hauron and ducked into the cabin. It took only a few minutes to don a fresh robe. Distractedly, Anqet snapped on hinged bracelets of gold and red jasper. There was a matching necklace, a pectoral in the shape of a falcon with outspread wings. Her fingers were cold as they arranged the crimson and gold pendant so that it rested between her breasts. As her hand touched the falcon, it pressed into the softness she had always taken for granted.

Damn him to fiendish torments. Damn him for making me feel unclean with his gaze.

"I don't like it," she said aloud. "This visit to the overseer of the fields."

"Neither do I," said Bastis as she combed Anqet's hair.

The woman sank to her knees. "You remember my cousin Tamit who went to serve Lady Gasantra in Thebes?"

"What?"

Bastis grasped Anqet's hands in her own. "My cousin Tamit. You must remember. She made a wig for one of your dolls before she left."

Anqet shook her head, her nerves on edge. "What are you trying to say?"

"I'm trying to help you. Tamit lives in the household of Lady Gasantra in Thebes. Gasantra is a rich woman of the court. Thebes is a great city, a city where one can hide. If we must, we can go to Thebes, to Tamit. The Lady Gasantra lives near the palace, in the Street of the

Scarab. Hauron would never find us there. Will you remember?"

"Yes. But I don't think he'll approach me until he gets me to his house."

Hauron's deep voice boomed outside the door. Her uncle's chariot and horses were brought ashore, and Anqet found herself Hauron's passenger. She cast an apprehensive look over her shoulder at the array of merchants ships, barges, and small reed canoes docked along the village shore. Aboard the yacht, Bastis stood at attention, her hand lifted in salutation. The woman's lips formed a word, but Anqet couldn't hear her over the barks of a foreman directing his crew to unload a cargo of oil and wine.

Hauron stepped into the chariot, in back of her, and grasped the reins of the team of horses. With a jerk that threw Anqet into his chest, he set the team prancing through and out of the village. She could smell the beer, even though she faced away from the man.

Anqet watched patch after patch of stubbled fields go by. Here in the Delta, the Nile deposited its soil in a wide fan instead of a narrow strip along the river bank. They passed more fields and herds of oxen on their way to byres near the village.

The sun had burst into a red death over the horizon by the time they clattered up to the overseer's house. Hauron left Anqet in the chariot while he went inside. He returned immediately with the overseer and helped Anqet to the ground. The overseer nodded to Hauron as he jumped into the chariot and drove off before Anqet had time to protest. She turned to Hauron. He had left her and was entering the house.

Anqet watched the receding vehicle. Perhaps the man was going to care for the horses and would bring them back later. She followed Hauron into the house.

The overseer's residence was a two-story mud-brick rectangle much like other village houses. Hauron waited for her in the combination storage room and office that made up most of the first floor. Beckoning to her, he led the way to the second floor where food and drink waited in a small living area. The whitewashed room was littered with reed mats and brilliantly colored cushions. Pottery lamps cast uncertain light, but it wasn't so dark that she couldn't see that there was no one else in the room.

"Where is everyone?" she asked.

Hauron delayed answering her until he had poured them each a glass of beer. He downed his own before answering.

"The family will be staying in the village for a while." He refilled his glass.

Anqet set her glass down without tasting the beer. "Will your overseer be long attending the horses?"

"I told him to come back in a few days."

"A few—why?"

Hauron sighed and set his beer down on the floor. Instead of replying, he stalked toward her. Anqet backed away until she was near the stairs. Hauron saw her intent and halted his advance. Still he said nothing. He merely stared at her.

Anqet could almost feel his gaze on her body. His eyes traveled from her face, down her neck, to her bosom and hips, and back to her face.

"No," she said. She raised her voice. She repeated the word with finality. "No."

Hauron's face was flushed now, his eyes hungry. "That's what she said eighteen years ago."

Anqet watched Hauron wipe a film of perspiration from his upper lip. Raising his hands, Hauron lifted his wig from his head and tossed it to the floor. His hair was streaked with gray like the black granite near the First Cataract.

"I'm sick of this obsession," he said.

"Uncle, I wish to return to the yacht."

It was as if she hadn't spoken. She didn't think he'd heard her at all.

"You won't refuse me as she did. You're so like her. You're even more beautiful."

Hauron's hand shot out. He grasped Anqet's wrist and pulled her to him. Anqet cried out and struggled to free herself, but Hauron caught her in both arms and crushed her to him, fastening his lips over hers in a savage kiss. He tasted of sour beer. Her fingers curled into claws, and Anqet dug them into the bare skin of her uncle's arms. He grunted and forced her arms down to her sides, pinning them there.

"Ah, Taia, you were always such a fierce little thing."

Anqet went still. She stared up at Hauron. "I'm Anqet."

Hauron pulled her closer to him until she could feel a hard pressure between her legs. He laughed raggedly. "I know who you are, but it pleases me to think of you as Taia. I live with her memory day after day, and since I saw you, drink no longer brings relief. It only allows the demon to settle more firmly in my loins."

Hauron smiled at Anqet while she gawked at him in disbelief. "I loved Taia, but she preferred the gentle Rahotep to me." Hauron tightened his arms around Anqet. "After all this time, I thought myself free of her, but over the last days I learned that the only reason I've been free of torture was because I never saw you." Hauron put one hand across her buttocks and pressed Anqet into his erection. His eyes closed, and he sucked in his breath. "Feel the demon you set loose inside me. By the gods, I can think of nothing but pleasuring myself with you. My phallus has swollen to the size of a bull's, and I can't endure the pain any longer."

Anqet writhed, fighting to escape this man and his ugly words, but Hauron caught her chin and drew her face close to his.

"Taia," he said. "You're going to help me get rid of the demon, and you'll enjoy doing it. You'll see. I'm much better than my dreamy oryx of a brother."

"No!" Anqet screamed.

She clawed and bit and kicked at Hauron as he half dragged, half carried her toward a pile of cushions. He lifted her off her feet, tossed her on the soft mountain, and dove at her before she could regain her balance. Anqet saw his body coming at her and in a reflex action lifted her feet and kicked straight at the man's groin. When Hauron crumpled to the floor, Anqet darted away from him, grasped an ale jar from its stand, and crashed it over her uncle's head. Amber liquid and shards of pottery sprayed her face and gown, and Hauron lay silent and still, blood oozing from the deep cut on the back of his head.

Anqet stood over him, panting and waiting. Gradually she realized that he wasn't going to get up. Then the isolation and helplessness of her situation overcame her, and she doubled over in tears. In that room filled with the smell of beer and old food, she cried until she had no tears left. After a while, she drew an uneven breath, straightened her shoulders, and began to think. First she must get away. Hauron's injury would keep him from pursuit for many hours. She wasn't sure how long he would be unconscious, but he wouldn't be able to travel for a while. He had arranged for this isolation. No one would come to help him for days. She would find a place to hide and then try to think of a way to help herself.

Having a plan was a great comfort. Sheltered and protected she may have been, but her parents had given her the skills to think for herself. She would use them. Swiftly Anqet explored the house for what she would need. She could hardly travel alone dressed in jewels and a fine gown. She found an oversized coarse sheath, a scarf to cover her shoulders, and a head cloth. She removed her jewels and sandals and thrust them in a sack along with some food and a bronze knife. Hauron was sleeping peacefully. Anqet hesitated before wrapping a clean cloth over his wound, then ripped a linen sheet and tied his hands and feet and gagged him. Dousing the lamps, Anqet pattered down the stairs and out of the house.

Many days later, Anqet stood in an alley near the palace district in the western section of the city of Thebes. Her journey had been a slow one, filled with agonizing delays. She had returned to the village where her uncle's yacht lay, even though she could not contact Bastis. She had to travel south to Thebes, and the only way to do that was by boat. Anqet sought out the company of a barber and his family on their way from Tanis to their home south of Thebes.

The barber had a modest craft, big enough to carry himself, his wife, and their eight children. She paid for her passage with her gown. Her jewelry was too valuable for such an exchange and would have caused unwelcome speculation about where she had obtained it. So she sailed with the barber and his brood, and they stopped frequently for the man to ply his trade in exchange for fresh food. Until she finally reached Thebes, with each day that dragged by, Anqet expected to see Hauron's yacht oaring after her.

Thebes, City of a Hundred Gates, home of Pharaoh, home of the great god Amun-Ra. The capital stretched along the east and west banks of the Nile in hodgepodge splendor. On the east bank lay the temple of Amun-Ra in its own miniature city. Greatest of all the temples of Egypt, its columns were encased in gold and electrum. They stretched high into darkness and dwarfed the hundreds of bald priests who scurried beneath them. On the west bank lay Pharaoh's palaces. Even further west lay the royal mortuary temples; the living and dead kin of the gods rested in close proximity.

Thebes was a city of temples. To Anqet, making her way on foot to the palace district, it seemed that every god in Egypt, and every prince and king since the beginning of the Two Lands, had a temple in this city. Each temple had its covey of fat, officious priests. She couldn't remember how many times she'd been forced to scurry to the side of the road to make way for some high priest or priestess as the worthy lumbered by in a chariot surrounded by a contingent of fledgling priests, servants, and guards. She had taken refuge in this alley to avoid yet another encounter.

Anqet waited for the procession to pass. She had asked for directions to the Street of the Scarab. If she was correct, this alley would lead directly to her goal. She followed the dusty, shaded path between windowless build-

ings, anxious to reach the house of Lady Gasantra before
dark. She hadn't eaten since leaving her barber companion
and his family earlier in the afternoon, and her stomach
rumbled noisily. She hoped Tamit would remember her.
They hadn't seen each other for several years.

The alley twisted back and forth several times, but
Anqet at last saw the intersection with the Street of the
Scarab. Intent upon reaching the end of her journey, she
ran into the road, into the path of an oncoming chariot.

There was a shout, then the screams of outraged
horses as the driver of the chariot hauled his animals back.
Anqet ducked to the ground beneath pawing hooves.
Swerving, the vehicle skidded and tipped. The horses
reared and stamped, showering stones and dust over
Anqet.

From behind the bronze-plated chariot came a stream
of oaths. Someone pounced on Anqet from the vehicle,
hauling her to her feet by her hair, and shaking her
roughly.

"You little gutter-frog! I ought to whip you for dashing
about like a demented antelope. You could have caused
one of my horses to break a leg."

Anqet's head rattled on her shoulders. Surprised, she
bore with this treatment for a few moments before stamping
on a sandaled foot. There was a yelp. The shaking stopped,
but now two strong hands gripped her wrists. Silence
reigned while her attacker recovered from his pain, then a
new string of obscenities rained upon her. The retort she
thought up never passed her lips, for when she raised her
eyes to those of the charioteer, she forgot her words.

Eyes of deep green, the color of the leaves of a water
lily. Eyes weren't supposed to be green. Eyes were brown,
or black, and they didn't blaze with the molten fury of the
Lake of Fire in the *Book of the Dead.* Anqet stared into
those pools of malachite until, at a call behind her, they
shifted to look over her head.

"Count Seth! My lord, are you injured?"

"No, Dega. See to the horses while I deal with this,
this..."

Anqet stared up at the count while he spoke to his servant. He was unlike any man she had ever seen. Tall, slender, with lean, catlike muscles, he had wide shoulders that were in perfect proportion to his flat torso and long legs. He wore a short soldier's kilt belted around his hips. A bronze corselet stretched tight across his wide chest; leather bands protected his wrists and accentuated elegant, long-fingered hands that gripped Anqet in a numbing hold. Anqet gazed back at Count Seth and noted the strange auburn tint of the silky hair that fell almost to his shoulders. He was beautiful. Exotic and beautiful, and wildly furious.

Count Seth snarled at her. "You're fortunate my team wasn't hurt or I'd take their cost out on your hide."

Anqet's temper flared. She forgot that she was supposed to be a humble commoner. Her chin came up, her voice raised in command.

"Release me at once."

Shock made Count Seth obey the order. No woman spoke to him thus. For the first time, he really looked at the girl before him. She faced him squarely and met his gaze, not with the humility or appreciation he was used to, but with the anger of an equal.

Bareka! What an uncommonly beautiful commoner. Where in the Two Lands had she gotten those fragile features? Her face was enchanting. High-arched brows curved over enormous black eyes that glittered with highlights of brown and inspected him as if he were a stray dog.

Seth let his eyes rest for a moment on her lips. To watch them move made him want to lick them. He appraised the fullness of her breasts and the length of her legs. To his chagrin, he felt a wave of desire pulse through his veins and settle demandingly in his groin.

Curse the girl. She had stirred him past control. Well, he was never one to neglect an opportunity. What else could be expected of a barbarian half-breed?

Seth moved with the swiftness of an attacking lion,

pulling the girl to him. She fit perfectly against his body. Her soft flesh made him want to thrust his hips against her, right in the middle of the street. He cursed as she squirmed against him in a futile effort to escape and further tortured his barely leashed senses.

"Release me!"

Seth uttered a light, mocking laugh. "Compose yourself, my sweet. Surely you won't mind repaying me for my inconvenience?"

Anqet opened her mouth to reply, but the count suddenly bent over her and took her lips in a hot kiss. She tried to pull away, but he kept her immobile by placing a hand at the back of her head.

In her short protected life, Anqet had experienced the loving embraces of her parents, the shy attentions of young or inadequate suitors, and the frightening lust of her uncle. None of these encounters matched the ravenous sensuality of this kiss. The count's mouth explored hers, inviting and exciting her senses before she understood what was happening. For a brief time, she responded, her desires awakened, driving her unprepared body. Then, unbidden, came the image of Hauron. Seth's hands became Hauron's, the count's mouth and body her uncle's.

Fear gave her the strength and the wits to ball up her fist and jab it under the bronze corselet and into the count's hard stomach. The blow did little damage but caused enough pain to make him loosen his hold on her. She backed away, kicked his leg, and fled, hearing the yelp that escaped the count's lips. Uneven footsteps pounded close behind her. She was sure that this green-eyed fury would catch her.

He almost did. Seth's long legs closed the distance between them, despite the ache in his shin, but as he reached for the girl, Dega called to him. He glanced over his shoulder to find Dega scrambling out of the path of a rearing horse and struggling to hold the other.

"Son of a crocodile!"

Seth bounded to the young man's side in time to avert another catastrophe. By the time the horses were calm, his lovely quarry had disappeared.

"Did you see which way she fled?"

"No, my lord." Dega ran a hand through his closely cropped hair. "I was busy avoiding a crushed skull."

"Bareka!" Seth cursed. He could still feel the effects of the passion she had stirred.

"My lord? Seth?" Dega's voice firmed and rose. "Seth."

"Hmmm." Seth strained his eyes down the length of the street.

"We are late," Dega said.

"I don't care."

Dega grinned at the young commander of the King's Chariots. "But lord, you are expected at the palace tonight, and there waits one whose goodwill you do care about."

Seth's hard expression softened. He allowed a rare, gentle smile to transform his features.

Anqet had found her way to Lady Gasantra's house and sat in the kitchen sipping beer while Tamit clucked and fussed over the tale of her misfortunes. Anqet closed her eyes in an effort to quell the images of Hauron and the beautiful Count Seth. Tamit waved plump fluttery hands.

"Terrible, terrible. That serpent! To drive you from your own home. You should petition one of the vizier's judges. Lady Gasantra is a relative of the vizier. She could speak for you."

"No! Hauron will destroy Nefer in revenge. I must hide until I can think of a way to regain my freedom and my home. Please, Tamit."

Her friend nodded and went on clucking and fluttering. She was a good woman, softhearted and bewildered by the presence of this fugitive. Her good-natured passivity and talent for hairdressing made her Lady Gasantra's favorite maid.

Anqet smiled her thanks when the cook set roast duck, leeks, figs, and sweetbread before her. She sank her

teeth into the duck as Tamit excused herself. The woman
returned as Anqet finished the bread.

"If you are determined to live as a servant, Lady
Anqet, what skills have you to recommend you to my
lady?" Tamit asked.

Anqet rested her chin on her hand and pondered this
new difficulty. She could clean and cook, but Gasantra had
many servants to do that. She could hardly rival Tamit as a
hairdresser. What skills would a court lady value?

"I can sing and play the harp."

Tamit raised her brows. "My lady has musicians,
but..." Her voice faded away at the sound of Anqet's
voice. High and clear, it rose above the clamor of scullery
maids and the scraping of clay pots.

> *Make holiday,*
> *Do not weary of it!*
> *Lo, none is allowed to take his goods with him,*
> *Lo, none who departs come back again!*

Tamit grinned at her. "Lady Anqet, my mistress will
be ecstatic. She entertains constantly, and her—" Tamit
lowered her voice, "her lover, the man she seeks to marry,
adores music. Lady Gasantra is always looking for ways to
entice him with her gifts as wife and hostess. Come, my
lady is alone now."

They walked across the grounds to the main house
and through a back door. Lady Gasantra's abode was the
largest home Anqet had ever been in. She passed suite
after suite of rooms filled with cedar and ebony furniture,
fine mosaics and statuary of the mistress's family, and a
small shrine dedicated to the goddess Hathor. Tamit motioned
to Anqet for silence.

They walked into a room lined with clothing chests
and across a bedroom to an adjacent chamber. Golden rays
from the fading solar orb bathed the chamber. To her left,
Anqet could see a veranda and garden beyond. Lady
Gasantra stood on the porch with her back to the room,
her attention riveted on something out of Anqet's range of

vision. She turned to the side, and Anqet was able to see her more clearly.

Gasantra was a tall woman, slim, with the long, almond-shaped eyes so prized by the people of the Two Lands. She obviously knew that they were her finest feature, for she had applied much brilliant green paint to her lids and outlined them in bold strokes that ended in a long gash of color at her temples. Her small lips were painted red, and henna stained her nails. Gasantra was dressed in the height of court fashion in a see-through pleated sheath that left one breast bare. Draped in gold and carnelian, she wore six pieces of jewelry for every one that Anqet would have worn.

Tamit made as if to enter the chamber but stopped at the sound of a masculine voice from the garden. The maid pattered back behind the door and whispered to Anqet, "I thought he'd gone."

Anqet peered over Tamit's shoulder. Lady Gasantra was speaking, softly at first, then in a voice edged with temper. As she spoke, a shadow loomed across the veranda. There was a low, malicious chuckle that tugged at Anqet's memory.

The lady's visitor glided into view. Anqet forgot to breathe. There was no mistaking that tall brown body, auburn hair, and those brilliant green eyes.

He moved past Gasantra with the grace of a hunting cat. Pausing beside the woman, he made a servant's bow with hands upraised, picked up a whip with an ebony-and-ivory handle from a table, and headed for the door.

"This is the third time this week you've left me early," Gasantra said.

Seth barely looked at her. "I must go."

Gasantra swept across the chamber and caught his arm. Anqet could see she was struggling to conceal a nasty temper.

"I know. You go to Pharaoh. The Living Horus commands your presence. Pharaoh must be taught strategy. Pharaoh must learn the art of the bow. Pharaoh wishes to consult you about the northern raiders. Always Pharaoh.

Does the king's majesty have no other companions? He should be bedding his wife and concubines, providing his empire with heirs."

Seth roared at the woman. "Silence!" Elegant hands twisted the lash of the whip. They strained against the leather, and Gasantra backed away from the count.

"Your jealousy becomes intolerable when it touches the king's majesty," Seth said "Be warned, Gasantra. My affection for Pharaoh surpasses any you may have evoked in me."

Gasantra clasped her hands together until the knuckles turned white. "Seth, forgive me. It's just that I know he presses you to take a wife. And there are several girls in the palace, daughters of princes."

"I told you. I want no wife " Seth's wide mouth curled into a smile. "We depraved barbarians don't believe in marriage, my little goose. My mother used to tell me her people mated where they chose and held all children in common. There were rites of fertility, men and women together, all in an open glen in the forest. She said only the adolescent boys had enough strength to satisfy the women."

"Seth!"

The count's sardonic expression deepened. He swooped down at Gasantra and enveloped her in a rough, vengeful kiss. When he stepped back, Anqet noted that he wasn't even breathing hard. He nodded regally to the shaken woman before him and left.

Anqet couldn't help but chuckle inwardly at the discomfort he'd created in Gasantra. She and Tamit waited for a discreet period before going to the lady. After all, it wouldn't do for Gasantra to suspect they'd witnessed the quarrel with her lover.

Not long after his visit to Gasantra, Seth, count of Annu-Rest and governor of the Falcon nome, lounged in an office in Pharaoh's palace. He had just finished a report on conditions at his majesty's fortress of Sile on the northern frontier. The king's great uncle, the vizier Ay, and Horemheb, general of the army, sat opposite him conferring over his news while a scribe sat on the floor and took notes. Seth hardly listened to his commander or the vizier. The two were old compatriots, and they solved problems—anything from land disputes to foreign alliances—by bickering with each other.

Seth's attention wandered back to the Street of the Scarab where a lithe, curved body writhed in his arms and ink-black eyes bore into his soul. His breathing quickened. He wet his lips.

"My lord Seth," Vizier Ay said.

Seth started and straightened in his chair. Was the girl a demon, to have bewitched him after so brief an encounter?

"Count Seth, are you ill?" Ay asked.

Seth cleared his throat. "No, Divine Father. Perhaps I'm not fully rested after the journey from Sile." A demon, that's what she had to be, to send him into fits of passion at the mere thought of her. What was he? A young stripling in his first kilt and belt? He would forget the girl. She was nothing. She was gone.

"One matter we would discuss with you," Horemheb said. "Then you must attend Pharaoh. He is anxious for the news from Sile."

Ay interrupted. A gentleman of falconlike dignity with silver hair and a prominent nose, he had been Pharaoh's regent and was also his foster father.

"Horemheb, I'm not convinced the lad is right for the task," Ay said.

Horemheb snorted at the vizier. "Who else shows so fine a disregard for convention and a desire to outrage priest and court alike? The boy already has half the noble families in Thebes convinced that he's corrupting the Living Horus and shouldn't be allowed near the king."

Ay cast an irritated glance at Seth before making a reply. "Tutankhamun says Count Seth is one of the few real friends he's allowed. He will listen to no one where your protégé is concerned."

"Not even to you, Divine Father?" Seth queried. He

knew full well that the serious statesman Ay didn't approve
of him. That knowledge gave him much pleasure.

"No, not even to me, you insolent tavern-hopper!"

Seth's delighted laughter filled the room. The scribe
winced and directed his gaze to the papyrus stretched
across his lap. Horemheb glared at Seth. Ay glared at
Seth.

"If you two are finished?" Horemheb asked. "We
must act on this information from Babylon."

The door crashed open under the huge black arm of a
Nubian bodyguard. A youth entered, and everyone fell to
his knees.

"General," the boy said to Horemheb. He nodded to
his foster father. His eyes found Seth, and an ingenuous
smile replaced the formal and remote facade that was
second nature to him.

No longer a child, Tutankhamun was a slender lad of
fifteen. He had the athletic build of his father, Amenhotep
III, and the regal beauty of his mother. Dressed simply in
a kilt falling to the middle of his thighs, he wore a short
wig and the uraeus crown, a gold diadem mounted with
the uraeus serpent, the sacred cobra. Pharaoh surveyed
the room's occupants and murmured a polite phrase to the
older men before turning to the commander of chariots.

"Seth." Tutankhamun held out a hand. "Come. Get
up. That tedious old high priest of Thoth fell asleep during
the audience, so I sent him home." As Seth fell in step
beside him, the king barraged him with questions. "Tell
me all the news from the Delta and from Sile. Do the
tribes of the western desert stir? I've always feared another invasion of nomads."

Ay and Horemheb watched the two young men walk
side by side out of the room and into an audience chamber
lined with guards. Count Seth spoke with easy respect as
the king listened intently.

Ay stared after them, then motioned for the scribe to
leave.

"I prefer Seth's half brother Sennefer," the vizier

said. "Lord Sennefer is thoroughly Egyptian and a devout follower of the great god Amun-Ra."

"Sennefer never got over being the son of their father's concubine and not inheriting the family title. He's a stuffy young prig, proud and vicious, and doesn't know a bow from a bottle of ale."

Ay gave the sneer of a dedicated civil servant. "You mean he doesn't sweep across the desert with a band of half-tamed aristocratic killers."

Horemheb's laughter boomed at Ay. He was a dark giant of a man, young for his rank, and protective of his most talented warrior. "Peace, my friend. Seth may be the offspring of a captive savage, but he's the most brilliant strategist and diplomat we have, and you know it." Horemheb held up a hand. "Yes, I know. We must find someone to help us solve our mystery, someone we can trust."

"Someone of loyalty, honor, and respect," Ay said.

Horemheb tucked his thumbs into his belt. "Someone with the guile to win the confidence of the traitor in our midst."

A sigh escaped both men. Each knew that the Two Lands was about to be scarified by a betrayal, an unparalleled blasphemy. They must find someone whom they could trust and in whom Tutankhamun would have faith.

3

Hauron lay on his side, his hands pressed to his head. He knew they crowded around his bed, these servants and slaves of his niece, but the pain in his head made it impossible to open his eyes. They'd put him in Rahotep's old bedchamber. He lost track of time because he spent most of his conscious hours fighting nausea, dizziness, and shooting pains in his groin.

"Physician." The word came out as a whisper.

"My lord?"

It was that old lizard Nebre.

"Physician. Tell him, more pain."

The voice of the physician burst upon him and made him cover his ears.

"I'm sorry, my lord. I can give you nothing else. Not until tonight. The head injury forbids it."

"Then get out." Hauron sucked in his breath and groaned. "Thanasa."

"Here, my lord. She hasn't sought out the nurse, and she hasn't tried to come home. We've searched the area around the village where she disappeared."

"Find her."

Nebre's voice hovered somewhere over his body. "My lord, it has been almost a fortnight. Your men have found no trace of the thieves who took my lady, and there have been no other attacks on houses in that village. Are you well enough to tell us how they appeared?"

Hauron gagged and pulled himself to the edge of the

bed where a slave held out a basin. He retched into it and fell back on his side.

"You have your answer, old man. Go away. My men will find her, no matter how long we have to search. Go away."

Anqet strummed the harp in her lap. She flexed her fingers and repeated a section of a love song she was to perform tonight. She had been in Lady Gasantra's employ for three days, and life was beginning to settle into a routine. Her main tasks were to serenade the mistress whenever requested and to sing for guests, especially at events such as tonight's feast. If she was not practicing, she was required to assist Tamit in any capacity the maid might require. So far, Tamit had not been able to bring herself to ask Lady Anqet to work for her, so Anqet quietly offered her help without being requested.

Each morning she would breakfast with Tamit and the house servants before practicing with the other three musicians kept by the mistress. None of the three could sing, and they were glad to have her in their group. Anqet enjoyed the musical mornings when she and the three women played lute, double flute, harp, and drums. Her enjoyment was usually short-lived, for the fear that Hauron would find her popped into her thoughts at unexpected moments. At night she had dreams of him lunging at her. Though it had been seventeen days since she had fled, she still woke in the middle of the night, certain that she could smell the fumes of beer and wine she associated with her uncle. Yet she was blessed by the gods with luck, for she took her place in Lady Gasantra's household easily.

Gasantra lived with her grandfather, an ailing old man who kept to his private garden and took pleasure in making constant, niggling demands on his granddaughter. Despite this inconvenience, Anqet envied Gasantra, for the woman was a widow who tended her own affairs and determined her own life as Anqet longed to do.

A woman of little curiosity, the mistress barely spoke to her, hardly even glanced at her, once she had heard

Anqet's voice. Anqet soon realized that Gasantra took no notice of servants or slaves, other than in a utilitarian way. The woman knew when service was satisfactory and when it was not. Beyond that, she interested herself not at all in the lives of those she employed or owned. Anqet was sure she wouldn't even notice if Tamit were to become ill until it was time for her hair to be dressed. Then the woman would be annoyed at the inconvenience.

Gasantra's attitude worked in Anqet's favor, for the woman never bothered to inquire into her background. In addition, she displayed no jealousy. Gasantra disliked pretty women, but servants, of course, were not rivals.

Anqet's main concern upon being hired had been Count Seth. The man was most unsettling, and dangerous, but after observing Gasantra's attitude toward her, she concluded that the fabulous count would have forgotten her existence moments after she escaped him. Besides, she had been so disheveled, indeed dirty, that he wouldn't recognize her in her musician's garments.

But Anqet couldn't help but feel an unexpected irritation at the thought that Count Seth had in all probability erased her from his memory like a misdrawn hieroglyph. Anqet squirmed on her stool and set the harp aside. It had been a piece of ill luck, meeting this auburn-haired creature. He had infested her dreams. She would see him swooping at her, reed-green eyes full of mockery and fire. He would catch her to his hard body and run his hands over her. . . .

Anqet moaned aloud and clenched her fists in frustration. The man was a tyrant, a seducer of women. Tamit had told her so. Anqet wanted nothing to do with such a man. Hauron had taught her a lesson. Far better to marry a boring old lecher like Oubainer than to be at the mercy of a man like Count Seth. What she would really like to do was to find a man who would be a suitable ally for both her and Nefer, talk to him, make agreements. It seemed to her a proper way to find a mate. No doubt Count Seth and his powerful friends would laugh at her if they knew her predicament.

Yes, Tamit had warned her about Count Seth. He was hereditary ruler of the Falcon nome of Annu-Rest, one of the provinces below Thebes. At twenty-four, Seth was one of General Horemheb's top military commanders and a friend of Pharaoh. This despite his tainted blood.

Tamit chattered to Anqet about Seth's scandalous background. His father had horrified the old pharaoh Amenhotep III by bringing back a foreign bride from an expedition to the Peoples of the Sea. A captured chief's daughter, the woman hated the Two Lands, and though she bore the old count a son, she never forgave her husband for keeping her away from her home. The woman raised her son with strange ideas from her tribal background. Seth's father saw the danger of filling his son full of ideas unwelcome in the Two Lands, and the parents fought. Seth was sent to court at the count's order. There the boy became one of the Children of the Kap, those sons of high lineage who were raised with the royal offspring and trained to take positions in the government of the Two Lands.

Eventually Seth came under the tutelage of General Horemheb. During the time of chaos, when Tutankhamun's older brother ruled, Seth had been the general's aide. It was said that the young warrior had a hand in making Vizier Ay aware of the impending collapse of the northern empire in Syria through the king's neglect of the army and his Syrian vassals. When Tutankhamun came to the throne, Vizier Ay needed someone to train the king in the arts of war, and Horemheb recommended Seth, who was already a friend to the boy.

Anqet got up and stretched. She should be dressing for tonight's feast, not sitting here in a trance. She knelt before a clothing chest and took out a sheer robe. She fished about in a casket for a bronze-and-faience broad collar and earrings borrowed from Tamit. She gathered her hair on top of her head and pulled on an ebony wig that fell past her shoulders. Taking up a bronze mirror, she began to apply her cosmetics.

Anqet giggled, remembering Tamit's avid face as she

described Count Seth. "Everyone knows he's a barbarian, my lady. Just look at him. You know why he's named after the god of darkness and evil? His mother found out that those born with reddish hair are thought to be under the god Seth's influence, and she named him that to show her contempt for our beliefs. But she was right to name him that."

Tamit lowered her voice. "That man is under the rule of the Dark One. Did you know that he seduced a priestess of Isis? Right in the temple. The vizier was furious. But then it turned out that the priestess was quite happy about being debauched."

"So he didn't force her?"

Tamit shook her head, her eyes wide with vicarious horror. "He didn't have to. Count Seth has never had to force any woman to grant favors." She leaned close to Anqet and whispered. "He and his wild friends had midnight chariot races before the palace. He even took the king to one, but the divine father Ay put a stop to that. And the worst, or nearly the worst, are those depraved nights at the Tavern of the Serpent." Here Anqet only caught hushed references to "many women," "leading other young men astray," and "strange, foreign potions mixed with wine."

Anqet blushed and stalled with a question. "What did you mean, almost the worst? There's more?"

"May Toth be my witness, my lady. There's too much to tell. The worst is what he did to his mother. They say he—he took her body from the tomb where it lay with that of his father."

A sickened shudder passed through Anqet's body. "Why?"

"Because he's evil. That's why." Tamit's voice shook as she spoke. "He took her body out into the desert and burned it. Oh, think of it! He destroyed the home of her ka. There's no place for her spirit to return to. She's lost. Lost forever."

"Did he do that to his father too?"

"No. He's half mad, don't you see? He buried his

father as a proper son should, here in the City of the Dead with his mother and all his noble ancestors. Perhaps his half brother Lord Sennefer wouldn't let him burn their father. They always fought. Sennefer hates Seth. The poor man was his father's only son until Seth came along. Just imagine. Burning your mother's body."

Anqet stared into her mirror and contemplated that horrific act. It was truly the act of a barbarian. Why did he have to be so beautiful and yet so evil? She buried the memory of his lean body as she had done all day and finished dressing.

When she closed the door to the room she shared with Tamit, she heard the busy sounds of a house in preparation for guests. For several days, a flurry of activity had disrupted the compound. An ox had been butchered, fresh waterfowl acquired. The cook and her assistants had been up before sunrise, baking bread and pastries. Extra servants had been hired to scour the house. Even the household children had been pressed into service. Three naked younglings rushed by her now, arms loaded with fresh flowers worked into garlands.

Anqet dodged the children and maneuvered through crowded passageways to the main hall. It was dusk. A slave lit alabaster lamps; another filled bowls with scented oil. The chief cook stood over her assistants while they decked small tables with food and flowers. Additional musicians waited in an alcove that opened onto the hall, hired by Gasantra to supplement the regular staff.

"Singer." Lady Gasantra stood at the entrance to the hall and called imperiously.

Anqet went to her and made a low obeisance. "Yes, mistress."

Gasantra's long slanting eyes barely touched her.

"You have prepared the song I requested?"

"Yes, mistress."

"Remember, don't begin it until I signal."

"Yes, mistress."

Gasantra turned away without another word. Anqet hastened back to her place behind a harp. The instrument, taller than she, was made of cedar overlaid with sheet gold. It was a costly piece, far finer than any she had ever played. She suspected that Gasantra had ordered it made only to impress her guests, for the woman was unmoved by music.

The lute player nudged her. Guests were arriving. She fought back an unreasonable fear that Hauron would be one of them. No, Hauron was far away. She and the other musicians struck up a sedate tune, suitable for the hostess to welcome her friends. Anqet could see Lady Gasantra standing beyond the hall entrance, groups of richly dressed nobles filing toward her. Over the strains of the music, she heard urbane, courtly greetings.

"May the grace of Amun be in thy heart, dear Gasantra."

"Welcome, welcome."

"I pray the gods grant thee health and life."

Anqet began to enjoy herself. She had never witnessed such an illustrious and sophisticated gathering. Her parents had entertained, but on a modest scale. Here in Thebes, the great worked far harder at having a good time. At first the men and women kept apart, as was fitting. Beflowered ladies sat in ones and twos nibbling daintily at roast pigeon, teal, and goose. She saw two young men playfully struggle to break a haunch of beef in half. Wine, beer, and liqueurs circulated freely, poured by serving girls.

"*Psst.*"

Anqet looked over her shoulder at the sound. The leader of the hired acrobats signaled that they were ready. A drummer beat a rapid tattoo. Anqet and her fellow musicians struck up a staccato melody. Five girls tumbled into the hall to the delighted cries of the crowd, for Gasantra had hired the best performers in Thebes. Anqet's jaw dropped as one girl did a series of backflips across the length of the room, her long, braided ponytail a black whip at her back.

The evening progressed with an ever-increasing consumption of liquor. The atmosphere in the packed hall became stuffy. Anqet, who had sung almost without respite, left the hall for a few minutes and downed a cup of beer in the kitchen.

The mood of the party changed from formality to familiarity. Men and women mingled freely now. Some wandered out into the cool darkness of the garden; others gathered around a line of dancing girls. Anqet returned to her seat at the harp in a mellow mood after a second cup of beer.

She enjoyed being a singer. It was good to give pleasure to people and to see their heads turn at the sound of her voice. There was a feeling of power when her music brought a smile or a tear to a stranger.

Lady Gasantra appeared. "Where have you been?" she snapped. "Never mind. Await my signal."

Anqet huddled behind her harp. This was the moment she dreaded, for she knew of only one person for whom Gasantra would want this song performed. There had been no way to refuse. Well, he wouldn't be looking at her anyway, not with Gasantra clinging to him. From behind the instrument, Anqet searched the hall. She caught sight of her mistress slinking up to a tall figure in a long, transparent robe that covered a white kilt. She recognized those muscled legs and brown shoulders, even though Count Seth defied fashion and left off the intricate wig everyone else was wearing.

Anqet squinted as Seth turned and lamplight flashed on the gold-and-silver collar that draped his shoulders. She noticed that even at this social gathering he wore a dagger at his belt. Anqet tried to keep her eyes on the blade instead of its wearer. The hilt of the weapon was decorated with an intricately beaded design of gold. The sheath glittered with midnight-blue lapis lazuli and green malachite inlay. Anqet's gaze traveled down the hilt to the firm muscle of a thigh, then flicked back to the count's face when he made a sudden movement.

Seth bent to catch Gasantra's words as the woman nestled close to his side. Anqet ducked her head behind the frame of the harp when he turned to glance at the musicians. When Gasantra clapped her hands three times,

Anqet swallowed hard and ran her fingers across her instrument. Her voice pierced the laughter and murmurs that hung in the room. Its strength and clarity, raised this time to command attention, brought instant silence. Seth raised his head.

He saw her. A puzzled frown made him seem quite forbidding. He ignored the whispered conversation around him, intent on the singer's voice. Gasantra smiled up at him, pleased with the success of her offering. When Seth moved toward the musicians' alcove, she clung to him. He seemed not to notice her company, so absorbed was he in the song. Gasantra's smile widened at this unlooked-for success and nestled close to the count, pressing her small breasts to his chest.

Anqet wished the man would pay attention to his hostess and stop that scarifying stare. She sang:

> *. . . apportioned to you is my heart,*
> *I do for you what it desires,*
> *When I am in your arms.*
> *My longing for you is my eyepaint,*
> *When I see you my eyes shine;*
> *I press close to you to look at you,*
> *Beloved of men, who rules my heart!*

Never had a song seemed so endless—or so embarrassing. Anqet lowered her eyes to the floor as a flush crept up her neck to her face. Her glance flitted to the count as the song ended. He was smiling maliciously at her. She blushed a deeper red and curled her fingers in the strings of the harp in annoyance. Seth swept a heated look over her body, then turned to answer Gasantra's impatient tug on his arm. Anqet sighed with relief as the lady swept him away with her to accept the greetings of new arrivals.

Unsure whether the count had recognized her, Anqet tried to quiet the hammering of her heart. It was rumored that his eyes held dark magic, that he needed no love-charms because of them, and that he used his power shamelessly. Perhaps he looked at all women that way. Yes,

that was it. She needn't worry. Oh no. He was coming
back, this time without Lady Gasantra. Anqet's hands
stilled on the harp. One of the hired musicians took up
her part in the tune without hesitation.

She pushed the instrument from her and was about to
rise and flee when she saw a man slide up to Count Seth.
A group of tipsy young lords swayed past and blocked her
way. Suddenly the two men were before her. The older
man had eased Seth back against a bronze winestand to
the side of the alcove entrance. Anqet could see and hear
them, but Seth and his companion were absorbed in their
conversation and took no heed of their surroundings.

"Younger brother, I haven't seen you since you returned
from Sile," the companion said.

When she heard these words, Anqet looked at the
newcomer curiously. Had she not been in such a frenzy,
she would have noticed the resemblance between the two
men. This had to be Sennefer, Count Seth's half brother.
Tamit had told her Sennefer was a few years older than
Seth, and it seemed to Anqet that the gods had fashioned
a classic Egyptian version of the lean good looks of the
ruler of the Falcon nome. Only a finger's width shorter
than Seth, Sennefer had the same high cheekbones and
long muscles of his brother. Like his brother, the older
man resembled the perfectly proportioned sculptures of
pharaohs she had seen in the temples and shrines in
Memphis. Yet there were differences. Sennefer's skin was
darker, his lips thinner, his eyes less hawklike and satirical.

Sennefer addressed his brother in gentle tones. "I
want to talk to you about Khet. Our dearest stepmother
tells me you've promised to take him on campaign against
the Bedouin if war comes. The boy is too young."

"Have some wine, Sennefer. You look thirsty."

Seth plucked an alabaster goblet from a table and
thrust it into his brother's hand. He took a step away from
the man, but Sennefer put an arm out to block him. Seth
sighed and leaned back against the wall beside the alcove,
an expression of boredom on his face.

"I want Khet to enter the House of Life here in Thebes," Sennefer said.

"Why this sudden interest in your youngest sibling?" Seth asked. "You've ignored the boy since he was born."

Sennefer lowered his head. "Mother died with his birthing. You know that."

"Spare me the story," Seth said. "It wasn't Khet's fault."

"I want him to study with the priests of Amun. The second prophet has consented to guide Khet's studies personally."

"Ah!" Seth grinned at his brother. "We come to the truth. You want to throw Khet to the priests as a living offering. A rich and well-connected pupil to be molded into a pasty-faced, sniveling devotee of the Hidden One. Another docile servant who will spend his fortune and his influence to further the temple's already overweening power."

Anqet shrank back in the alcove in horror at the blasphemous words. Evidently Sennefer was used to his brother's sacrilege, for he endured the mocking words without losing his temper.

"As a priest of Amun-Ra, Khet's future would be assured, and he would be safe from the hardships and dangers of warfare."

Seth straightened and pushed himself away from the wall. He laughed a quiet yet derisive laugh. "Khet is not priest material."

"All good men are servants of the great god. They hold in their hands the harmony and balance that rules the Two Lands."

"Bareka! You depress me with your piety, Sennefer. You forget. I know you well." In a flash Seth snatched his brother's wrist in a cruel grip. "I know you, pure-blooded brother. I remember the year of the high flood and the wild-bull hunt."

"That was an accident." Sennefer jerked his wrist, but it stayed imprisoned in Seth's hand.

"Was it?" Seth asked. Thick lashes swept down to

conceal the expression in the count's eyes. In a suddenly exhausted voice, he went on. "Was it? I thought so at the time."

Seth released Sennefer's wrist, brushed past the man, and joined the equerry Dega and Lady Gasantra. Lord Sennefer moved away too, and Anqet considered the scene she had just witnessed. How blessed she had been in her family, surrounded by love; it had never occurred to her how terrible its lack would be. Seth's family was divided by rival allegiances and old hurts, divided by the lineage and power that made it great. She'd rather be an obscure, modestly prosperous farmer. She missed Nefer, Bastis, and Nebre, and was beginning to miss even Oubainer. Pleading fatigue, Anqet slid out of the alcove and headed for her room.

In her chamber, Anqet discarded her jewelry and wig, scrubbed her face, and combed her hair. It was late enough that no one would miss her services. Soon the guests would all depart. Gasantra would be occupied with Count Seth.

That woman, Anqet thought. She made rapid strokes through her hair with the wooden comb. *Such behavior. Rubbing herself against him. Running her hands over him.*

Anqet blushed when she thought of them together. Why was she so shocked? Gasantra hadn't been the only woman at the feast to exhibit herself, but she was the only one who made Anqet want to stuff her down a cistern. *Why didn't she just drag him to her bed and be done with it?* Anqet slammed the comb down on the cosmetic table and drummed her fingers against it. The room was stuffy, and she was hungry.

With a snort, Anqet set out for the kitchen. After a small meal she took a pastry and wandered toward the rear of the compound. Most of the people still about were cleaning up inside the house. She paused to eat her pastry and wash her hands with water from a storage jar, letting the breeze cool her wet skin. Relaxing, Anqet strolled toward the granaries, sat down on a mud-brick bench, and stared up at the sky. The red star was visible. Called Heru-Khuti, its god was Ra. The moon hung in the sky; it burned white and full.

"Singer."

Startled, Anqet whipped around to face Count Seth. He had discarded his outer robe and wore a kilt and sandals. Standing in the darkness of the granary looking up at him, she could barely make out his face, but she could see that he was smiling.

He purred. "So the street urchin is a singer. We have unfinished business."

Anqet stood and cleared her throat. He was between her and the house. She must play her part and get rid of him.

"I beg forgiveness, my lord." She bowed. "I was thoughtless."

"Forgiveness. Oh, yes."

The count moved toward her. Anqet took a few steps sideways as a precaution. Seth hesitated, then spread his arms wide.

"I intend you no harm, girl," he said. "What's your name?"

"Anqet, my lord."

Seth pulled her down on the bench with him. She could see him clearly now. His eyes were fastened on her face with that unnerving intensity, but his body was relaxed. He gestured to a place beside him. Anqet shook her head and stayed where she was. He leaned on his arm so that he was closer to her.

"I am called Seth."

"I know."

"So you've heard of me?" Seth sighed. "I see. Alas, this city is a nest of evil tongues."

"My lord, I am needed in the hall."

Seth shook his head. Soft hair swayed and cast shadows on his face. Anqet stood, but in one easy movement he was against her, holding her hand in his. Anqet tried unsuccessfully to free her hand, her fear growing steadily with the seconds. Seth turned her hand and traced a line from her wrist up the length of her arm with his fingers. She shivered.

"There is no need to be frightened. I have forgiven you." He pulled her close. His arms held her firmly but gently. Anqet placed both hands against his chest and pushed; his arms tightened around her. "Easy, my little goddess."

Anqet twisted in Seth's arms. She tried pushing with her trapped hands again, but that only forced the lower part of her body against him. Seth braced his legs apart, put a hand on the back of her neck, and captured her lips with his. Her startled cry was cut off in her throat. Anqet's eyes widened as she felt his tongue inside her mouth. He kept one hand at her neck, but the other traveled lazily across her back, down to her hip and leg, and back up to press her buttock.

Anqet felt a slow building of fire in her veins. It spread everywhere Seth touched and to the places where their bodies melded. The count released her lips only to spread kisses over her eyes, cheeks and neck. She could hear his breathing quicken. His skin was as hot as her own. Her hands roamed over the smooth skin and hard muscles of his back and shoulders. Seth shifted his weight. Running his tongue down her neck, he slipped his hand inside her robe and cupped her breast. His mouth fastened over her nipple.

Without thought she wrapped her arms around Seth and pressed her breast into his mouth. He caressed her hips and belly. His hand travelled lower, and there was a strange sensation between her legs where his hand had roamed. What was this feeling? Seth slipped his hand beneath the skirt of her gown and stroked the inside of her thigh. His fingers drew a line of delicious torment up to the hidden place between her legs and nearly drove her mad.

It was this madness, this unexpected torture of pleasure, that drove Anqet from passion to panic. As Seth's hand touched her, she started and cried out. Immediately the count lifted his head and caught her before she could wriggle away. He murmured soothing words to her, but Anqet was frightened, frightened of passion and of him. She fought him, her struggles growing more violent when they proved useless. Seth swore under his breath and twisted both her arms behind her back.

"By the gods, what ails you? You wanted me a moment ago."

"Let me go!" Tears of fright welled up in Anqet's eyes. No! She mustn't cry. She was angry. How did he dare try his seductive tricks on her in the house of his lover? He had no right to approach her. No right at all.

Seth held her against him and peered at her. His breathing was ragged, and she could feel the tension in his body. All at once, a cynical smile curled his lips.

"I forgot. You're a singer. I have never asked this question before, but I will for you. What is your price?"

Anqet stared up into Seth's amused eyes. "Price," she repeated in a dead tone.

"Come, you must have settled on a fee before you sang this evening. All singers have their price, although I have never had to pay it. What is yours?"

"Son of a crocodile!"

"You're changing the subject."

Anqet wanted to claw those magnificent eyes from his head. Pulling one arm free, she drew back her hand and took a swipe at the count's face. He caught her hand and laughed.

"Is it to be combat?" he asked. "I've never had a woman that way either. You are indeed full of surprises, singer. Let us begin the battle now and decide your fee later."

Anqet snarled. His nasty assumptions and heartless sensuality turned her into an inferno of rage, rage that inspired her to rake her foot along the inside of Seth's leg and crush his foot. He grabbed for his leg, and Anqet escaped, charging full force into Lady Gasantra, who was coming toward them from the house.

Lady Gasantra thrust Anqet away from her. "What is

this?" She saw the count, who had limped to the bench and sat rubbing his leg. "Seth?"

Seth cocked his head to one side and regarded his lover with mock felicity.

"It isn't your concern, Gasantra. Go back in the house. I'll join you shortly."

Gasantra looked from Seth to Anqet. Anqet was standing with her arms clasped around her body, her eyes on the ground. A killing gleam came into the older woman's eyes. She swooped at Anqet and slapped the girl across the mouth.

"Little slut! You're already spreading your legs for the best you could find."

Gasantra drew her hand back to strike Anqet again, but strong fingers closed over her arm and forced it down. Seth stood over her, his body tense with anger.

"Touch her again, and I'll throw you in the cattle pen," he said.

Gasantra hissed at him. "She's a conniving whore."

Anqet held a hand to her bleeding mouth. She was about to lose her place with Lady Gasantra. She didn't like the woman, but where would she go?

Gasantra was in a fine temper. Seth half reclined on the bench and listened to the woman's tirade while Anqet stood between them in miserable embarrassment and fear.

"I don't see why I should share you with one under my own roof." Gasantra paused for breath.

"Neither do I," Seth said. He got to his feet and headed for the house with the easy walk of a leopard.

"Seth, where are you going?"

"Out from under your roof, of course." He didn't even turn his head.

Gasantra pattered after him. She had lost all semblance of anger. "Seth, wait!"

Anqet watched Gasantra hurry after the count. Seth stopped and stood in the moonlight, cool and distant, while Gasantra pleaded, bringing a gentle hand up to his cheek. Seth bore her caress patiently but remained unmoved. When Gasantra released him, he turned away once more and strolled around the corner of a storage building toward the gardens and the house.

Gods! He'd wanted her and had the temerity to assume that she would return his advances for a price. And now his attentions had probably cost her her livelihood. One moment he was obsessed with passion for her, and the next he had forgotten her for that woman.

Anqet sank down on the bench and rested her head in her hands. How could she have been so foolish? How could she have forgotten what he was—a foreign, depraved demon, a man who would destroy his own mother's soul, a man who kept one brother from the priesthood and tormented the other with his heartlessness.

Black, sluggish depression settled over Anqet. She had to put Count Seth out of her mind. She mustn't forget that neither he nor anyone else except Tamit knew she wasn't really a singer. It wasn't pleasant, being a commoner. She didn't like being treated like a toy. She would forget the nasty, beautiful count and go to bed.

Wearily she got to her feet and trudged across the yard to the kitchen door. Tomorrow she must search for other employment, and somehow she must think of a way to return to her beloved Nefer without falling into Hauron's power again. Perhaps she could hire her own warriors who would protect her from him. To do so would require payment, and her valuables were at Nefer. What little jewelry she had with her would not be enough. No matter. She was going home if she had to steal a reed skiff, paddle all the way by herself, and fight a small war when she got there.

Picking up a pebble, Anqet hurled it at the side of the house. It hit the mud brick with an angry snap that echoed her thoughts. Yes, she would think of a plan that would allow her to go home. She had had enough of Thebes and its cruel aristocracy.

"And thus, might Pharaoh, I feel confident that we have enough surveyors to attend this year's Inundation.

We will have the whole of the Two Lands measured without difficulty."

In the king's audience chamber Seth set his jaws together and willed himself not to yawn. He leaned against a column shaped like a papyrus stalk. His eyes drifted from the overseer of surveyors to the king. On a dais, Tutankhamun sat on his golden throne, crook and flail scepters in his hands. Like Seth, he wore a linen head-cloth that fell over his shoulders, but his was held in place by a gold uraeus diadem. Seth marveled at the boy's expression of polite attention. The lad had been in counsel for the whole morning, and old Huy was particularly long-winded. What amazed him more was that Pharaoh would recall every detail of the man's report.

Huy knelt on the floor. Tutankhamun inclined his head, and Huy backed out of the chamber. The double doors, taller than two men, closed with a boom that echoed in the vast hall. Tutankhamun set his scepters on a tray carried by a servant, let out a sigh, and stretched his legs. As the pharaoh got to his feet and worked his shoulders free of kinks, the group of ten councelors clustered around him drew closer.

General Horemheb motioned for Seth to stand beside him. Vizier Ay, Treasurer Maya, and Lord Sennefer stood together at the foot of the dais. The Nubian prince Hiknefer of Aniba handed Tutankhamun a goblet of water. He and Prince Khai were two of Pharaoh's companions. Seth's eyes found the overseer of the audience hall and the viceroy of Kush as well as the high priest of Amun-Ra. He wondered why Horemheb had requested this so-called private meeting. He didn't wait long in ignorance, for Tutankhamun settled himself on his throne again and beckoned for his chief counselors to come near. Pharaoh nodded at Horemheb. The general strode to the king's side and faced the group.

With Seth standing beside him, he waited for their attention. When he had it, Horemheb held up a miniature gold statuette of the jackal-god Anubis. Seth's expression remained impassive, though he noticed the funeral inscription at the base of the figure.

"The divine son of the god has asked me to address you in a matter that has shocked him beyond speech," announced Horemheb.

Seth cocked a skeptical eye at the king. Well, the boy certainly looked worried, so the matter had to be serious.

Horemheb handed the statue to Seth. "King Burnaburiash of Babylon sent this image to the king's majesty. One of his men found it on the leader of a caravan raid. Burnaburiash doesn't take kindly to nomads disrupting his Egyptian gold supply. Anyway, he questioned the man. Before he died, the man spoke of tomb robbery."

There was a strangled cry from the high priest of Amun-Ra. The old man was steeped in the occult traditions of his country and like all good Egyptians, believed in the cult of the dead of the god Osiris. Several councilors made the sign to protect against the vengeance of the dead.

"There have been defilements before," Horemheb said. "But this instance is different. That Anubis image comes from the necropolis at Memphis, some eleventh-dynasty lord. Treasurer Maya went personally to the city. He had the necropolis police search. Nine old tombs had been stripped of all their portable wealth. All the gold, silver, electrum, and precious stones. The coffins were rifled." Horemheb stopped and muttered a charm.

Seth spoke up. "I told you it would happen sooner or later. Of course, being only half Egyptian, I can appreciate what a temptation all that lovely gold must be, especially if your belly is empty and your lord takes much of what you raise in taxes."

There was outraged grumbling. Tutankhamun cast a startled look at Seth. Sennefer took two steps up the dais toward his younger brother, but Horemheb was quicker. The general lunged at Seth and yanked his junior officer to him by one arm.

"Spare us your provocative wit," Horemheb said. "This is not a matter for levity."

"Yes, my general." Seth knew when not to try his commander's patience.

Ay cleared his throat, and silence immediately fell over the men.

"General Horemheb and I will begin investigations. We ask that each of you be aware that Burnaburiash of Babylon made one last comment in his letter. His words were, 'Let my brother Tutankhamun beware. The vultures who prey upon the dead lodge in his house and partake of his bread and beer. Let the Living Horus take heed, for he has taken to his breast a scorpion.'"

A sibilant hiss traveled around the group. No one could mistake the words of the Babylonian king. The corruption and thievery reached into the court itself.

Seth was intent on the king's response to the news. The boy's life had been filled with intrigue and betrayal during the reign of his older brother.

When he looked around, Seth noted the suspicious glances directed at him. He met the eyes of his half brother and found Sennefer looking at him appraisingly. Seth grinned at his sibling as the king spoke.

"My majesty is determined to stop this blasphemy, my lords. There has been too much heresy in the Two Lands. Now that the gods and the people are in harmony and balance again, we do not intend to have that balance destroyed."

It was one of the few times Seth had heard the boy refer to the rift caused by his brother's disastrous persecution of the old gods.

Tutankhamun rose and made his way toward the doors. "Count Seth, we are to practice at the bow this afternoon."

"Yes, Divine Majesty."

Seth followed the king out of the room, past the silent and pensive group of men. Pharaoh led him out to the waiting royal chariots. The king's war band stood ready, fifty of Egypt's best warriors drawn from the ranks of the nobility.

"Life, health, strength!"

Tutankhamun raised his hand in response to their greeting. Seth jumped into his own vehicle and followed the king out of the city into the desert practice field. Soon they were racing across the rocky surface of the land. Each chariot had a driver and a bowman who aimed at stuffed leather targets on wooden stakes. Stones and dust churned under the horses' hooves and the wheels of the chariot as Seth drove the king's chariot at top speed down the course. Beside him, Tutankhamun let fly an arrow from his compound bow. It found its mark, along with twenty others just like it. The king shouted in triumph.

"All of them! Seth, I got all of them!" He clutched at the rim of the chariot as Seth slowed the horses to a trot. "That's the first time."

"Didn't I tell Your Majesty it would happen? You have the patience to practice and the skill."

"Patience! It took years."

Seth pulled the team to a walk and guided the chariot in a circle. The yells and jeers of the war band bounced off the cliffs to the west as the men continued their practice.

"My pharaoh, you have only this year attained the necessary height."

"Yes, yes. I know." Tutankhamun thrust his bow into the case attached to the side of the chariot. "Seth, I'm worried."

"I know."

"But you don't take this tomb robbery seriously," the king said. "I fear for your ka, my friend."

Seth looked down at the king, his face a blank mask. "Majesty, my soul is split down the middle. Half of it is Egyptian, half barbarian." He leaned toward the boy, his lips twitching. "Perhaps my soul will go to two heavens. I am doubly assured of the afterlife."

"You could go to double hells."

Seth threw his head back and laughed. The king hopped from the chariot. Seth followed, and they walked before the horses.

"My pharaoh, I would ask a favor."

"How may I serve you?"

"I would like to borrow the chief royal harpist for a few hours, and also make an addition to your staff of musicians."

The king glanced at Seth with a perplexed frown on his lips. "If you wish. It seems a trifling favor."

"Hardly worthy of your notice, Majesty, but the chief harpist is temperamental. You know he can be uncooperative if he's in a mood."

"What are you up to?"

Seth turned to the king, his eyes wide and innocent.

"Oh no." Tutankhamun raised a hand in protest. "Don't say anything. I know you. You're not going to tell me, so don't bother with that performance. Let's go. My difficult royal spouse expects me to join her for the evening meal."

4

Anqet scurried along the busy avenue after the blind man and the youth who led him. Two royal guards followed her, scimitars dangling at their sides.

She called to the blind man. "Master Harkhuf."

Her bundle of possessions slung over her shoulder, she trotted to catch up with the two. Harkhuf might not be able to see, but he traveled as if everyone knew it and would get out of his way. In most cases they did. He paced along with a sure gait, one hand on the boy's shoulder, the other holding a walking stick with a silver top shaped like a duck's head. Anqet managed to overtake the man as he turned a corner.

"Please, Master Harkhuf, I don't understand. How can I be a singer for the divine pharaoh?"

Harkhuf stopped abruptly, forcing his guide to totter off-balance for a moment. Pedestrians filed around the guards and their charges.

"How?" the man snorted. "Foolish girl, the son of the god has spoken."

"But Pharaoh has never heard me."

"Presumption! Of course he has never heard you. I received instructions to acquire you. It has been done."

"But whose instructions?"

Harkhuf swiveled his head in her direction. Wrinkled eyelids remained closed over sightless eyes.

"One of Pharaoh's servants brought commands. Don't dawdle, girl. My time is precious to me, if not to you."

Anqet walked beside Pharaoh's chief harpist, determined to make the man listen to her. "Master Harkhuf, I have no wish to be a court singer."

The blind man paid her no heed other than to swat at her with his stick. Anqet cast a glance over her shoulder at the two guards. Their faces were blank, but she knew they wouldn't allow her to leave.

A few minutes walk took them to a sentried gate set in a high white wall. Inside the gate was a small city. Single- and two-storied blocks of buildings lay on either side of a central path. As she rushed after Harkhuf, Anqet passed the workshops of stonemasons, lapidaries, sculptors, metalworkers, carpenters, and leatherworkers. At the lapidaries' she paused to eye a pile of stone flakes: the red-orange of carnelian, the azure blue of turquoise, the deeper blue of lapis lazuli, and the flamboyant green of malachite.

Shepherded by the harpist, Anqet quickly arrived at the living quarters of the female singers of the royal household. There Harkhuf left her. Anqet couldn't understand what had happened. This morning she'd risen, fearing Lady Gasantra would have her beaten. The night's events between herself and Count Seth had convinced Anqet that she must leave. In a way, she was grateful that she was forced to make a plan.

Last night Anqet had decided she would appeal to her old suitor, Menana. He was young and shy, but a good boy. She would go to his estate first. They would marry. She had visions of them marching upon Nefer with a hoard of retainers, casting Hauron's minions into the Nile. If Hauron was there, she would throw him to the crocodiles.

Menana was the answer to her problem. He knew of her love for Nefer and wouldn't stand in the way of her desire to keep her home. If she allied herself with him, she would be safe from commanding green eyes and licentious hands.

With her plan set, Anqet was saying good-bye to Tamit when Harkhuf descended upon Lady Gasantra's household like a hawk upon a flock of pigeons. The old musician announced Pharaoh's commands, and Pharaoh's word became reality. Anqet was now a member of the royal household; there was no other course open to her.

The singers' quarters where Anqet now slept were in the same block of rooms as the personal maids', in the rear of the palace. Segregated from the male retainers, the inhabitants could go for days without seeing a man, for they were servants attached to the large royal harem. Unused to such isolation, Anqet became bored with the routine of the female relatives and wives of Pharaoh within two days of her arrival.

From the time they rose until they retired, these women spent their time in personal grooming, eating, lounging, and gossiping. For diversion they would take chariots to other noble ladies' houses where they would eat, lounge, and gossip again. Rumor and scandal were life breath to these women. Many were mothers of royal offspring by the old pharaoh and spent much time plotting their children's advancement.

None had children by the new pharaoh as yet, not even the Great Royal Wife, Ankhsenamun, daughter of the heretic. Anqet knew that Pharaoh had no heir, but whispered conversations in the servants' quarters made her aware that many of the harem vied to be the first to present the living god with a son. To their frustration, the divine father Ay hadn't allowed Pharaoh to test his strength with women until last year, for fear of taxing the boy before his time.

The rumors about Pharaoh fascinated Anqet, yet they failed to concern her. She had never seen Pharaoh and probably never would. Her main goal was to leave the palace complex and find her way to the estate of Lord Menana without running afoul of Hauron. She had been away from home almost two fortnights, too long.

Her most exciting activity in the four days since Harkhuf had left her was singing for the Great Royal Wife. Ankhsenamun had heard Anqet sing once and commanded her presence again the following evening. Anqet was doing so now, on a night heavy with still, warm air and incense, in a chamber that gave onto a pleasure garden

Anqet had just finished a song and was listening to a melody by one of her fellow singers when one of the women who waited on the queen ran into the room. She went to the pile of cushions where the queen lay and threw herself at her mistress's feet Ankhsenamun narrowed her eyes, got up, and faced the door. Everyone got up. Quiet filled the room.

Anqet heard the distinct sound of male footsteps, then butts of spears tapping the floor as sentries saluted along the hall. There was a murmur, the sound of deep laughter, and then a group of about twenty young men burst upon the silent chamber. Immediately the Great Wife sank to the floor along with her women

Anqet dared a peek from her position on the floor. All she could see was a pair of broad-toed feet in gold sandals. At a command, everyone rose. With no further ceremony, the two groups blended into one. Music resumed. Anqet played her harp as dancers appeared. The queen sent for wine and poured it into a golden cup for her lord. Anqet noticed that although Pharaoh sat close to his wife, neither he nor his spouse spoke. Neither smiled.

"Singer."

Count Seth leaned over Anqet, and she jumped and missed a note on her harp. He'd worn a wig, and she hadn't noticed him. Curse him.

"You. It was you. It's your fault I'm here."

Seth grinned his evil grin and tossed a length of black wig over his shoulder. "You needn't thank me. I did it for my own convenience."

"I don't intend to thank you, my lord," Anqet said through clenched teeth. "I'm a free woman. Your plottings are of no use. I don't want you."

The count laughed, dropped down beside her, and lowered his voice.

"You don't want me? Ah, singer, you shouldn't lie. It is an abomination to the gods. Besides, the patron goddess

of singers is Hathor, mistress of love. I intend to see that
you fulfill your destiny as an acolyte of the divine Hathor."

Before Anqet could reply, the count melted into the
crowd. She glared after him as he approached Pharaoh.
The king reached out a hand. Seth took it and knelt beside
the boy. Anqet's hands went cold and numb on the strings
of her harp, for the king listened to Seth's whisper and
then settled two distant and troubled eyes on her. On her!
Anqet wanted to sink into the earth. She lowered her
eyes. Hands clapped. She looked up to find the Great
Wife signaling for her. Her knees about to give way, Anqet
stood reluctantly. Frightened, her throat and mouth dry,
Anqet could think of nothing to sing before the son of the
gods.

Oh, she wanted to kick that aristocratic conniver who
sat at Pharaoh's feet and smiled at her like a hungry
crocodile. Anqet lifted her chin and tossed an order over
her shoulder. Music started and she began a triumph song:

> Twice joyful are thy ancestors before thee,
> Thou hast increased their portions.
> Twice joyful is Egypt at thy strong arm,
> Thou hast guarded the ancient order. . . .

As she sang, Anqet's fear lessened its grip. After all,
Pharaoh seemed somewhat human. True, he was the
offspring of the gods, but he was the son of a man as well.
Why, he even looked sad. Sad and a little frightened. As
Anqet digested the novel idea that the king might feel
grief and fear, she saw Count Seth excuse himself. Pharaoh
let him go with reluctance and fastened his remote look
once more on Anqet. The royal attention so flustered
Anqet that she didn't see Count Seth move off among the
ladies and men of Pharaoh's court in search of someone.

Seth struck a leisurely course that meandered over
the entire room. He alighted here and there to share a jest
with a friend, exchange lustful compliments with a woman.
He dared not look at the beautiful singer. He must keep

his head clear and his passions in check. Seth finally settled beside a man who sat alone against a wall and popped chunks of coconut into his mouth.

The man was of middle height with a face like a granite slab. His nose was flat and wide, and his mouth too small for his face. He crunched and slurped, devouring handfuls of white fruit. Between crunches, the man spoke to Seth.

"I am indebted to you, Count. Your warning saved a valuable shipment of mine. However, I think I shall have to kill you for knowing about it at all."

"Why kill a useful ally, Merab?"

"Because," said Merab, "I still can't trust you."

Seth seated himself on a stool and let his eyes roam over the people in the room.

"You know me by reputation. You know I'm not a pious temple lover. How can I prove myself trustworthy?"

"Why would you want to prove it?" Merab asked.

"Revenge." Seth cracked a humorless smile when he saw Merab's confusion. "I want revenge on all the holy, self-satisfied puritans who sneer at me for my tainted blood. I want to see the looks on their faces when they find out the gods can't protect them from defilement." Seth ignored the sensual rhythm of a drum that came from the center of the room. He hissed the words. "There are a few whose names I want to add to your list, since you're about this work anyway."

Merab's teeth clicked. He regarded Seth without surprise. "What surety?"

"Why, my life, to be certain. I'm not a child, Merab. I know what will happen to me if you are discovered, for whatever reason."

Seth was on his feet as a dancer wove her way toward him. She kept her eyes on his face and jerked her shoulders so that her breasts bounced. Seth let out a war cry that was taken up by several men. The count swept the dancer with him toward his friends. Merab stayed where he was and watched Seth, Dega, and Prince Khai surround the woman's gyrating body. When the dancer caught

Seth's belt and leaned backward, bracing herself against his thighs, Merab slipped out of the room unnoticed.

As Anqet watched the erotic performance from a corner she thought of all the horrible ways a dancer could die. She could slip and break her neck. She could impale herself on the dagger of a certain libertine count. A shadow fell across her line of vision. She looked up into the dark eyes of Lord Sennefer. His clean jawline was disguised by the fall of a heavy wig as his head tilted down.

"You are the new singer. The Royal Wife has spoken words of praise for your voice. The beauty of your song is dimmed by the loveliness of your body."

Sennefer moved in front of her, blocking the sight of his brother and Dega with the dancer between them.

"My name is Sennefer," he continued. "You are Anqet."

"Yes, my lord." Anqet blushed at the now-familiar light in Sennefer's eyes.

"You are young," Sennefer said. He assumed a puzzled frown. "And you seem quite unlike most singers." His hand indicated the brazen antics of her sisters. "Am I right? You are new to these games?"

He understood, and he knew that she didn't belong here. How sensitive of him. Tears threatened to embarrass her.

"M-my lord," she said. "I am a singer through hardship. Not a month since, I was in my home near Memphis. Indeed, I know little of the ways of singers or of the court."

Two words came snarling at them: "Dear brother." Seth was beside Sennefer, his arm around the older man's shoulders. "How kind of you to get her to talk. You've gotten more out of her than I have, and in half the time."

Sennefer disengaged himself from Seth and rubbed his arm where Seth's hand had gripped it. "It's plain to see she's frightened."

"And you came to offer comfort," Seth said. "How generous. Now go away."

"Why must you always assume I mean to offend you?"

Sennefer asked. He took Anqet's hand. "Don't let him scare you. His attention is easily distracted, and he is a good lad when he's not trying to feed on everyone's sensitivities."

Sennefer left them. Anqet turned to Count Seth, ready to do battle, but he wasn't looking at her. He was looking at the retreating back of his brother with the eyes of a lost child. Heavy lids came down almost before she was certain of what she'd seen. Seth whirled and caught her wrists. This was no lost child. Wrath ignited a green blaze in those eyes. His voice shook with suppressed anger.

"Whoever heard of a virgin singer?"

Surely it would do no harm to retrieve her harp. Anqet lay on her pallet in the room she shared with five other singers, unable to sleep. She had fled Count Seth's wrath earlier that evening and still couldn't understand its cause. Who was he to question her honor? Why did he care if she'd bedded a man before? Cursed philanderer. He stirred up her desires and insulted her at the same time. He'd made her forget her new harp in the queen's chambers.

It was a small instrument, made to rest on her lap. Though far less costly than the one she'd used at Lady Gasantra's, Anqet treasured it. Harkhuf had given it to her upon hearing her sing one of his compositions. She was loath to forfeit the old man's tribute to her talent. She would sneak into the queen's apartments and get the instrument.

Like the ba bird, spirit of a dead soul, she flitted down the corridors of the palace. The women's quarters were guarded against intrusion from the outside, but not from within. Anqet gained the queen's lounging chamber without incident. A life-size sculpture of Pharaoh and the Great Wife loomed dark and forbidding to her left as Anqet entered. Filmy hangings that screened the entrance to the garden stirred as she tiptoed past them. Moonlight cast the musician's corner into blackness. She crept toward it.

A moan Anqet stopped. There was the sound again—a low sob, chopped off almost before she could hear it. It came from the porch. On silent bare feet, she moved to the corner and edged her head around it to peep outside. She saw nothing but the eight blue-and-white columns that supported the roof of the portico and carefully molded walkways of packed earth that led to groves of palms and sycamores. A fish jumped in the pond to her right.

There was a sharp rush of indrawn breath. Anqet noticed a slick black stain marring the perfection of the column slightly to her left. She was across the porch and around the column before she had time to be afraid of what she might find

Leaning against the pillar, head down, was a man. He wore only a thin robe that hung about his shoulders like a cloak. His hands pressed tightly over a long cut from his lower ribs almost to his groin. His head came up as Anqet rounded the column. She couldn't see his face, for he moved into the shadows deliberately. At the sight of his wound, Anqet went to him.

"You are hurt. Let me help."

Without waiting for an answer, Anqet slipped her shoulder under his arm. At her touch, her patient gave a startled gasp and began to pull away, but Anqet was used to the proud and stubborn ways of injured men at Nefer. She hushed the man's protests and forced him to walk with her, seating him in a chair where the moonlight fell on his wound. It was a clean cut, not shallow but not deep enough to threaten life. Jagged scratches decorated the smooth skin on either side of the wound.

Anqet tore a strip from the hem of her gown and made a pad. She laid it over the cut and had her patient hold it there

"I must get help," she said.

"No."

The word was barely audible, but the tone of command behind it made her stop.

"They mustn't see me like this. No one must know."

Suspicions formed rapidly in Anqet's mind. She was a fool. This man was in the queen's rooms! Anqet tensed, ready to sprint away, but he managed to grasp her arm and stand up, using her for support. As he moved, his face came into the moonlight.

"Pharaoh!"

"Hush."

Anqet fell to her knees. "M-Majesty. Merciful Horus! Majesty—"

"Stop that. I don't need your groveling and your worship now."

Anqet clamped her mouth shut and managed to lift her eyes to the beautiful face of the king. His wideset eyes were large and pained. Compassion did much to still her awe.

"Shall I fetch guards, Majesty?" she asked.

"No. Do you think I want the whole palace to know what she did to me?" The king stopped, then swore. "I must be worse off than I thought. My tongue is loose."

Anqet ignored his angry words.

"What is your will, Pharaoh?"

"I must leave, but I must not be seen in this condition. Find a place where these wounds may be bound."

"There is a room where cushions and mats are stored," she said. "Through that door, my Pharaoh."

Tutankhamun extended his hand. Anqet took it reluctantly. She had treated the living god with familiarity. Amun-Ra would strike her dead. To her surprise, she lived to support the king through a door and into the storage room.

As she helped him to a seat among the piles of cushions, Anqet realized that she would have to bind the king's wound, for they would never be able to hide the stains if his blood got on the floor.

"I must have bandages," she muttered.

Casting a nervous look at the king, she bowed and went out the door. Anqet returned with a lamp from the hallway and a curtain she had jerked from the wall. She tore the material into bandages and wrapped Pharaoh's wound as best she could. When the last knot was tied, she sat back and found Pharaoh staring at her—or through her. She was struck by the change in him. Gone was the remote majesty, the formality, the maturity. Here was a lad tortured by shame and fear, trying desperately not to show it.

"Majesty, you must send for someone," she said. "I will go. Tell me what to do."

Tutankhamun drew a deep breath. His full lips pursed as he moved in pain.

"You know the main entrance to the queen's apartments? Go there. Say these words to the chief of my bodyguard."

Anqet memorized the king's cryptic message. It took all her courage to skulk down the guarded main hall and speak to the silent black giant before the queen's doors. At her words, the Nubian made a quick hand signal, and sentries filed out of the hall. The black man lifted a massive arm and pointed back the way Anqet had come.

She ran back to the king. He was tugging at his makeshift bandage. Anqet pulled his hands away.

"Please, Majesty. You will start bleeding again. The writings of Physician Ahmose say that such a wound must be sewn."

"You can read? How is it that a singer can read?"

Anqet was never required to answer, for the door opened. Pharaoh's bodyguard slipped inside, followed by Seth. The count carried a bundle and a drawn scimitar. He rushed to the king, anxiety plain on his face.

"Majesty, are you all right?"

Seth glanced at the bloodied robe, the bandage, and Anqet, who had retreated to a far corner. A low, urgent conversation followed, to which Anqet was not privy. Seth put his scimitar on the floor, took from the bundle a robe of heavy linen, and helped Tutankhamun dress. Their voices rose in argument.

"No," the king said. "We'll wait until tomorrow to send for the physician. I want no rumors started."

Seth bowed his head. It was the first time Anqet had seen him submit to anyone. She would have doubted even Pharaoh's ability to command the count. Seth helped the king to his feet and escorted him from the room. Anqet was left standing by herself with Pharaoh's bloodied robe in her hands.

Seth reappeared and picked up his scimitar. He took the king's robe from her. "Why are you here?"

On the defensive, Anqet frowned at him.

"I came to get my harp. I forgot it. I heard the king." That was all she was going to say.

Seth put a finger under her chin and tilted her head up so that she was looking at him. Anqet jerked her head away.

"Do you know what happens to people who come upon the secrets of the great?" Seth asked. "Sons of pharaohs have been killed for learning too much."

Anqet shrank away from him. "Pharaoh told you to kill me."

"No. I only want to make sure you understand that it is a possibility. Pharaoh asked me to thank you, and commands your silence."

Anqet nodded. The count studied her, letting his eyes roam over her body. Anqet could feel a blush spread over her face. Seth leaned down and kissed her on the nose.

"Remember this, sweet one. Kindness and intelligence can get you killed. Tend to your singing, and do not force the Living Horus to cut out your tongue by using it too freely."

Seth traced a long finger over her lips, then kissed them and vanished. Anqet suppressed a shiver. She looked around the room to make sure there were no traces of their visit, but Seth had already taken care of that.

Why had she gone out on the portico? Inexperienced as she was, she should have known that only one man would be present so close to the queen's apartments. She was fortunate that Pharaoh was young and softhearted. His brother Akhenaten or his father, Amenhotep III, would have made her mute for hearing such secrets. Anqet had no doubt that the queen had attacked Tutankhamun in bed. The woman must be mad. She was the daughter of the heretic Akhenaten; she was probably insane.

Anqet made the sign against evil and resolved to obtain a charm that would protect her from further danger. She would see one of the magician priests tomorrow.

That evening, on the right bank of the Nile in the temple complex of Amun-Ra, the adoration of the god was over. Priests of all ranks, Divine Servants, Pure Ones, Prophets, Seers, and Sem Priests had long since scattered to their homes within the walls of the god's city. Deep within the god's house, behind the pylon of Thutmose III, in a tiny windowless room off the main shrine, sat Lord Merab's leader. The man was known simply as the master. He read from a brightly painted papyrus. Air circulated in the chamber through grilles set high in its walls. The breeze made the flames from alabaster lamps flutter. The master rolled one page closed and slipped it into the compartment of a stiff leather case. As he reached for another page, Lord Merab entered. The master looked up, his face registering surprise.

"Something has happened," Merab said.

"I assumed that you had a good reason for coming to me here."

His sandals creaked as Merab rocked on his feet. He had put off reporting to the master about Count Seth, for he knew that his leader had the temper of a possessed cobra, hide it as he might from most. Merab had seen the master deliberately unleash his rage—and kill. Stuttering, with many hesitations, Merab revealed that Count Seth, nomarch of Annu-Rest, knew of his activities and wanted to join their association.

The master said nothing, even after Merab had finished. "He doesn't know about you," Merab said uneasily.

"Offal-head. Of course he doesn't know, or he would have dealt with me, not you."

The moments passed in quiet tension. Merab thought the master had forgotten his presence, the man was so intent on his own thoughts. Something brown came flying at him, and Merab jumped back as the master hurled the leather case across the room.

"Him! He will ruin everything with his pernicious urges to affront the true order." The master pointed a finger at Merab. "You say he suspects nothing more than simple thievery. I tell you, we have to be sure. Our plans for the venture in the North will mature soon. I want to make sure of him before that. We can't afford to leave him loose around the king with his knowledge. Either he becomes one of us, or he dies. Once he's committed a crime, he won't betray us, for fear of exposure."

Merab stepped around the leather case. "Unless he serves Pharaoh."

"Seth wouldn't bestir himself on behalf of the dead, even for Pharaoh," the master said. "Remember his mother."

"Body of Osiris, who does not?"

The master picked up a bookroll and tapped it idly against the tips of his fingers. Merab relaxed, now that his life was no longer in danger. His confidence in his ally was unquestioning. For years the man's ingenious plans had brought them riches, riches carefully concealed and used to buy adherents and favors among the state's bureaucrats and greedy priesthood. The master's hidden influence was felt throughout Pharaoh's kingdom.

Merab's leader dropped the papyrus. "Perhaps the gods have done us a favor, my friend." The master ran his fingers lovingly over the roll where it lay on the table. "Yes. I begin to think Amun-Ra, the Hidden One, has put Seth in my power for a reason. I'll think upon this. I must consider how best to take advantage of our dear count's indiscretion. I'll have instructions for you soon. We will meet in the customary place. Don't come here again."

Merab bowed to the master and withdrew, leaving the man staring into a lamp flame with a peaceful expression on his face that boded ill for Count Seth. As he walked through the quiet shrine past a black basalt statue of Sesostris I, Merab again counted himself lucky. He had been sure that the sound of Seth's name alone would produce one of the master's killing rages. Once Merab had seen him plunge his dagger into a man's throat because the unfortunate had questioned his orders.

One did not question the master. One obeyed without inquiry—and became wealthy. It would be a pleasure to watch his leader wrap Count Seth in his powerful coils. They hadn't expected Pharaoh's friend to come within their reach. The master wasn't that secure in his power yet. Merab's grin widened. As long as his own hide wasn't endangered, he would enjoy the contest between the count and the master whose lethal vindictiveness was as hidden as the Hidden One himself.

Where could one find the privacy to pen a letter when one wasn't supposed to know how to write?

Anqet had obtained a scrap of papyrus, a reed pen, and ink from the magician priest who gave her the amulet of the buckle that would protect her from harm. It was a charm of red glass shaped like a miniature buckle. She wore it suspended from a copper chain. In return for the amulet, Anqet had transmitted a love token to a dancer for the priest.

Anqet twirled the reed pen in her hand. The problem was not to reveal her education. Gossip of a court singer named Anqet who was also learned might reach Hauron before she could gain the safety of Menana's house. Anqet stuffed her writing materials into a bag, along with a vial of water.

She decided to take a walk. She would keep her eyes open for a good hiding place. She had more free time now, for today the Great Royal Wife had suddenly gone to Abydos with most of the harem. Ostensibly the queen went to dedicate a new wing of the Osiris temple. Anqet was sure that Pharaoh could no longer abide his wife's presence under his roof. One of the queen's women had commanded Anqet's presence on the royal barge, but the

order was countermanded by Pharaoh's steward. So here
she was, stuck in the women's quarters with a reduced
contingent of singers, dancers, acrobats, and musicians
who had nothing to do because Pharaoh was indisposed
and the court's activities in abeyance.

It was dusk. Heat from the afternoon sun still baked
the bricks of the living quarters. Anqet sauntered toward
the east side of the compound where little-used storehouses hugged the outer guard wall. She passed artisans,
laborers, and slaves headed for home and the evening
meal. In the distance she could hear one of the king's
horse masters swearing at a stallion newly arrived from
some desert kingdom.

Anqet glanced up and down the path that led to the
storehouses. Ahead lay a block of buildings in disrepair. A
dumping ground for everything from broken harnesses to
flawed stone from the sculptors' workshop, the place was
deserted. Holes had begun to appear in walls and in the
exterior staircase at the end of the building. These stairs
led to the roof and had three steps missing at the base.

Anqet paused beside the stairs and inspected them
under the guise of adjusting the strap of her sandal. No
one was around. Who would look for her on the roof of a
storehouse? Pleased with her cleverness, she hopped up
the steps and onto the roof. There were holes in it, so
she'd have to stay close to the edge. The walls of the
building extended above the surface of the roof, so that
she was hidden from anyone on the ground. Anqet sat
down and leaned back against the wall. Taking out her
supplies, she mixed ink while she thought of the best
way to explain to Menana that she wanted to be his
wife after all and that they had to hire a small army as
soon as possible.

Anqet swirled the tip of her pen in the ink and tried
not to worry. Each day she was absent from home risked
the souls of her parents. She was afraid Hauron would
take vengeance upon her by destroying the eternally
preserved bodies of Rahotep and Taia. It was the threat of

this horror that gave her the courage to propose to the unexciting Menana.

The failing light was causing her eyestrain by the time Anqet was halfway through the third sentence of her letter. She packed up her utensils and was about to swing her leg over the wall when a man walked past the stairs. Anqet crouched behind her wall and raised her head barely above it. The man stopped to adjust his sandal, just as she had. The coincidence sparked her curiosity. To her dismay, the intruder went around the staircase and leaned against its back as though he intended to remain there for some time.

She heard a crunch and peeped over the low wall. She could make out the man's form only as a blacker mass in the darkness. He was popping bits of whiteness into his mouth. Coconut. The noise of his chewing was loud. Anqet groaned inwardly and sat down with her back to the wall. Why did this man have to choose her refuge as a place to snack?

The time passed, enlivened by lip smacking. Someone else came near. She could tell because he was humming a pastoral tune in a low, vibrant voice. Anqet once more peered down at the intruder. A tall, sinewy man, the man who hummed, had joined him. He still hummed and watched the other man calmly munching coconut. The tune was familiar. It was the song of a lovesick cattle herder. Anqet blinked. She almost giggled. The insult was completely lost on the coconut eater. The newcomer broke into song:

> *The cattle are my companions,*
> *I have no others.*

Anqet shrank down in her hiding place. Not him again! It was a curse. The count finished his verse and eyed the other man.

"Merab, you have news. Control your appetite and tell me."

"I have need of transport for my goods," Merab said, his mouth full of coconut. "Seagoing vessels and cargo ships for the trip downriver."

"What you mean is, you've robbed a few tombs and want to get rid of the spoils before Pharaoh sends his agents throughout the Two Lands looking for purloined grave furnishings."

Merab swallowed a bunch of coconut in one gulp. He waved at the count to silence him.

"Don't you think Osiris knows what offense we commit against his land of the dead?" said Seth. "The god who rose after his death surely sees what you do."

"I'm more concerned with making sure no mortal hears of it, my lord." Merab poked his head around the corner of the storehouse. He rejoined Seth. "I need cargo vessels. In ten days they must be at Edfou."

Anqet listened, horror making her stomach churn. She clutched the amulet of the buckle for protection. She repeated to herself a prayer in the words of power given to her by the magician: *Blood of Isis, and the strength of Isis, be mighty to act as powers to protect me, and to guard me from him that would do unto me any abomination.*

They were grave robbers. She had heard of such people. In one of the villages near Nefer, an old man had been caught stealing food from graves, but he had been poor and without family to care for him. These men were different. They robbed out of greed. No. Count Seth was many things, but not greedy. He ravished eternal houses because it pleased him to do so. So much was plain from the mocking way he talked of the business.

As she came to this last conclusion, heaviness settled over Anqet. It was as if her twin spirits, her ba and her ka, grieved. Had she hoped this man might turn out to be something other than what he was? Tears stung her eyes. She dabbed at them angrily with a corner of her shift. Why was she so stupid—to hope that Seth's body housed a soul equal in beauty to that pleasing exterior?

They were leaving. Merab lumbered off in the direction of the palace. Seth made his graceful way toward the rear gatehouse, humming the cattle herder's tune. Anqet watched him go, but made no move to leave her rooftop. What should she do? Should she tell someone of her

discovery? Whom would she tell? Who would believe her,
a singer? Wisdom born of danger and hardship told Anqet
that she would be dead before the truth of her story could
be verified. She was in the palace, and the palace was
Seth's domain and Merab's, not hers. Yet she could not let
them continue to commit atrocities.

Anqet chewed her lip, deep in thought. She heard
the scurryings of rats in the room below. Somewhere she
heard the crash of broken pottery and a muffled curse.

If she could get word to Pharaoh—but no humble cup
bearer such as herself spoke to Pharaoh. Even the king's
thanks had come to her by way of Count Seth. The Great
Royal Wife was as unreachable. Anqet thought of the
glamorous young lords who served the ruler of the Two
Lands. Not one would listen, and many served under
Seth, commander of the king's chariots. Perhaps she should
speak to a priest. There were many Divine Servants and
Pure Ones in attendance at the palace. They served
Pharaoh, especially when the king went to the temple of
Amun-Ra to converse with the god. Surely one of them
would listen and speak to his superior, the high priest.
The high priest could certainly approach Pharaoh.

A course of action, that was what she needed. She
needed proof of her accusations. If only she knew where
these criminals hid some of their stolen riches. She should
have listened to the two men more closely instead of
cowering in fear. She remembered that some of Count
Seth's vessels were to travel downriver, picking up concealed
shipments. What had been their parting words? Ah! The
one called Merab had asked for another meeting. Tomorrow
night they would meet behind this same building. Anqet
would be in her perch above them and listen.

Aghast at her own daring, she slinked down the
staircase. As her foot touched ground, Seth's menacing
words came to mind: "Do you know what happens to
people who come upon the secrets of the great?"

She would be sure that she was well away from
Thebes before the magnificent lord of the Falcon nome
discovered that she knew his secrets.

5

Clad only in a loincloth, his body sweating in the afternoon sunlight, Seth gripped his dagger, crouched low, and circled Lord Dega so that the younger man's face was to the sun. Seth was breathing hard, but Dega was breathing harder. With deliberate cunning he let his eyes focus on the left side of Dega's abdomen while he lunged and struck at his equerry's throat. Dega leapt backward, but not quickly enough. Seth continued his assault and brought Dega to the ground under him. He grasped the warrior's slippery dagger arm and brought his own weapon to rest on the exposed throat.

Dega went still, and the two men stared at each other, lungs gulping in the heated air. Drops of sweat beaded on Dega's upper lip. An animal gleam came into Seth's eyes, and he shifted his weight so that Dega's body was pinned beneath him. He drew the blade lightly across Dega's skin, and a thin red line appeared.

Seth crooned to his captive. "Among my mother's people, when a chief dies, his closest liege men are put to death. Their throats are slit. They are disemboweled and stuffed with straw. They are set on their horses with their weapons inside the chief's tomb," Seth said.

Dega met his commander's burning gaze without flinching.

"I can't help it if your singer is a virgin."

Seth's lips drew back over his teeth in a snarl. He hurled the dagger across the practice yard and released Dega. The warrior got to his feet, gathered their weapons, and followed Seth across the yard and into one of the palace barracks. They headed for the bathing rooms, but Seth was stopped by a group of three men. One, a young man with the bearing of a pharaoh and eyes with the welcome of a scimitar, stepped in Seth's way, his hand playing with the hilt of a dagger in his belt.

"You can't send me to Sile," the officer said.

Seth raised his brows. "Oh? I thought I could. I am your commander." The count appeared to think about the matter. "Yes. Yes, I'm almost certain that I can send you there, Prince Bakenkhonsu." Seth smiled happily at the young man.

Bakenkhonsu turned as red as watermelon fruit. His hand closed over the dagger at his side. Before he could draw, Seth stepped close to him, planted a short punch in his stomach, and sent the dagger flying into Lord Dega's waiting hand. The other two officers closed in to support Bakenkhonsu by the arms while he gasped and grunted in pain.

Seth lifted his opponent's chin with one hand and spoke to him in a voice as hard as the stone of a sarcophagus.

"You mistreat the warriors under your command. You have allowed your chariot driver, who should be as your second self, to be injured because you thought it was more important to kill a worthless bandit than to protect him. You will go to the fortress of Sile and learn what it means to value your fellow warriors as comrades. You'll learn to work with them and to be worthy of their loyalty and respect. You will learn these things, or the Bedouin will bury you alive in the desert with your head just above the ground, so that you can be eaten alive by scorpions, ants, and the demons of the wasteland."

The count dropped his hand and stalked off to the bathing stalls with Dega close behind. As water was poured over their heads, Dega took a handful of soda and rubbed it into his chest and back to remove the grit and dried sweat.

"Bakenkhonsu is royal. He can make trouble for you," Dega said through a stream of water.

Seth parted his drenched hair and looked at Dega. His friend was slender, almost fragile-looking in bone structure, with calm eyes, a wide, rounded face, and small nose. Dega's appearance was deceptive. He had the strength and agility of a leopard. More than once he had bested the count in the practice yard. Seth grinned at his equerry.

"Bakenkhonsu is a royal ass. Pharaoh knows it and asked me to break him before he got himself killed."

"He is like to do that anyway."

"Pharaoh has spoken," Seth said.

That ended any discussion. Dega handed an oil jar to his commander. A slave dabbed at the younger man's throat with a salve. Dega shoved the boy's hand away impatiently and toweled himself dry. He started at the feel of oil trickling down his shoulder and turned to find the count pouring the scented stuff from the jar. Dega made a grab for the container, but Seth switched hands and emptied it on his other shoulder. Dega cursed in frustration and padded out of the chamber, leaving a trail of oil behind him.

"Do me a service," he called from the robing chamber. "Bed that girl before you drive me to take refuge among the nomads."

Seth swept into the room and stood looming, wet and angry, over Dega. "What are you talking about?"

"It's been over a week since you almost ran her down," Dega said. Since then, you've been as nervous as a student on his first visit to the taverns." The slave rubbing his shoulders stepped back in alarm at the look in Seth's eyes, but Dega merely eyed the count. "You've refused Gasantra's advances, yet you won't bed this new fancy of yours. Instead you devote yourself to Pharaoh and torment the rest of us with desert drills and naval exercises that we went through last month. And now you try to flay me in practice. Your lust for this girl will be my death."

Seth waved the attendants out of the robing chamber. Walking around the bench where Dega sat, he began to rub the kinks out of his friend's shoulders.

"My poor Dega, I've used the whip on you a lot lately."

"Let's go to the Blue Ibex tonight." Dega winced as the count's fingers dug into his muscles. "You can repay me with their best wine."

"I have letters to write. My stepmother is complaining about her allowance again, and about Khet."

Dega twisted around and looked up at the count. Seth was looking off into space, his hands still on Dega's shoulders.

"Baba has returned from Nubia," Dega said. "She'll be there tonight. She asked for you. Ouch!"

"I don't want Baba. I don't want Gasantra. I want her."

"So what delays you?" Dega rubbed his shoulder where Seth's strong fingers had worked vigorously.

"She delays me, the little beast. First I couldn't find her. Then she refused me. Then she turned out to be a virgin. Now she—she has put me in her debt. What are you laughing at?"

"You." Dega tied a belt around his kilt and handed Seth his garment. "Someone finally refused you. I think you're in a daze from the shock of it " Dega chuckled.

"How would you like duty on the First Cataract?" Seth asked. "You could entertain the water buffalo and baboons with your sense of humor."

"I'm staying right here and watch the singer play with you."

Seth pulled his belt tight around his waist and scowled at Dega. "Your entertainment won't last much longer. This virgin's game ends tonight."

"And if she's not playing a game?"

"There will still be no virgin among Pharaoh's singers tomorrow. I can play the supplicant and gentle lover if I set my heart to it."

That evening, Seth was in the outer chamber of his apartments in the royal palace preparing to fulfill his words. The sun died behind the western cliffs of the necropolis. He stood on the balcony and gazed into the branches of an old sycamore that grew in front of it.

Behind him, the room had taken on a warm and aureate glow from the lamps lit by the servants. The walls of the room were decorated with scenes of himself and his brothers fowling in the papyrus thickets, hunting wild bulls, and sailing on the Nile. The greens of the papyrus marsh, and the deep, almost lapis-blue of the Nile's water gave the whole chamber a feeling of vibrancy. Seth could almost hear the slap of water against the reed skiff and Khet's excited whispers as they lay in wait for a flock of game birds. The memory made him long for a few weeks at home with Khet, away from the tedious decorum of the court. Perhaps after he finished with Merab, he'd go to Annu-Rest.

Seth glanced at the door. He'd sent a maid to fetch Anqet, and it was taking the woman a long time to bring her. Walking back into the room, he stopped to touch one of the lotus flowers floating in a gold basin. Anqet's skin was as soft as the lotus. His electrum wristband slid down to his hand when he touched the flower. It was inlaid with a scarab of lapis lazuli and matched the blue stones in the collar that covered his shoulders. He had deliberately dressed in a soft robe of revealing white linen that hugged his hips. Gone was the armor, the protective leather and bronze of the soldier. He didn't want to intimidate Anqet. He always seemed to be scaring the girl when all he really wanted was to make love to her.

The door opened, and Seth looked up from the lotus blossom to see Anqet walk in. She wore a simple, sleeveless gown that fit snugly around her body in a way that made him want to tear it off and run his hands over the curves it revealed and hid at the same time. Anqet wore none of the ornate jewelry flaunted by Gasantra and the other court beauties. Seth realized that no man would notice its lack.

When she saw him, her eyes widened, and she turned to go. He resisted the urge to pounce on her; he'd done too much of that "Please don't go." He made his voice gentle and calm. "I won't hurt you."

Anqet muttered something he couldn't hear and put her hand on the door He was beside her before she got it open, leading her back into the room. He fought the impulse to slip his arm around her shoulders. By the gods! She had only to come near him, and he throbbed almost uncontrollably. She smelled of jasmine and some fragrance that reminded him of fresh water and wildflowers. Curse it. He would not lose control. He would not.

Seth escorted Anqet to a chair and took her hand. She looked at him nervously when he sank to a stool at her feet, blocking her path to the door. Her hand was cold, and trembled. Had he frightened her that much? She was young.

"Anqet, I want to beg your forgiveness. I have treated you like an experienced singer or tavern girl, and you are not." Seth smiled. "I know. I never gave you the chance to tell me you weren't. I'm afraid when I saw you at Gasantra's house, I assumed you were like the others you were with. I have had occasion to enjoy the talents of one of them. So you see, I was under a false impression. Can you forgive me?"

"That's why you sent for me?" Anqet asked. Her great dark eyes bore into his own—searching, questioning.

Seth squeezed Anqet's hand and brought it to his lips. He sighed when she pulled it away. "Yes, to apologize and to talk. I would like to know something about you. Something besides the fact that you are more beautiful than Isis and that your voice could charm a man's ka out of his body." He leaned back on the stool so that he could see her face. She was staring at her clasped hands. "Do you have family in Thebes?"

"No, my lord."

"Where is your home?"

"In the North."

Seth persisted. "Where in the North?"

"It is many days' sail from here."

Seth looked at the girl's tense body and guarded face.

There was more to her reticence than virgin shyness. She was concealing something. Probably she had run away from an overbearing father, or she might be a thief. Impossible. A girl this beautiful would have no need to steal. Still, her reluctance to speak about her home was intriguing. Most Egyptians were quick to tell you their family, their lineage, clan, village, nome. They were enthusiastic visitors and exchangers of genealogical information. Yes, Anqet had something to hide. He would find out what it was.

"Pharaoh tells me you can read. Not many singers can read. How did you learn?" Anqet paled. Seth watched her slim fingers press together. "Be at ease. I only asked because, now that I think of it, you do not act much like a singer. You are quiet, and when you speak, your words are those of a girl trained in manners and propriety. Yet you sing for strangers, as any common woman. Tell me, have you and your family come upon misfortune?"

Seth placed his hand over Anqet's, and she let it rest there. "My father died several months ago, my lord. I earn my keep as I can, for although he was a loving man, he was not a wise one in the ways of evil. My home and possessions have been taken from me." Her voice faltered. "But I would give the whole estate and more to have him back, to see him laugh and smile with my mother, to see them together and happy. May I go now?"

"Do you really want to leave?"

"Yes."

"Why? Please don't. I can see you're unhappy. I know what it is to lose a father. The world loses its underpinnings. One is a barge adrift on rapids." Seth leaned toward Anqet. He slid a hand up her arm and rested it on her shoulder. "You have lost much, and you seem so frightened. I chastise myself for adding to your fears."

Seth pulled her firmly toward him. "My sweet one, let me ease your fears. I would give you pleasure and care for you. If you would let me. Let me." He held those earth-black eyes with his own and let his words soothe the girl while he drew her to him. He slipped his other arm

behind her and brought her lips down on his. He could
feel her trembling. Was it only out of fear? He would
make her tremble for a better reason. Seth gently forced
Anqet's mouth open with his own and lost himself in warm
moistness.

A shadow blocked the lamplight. Seth opened his
eyes and twisted, his hand already reaching for the dagger
at his belt.

"Sennefer, you fool, I could have killed you. Get out."

"I knocked. You didn't hear me."

Seth turned back to Anqet. The girl had risen and
was edging toward the door. He placed a hand on her arm.
She jumped and uttered a small cry.

"Please, Anqet, don't go."

"Seth!" Sennefer moved his tall body between them
and brushed Seth's hand from Anqet's arm. Imprisoning
the offending arm, he faced his younger brother. "Do you
still pursue this child? Look at her. She's quivering. What
have you done to her?"

As always, Sennefer's presence set a pack of howling
jackals loose in Seth's heart. The anger and bewildered
hurt of eleven years ago lay buried until he was forced to
deal with his brother. And as always, Seth sought to
conceal his desperation and the pain.

"I've done nothing to her. Yet. Do you want to watch,
brother?"

Sennefer's reply was interrupted by Anqet's gasp.
The singer turned and ran out of the room. Seth muttered
an obscenity. He jerked his arm free of his brother's
restraining hold. He turned his back on Sennefer and
went to a table against the wall where he poured a goblet
of wine.

"Get out."

"I'm sorry, Seth."

"It's nothing. One more night without sleep. She's
like an infestation in the blood."

Seth looked over his shoulder. Sennefer was watching
him with that sad, forgive-me look. Seth turned away.
Beside the winejar lay a jewel box of polished, red-brown

wood. Its top was carved with the figure of a warrior on a leaping stallion. His grandfather, the chief. Where was that other family now, his barbarian blood? Did their women raise brothers to hate each other as Seth's and Sennefer's mothers had tried to do?

"Go away, Sennefer. I have an itch in my loins that will drive me into a rage now that you've taken my satisfaction from me."

"Drink some more wine. Better still, visit Gasantra."

"I don't want Gasantra. Bareka! Can't you leave me alone? Go play with your priest friends. Sacrifice a lamb or whatever it is you do with all those sheep at the temple. Priests seem to have an unhealthy liking for woolly pets."

"Seth." Sennefer's tone was hard, a stern older-brother warning. "You can leave off the insults. I'm used to them. You forget I watched you grow up. You'll have to do more than spout heresies to shock me. Now sit down. I'm going to talk to you, whether you want it or not."

Seth gave an elaborate sigh. He took the chair Anqet had vacated. Unfortunately, Sennefer chose to occupy the stool at his feet. Seth curled his lips. "Afraid I'll bolt like she did?"

"Yes. Hold your tongue and listen to me." Sennefer linked his hands together and rested them on the white pleats of his robe. He wore thick gold bracelets and anklets engraved with the falcon emblem of their family. His brown skin caught the burnished light of the metal. "Seth, are you involved in this tomb-robbing obscenity?"

Jewel-green eyes widened in amusement. A rapturous laugh bubbled forth. "Oh, thank you Sennefer. That was lovely. You're so worried."

"Stop it," Sennefer said, a flush creeping into his face. "If you have desecrated houses of eternity, you will ruin our whole family. Pharaoh will burn every house and field we own, and you'll be lucky if he takes your head instead of letting the priests have you. And what of the rest of us? Have you no care for what happens to Khet or our stepmother—or me?"

"Calm your frenzy. I'm always careful in what I do."

Sennefer regarded his brother in silence. "Have you sinned in this horrible fashion, little brother?"

"The transgressions of my ka are not your concern. I told you that long ago."

"I'm the one who first instructed you in religion. Should you die, I will have responsibility for the care and feeding of your soul." Sennefer's voice rang out in the quiet chamber. "I ask you again. Have you sought to destroy the harmony and balance of the Two Lands to feed your sick cravings?"

Seth stared at the man at his feet. He let the quiet soothe his urge to kick his solicitous brother. He bent down to Sennefer so that his face was a finger's width from the other's ear.

"Hypocrite," he said. "You're worried about your own devout skin. Don't try to convince me you'd mind becoming nomarch if I died."

"Will you never forget that?" Sennefer said. He backed away from Seth. "I was young. Mother taught me to hate you. You don't know how it felt to see Father come back with that foreign usurper. He forgot us and took her to wife. Later, you would look at me with her eyes, witch's eyes, and want to be friends. I was trying to hate you. You nearly drove me mad, following me around, trying to do the things I did. I didn't want you."

"So you decided to kill me."

Swift as a cobra's strike, Sennefer's blow gave Seth no time to duck. The older man's hand struck him across the mouth and drew blood. Seth's head snapped to one side. The yellow glow of the room brightened to silver for a moment. He waited for the floor to stop chasing the walls and settle back under his feet. Then he brushed a strand of auburn hair from his eyes, sat up, and wiped the blood from his mouth.

Sennefer was on his feet and bending over him. "Falcon, I'm sorry." He tried to turn Seth's head, to look at the damage he'd done. His hand paused as it touched his brother's chin. "Are you trying to make me hate you all over again? Don't do it, brother."

They engaged in wordless combat until something in Seth's face made his brother sigh and drop his hands. "Inundation approaches. Will you be here for the festival of Opet?"

"I don't know," Seth said. He relaxed now that they spoke of impersonal things. "Pharaoh wants me to stay, but I haven't been home yet."

Sennefer inclined his head and moved away. He went to the door and stopped outside for a moment. When he returned, he was followed by a black shadow. It was a hunting dog, a purebred hound. All bone, sinew, and muscle, the creature had long, soft hair as dark as Sennefer's own and a narrow, aristocratic head dominated by enormous eyes. The hound walked into the room as if he were master and sat down beside Sennefer next to Seth's chair.

"His name is Meki, protector. He's a hunter and will make a good friend, I think. He's young, but then so are you."

Seth eyed the dog. The animal cocked its head to one side and sniffed. Then he moved closer to Seth, put one paw on his knee, and stared straight into Seth's eyes. Seth couldn't help stroking the sleek head.

"Did you teach him to do that?" he asked.

"I haven't taught him anything. I didn't think you'd take him if I did."

Meki shifted his weight and rested his other paw on Seth's knee.

Sennefer laughed. "I don't know where he got that from. Will you accept him?"

Seth nodded. He followed his brother to the door. "You deprived me of my evening's companion. It's only fair that you provide me with another, although I'd rather—"

"Enough, Falcon. I don't want to hear your plans for that poor child."

"Don't worry. I'll make her happy. For a while, anyway." Seth's grin faded into one of his infrequent expressions of solemnity. "My thanks, Panther."

Sennefer threw back his head and laughed. "You

haven't called me that in over ten years. I should have bribed you long ago."

Seth smiled back at his brother. He watched the older man walk down the hall. He shut the door and leaned against it

Panther and Falcon. Cat and bird of prey. Could they exist together without enmity, two such unnatural companions?

He returned to his chair. Meki set a paw on his knee again. Seth stroked the dog's head absently and let his thoughts drift back to Anqet, the mysterious, learned, and beautiful Anqet. He had to find a way to be with her. She needed someone to look after her. Seth's hand froze on Meki's head. A warm, rushing feeling came over him. Anqet was a lady, and she needed protection. What was she doing in this city alone? An unaccompanied woman in Thebes was prey to all the cutthroats and perverts that any great capital attracted.

Bareka! What was wrong with him? The agitation in his heart was like the frenzy of a feeding crocodile. That settled it. He would take the girl to his town house near the palace. She would be safe there; he could have her whenever he wished. And he wouldn't worry about some other warrior or noble getting his hands on her.

Having decided Anqet's future for her, Seth turned his thoughts to his impending encounter with Lord Merab.

Not long after she fled Count Seth, Anqet sat beneath a palm tree in one of the gardens on the palace grounds. She hugged her knees to her chest, rested her cheek on her knees, and shivered with anger, anger at herself. She had let Count Seth make love to her.

You were frightened. You were sure he knew that you'd discovered his secret. By the time you figured out that he had not, it was too late. He tricked you by being nice. It isn't fair. He's a criminal. You know he's vicious, yet he still makes your blood turn to hot wine.

She heard the rustling of leaves and feared that Count Seth had followed her but as the man came closer, she saw that it was Lord Sennefer It was annoying that the count, his brother, Dega, and General Horemheb were all of similar height and build. At a distance she could hardly distinguish between them.

When she realized that her visitor was Lord Sennefer, Anqet felt secure To her, Seth's brother carried with him the aura of a priest of Osiris, the god of hope and renewed life. He was a gentle and devout man, a mature and sane version of his cruel brother.

"Ah, dear child, my servant said you ran off in this direction." Lord Sennefer motioned for her to remain seated and gave her a smile that radiated peace. "I was afraid I wouldn't be able to find you."

Sennefer sat beside her. He rested his weight on one arm and looked at her with worried eyes. Anqet noted the hair-thin lines at the corners of his mouth, but it was the same wide, sensual mouth that had invaded her own so devastatingly not long ago. Its corners turned up in a deceptive way that implied good humor where often there was none. Anqet tore her eyes from Lord Sennefer's lips and concentrated on his words.

"I know how shattering my brother's attentions can be. I fear he has developed a craving for you." Sennefer shook his head. "I can not influence him, but I can offer you my protection."

"You are kind, my lord, but you don't know me. Why should you bother?"

Sennefer averted his gaze Anqet saw his shoulders hunch, as if some unpleasant demon had settled on them.

"I'm to blame for much of what my brother does. If I had been kinder to him when we were growing up, perhaps he wouldn't be so vicious now. After I married, I saw to it that my wife knew my feelings for Seth, and she adopted them. She avoids him as a Bedouin avoids cities." Sennefer turned back to her with a sad smile. "In the last years I've tried to repair the bright jewel I crushed beneath my heel."

Lifting her brows, Anqet tilted her head to one side. "He doesn't appear crushed to me."

"He isn't your brother," Sennefer said. "In any case, the honor of my ka demands that I help you. I have a daughter. She is younger than you, but I wouldn't like to see her corrupted. I could have someone take you home. You don't belong here, Anqet. At least, you don't belong here alone. Seth isn't the only man who wants you. He's just the most dangerous of them."

Anqet warmed to the compassion in Sennefer's voice. He too had suffered from Seth's aggression. How kind of him to feel responsible for her, a stranger. Would there be any harm in letting Sennefer send her to Menana's house?

"Near Memphis there is a town called South Wall. I would like to go there in a few days to see the man who wishes to marry me."

There was a small pause while Sennefer examined a ring on one of his fingers.

"I will arrange an escort," he said. Sennefer put his hand on Anqet's forearm. "When you are ready to go, come to my house in the Avenue of the Sacred Sycamore. Are you sure you won't come at once?"

Anqet lowered her eyes. Sennefer's hand was still on her arm, and she noticed the heavy silver ring on his third finger. It had a flat bezel into which was etched an ostrich feather, symbol of truth. A strange design, to show only the one hieroglyph and nothing else. In order to invoke the magical protection of Maat, goddess of truth and patroness of justice, one usually wore the image of the deity herself.

"You're upset and confused. I shouldn't let my urge to reform my brother blind me to the fact that you know less of me than of Seth. I'll wait until you ask for help."

Anqet felt a wave of gratitude that threatened to send her into tears.

"You are kind, my lord. May thy ka find peace."

Sennefer brought his hand to her cheek. Anqet didn't shy away when he kissed her lightly on the forehead.

Lord Sennefer stood up and gave her his hand to steady her as she rose. Anqet was surprised to feel his hand shake as it lay on her arm. She was about to ask if he was ill when Seth's brother excused himself abruptly and plunged down a path toward the palace.

Anqet didn't wait for anyone else to come searching for her. She found her way to the workshops and slipped down the black path to her storehouse hiding place. She put her foot on a crack in the roof in climbing over the ledge of the building. Her leg plunged into the wood and mud-brick beneath. Luckily she caught the ledge and pulled herself back before she lost balance. Her leg was scraped a bit and bruised, but not seriously hurt. Anqet knelt down and propped her arms on the ledge to wait for Count Seth and Lord Merab.

There was no moon by the time Merab slunk around the corner of the storehouse. Anqet's eyes were heavy-lidded and dry. She had to force them open to make out the square blob of darkness that was Merab. Leaning over the edge of the roof, she heard a curious smacking sound that helped her locate him.

What was that noise? It was a wet, mouthy sound. Merab was eating again, but he'd chosen to vary his diet. Probably dates. Sticky, mushy dates.

A tall silhouette floated up next to Merab. In the darkness, Anqet could see little more than the vague froth of a court robe, but the height and slender grace of the figure spoke for itself.

She leaned out over the edge of the wall. They *would* decide to whisper. She couldn't hear them. Plague take them. They hadn't been so quiet before.

Ah! If she laid her head sideways, she could just make out a few words.

"Heretic." "Old heretic . . . one large haul . . . place to store . . . dupe."

There was a pause. The two moved away. Count Seth started to leave first, but turned back.

"Change . . ."

What had he said? "Change" something, and "further," or was it "father"?

Anqet sat down on the roof. What was she going to do if Count Seth and Merab continued to speak so softly?

There wasn't anywhere else that offered a chance to eavesdrop. She couldn't lie on top of the wide outer wall; they might see her. Anyway, she wasn't sure she could leap the distance between it and the storehouse. The gap must be over six cubits. She would have to ask the god Osiris to make the criminals speak a little louder in the future.

Seth had fed Meki roast duck and left him curled up on the balcony. He was a few paces outside his room when the treasurer of the Two Lands came charging down the hall and almost collided with him. Maya was a small man with a slight paunch and flat feet that reminded Seth of bow cases.

Seth stepped out of the way of those feet. "My lord Maya, what causes this haste?"

"Com—Commander. Pharaoh—" *Puff, puff.* "Pharaoh—" *Puff.*

Seth scowled at the treasurer. "Say it, man. Has Pharaoh sent for me?"

Maya shook his head. His wig was askew, and he was sweating.

"Hurry, my lord. Terrible."

"Terrible?" Seth raced toward the royal apartments with Maya in tow. "Is the king hurt? Talk!"

"Not hurt. It was the message. He turned so pale. Threw everyone out, even Prince Khai. Won't speak. Not to the Divine Father, not to General Horemheb, not to me."

Seth rounded a corner and charged at the great double doors where the chief bodyguard was already waiting. He left Maya behind as he ran through the state rooms and into the foyer that led to the king's bedchamber. Ay and Horemheb stood before the closed door. The vizier stared at the door as if it could speak while Horemheb paced in front of it.

Horemheb stopped as Seth approached. "Maya told you? He won't speak to us. He read the message, and now he won't even let us stay in the room. Seth, lad, you must try."

The vizier made way for Seth. As the younger man passed, Ay spoke. "Be careful. Whatever is wrong touches him intimately. If you hurt him, I'll have you torn apart by your own horses."

Seth didn't bother to reply. He slipped inside the bedchamber. The only light came from a lamp of alabaster set on a table beside the canopy that surrounded the king's bed. Seth glanced around the room, but it was larger than three ordinary bedrooms and the lamp cast an aura of light only in its immediate vicinity. He went to the lamp. It rested on a table of the same gilt wood as the king's bed. Tutankhamun wasn't within the curtains of the canopy. The sheets on the bed were in disarray. Seth stood still. He waited and listened.

"An odd chance that they should send you."

Seth sank to his knees. Tutankhamun moved toward him out of the blackness to his right. The king stopped beside Seth and stared at the lamp. In profile, his face was immobile, stiff. Framed by softly curling hair cut short to accommodate his heavy wigs and crowns, there was a pinched look about the boy's face, and especially the mouth. Seth could see the king's jaw clench, the muscles below his cheekbone twitch. He knew from experience that these signs indicated great trauma in the youth's soul.

"An odd chance," the king repeated. He held out his hand and helped Seth rise. In his other hand he held a papyrus roll tied with a gold cord. Tutankhamun loosened the cord and spread the ends of the sheet. It was the hymn to the sun-god Aten written by the boy's dead brother, Pharaoh Akhenaten. "He gave this to me the year before he died. I was too young to appreciate it."

> *O Sole God, beside whom there is none!*
> *You made the earth as you wished, you alone....*

Tutankhamun's voice shook as he recited the words from memory. "Your brother and the priests of Amun-Ra would be horrified to know that I still keep this." The king let the roll drop to the table and covered his face with his hands. "They broke into his tomb, smashed everything they couldn't take with them. They even ripped open his coffin to get at the jewelry. They t-tore him and tried to destroy his body so that his ka couldn't seek revenge. I d-don't even know if there's enough of him left to rebury." Tutankhamun's head shot up. "You don't understand, do you."

"I understand that you grieve, my Pharaoh. No matter how I feel about gods, I understand grief all too well." Seth placed a hand on the king's arm and guided him to sit on the edge of the bed. He sank to the floor beside the youth. "You thought you had given him the peace he never found in this life. You thought that by leaving him near the city he built for his god, you would make him happy, and at the same time lay to rest the wounds he made in the harmony of the Two Lands. You thought he would be safe and free, as you cannot be, being pharaoh in his place."

As he had intended, the bald truths unleashed Tutankhamun's pent-up sorrow. Seth held the boy and stroked his hair as the tears flowed. Tears that no one must see, for since becoming pharaoh, Tutankhamun was not allowed mortality.

"My wife," the king said after a while. "She already blames me for his death."

"You were nine when her father died."

"I was the one everyone wanted in his stead. Now she will hate me even more."

Seth shook his head. "Majesty, you know she is unbalanced. Look elsewhere for woman's love."

"She is my duty," the king said. He pulled his body erect and wiped his wet face with the corner of a sheet. "I know. You are going to say that I have more than enough to worry about. You will tell me to dismiss her from my mind as I have from my presence. You are right."

The king stood up. "Ay and Horemheb were wise to send you, after all." Tutankhamun gestured for Seth to stand. He faced the older man, trust plain in his young-old eyes.

"Find the ones responsible. Do this for me, as my friend, not as my subject."

"Majesty." Seth gave the king a smile that reflected a ravenous desire for vengeance. "I would like nothing better than to meet the man responsible for your sorrow, the man who dares the curse of the gods."

Count Seth's laughter could cut as deeply as his dagger.

Anqet watched Lord Merab writhe under an onslaught of acid wit. Eager to be done with spying, she balanced on the ledge of the storehouse two nights after her encounter with Seth in his chambers. Last night no one had appeared. Tonight the two men were being quite accommodating. They stood where moonlight struck them and spoke so that she could hear almost everything they said

"I'm surprised you had the courage to try it," Seth said. "But then, you must have had help. I'm beginning to think you have help from someone most highly placed. After all, there are the necropolis police to be bribed, and mortuary priests to suborn."

Merab squirmed. "I manage."

"No you don't," Seth said. "Someone with much more influence than you rules this kingdom of thieves. If I'm to risk my head in this venture of yours, I want to know who benefits." Seth's voice lashed through the night air. "Who is your master?"

"No one may know that. Not even you."

Anqet leaned out over the ledge, engrossed in the confrontation below. The count lounged against the wall of the storehouse. He wore a short kilt, and a leather soldier's corselet molded itself to his chest. His lean body and his elegance made Lord Merab look as common as a pair of muddy sandals.

"Merab," Seth said with the caressing tones of a snake's hiss, "if you want to use one of my estates as a storage depot for this royal booty of yours, you will arrange for me to meet this prince of tomb robbers. Come, I know your arrangements for a warehouse fell through."

"You can't refuse to help now! I've passed instructions along. It's too late to change."

Seth wrapped his hand around the thief's neck. Merab gurgled and pawed at the count's arm, but Seth only increased the pressure on his throat.

"*Ghhhhh,*" Merab said.

"I don't believe I understood you."

"*Aaaaaaath.*"

Seth let the man go. Merab heaved and choked, clutching his throat.

"How would you like to work in the gold mines of Nubia, Merab? Think of it. Desert heat, no water. Day after day of heating rock and then hammering it out of the earth alongside murderers and thieves. It is said that few last as long as two years in the mines. In the season of Drought, it's so hot that the color of the rock fades."

"You can't."

Seth went on as if Merab hadn't spoken. "No one would know where you'd gone."

Merab took an involuntary step backward. Anqet leaned even further over the edge. She braced herself on the corner of the ledge, avid to learn the name of Merab's leader.

Merab swallowed. He looked like an oryx caught between a bull elephant and a lion. "He would kill me."

"It's always difficult to decide by whom you would like to be killed. Personally, I'd chose me. Sometimes I can be creative in my killings."

"Curse you. I can't say anything without his permission. I cannot."

"Then get his permission," Seth said. "Tell your master that your life span will be much extended if he will honor me with his acquaintance."

"Even that suggestion could be my death."

"Do it, and I'll let you use some old storehouses on my estate in Annu-Rest."

Anqet gawked at Seth, as did Merab. To bring the stolen funerary objects to his own seat. Anqet could hardly believe that even Seth would dare such a thing.

In her shock, she forgot her precarious position and leaned a little too hard on the corner of the ledge. The corner broke. Anqet's hand shot out from under her, and she landed hard on her chest. The broken mud brick dropped in fragments on Merab's head. Seth leapt away from the wall and looked up at her. Merab followed the direction of Seth's gaze. He met Anqet's eyes and gave a low yelp.

"It's that singer. Get her!"

They stared at each other, and Anqet remained frozen. When Merab bounded toward the stairs, Anqet leapt to her feet, turned away from the stairs, and took a running jump across the abyss that separated the storehouse and the guard wall. She landed on the other side with one foot barely on the edge. Teetering for a few seconds, she heard two voices raised in argument and footsteps on the stair. Anqet saw the top of Merab's head bob up over the ledge.

Light quick steps took her along the wall. She had to find a way down. It was too far to jump. As she ran, her eyes skimmed the dark outer perimeter. It was a sheer drop to the ground. The two men were leaping across from the storehouse. Desperate, Anqet sat down and lowered her body over the edge, took a deep breath, and dropped. She landed on her side, breathless, her arm throbbing, and stumbled into the darkest shadows she could find.

Two thuds and feet pounding the ground brought Anqet to her feet and down a dark alley as fast as she could go. If she wanted to live, she must evade her pursuers. After what she'd witnessed tonight, Anqet had no doubt that Count Seth would calmly plunge his jeweled dagger into her heart to protect himself.

An old city, the streets of Thebes presented no coherent pattern. Avenues and alleys, paths and streets appeared in haphazard fashion as the need arose. Monuments of kings huddled close with houses and shops. Anqet raced past the base of a limestone obelisk set in the middle of an intersection and into a district of taverns and inns. She finally ducked into a road that boasted less light and traffic lest her pursuers catch sight of her. Strains of music and harsh laughter chased after her, but her legs churned on, even though they were almost numb. On she ran until, turning a sharp corner, she came up against a featureless wall. There she listened for her pursuers.

She heard Merab's angry shouts from nearby, and terror shot through her. On either side of the street sheer walls loomed high. Anqet retraced her steps and peeked around the corner to find Merab lurking beside the obelisk, obviously unsure of her whereabouts. Her heart did a somersault. Count Seth cut through a group of foreigners as a scimitar cuts papyrus stalks. An Assyrian merchant in a garish red-and-yellow robe staggered down the street past Anqet. She shrank into the shadows. When she looked at the obelisk again, Seth was pointing toward the tavern district. Merab nodded and set off in that direction, away from Anqet.

Hugging the wall like a moth, she peeked at the count around the corner of her shelter. He circled the obelisk, eyes roving over the dark streets lit only by a few torches outside the taverns farther down the street. Seth reached the side of the monument nearest Anqet and stopped. She edged back as the green stare focused straight at her. A millennium passed while he stood there, the long fingers of one hand spread out on the stone of the obelisk, his other hand resting absently on the bronze dagger at his belt. She held completely still until Seth's angular face turned away. He stood there as if undecided, then struck a path that would take him back to the palace.

Anqet let out her breath. She rested her forehead on the wall in front of her, rubbed her aching arm, and tried to figure out where she was, now that she had time to think. Where? Near the commercial district probably. She had to leave the city at once. Anqet pulled her buckle amulet from beneath the neck of her dress and rubbed it.

Sennefer! She would go to his house and beg his protection. All thought of exposing the criminals must be abandoned until she was well out of their reach. She recalled that Lord Sennefer's house was near the palace.

Anqet peered around the corner once more. The intersection was deserted except for three tipsy students who had collapsed at the foot of the obelisk. Anqet slipped out into the street and began a circuitous route that would take her to the area where Count Seth's brother lived.

She was making progress down a quiet avenue lined with modest two-storied houses when she heard a donkey bray. The animal plodded behind her, pulling a cart and followed by a sleepy boy. Beyond him she caught a glimpse of white as someone stepped behind a high stack of baskets.

That glimpse was enough to impel Anqet down the avenue and into the nearest maze of side streets. Had they found her? She couldn't risk it. In desperation, Anqet pushed against the door of a house with her good arm. It opened, and she stumbled across the threshold. Blackness greeted her. And smells. Pine, cedar, fir, and cypress—the wood scents mingled in the air. Her hand touched a wall and felt the sharp edge of an adze. She was in a carpenter's workshop. The owner and his family would be asleep on the second floor.

Anqet placed a hand on the door through which she'd come and eased it open a crack. Night was dissolving into the gray of morning, but she couldn't see much of the street unless she opened the door a little wider. She pushed.

A hand snaked inside the gap and grabbed her wrist. Before she could cry out, someone was inside and had clamped a hand over her mouth.

6

Anqet screamed into the hand that covered her mouth.

"Quiet," Count Seth hissed into her ear. "Merab is back, and he's not far away."

She didn't listen. Terror gave her the wits to lay hold of the adze hanging on the wall beside her and slam it flat against Seth's head. He saw the blow coming but wasn't able to dodge it entirely. The tool glanced off the side of his head. He gasped and stumbled. Anqet wriggled free and dashed into the streets of Thebes again.

It seemed as if she ran for hours, although the world was still gray and cool when she finally stopped to rest. Her mouth was parched, her legs trembled, her injured arm ached, but she was free of pursuit. And lost. Over the tops of the squat hovels in front of her, Anqet could see the face of a colossal statue of a long-dead pharaoh. The double crown of Upper and Lower Egypt rose above a face of black granite. She decided to make for the statue in the hope that it was set in a square or marketplace with which she was familiar.

Anqet took several steps. Count Seth swooped at her, but she crouched, spun around, and fled down an alley. She went five steps and felt her foot sink into mush. Another step. Her other foot stuck fast in something equally slimy. Anqet tottered, arms flailing, knees shaking, and fell on her hands and knees. Pain shot up her bad arm. Mud squirted up onto her face and chest. Through a screen of brown ooze, she saw that she had tripped on the first of a double row of molds that held mud brick set out

101

to dry. A homeowner was making repairs to his house, and she had failed to see the trap.

A masculine chuckle startled her, and she collided into hard brown arms. She pushed, scratched, bit, and kicked, heaving the count backward into the shallow mud pit.

Anqet hit the basin of slime with Seth's arms wrapped around her. Covered in mud, their bodies slithered against each other. Seth held her fast to his body and let her fight him until she had no strength. When Anqet lay pressed to him, gasping for breath and quivering with fear, he gave another quiet laugh and spoke to her.

"Come, little mud-beetle. I'm enjoying this contest, but we must end it."

Anqet stared up into the count's smudged face. The dark mud made his eyes an almost iridescent green. He smiled at her and ran his hand along her grimy cheek, down her throat. Anqet closed her eyes and waited for those strong fingers to close about her neck and choke her to death. Instead, the hand moved across her shoulder and down her arm in a gentle caress. Seth's weight pressed on her for a moment. Anqet's eyes popped open at the feel of his hips and legs against her own. As suddenly as he had pressed against her, he pulled away and brought Anqet to her feet. He imprisoned her wrist in an unbreakable grip and set off, dragging her behind him.

Fevered thoughts swam through Anqet's head. Why hadn't he killed her? Maybe he wanted to do it where he could get rid of her body quickly. Maybe he was going to let Merab do it. Anqet prepared to scream, drawing air into her lungs, but Seth masked the lower part of her face with his hand and whispered to her.

"If you try to scream, I'll have to hit you. Please believe me when I tell you that I will do that, much as the idea repels me."

Anqet nodded. Seth shifted his grip to her arm. This time he walked with her at his side, an arm around her waist. Anqet saw that he was heading for an area of town inhabited by some of the most skilled artisans in Thebes.

They were walking down Udjet Road. The citizens of
Thebes went about their morning business. Anqet could
smell bread baking in outdoor ovens and hear the long,
raucous bray of a donkey as it ascended the musical scale.
Three young boys trotted by on their way to scribal school,
palettes containing writing pigments clutched in their
hands. Two city police with bronze-tipped spears strolled
past and glanced at them curiously, but Seth's face was
well known to them. They did not question Pharaoh's
commander of chariots.

They entered a crossroads between Udjet Road and
Painter's Row. Seth stopped, swore, and pushed Anqet
backward, behind the column of a porch. Seth pressed her
between his own body and the column. His lips brushed
her ear.

"If you would keep your ka attached to that magnificent body, be silent."

Anqet tried to look up at the count, but he pointed at
something in the street. She followed his gesture and saw
a gang of men trotting down the road. In their lead jogged
the blockish, sturdy form of Lord Merab. Anqet's skin
crawled at the sight of these men. Armed with spears,
curved swords at their sides, they bore a collection of scars
that marked them as mercenaries or hired thugs who
earned their living by violence.

"You have a choice, singer," Seth said. "Me or them.
Life or certain death."

The meaning of Seth's words and actions finally pene-
trated Anqet's understanding. She tilted her head up to
look into her captor's exotic face and encountered amusement.

"You aren't going to kill me?" she asked.

A frown pulled at the corners of Seth's mouth. "Kill
you? You thought I was—I see. No, I have other plans for
you, my over-curious singer. And I do hope that inquisi-
tiveness is the reason for your presence at the storehouse.
Merab is gone. Come."

They negotiated Udjet Road without interruption.

Seth knocked on the door of a house on a corner. They were admitted by the owner.

"Kakemour," Seth said. "I seek refuge, old friend."

Kakemour took in Seth's mud-covered body and Anqet's silent presence without a murmur. "Of course, my lord. I am your humble cupbearer."

"Your ka will never become as light as the feather of truth if you keep calling yourself humble, Kakemour." Seth pulled Anqet forward. "My new slave has led me on an unexpected hunt. I'm not used to dealing with runaways."

"Runaway!" Anqet pulled away from Seth. "You dare call me slave? You criminal. You hunt me down for your own vile purposes and think to make me your slave."

Seth clamped a hand over her mouth and held her effortlessly while she fought. He resumed his conversation with Kakemour as though she had said nothing.

"As you can see, we'll need to bathe. I must send for Lord Dega and make certain arrangements." Seth lifted Anqet off her feet as she kicked at him. "And I would be grateful if your wife would look after my slave. Ouch! She is new and unused to a master. She needs discipline, but she's worth the trouble."

Kakemour gave Anqet a dubious look. "As you wish, my lord. Any service I can do will be little enough repayment for what you've done."

"My thanks," Seth said. "If you will lead the way, I'd like to deposit my dirty treasure in a secure place."

Hours later, Anqet sat on a flat stone in the courtyard behind Kakemour's house watching the man's wife supervise the day's baking. Bathed and wearing one of the woman's old dresses, she was tired and anxious. That Seth didn't intend to kill her had only partially alleviated her terror. There was no telling what that man might do to her. He seemed to know exactly what she was thinking and anticipated every attempt she made to escape. He was too clever. She realized now how he had managed to imprison her without having to tie her.

No one listened to slaves. No one trusted them to tell the truth when they were obviously runaways. She had tried to appeal to Kakemour's wife, but the woman paid her no heed. She clicked her tongue at Anqet and scolded her for being disloyal to such a kind and honorable master as Count Seth. The woman hadn't let Anqet out of her sight since she had arrived.

Seth had disappeared into Kakemour's apartment. There had been visits to the house by several men. Each reported to the count and went away without communicating with anyone else. Kakemour's youngest son came and went on errands for Seth that had the boy strutting about proudly at the honor entrusted to him. The youngster appeared in the courtyard now and gave a message to his mother. Anqet was promptly escorted into the house and deposited in front of Count Seth in the master's chamber.

Beside the count stood Lord Dega, whom Anqet had seen a few times at court. Seen together, the two young men looked like fire and gentle rain. Seth and Dega looked her up and down. Anqet was suddenly glad that the shift she was wearing was too big for her.

"You see what is needed," Seth said.

"Aye, my lord. The men will be here at sunset with what you require." Dega cast a glance of mingled pity and admiration at Anqet before leaving.

Seth came toward her. Anqet edged away, but he took her wrist and pulled her to a stool. Pushing her down, he stood before her with his hands on his hips. He too had bathed and donned clean clothing. Once more sparkling and neat, every flamboyant auburn tress in place, Seth wore a simple kilt that bared his long legs. They were perfectly porportioned specimens, with lean muscles that spoke of constant hard exercise. Anqet dragged her eyes away from a brown thigh only to have them wander to Seth's hips. The kilt wrapped around them securely, concealing and protecting what lay below. A flush made her cheeks hot. Anqet looked away, cringing at the count's soft laugh.

"Virgin singer, you're not as afraid of me as I thought."

Anqet glared at him. "What are you going to do with me?"

"At the moment, I'm going to ask you questions. What I do with you depends on the answers you give. Why were you spying on me?"

Pursing her lips together, Anqet said nothing. She wouldn't say anything that might help this conceited barbarian.

Something sharp pricked her neck. Anqet cried out. Seth held a knife to her throat with one hand and steadied her with the other.

"I said I wouldn't kill you. I didn't say I would not hurt you. You've appeared twice at the scene of great events. I'm beginning to think it might not be by accident. Convince me that I should not sell you to a Babylonian slave merchant."

Anqet swallowed. The knifepoint moved with the convulsion of her throat. Would he do such a thing? Of course he would. He'd done things far worse. If he'd steal from the dead, he wouldn't mind slicing her up and then selling her into foreign slavery. She must answer him. If she appeared cowed, he might relax his guard enough for her to escape.

"Answer me."

"I was writing a letter," Anqet said.

"What are you talking about?"

"To my suitor, Lord Menana. I was writing a letter to him. I had this plan to get rid of Hauron, only you ruined it."

"Suitor?" The count stared at her. His frown made him even more formidable.

Seth tossed the knife onto a table and knelt in front of her. Resting his weight on the backs of his heels, he put a finger over her mouth.

"Begin again." He scowled. "Tell it from the start."

"You won't believe me," Anqet said in protest.

"My sweet one, you don't have much choice." Seth took her hand. "And I have no choice at all. I must have the truth from you. Many lives depend upon the secrecy of my activities. If you've jeopardized that secrecy, I'll know of it."

The man was obnoxious and domineering, and she hated the way he gave her orders in that gentle voice with that air of quiet certainty that he would be obeyed.

"I suppose telling you about myself can't get me into any worse trouble than I'm in already," Anqet said.

Seth grinned at her, but when she started talking, he listened without comment. He nodded and squeezed her hand at the mention of her parents' deaths. By the time she got to Hauron's attempted rape, both Anqet's hands were in his. She stuttered to a halt, unable to describe Hauron's lust-bloated face and invading hands to this man who might well treat her as her uncle had. Anqet lowered her head and wished she could burrow into a deep hole, away from those mocking eyes.

"Did he rape you?"

The question was voiced in a calm, matter-of-fact tone that startled her out of her misery. She looked up to find Seth's eyes on her. How strange that she should find honest sympathy there instead of derision.

"No," Anqet said. She cleared her throat. "I fought him." She frowned. "I think he'll still be able to father children."

"Still be able to father children. Bareka! You have the courage of twenty warriors, little singer."

Anqet peered at the count, sure that he was making fun of her. Seth regarded her seriously and bade her finish the tale.

She decided to edit the latter part of her story. No use letting him know about all the times she'd spied on him. She spoke only of the latest, disastrous eavesdropping.

"So I know all about your plans to help rob tombs, my lord count. If I hadn't been careless, I would be exposing you to the high priest of Amun-Ra at this moment." Anqet shook his hands off and looked down her small nose at him.

"By the myriad gods of Egypt, I do believe you would be," Seth said. He gazed at her admiringly. "What I don't understand is why. Is your soul that honorable?"

Anqet jumped to her feet. She stood over Seth.

"What would you know of honor? You scoff at the laws and ways of the Two Lands even as you bask in the friendship of the Golden Horus Tutankhamun. How could you betray Pharaoh, who trusts you? Even I can see that the living god has a great love for you. You defile him by using that love as a shield behind which you hide and thieve and corrupt the honorable to the destruction of his peace." Seth tried to interrupt, but her rage swept over his words. "And as to why I should concern myself with tomb robbing, I couldn't stand by and let such a sin go unchecked. How would I feel if someone desecrated my parents' tomb? Did I tell you Hauron threatened to do just that?"

Anqet poked a finger at Seth.

"You, my lord, are cast of the same metal as my uncle. Both would take from me what should be given freely and shared. You would as cheerfully deprive my parents of eternal life. You disgust me."

Seth stared at the angry young woman in front of him. He'd thrown his most seductive lures to her, and she declared that he disgusted her. His eyes absorbed the sight of her—the flush that spread from her cheeks to her chest, her glittering eyes and erect posture, her look of contempt. It was true; she didn't want him. She didn't like him.

Seth looked away from Anqet and pressed his lips together until they hurt. He felt himself at the mercy of a new emotion. Unidentifiable, it started a small inferno in his chest and stayed there, baking his reason, his intellect, and his anger. This young girl with her innocence, her forthright honor, and large-eyed beauty—what had she done to him? He'd known her but a fortnight. Why did he suddenly value her opinion of him? He hadn't cared what women thought of him since—since he'd broken his betrothal.

Scorpions take the girl! He wasn't letting anyone devil him so. His parents had tortured him like this, torn him apart with their demands that he love one more than the other, obey one and not the other, live for one and deny the other. He would make this scornful enchantress resume her proper role. He would not care. She had no right to make him care.

Seth smiled his lazy, hot smile and began a slow, sensuous walk toward her. "Your anger excites me. Were you Gasantra, I would say you lose your temper deliberately."

He was beside her in three steps, catching her shoulders from behind, whispering in her ear, drawing her close. He could feel her soft buttocks move against his loins. The throbbing ache caught him by surprise and made him grind his teeth together.

Impatient, nerves strained, he turned Anqet in his arms and forced a savage kiss on the girl. Grasping her buttocks, he pressed her against his hips. From a long way off he heard wordless protests. He ignored them and concentrated on exploring the girl's mouth. He would have her passion. He would make her want him again. Bracing Anqet with one arm, Seth placed his hand on her breast. He lifted his mouth and spoke against her lips.

"You are named for a goddess of fertility. We'll see just how fertile you can be."

It was as if the girl had turned to cedar. All the softness was gone. Seth raised his head. Loathing had replaced desire in those dark eyes. He dropped his arms, and for the first time in his life, experienced the fear that a woman might not want him, that this woman might come to hate him. That fear was quickly masked and denied. It would have remained unacknowledged if Anqet hadn't dug it up for him.

"My lord Seth," the girl said in an expressionless voice, "you may try to force me, but I promise you by my twin souls that I will not have it so." She pointed at him. "Remember. To have me you must make yourself vulnerable, and this time I won't promise that afterwards you'll be able to father children."

Anqet stalked out of the room, leaving Seth to stand by himself like some forgotten pylon in the desert. He stood there fuming until Dega returned from his errands.

*   *   *

Anqet sat on the lid of the rectangular wickerwork box in the middle of Kakemour's storeroom.

"This is ridiculous," Anqet said. "I won't do it. I won't go, especially like this."

Dega looked unhappy but determined. "Please, Lady Anqet."

"How do you know my title?"

"The commander mentioned your circumstances. My lady, this is the best way to get you to the docks in safety. Lord Merab is still looking for you. Count Seth has decided to take you to Annu-Rest where you won't be found." Dega stepped closer to Anqet. His voice held a kind, sympathetic note. "I am sorry, but you must go."

Anqet clenched her fists, aware of how powerless she was. She mustn't let Lord Dega see her fear.

"No. I'll be even more at his mercy at his estate." Her own words sent her tumbling into outrage. "You expect me to consent to my own debauching by that—that dissipated vandal! There's nothing he wouldn't do. After all, he murdered his own mother's ka."

Dega paled. Anqet watched the young man's eyes erupt with demon-fire. At once she realized that Dega could be as dangerous as Seth. The count's equerry favored her with silent scrutiny, then addressed her in a deadly quiet voice.

"Did it ever occur to you that if Lord Seth was as depraved as you say he is, he would have forced you long ago? Even that first day, when you ran in front of his chariot, he could have kept you. Had he been willing to hurt you, he would have knocked you out and taken you to a place where he could use you at will. Do you really think anyone can stop Seth if he wants something?"

Anqet looked at him, silent and confused.

"Consider this, lady. Does a criminal, a murderer, and a libertine risk his own life saving a foolish girl who, through her misplaced curiosity, jeopardizes his most important affairs and even himself? Does an evil man spend days in a distracted love frenzy because of a woman he has seen only once and cannot find again?"

"Love frenzy?" Anqet blinked in disbelief. She was about to ask about this frenzy, but Dega took a seat beside her and plunged on.

"Lady Anqet, I've known Seth since we were boys being raised at court. We've served together under General Horemheb since the days of the heretic. I've seen him hunger after many women. I have seen many women at court hunt him. Never in all this time have I seen him denied. Until now. You bewilder him."

Anqet tossed her head. She hitched one leg over the corner of the wicker box. "I bewilder him because I won't submit and be grateful for his attentions."

"I never said Seth didn't need instruction in humility." Dega smiled at her.

She laughed. "You would have me believe him to be misunderstood, a noble heart concealed behind a mask of licentiousness and corruption."

"I would have you know Seth for what he is."

"Why?" Anqet asked.

Dega stood up. "I've already said enough to make Seth put me to the whip." He gestured to the crate where Anqet perched.

Anqet found herself packed away like a sack of lettuces and hauled through the dark streets of Thebes by Lord Dega's bearers. The crate tilted, then leveled. When one of the men stumbled, she banged her head and was thrown from side to side until the trip ended with a jolt.

The lid of the crate flew open, and Anqet popped up, weary and light-headed. She lifted one leg over the edge of the box, her skirt raised, baring her leg almost to her hip. Count Seth stood waiting, in full court dress, eyes alight with amusement and appreciation. Anqet yanked her dress down, removed herself from the container, and scowled at Dega.

"As much nobility as a jackal," she said.

Leaving Dega to explain her remark, Anqet stalked to a place near the prow of Count Seth's galley. Depression came upon her as she realized she would soon be farther than ever from Lord Menana and home. For all she knew,

Hauron had already carried out his threat to sell Nefer and desecrate her parents' tomb. Even now, Bastis, Nebre, and all her people could be homeless, her parents' kas abandoned to wander the desert in torment.

Anqet balled her fists and stepped close to the ship's railing. The water lapped rhythmically against the side of the galley. The gentle slap of the waves reminded her of the time she and her mother had taken a skiff to gather lotus blossoms in the marshes near Nefer. They took meat, fresh bread, and wine, and floated lazily among the high reeds. They made a game of trying to find as many pintail ducks as they could. She had fallen asleep in her mother's lap, to the calls of waterfowl and the creak of the skiff rocking on the water.

Anqet tried to fight back tears. They came anyway, so she covered her eyes to hide them from any curious sailors who might be watching. A light touch on her shoulder pulled her from her misery.

"My lady's quarters await her," Seth announced, with a too-gallant flourish. "I regret there are no handmaidens to attend you."

But when he saw her, his voice faltered, and he gripped her sagging shoulders.

"Little singer, what's wrong?"

That softly voiced question and the strong arms around her robbed Anqet of the last of her reserve. Sheltering her face with both hands, she wept. A hard knot of pain formed at the base of her throat as she tried to swallow the grief. It was no use. All the terror and isolation of the previous night returned and fed her distress. Seth gathered her in his arms, and as if she had sought comfort there all her life, she buried her face in the smooth angle between his neck and shoulder and sobbed while he stroked her hair and murmured words of solace and endearment.

The steady hand at the back of her head, the strong arms and tender voice, brought forth an elemental sense of asylum, of a sturdy male sanctuary, impregnable and built specially for her. In all the time since she'd run from Hauron, Anqet had found no one capable of such a feat, yet Seth was holding her, giving comfort in a way she would never have thought possible for him. Could she have been wrong about him? No. She had witnessed his baseness only the night before last. It wasn't right that she felt so safe with him when she knew what he was

Confused, Anqet was barely aware that Seth had led her inside the cabin amidships. They faced each other in a room filled with portable furniture. Seth's clothing lay strewn across a folding bed. A gold-and-amethyst broad collar lay draped over the lip of a jewel casket. Anqet snuffled and wiped at her flushed face.

Seth regarded her with a look she now knew, thanks to Dega, to be complete bewilderment. His brow wrinkled, he tilted his head to one side and frowned in a way that Anqet somehow knew was the sign of intense internal dialogue. After a moment, Seth turned and vanished, only to return with a damp cloth that he dabbed tentatively on her face.

"What's wrong, sweet one?"

She hiccupped and took the rag from him.

"I'm worried about my people. If Hauron turns them out of Nefer, I don't know where they'll go. Nebre and Bastis aren't young. Who would employ them? The tenants and laborers will go hungry. You don't know Hauron. When he drinks, he becomes possessed, and he drinks most of the time. He might take out his anger with me on them—or on my parents' tomb." Anqet cast a glance full of misery at Seth. "I don't suppose that means much to you."

Seth gave a sigh. He led her to a corner filled with cushions and seated her. "Why do you think me incapable of sympathizing with your grief?" He touched her arm with the tips of his fingers. He leaned toward her. He kissed her forehead.

"How can I expect sympathy from you after all that's happened between us? You torment me." She rushed on without thought. "And how can I trust you? You murdered your own mother's ka."

She hadn't thought it possible for a face to resemble a blank sheet of papyrus. Seth didn't move. He said noth-

ing. As if he were a mural painter, he smoothed a layer of
plaster over his features that concealed every emotion,
and then, in a fluid motion, Seth moved away from her.
The light from a lamp turned the brown of his skin a
golden hue. Anqet watched the angular planes of his face
tighten. The color of his eyes deepened until it glowed
like the green flame produced by melting copper.

"I'm overdue at the palace," he said. "Pharaoh wishes
to bid me farewell and tells me he has a parting gift. Last
time it was a Sardinian slave. Quite beautiful." Seth
turned and put his hand on the door of the cabin.

Anqet couldn't resist a taunt. "Poor slave, to be the
property of a lecherous wanton. She must be unhappy."

Seth laughed and tossed a reply over his shoulder as
he stepped out the door. "Dear innocent, I didn't say the
slave was female, and he is content—you might even say
pleased—to be my property."

The door shut. Anqet loosed a cry of outrage, grabbed
the nearest cushion, and hurled it at the entry. She took
another cushion and began to twist it like a wet rag until
her anger subsided. Once she'd calmed down, Anqet
realized that Seth had again enticed her despite her anger.
It was her own fault for giving in to this weakness in her
heart. She seemed to be permanently enthralled by the
man.

She'd been a fool to speak of his mother. Her sense
was deserting her. She should have known the subject was
forbidden. Seth had reacted with his special brand of lurid
self-defense, and she had responded in the intended manner.

Anqet threw the cushion to the floor and kicked it.
"He's as difficult and obscure as a mortuary text. He
reminds me of a bad pomegranate: lush and beautiful on
the surface, rotten within."

Seth watched Tutankhamun's body servant divest the
king of the heavy double crown of the Two Lands, the
white symbolizing southern Egypt, the red the Delta.
Tutankhamun sighed as the weight left his brow. He
rumpled his curly hair and buried his face in a wet cloth.

The heavy cosmetics on his eyes smeared. He was about to say something to the count when another servant wiped his face with an oily cleanser. Seth snickered at the boy.

"Patience, my king."

Tutankhamun's voice floated out from behind a cloth. "You don't have to wear these things. The crown presses down on my ears. Someday it will chop them off."

Further teasing on Seth's part was forestalled by the entrance of Divine Father Ay and General Horemheb, deep in argument as usual. Ay cut off his last statement, clapped his hands to scatter the servants, and assumed the role of body servant. Beneath a thick court wig, his face was set in lines of disapproval. He lifted a coronation pectoral from the king's shoulders. Gathering the gold chain in one hand, he glared at the turquoise, lapis, and malachite symbols of the pendant and frowned at Tutankhamun.

The king looked to Seth for support. "He hasn't forgiven me for not coming to him when I found out my brother's tomb had been entered."

"You frightened me, beloved Pharaoh," Ay said. "I pray to Thoth, god of wisdom, to help me understand."

Tutankhamun looked at his gold sandals, his face bleak and weary. Horemheb distracted Ay by removing the lid of a jewel box and holding it out to receive the pectoral. Seth maneuvered the king far away from the Divine Father under the pretense of helping with the clasp of an electrum armband mounted with winged scarabs. Seth snapped open the hinge of one band.

The king stared at the silver signet ring on the count's hand; it was inscribed with Seth's name and titles. Tutankhamun lowered his voice. "Why have you not told me of your association with Lord Merab?"

Seth's hands froze on the king's arm. He looked past the youth at a gold drinking vessel on a table.

"Majesty, has General Horemheb mentioned the task he set me?"

"The Eyes and Ears of Pharaoh are numerous," the

king said. "My majesty doesn't depend only on Horemheb and Ay for knowledge."

Seth's eyes took on the luster of ceramic glaze. "Bareka! Golden One, does someone else know too?"

"You mean besides me?"

"Majesty!"

Tutankhamun pulled his arm free of the second electrum band and took it from Seth. A fighter's gleam came into his eyes. "You three saw fit to keep me in ignorance. I'm no longer a child. You will not decide what I should know. You've caught the ringleader of the tomb robbers, and I wasn't told."

"Divine Ph—"

"I'm angry with you, Seth. I asked you to find the man responsible for the atrocity on my brother, and you had already found him." Tutankhamun's hands flexed as he glared at Seth.

At the sound of the king's irate voice, General Horemheb left Ay and crossed to the younger men. "I beg Your Majesty's pardon. It was I who bade Count Seth to keep silent. Knowing how the robberies cast a pall upon the well-being of Pharaoh, I didn't want to burden Thy Majesty with petty intrigues. The Divine Father and I wished to present the criminals bound and prostrate before thee—not just the henchmen, but the real leaders."

The king growled and spread his arms out to Seth.

"Forgive me. I should have known you would keep nothing from me."

Seth smiled at Tutankhamun. "It isn't for me to forgive the living god, Divine One."

Tutankhamun turned on the two older men. Before he could open his mouth, Ay held up his hand.

"We were wrong, Majesty. It won't happen again."

"That is all?" the boy asked. "You aren't going to argue?"

Ay shook his head.

"Why not?" Tutankhamun asked.

"Because you are right, Pharaoh," Ay said. "We try to

protect you from all harm and forget that you are almost a man. A man must protect himself."

Tutankhamun smiled at Ay. The vizier's stern countenance crumpled at the sight. The king laughed, went to his mentor, and gave him a rough hug.

"Seth," the youth said, "explain these clandestine meetings with that dog Merab. And while you're about it, explain why you're holding my singer-physician prisoner on your galley."

A royal armband clattered to the floor. Seth cursed and picked it up while Tutankhamun chuckled. Seth scowled. He wondered how much the boy knew about his dealings with Anqet. Feeling like a magician whose apprentice has suddenly begun casting spells without aid, Seth told the story of Merab.

"When will you have the leader?" Tutankhamun asked.

"I can't be sure, Divine One. Merab says his master will find me on his own. I can't close the snare on Merab or his cohorts until we have the leader." Seth smiled a grim smile. "I'm sure this leader is the one responsible for the attack on your brother's tomb. I expect the man to contact me after the delivery of the booty to my estate. Once we have the master thief, the royal troops can board my ships and take the whole pack at once."

Tutankhamun paced back and forth between his two advisors and Seth. "I don't like it. You invite the jackal into your home and leave yourself open to his attack."

"Dega will be nearby," Seth said.

"Near, but not by your side as he has always been."

"I'll be careful, Majesty."

Tutankhamun threw up his hands. "Very well. I can't be there myself, so I'll have to trust in the gods to see that you don't take foolish chances." The king turned to Horemheb. "I will expect a company of archers and one of spearmen to assist the chariot corps. They must be ready to leave for Annu-Rest at any moment."

Dismissed, Horemheb bowed, and both he and Ay walked out. The sound of the bickering made the two young men grin at each other.

"What about the singer?" the king asked.

Seth fiddled with one of the electrum armbands. "She accidentally witnessed a conversation with Merab. She has to be kept hidden, or the man will kill her. I dare not let her out of my sight for long. She tries to escape me constantly." Seth cleared his throat. "She doesn't approve of me. She thinks I'm Merab's ally."

"I suppose you have done nothing to encourage this false impression," Tutankhamun snapped. "Put the armband away before you break it."

With elaborate care Seth put the band on top of a pile of jewelry in one of the caskets on a side table. When he turned around, Tutankhamun had arranged his long body in an ebony-and-gold chair and was watching him. Seth approached the king. He dropped to the floor beside the boy, facing away from him. Tutankhamun's amused expression made him cautious. He hooked one arm around a bent knee.

"The Living Horus should not concern himself with such trivial matters."

"After all these years you've cared for me?" Tutankhamun replied sweetly. "Anyway, you help me deal with the queen."

"You aren't going to leave me alone, are you, Majesty?"

"No."

"She's a lady. I treated her like a woman of the taverns."

Tutankhamun rested his hand on Seth's shoulder. "Do you know how your voice changes when you speak of her? There is a gentleness you never allow. I think few know it exists in you. I have known the gift of that gentleness. You give it to Khet. You never give it to your women, at least not until now."

"The gods have made Pharaoh too wise. I could wish you were still a little boy, too young to perceive my shortcomings."

"Pharaohs have few friends. They must guard them well." Tutankhamun gave Seth's arm a shake. "So you suspect the singer of complicity with the robbers?"

"No, Majesty. She is innocent." Seth told Anqet's story. "I've sent someone to this house called Nefer, but I believe her. She's not a good liar, and she has no powerful connections. In time, I'll deal with her uncle; perhaps Thy Majesty will allow me the use of two or three of his leopards for the purpose. Am I so different when I speak of her?"

The king grinned at him. "If a lion could transform into a kitten, you would see a like change."

Seth's eyes became two slits of jade. "Hardly a flattering modification."

"I like it. You have my permission to marry the lady."

"Marry!" Seth nearly fell over so quickly did he twist around to stare at his monarch.

"Only if you want to. It's not a command."

"I thank thee, Pharaoh, but marriage won't be necessary," Seth said. He ignored the laughter in Tutankhamun's voice.

"Perhaps it is. You can't keep preying on my noble-women forever. This singer is an enchantment of a woman. Had I not known you wanted the girl, I would have taken her for myself. Don't look so shocked. You told me to look elsewhere for love after the queen tried to kill me. Be comforted. I'm not yet recovered from my last so-called lovemaking."

Seth eyed the king. "You're serious."

"She nearly made me forget my injuries the night Ankhsenamun cut me."

Seth gawked at the youth sitting above him. He fought with the disconcerting urge to strike the living god. The king wanted Anqet. It had never occurred to Seth that anyone would be a threat to his possession of the girl. Pharaoh had but to lift his hand, and Anqet would be his, not Seth's. That thought sent wrath bubbling like liquid metal through his veins. He got to his feet, bowed to the king, and asked leave to retire. Tutankhamun nodded, a pleased smile on his lips. At the door, Seth turned back to the boy who watched him so closely.

"My vow of secrecy, Pharaoh. I would be released

from it so that Lady Anqet may be told that she need not make these annoying breaks for freedom."

"You have my permission However, I don't think she runs from you only because she thinks you're a criminal. After all, she knows about Gasantra. And someone's bound to have told her about all the others."

"Majesty, don't people have anything to do but spy on my private affairs?"

"But Seth," the king said, "you give them such a splendid spectacle. Ay wanted me to banish you after you seduced that priestess. I told him half the ladies would follow you into exile and the other half would expire from boredom with no one to tantalize their rigid little sensitivities. Have a pleasant trip home, my friend."

7

Count Seth's galley was an elegant craft, as sleek and sinister as its owner. Larger than most pleasure ships, its sides were painted black, with gold trim at the railing and at the floriform tips of the prow and stern. The sleeping cabin amidships had a pavilion attached to its front hung with transparent curtains. The galley carried twenty-two oarsmen and two helmsmen to handle the great steering oars at the stern. On such a large ship, Anqet reasoned, it should be possible for one small woman to slip overboard and swim away.

After Seth left for the royal palace, Anqet stayed in the main cabin until well after moonset. The count had posted a sailor outside the cabin, and it was some time before she saw him walk forward a few paces to stretch his legs. In that brief time, she scuttled outside and around the corner of the cabin with one of Seth's whips grasped in her hand as a makeshift cudgel. Keeping to the shadows beside the cabin wall, she tiptoed past the bodies of the sleeping crew. Ahead lay the stern with its railed platform. It was deserted.

Anqet paused at the end of the wall that concealed her. She could see nothing beyond a stack of crates set before the stern. Anqet checked to port and starboard, then ran for the crates. She swept around the boxes and skidded to a stop before a man leaning over the side of the galley. He straightened and weaved around to face Anqet.

Count Seth breathed his words at her. "Ah, it is the

small needle that pricks at my heart, come to practice further savagery on my ka."

The words were only slightly blurred. He kept one hand on the rail to steady himself and caught Anqet's hand with the other. Drawing her to him, he kept her hand as he took a perch on the railing, with his feet hanging over the side. Seth turned slightly and invited Anqet to join him. She thrust the hand with the whip further behind her back and shook her head. Letting go of her Seth turned to face the water. Anqet took in the smell of liquor and the odor of women's perfume.

Seth stared out at the night sky. In profile his jawline was clean and angular, his cheek hollow, and his mouth full and upturned. Anqet resisted the urge to trace the angles of his face with her finger. She must keep her thoughts on escape. If she started thinking of his body, she was doomed.

The hard grip of the whip in her hand made her brave. She would hit him. Just a little. She didn't want to hurt him, but after all, he was a thief and a defiler of the dead. Trembling with apprehension, Anqet lifted the butt of the whip high. Seth sighed and began to turn his head in her direction.

"Sweet one, is there no physician who can cure me of this illness? You are a delicious poison—"

Her improvised club came down on the count's head before he could finish. Without a sound, Seth crumpled forward. Anqet wasn't practiced in violence and hadn't thought out the consequences of her attack. Seth's body started to fall over the side. Dropping the whip she clutched at him. She managed to hook him under the arms and pull, but his hips and legs slipped down. Although slender, the count was tall and muscled, and Anqet was no match for him. Inexorably, she was dragged along with him until she was bent across the rail with Seth hanging in her arms. It didn't take long for her strength to give out. She lost one arm, then the other, until she held him only by one wrist. The ship swayed, and he slipped out of her grip into the water.

"Mother of Isis!"

Anqet strained to see Seth's body floating facedown in the water. All thought of freedom vanished. Fear paralyzed her for only a moment. Anqet jumped up on the rail, shouted for help, and plunged into the black water. She landed near Seth, grabbed a handful of hair and dragged him close. He was still, and she listened for breathing. Treading water with Seth's head held above the surface, Anqet said a fervent prayer that she had not managed to kill him with her stupidity.

Shouts and splashes cut through the night air as Dega and a helmsman swam toward them. With the aid of a rope, all were soon back aboard. Anqet pushed the anxious Dega and several crew members away from Seth's unmoving body, turned him over on his stomach, and pushed on his back. Nothing happened. Anqet caught her lower lip between her teeth and pushed harder. Seth coughed.

Dega knelt beside her. "Lady, let me help."

Together they forced the water from Seth's lungs until, with a wrenching gag, he began to breathe normally. Dega helped her turn the count over. Oblivious of everyone else, she pulled Seth into her arms. Anqet searched his face in an effort to assess the damage she'd done. He lay quietly, his head resting on her breast. Dega ordered the crew about their own business. He lifted Seth over his shoulder and carried him into the cabin. Anqet followed.

Dega laid Seth on the bed. He stripped the count, ignoring Anqet, who was so worried about Seth that she had no time to consider that this was the first time she'd seen him nude. She watched his chest with its molded contours and tight hills of muscle, anxious at any gap in the steady rise and fall of that perfect male anatomy. Wrapping his commander in a clean sheet, Dega motioned for Anqet to bring a lamp, then turned Seth's head to the side. He leaned close to examine a small lump near the back of the skull. Bending near, the equerry listened to Seth's breathing.

What he heard must have satisfied him, for he straightened and turned to Anqet. "Tell me why my lord is unconscious and half drowned. I didn't hear him fall from the ship."

Anqet set the lamp on the floor. She cast an embarrassed glance at Dega. Wet and miserable at the thought of what she had almost done, the last thing she wanted was for Dega to be angry at her for injuring his precious commander.

"You tried to get away again, didn't you?"

Anqet shivered and nodded.

"But you couldn't leave him to die."

Anqet stared at her damp feet. Her head shot up at Dega's laugh.

"I suppose I can't blame you," he said. "I've been tempted to crack his skull more than once these past few weeks." Dega fastened a severe look on her. "May I have your promise that you won't hurt him again?"

"I won't. I only hit him once." She hunched her shoulders. "But he slipped out of my arms."

Dega grinned at her. His eyes lowered to her hips and slid away. Anqet blushed. She must look ridiculous in her wet, overlarge gown. Dega muttered something about clothing and rushed out of the cabin. He returned with a bundle that turned out to be her belongings from the palace. She changed while Dega went in search of medicine.

She was combing her hair when Seth stirred. Anqet flew to the bed and took his hand in both of hers. Seth moved his head. She bent over him, uncertain what to do. As she examined his face, Seth's brows drew together as if he were in pain. Anqet patted his bare shoulder. At the fifth path, Seth's eyes opened, slowly, as though weighted with lead. Anqet brought her face close to his. At first his expression was blank, but gradually the verdant eyes focused, and Seth smiled at her. She had to lean closer to hear him.

"Beloved," he said. "Forgive."

Anqet put a finger to his lips, but he went on.

"There's something I must tell you." The words trailed away. He grimaced. "Bareka! I drank too much cheap ale, and it's given me a demon of a headache."

"Serves you right," Dega said. Anqet looked up. Seth's friend stood over them. He held out a cup full of an amber liquid. "Drink this. It will help the pain."

Anqet held the cup to Seth's lips. The count drained the cup and lay back.

"I don't understand," he said. His hand shook, and he didn't quite manage to lift it to his head. "I don't usually have this trouble. Must have been something in the ale." Seth blinked at them and yawned. "Dega, my lips are . . . heavy. What was in that drink? Never mind." Seth squeezed Anqet's hand. "Dega, don't let her out of your sight."

Making a determined effort to stay awake, the count beckoned to his equerry. "Keep her here, Dega. He said I could tell her. Released me from my pledge . . . of . . . of silence. Have to tell her the truth."

Dega put his hand on Seth's shoulder. "Yes, lord. Sleep. She will be here when you wake."

Seth's eyes were shut, but he smiled. He drew a deep breath and let it out as though a heavy burden had lifted from him.

"Tell me what?" Anqet asked when it was apparent that the injured one slept.

"It is for Count Seth to speak of, lady," Dega said. He bowed and left her.

For a long time, Anqet stayed beside Seth and watched him sleep. In rest, his face lost its haughty, taunting expression, and his mouth relaxed into a half smile that spoke of a gentle innocence one dared not trust.

Anqet sighed, exhausted and angry with herself for feeling so protective of this perverse wanton. What did he have to tell her that was so important? He was so anxious to speak to her. Seth said he'd been released from a pledge of silence. That could have taken place only since she last saw him. What had happened to make him want to confide in her?

Anqet's heart pounded in her chest. Seth wanted to tell her the truth about himself. Did she want to hear it? Anqet drew the sheets up under the count's chin. She settled on a pallet close to his bed after putting out the lamp. She slept lightly, always alert to any change in Seth's respiration, any shift in his position. She dreamed of Seth's eyes glowing at her, and his voice calling her Beloved.

Hauron bowed to the departing guests and watched them drive away from his dead brother's house. He'd been the eiptome of bereavement. Rahotep's friend, a priest of Ptah, believed him. He wasn't worried about Oubainer; the man had the wits of a grasshopper. Lord Menana was different. The boy was shy, but Anqet's disappearance had brought forth a hidden strain of temerity and distrust that Hauron couldn't afford to arouse to greater levels than he already had by losing the girl in the first place. He'd have to watch Menana.

The rustle of luxurious cloth signaled the approach of Thanasa. Not bothering to look at the man he'd installed as Nefer's steward, Hauron walked back into the house. Thanasa followed him to the hall and stopped before him when he sat down. A slave poured wine, but Hauron growled a dismissal. The steward waited in silence while Hauron drank a whole goblet. Running the back of his hand across his lips, Hauron at last looked at the man.

Thanasa bowed. His electrum necklaces swung forward. Bracelets clanked together. Thanasa straightened and put a hand to his chest to still the swing of jewelry. Hauron noted the smooth slickness of the steward's skin and curled a lip in disdain. Unguents were one of Thanasa's favorite indulgences.

"Don't stand there with your knees stuck together like a simpering concubine. What news?"

"There is none, my lord."

Hauron finished off another goblet of wine.

"It's been weeks. She has to be somewhere, you leg-spreading hornet. I pay you well, and I'm beginning to think you're not worth it. That girl nearly made me a eunuch, and while such a fate might not bother you, I nearly died from fear alone. I want her back."

"But my lord, the men have searched every village between the place where she disappeared and Nefer. She's never been seen."

"Shut up."

Hauron took the flagon and lifted it to his lips. Downing its contents failed to wipe memory of the eternity of pain he'd suffered because of his niece. It didn't help that he had to put on a mask of concern when he wanted to howl his rage. The anger built in him. He could feel it churning in his breast and in his groin. He was in no mood to be subjected to the spectacle of Thanasa's mincing walk and whimpering voice. If the man wasn't good at managing rebellious slaves and organizing households, he wouldn't put up with his prissiness.

"I beg the master's indulgence," Thanasa said.

Hauron grunted.

"A few moments ago, I was with the scribes directing the reapportionment of the harvest according to your desires when I noticed the woman Bastis. She was bringing flowers in from the garden, she had one of the most beautiful lotuses I've ever seen." At Hauron's curse, Thanasa left his elegy to the lotus. "My lord, as I watched the woman, it came to me that she wasn't worried."

"What has she to worry about? I haven't thrown her out, or any of the other useless old ones. Not yet."

"But lord, you said yourself the woman is like a mother to Lady Anqet. It's been almost a month. If Bastis doesn't wail for her mistress, it must be because she knows there is no need."

Hauron paused in lifting another flagon to his lips. He set it down and perused the bedecked, clever man in front of him. "Send for Nebre and the woman Bastis. Have them brought to the workroom, and get rid of the house slaves for a while. Bring three of your guards."

It wasn't hard to make Bastis speak. Hauron had but to ask questions while Thanasa held a white-hot brand close to Nebre's eyes. The old man's skin was only singed a bit before the woman broke. Nebre's sight was unimpaired.

He'd need it when Hauron threw both of them out without even clothing to protect them.

Hauron left the workroom in a fury Thebes was the last place he'd have searched. It was far away, and he would never have known that Anqet had taken refuge there. A pity she hadn't told the old woman where in the city her former servant lived. Still, finding her wouldn't be so hard now. Anqet gathered notice as easily as an ostrich grew feathers.

Throwing himself down on a couch in his brother's old bedchamber, Hauron let his wrath bubble and churn while he drank wine. It grew harder and harder to subdue as he realized how close he was to finding Anqet. He was near revenge, so close. She'd made the obsession worse, the little whore. He'd taken three successive wives to enhance his wealth and his standing and had five concubines to fulfill his pleasure, yet he couldn't forget the two women who'd denied him.

Gods! For a while he'd been sure he was impotent. He'd sent for three of his women to pleasure him, and it took days for their attentions to take effect. With blurred vision, Hauron looked around him.

It was dark. Someone had lit the lamps and gone away. Three empty flagons lay about the couch on which he reclined. He levered himself to a sitting position, then stood. Shuffling into the corridor, he pushed open the door to the women's room. They were all asleep And he couldn't rest for fear of dreaming of pain and Anqet.

"Lazy sluts."

Hauron swept across the room to the nearest concubine. Grabbing a handful of black hair, he jerked the woman upright. Hauron slapped her, and she began to cry. Hauron dragged her back to his chamber and threw her on his bed. She was naked. Hauron kept his hold on her hair while he tore at his own clothing. Baring his penis, he shoved it inside the woman as she wailed.

Hips pumping, lungs heaving, Hauron rammed inside her and pulled out, shoved in again and withdrew, while he grunted at the woman beneath him.

"This is what I'll do, Anqet. Do to you. Ram you, pound you until I burst. Use you until I'm purged." Hauron groaned rhythmically as he came to orgasm and dropped on top of the concubine. The woman whimpered and moved her arms.

"Be still. I'm not going to bother with mounting you again." He sucked in his breath as he swelled with another erection. Grinding his hips, Hauron let the image of Anqet fill his heart. It would be thus with him—this unending arousal—until he sated himself on the one he couldn't forget.

The day after her attack on the count, Anqet stood beside Seth in a chariot as he drove down a tree-lined path to his estate at Annu-Rest. The late-afternoon sun cast dappled shadows across their path. Dust billowed under the hooves of the pair of thoroughbreds that trotted before the vehicle.

Anqet had awakened that morning to find Seth missing from the cabin and the galley under sail. Dega had been left in Thebes. She spent the day in Seth's company. As always, it was an unpredictable and enticing experience.

Overcome with guilt at almost killing the young man, Anqet was surprised to find that Seth remembered nothing of the attack. Dega hadn't enlightened him, and the count assumed he'd fallen by his own clumsiness.

Seth devoted himself to Anqet throughout the short voyage. He displayed an uncharacteristic shyness and uncertainty around Anqet that both startled and intrigued her. He stood with her at the prow and pointed out ships that passed on their way downriver. Once he spotted one of his own headed north bearing a cargo of Nubian goods: ostrich eggshells and feathers, ebony, ivory, leopard skins, and a dog-faced baboon.

He described his visit to Prince Khai's tribe far to the south, and the strange circular houses the prince's people built. Seth's recounting of a leopard hunt was so vivid that she felt herself with him and the prince as they crouched

in the tall yellow grass. She suffered with him in the heat
and flies as he waited to catch sight of the cat.

Seth's eyes had their own catlike brightness when he
finished his tale. He looked down at her. They shared
smiles. He seemed about to say something. Instead he
stuttered and looked away. A flush crept across his face,
and he excused himself from her presence.

A few more such occurrences assured Anqet that
Seth, the brilliant commander and self-possessed sensualist,
was ashamed. After he spent an hour looking at her as if
she were one of the seven-headed reptiles of the underworld, Anqet resolved to ask him about his pledge of
silence. With a newborn optimism, she let herself hope
that whatever Seth had to say would explain why he had
corrupted himself.

With a shake of her head, Anqet admonished herself.
The reason he's a criminal doesn't make him less of one.

They fought once when she tried to explain her plan
for returning home.

"You think this little colt Menana will stop someone
like Hauron? What an absurdity. I forbid it."

"'Forbid,' do you? I have dependants to think of, and
Hauron won't be able to go against me when I'm no longer
a maiden. I'll do as I think wise, and that means going to
Lord Menana."

"Enough! If I hear that name from you once more, I'll
put you back in that crate."

A change in the horses' pace brought Anqet out of her
reverie. They had reached the end of the road that cut
across Seth's lands. Ahead lay a gateway of limestone set
in a thick, high wall that enclosed the main house, servants' quarters, outbuildings, and gardens. Passing several
gardeners and a laughing group of children, they drove
through the gate and up to the front portico of Seth's
home.

Anqet surveyed the seat of the counts of the Falcon
nome. She immediately felt at home, for Annu-Rest was in
many respects a larger version of Nefer. Although double
the size of Nefer, it too had papyriform columns that

supported the roof of the portico, and the entrance was painted with a border of red and blue palmetto leaves. A colonnaded terrace ran completely around the house. Surrounded by palms and old sycamores, the effect was one of shady and classic Egyptian symmetry.

Beneath the columns of the entryway stood several people. Anqet recognized one as Seth's personal body servant, who had come ahead of them to prepare for their arrival. Suddenly Anqet realized that the count had taken none of his military staff from Thebes with him. She was wondering why he would leave his men behind when she caught a glimpse of the others waiting in the portico.

They were women. Two of these were servants who plied an ostrich-feather fan and a fly whisk over a tall female. The woman was slender, with pale skin and a permanently dissatisfied frown on her painted lips. She was hung about the neck and waist with gold jewelry. Anqet took in the woman's pampered skin and long-legged prettiness. She glanced at Seth, who was busy controlling the horses. She had never considered that he might have a wife.

A slug. That's what she looked like. A white slug.

Seth pulled the horses to a halt and helped Anqet from the chariot. Anqet prepared herself to display cool politeness. Together they walked toward the portico. Anqet was aware of curious, laughing eyes watching them from all directions. Without fear or awe, the maids, gardeners, grooms, cooks, and other inhabitants of the estate hovered at a distance and called greetings to the master. Seth answered with easy camaraderie.

They were two paces from the step that led to the portico where the white woman awaited them when a shrill war cry assaulted their ears. Anqet heard a hollow *whoosh*, and a spear buried itself deep in the ground a palm's width from Seth's foot. Leaving Anqet crouched on the ground, Seth yelled a challenge. He plunged into the house and up to the room over the entryway from which the spear had been thrown. The sounds of a chase echoed out to the crowd. Seeing that no one else was disturbed,

Anqet stood up. She heard furniture crash, crockery splintering, and a dog barking wildly.

A thin streak of lightning shot out of the house, down the steps, and past Anqet. Seth raced after it. Anqet turned and watched the count scoop up the racing figure in both arms as it tried to dodge him. Seth uttered a loud growl, lifted his victim into the air, and crushed him in both arms. An exultant laugh escaped the boy who wrestled with the count. Anqet relaxed and smiled, along with everyone except the pale woman. This had to be Khet, Seth's younger half brother. Seth released the boy and led him back to stand in front of Anqet. Seth whispered to the youth.

Anqet studied the boy. Khet was thirteen and had reached the age when boys abandon the nudity and side lock of childhood. Long of arm and leg, his hands and feet were disproportionately large, reminding Anqet of the paws of a young hunting dog. Khet had Seth's upturned wide mouth, and shared the count's athletic build and animal grace, yet his face lacked the angularity of Seth's features. It also lacked the older man's look of cynicism.

Khet straightened the short wig that framed his face. His heavy-lidded eyes took on a momentary gravity as he listened to Seth's introduction. He bowed to Anqet.

"Welcome, my lady," he said. "May thy ka find pleasure in this house." He almost managed to utter the courtly formula without smiling, but as he finished, the boy broke out in a chuckle. "Seth! You're home. I missed you so. Take me with you when you go back to court. Please. Lady Anqet, Seth says you've lost your home to a greedy relative. Don't worry. You can stay with us. Seth will protect you. Did you know he saved me from a lion once?"

Over the boy's head, Anqet looked at Seth. The count was smiling at his brother's ingenuous chatter. Khet linked his arm through Seth's and walked between the two of them into the shelter of the portico where the white lady stood patiently.

"You'd think as Seth's stepmother I would be accorded more respect. All I ask for is a small addition to the town house at Memphis. We can buy the houses on either side of us and knock them down. Why, my father's guest home in Abydos was much bigger."

Anqet tried not to stare in wonder as she listened to the woman's monologue. Rennut was the third wife of Seth's father, whom he had married shortly before his death. The moment Rennut opened her mouth, Anqet's burgeoning jealousy disappeared. With hardly a word to Seth or his guest, Rennut launched into a litany of complaints. Anqet was sure the woman kept a scribe whose sole duty was to record the trivial criticisms and lamentations she collected between her stepson's visits.

The family was seated in one of the smaller chambers off the main feasting hall. Servants poured beer and served cold meat and fruit. Ignoring his stepmother, Khet stuffed food into his mouth until Seth took it away from him and sent the boy back to his instruction with his tutor.

The count listened to Rennut for the time it took to consume one beer. Then he excused himself. He took Anqet through the feasting hall, a reception room decorated in turquoise and gold tiles, and into the portion of the house reserved for the family. As they passed a set of double cedar doors, they opened to reveal a Nubian in Egyptian garb. With an elongated build that made him resemble one of the columns on the terrace, the man had creamy brown skin and aquiline features that spoke of mixed blood. He said nothing to the count, but fell in step behind his master as the count walked to the next door.

Seth paused before the chamber and said, "This is Uni. He is your bodyguard. I don't think you will need him, but I'll sleep easier knowing he's outside your door."

"I'm sure you will," Anqet said.

Seth laughed. He preceded her inside. There was an antechamber decorated in a geometric pattern of blue-grey interspersed with the ankh, symbol of life. Beyond lay a bedchamber that brought forth memories of Nefer.

Illuminated through windows sporting stone grill-work, the room had been painted with scenes of a young man and woman. On one mural, the two sat side by side, sharing a golden cup. On another, they embraced while standing beside a garden pool. On yet another, they sailed in a yacht on the Nile with two boys. The man was bearded and tall, with the wide shoulders and narrow hips that were the legacy of the males of Seth's family.

The woman was green-eyed. Her auburn hair flowed freely down her back, a curious departure from the formal hairstyles of most noblewomen in portraits. Seth's mother stared out from the paintings with burning intensity, eyebrows arched. The murals filled the room with brightness from the rich red-brown and cream of the skintones to the deep blue-black of the painted grapes that trailed in vines up the walls and across the ceiling.

"This was my mother's room," Seth said. He touched one of the images of his parents. "Father had these scenes painted. I wish our life had been as peaceful as it's shown on the walls."

Anqet drew closer to Seth. They looked at the couple sailing with the three children. Without his telling her, Anqet knew he was thinking of the devotion of her own parents. She also sensed an internal skirmish in the man standing next to her. A newly acquired urge to confide and share warred with the old shield of reticence. Suddenly Anqet knew that she must break through the flamboyant and provocative disguise he employed against the world. It got in her way, and she was tired of it. She eyed the count as he contemplated the mural.

Gently, with concern plain in her face and voice, she put a question to him. "Your father and mother fought?"

Seth's hand made a fist against the painting. He was quiet for so long that Anqet thought he wasn't going to answer.

"This house was a battleground," he said without looking at her. "When they weren't making love, they fought. She never forgave him for taking her away from her tribe. She hated the Two Lands—the heat, the desert, the lack of rain. She would punish my father for bringing her here. When I was born I became the prize for which their battles were fought."

Seth moved his hand to the spot where his father touched his mother's shoulder. "They would fight, and each would tell me a different version of the quarrel. I remember each of them expecting me to side with each. They fought over what to plant in the garden, who to invite to feast, when to go to court, everything. But most of all, they fought over me."

Seth stopped He glanced down at her as if surprised at his ability to confide in her. She could see his effort to stop the words, but they tumbled from him as though compelled.

"I grew up feeling that if I hadn't been born, they wouldn't have fought. I kept thinking that without me to fight over, they'd have been happy. I was almost a man before I realized that the battles had nothing to do with me."

Seth stopped again, but Anqet nodded her head in understanding. Her attention drew him on.

"And then there was Sennefer. And Sennefer's mother. You know, he was six when I was born. His mother raised him to think he'd be Father's heir. She thought she was going to be a wife instead of a concubine. I suppose I can't blame her for hating us. Father tried to be fair. He made no difference between Sennefer and me, or Khet when he was born. It didn't matter. Sennefer thought I stole his place.

"Father made us share the schoolroom and would take us hunting together," Seth said. "Sennefer cooperated, for Father's sake, but he couldn't help resenting me. I didn't understand at first. Then one day Father mentioned that it would be my duty to provide for his ka. I was watching Sennefer. He looked as if Father had driven a javelin through his heart. I was only ten, but I knew then that Sennefer believed my birth had cost him Father's love. After that, I swore he'd never regret—"

Anqet watched Seth frown at the wall painting, deep in the memories of his wrecked childhood, so different from her own, so impoverished of trust and unselfish love.

Forgetting her own wrongs at Seth's hands, Anqet slipped her hand in his.

"I'm sorry."

She had a vision of a loving and lonely boy, torn between a father and mother too concerned with their own grudges to see what they were doing to their son. For that boy, love was an occasion for betrayal, guilt, and divided allegiance. Anqet's heart burned with empathy. No wonder Seth had turned to his brother for affection. What had destroyed their precarious trust?

Anqet squeezed Seth's hand. Perhaps now was the time for confidences. "Will you tell me about your pledge of silence?"

The count jerked his hand away and backed up. His lips pressed together. He forced them apart.

"I wanted to . . . we have misunderstood one another from the first. Bareka! What is it about you that crumbles my will like sandy brick?"

"Seth!" Khet burst into the chamber, his face flushed. "That dung-beetle of a tutor says that if I want to be a soldier, I have to be a scribe first. I know how to write. Mostly. Enough for a soldier. I won't sit in a schoolroom for another two years. Please, brother. I want to train under you."

Seth took the boy by the shoulders, spun him around, and marched him to the antechamber. "We'll talk about this somewhere else, but first we're going to embark on an instruction about the correct manner of invading a woman's bedchamber. By the infinite pantheon, I don't think I was ever as much trouble as you are."

Khet patted Seth's arm, his brown eyes alight with humor. "Yes you were. Sennefer says you were worse than locusts at harvest. He told me about the time you took his body slave's place and poured wine over him instead of water in the bathing chamber."

Anqet was proud of her restraint. She didn't burst out laughing until the sound of the brothers' bickering faded down the hall. She was still grinning when a maid came in with her possessions and offered to assist her in bathing.

Three days passed in an odd domestic hiatus that Anqet would have appreciated had she not been a prisoner, homesick, worried about where her uncle was and if he knew where she was. The only discomforting event was her discovery that Seth had placed her in the room that adjoined the master's suite. The first night, she opened a door in her bedchamber that led to a short hall. She crossed the corridor into an expansive bedroom with its own terrace and garden. She was examining a rare incense tree when Seth came up behind her. He bent and whispered in her ear, causing her to squeak in alarm.

"At last you've found your way to my bedchamber. And without my even inviting you."

His laughter pursued her all the way back to her own room where she slammed the door shut. There was no bar to seal the count out, so she settled for stacking two heavy chests against the door. She spent the night restless, wakeful, and all too aware that Seth could invade her chamber and that no one would stop him. But he never did.

At midmorning on the third day after her arrival, Anqet prowled the sprawling garden that stretched over two acres. Uni was there too. He went wherever Anqet did. The grounds were divided into square and rectangular plots. Seth's ancestors had brought trees from throughout the empire to augment the native stock. In addition to sycamores and date and coconut palms, there were sidder, persea, pomegranate, acacia, and yew trees. Anqet could see tamarisks and willows as well as several balonos trees from which came an oil used in perfume. In a special section she spotted myrrh trees from the land of Punt.

Anqet wandered down paths that ran beside beds of flowers and vines. Some led to fragile pavilions where food and drink were served. Three pools, one large enough to accommodate a small boat, were fed by narrow canals. Water lilies floated on the surface of each pool, and they were stocked with fish and ducks. Wooden shelters with leafy roofs were scattered throughout the grounds. These protected porous water jars that kept drinks cool by evaporation.

Although more luxurious than many gardens, Seth's still adhered to the formal arrangements of Egyptian tradition, except for one area in the northwest corner. There, behind a screen of climbing vines, Anqet found horticultural chaos. There was no plan; trees and shrubs grew where they willed. Vines tangled up the trunks of saplings. She could inhale the aromas of wet soil and crushed, damp leaves. Beneath the shade of a thick stand of trees grew exotic flowers of brilliant violet and blue-green.

Used to orderliness and balance, at first Anqet found this jumble of vegetation disturbing. However, as she roamed the secluded spot, she grew to appreciate its natural wildness. She resolved to ask Seth why he kept such an odd place in his garden.

Anqet was headed back to the house along a path that ran by the largest pavilion when she heard a cry of annoyance. Rennut sat inside the structure holding one of many papyrus rolls from a case on the floor.

Anqet strolled over to the woman. "Is anything wrong, Lady Rennut?"

"My accounts," Rennut said with a wail. "Nothing balances. I'm supposed to check the steward's figures, but who can make sense of all these numbers? I don't see why I can't just take the man's word that everything is correct. Why do we have him if I have to do all his work for him?"

Anqet ran her eyes over the sheet in Rennut's hand. "Would you like me to look at them? I'm used to keeping records. I did for my own estate."

Rennut's pale hands snapped the papyrus closed.

"Would you do that?" She stood up. "I am so grateful, child. Seth gets furious each time we go over the records, and it takes so much effort to unsnarl the messes I make." Rennut wasted no time. She smiled at Anqet and scurried back into the house.

Grateful for something to occupy her time, Anqet took up a reed pen and started adding. The sun was high overhead when she finished the linen inventory. The rumble in her stomach reminded her of how long she'd been working. She was about to go in search of food when Seth appeared at the pavilion steps. Eschewing heavy pleated court robes, he wore a plain kilt and no wig or jewelry. To Anqet it seemed that his eyes outshone any jewels he chose to wear.

Seth leapt up the steps of the shelter and halted before her. "Anqet? I was expecting my stepmother. What are you doing?"

"Helping Rennut. From the looks of these inventories and ledgers, she needs it. Seth, the woman can't add."

"I know." Seth sighed. He waved a dismissal at the ever-present Uni and held out his hand for the papers. "Give them to me. I'll have to go over them myself."

"No need. I've done most of them already."

Seth felt to his knees and lifted his arms to her. "Thoth has blessed me. I thank you, learned lady. You've saved me from hours of listening to Rennut whine and howl about her burdens. Name your recompense."

"Send me home with a company of warriors."

The count rose. He drew Anqet to her feet. "I can't. Certain things are going to happen soon, and I must know where you are and that you're safe. You don't know Merab. The man is an insect, but a deadly insect. Shhh. We'll speak of going home when my business in Annu-Rest is finished. Come. Time to find something to eat."

In the end, Seth had to excuse himself from their meal, for he had a visitor. Directing that the newcomer be placed in a room in the back of the house, he stayed closeted there for several hours. Uni reappeared as soon as the count left her side. He was still with her when Anqet decided to take a ride in the boat in the great central pool. The Nubian stood quietly beneath the shade of a willow. Anqet floated about, dodging water lilies. She contemplated an insect as it slid across the surface of the pool.

A dark head popped to the surface in front of her. Water splashed in her face. Anqet gasped as Seth bobbed in place and clung to the boat.

"You!" Anqet placed both hands on Seth's head and pushed down.

The count sank, taking in a mouthful of water, but as he went down, he grabbed Anqet's wrists and pulled her out of the boat into the water after him. Seth pulled Anqet to him. She could see that familiar blaze of desire in his face. Taking advantage of her body's buoyancy, she shot up and out of his grasp before Seth realized what she was doing.

Despite her long skirt, Anqet swam quickly to shallow water at the edge of the pool. She grasped the tile ledge that framed the basin and hoisted herself up. Hands fastened around her waist. She was hauled back and twisted around. Seth imprisoned her between the side of the pool and his wet body. As Anqet squirmed, trying to slip away, Seth gave a gasp of pleasure that made her realize what she was doing to him. Chest to chest, thigh to thigh, their bodies thrust against each other. Seth busied his mouth in exploring hers while he ran his hands up and down her rib cage and thighs.

Anqet felt her muscles quiver. The water, waist high, felt cold on her warm skin. Through the thin linen of their soaked garments she could feel Seth's erection pressed between her legs. An answering knot of tightness formed in her groin, and Anqet perceived the danger of her own weakening resistance.

She tried to prevent it, but her legs seemed to open of their own will. Her hips drove into Seth's groin as if impelled by some thought-erasing force. Gods, she was losing control. And soon she wouldn't care.

Seth's tongue darted in her mouth. He sucked at it, trying to swallow her as his hand sought that knot of tightness between her legs. He found it and stroked. Anqet gasped and pressed her breasts hard against the moist brown muscles of Seth's chest.

A heady mist of passion enveloped her but Anqet had the will to pant two words. "Your pledge."

Seth's hands paused only a moment. Anqet repeated

the words, louder, even as she fastened her hands on his buttocks.

"Your pledge. Your pledge of silence. To whom did you give it?"

Seth's hands stopped their tantalizing motions. He lifted his mouth from her neck and glared at her.

"No," he said.

"Yes."

Seth tried to pull away, but Anqet gripped his buttocks and ground him to her.

"Let go. You're torturing me, curse you!"

Seth pulled away from her. He faced Anqet, his hands balled into fists, water swirling around his hips. Anqet eyes dropped to the hard bulge there. She blushed but lifted her eyes to his. Seth's anger was gone. He searched her face, and what he found there made him wade back to her. He stood with his body just touching hers.

"Sweet one, don't worry so," he said. "You and I are like bottle and stopper." He gave a soft laugh and found her mouth again.

Anqet put her fingers on his lips. She gathered her courage. "I will not make love to a thief and a defiler of eternal houses."

"Damnation of the gods! Won't you now?" Seth's voice echoed across the pool. His fingers pressed into the flesh of her arms. He sneered the words at her. "And if I were honest? The agent of Pharaoh, the high and puissant legate of his revenge? If I were his spy, sent to ferret out the hyenas that befouled his kingdom's dead, and even his own brother's tomb, then would you couple with me?"

Seth released her so abruptly that Anqet fell back against the side of the pool. "I think not. I think some underworld fiend sent you to make my life an abyss of misery."

The count was out of the water before Anqet had time to answer. He stood above her. The wet film that clung to his skin accented the lines of his body. He pointed at her and spoke in a voice of suppressed fury.

"I was named for the god Seth. He's not only the

ruler of desert and storms. He is also the lord of carnality,
governor of the sensual pleasures. He and I won't wait
upon your haughty honor much longer."

Self-righteous and bristling with offended pride, Seth
turned away.

Anqet collected her wits. She called to him. "You
mean you're not a criminal?"

Seth didn't look back. "I don't rob the dead. Demons
take me if I intend to defend my integrity to a young witch
of a beauty who knows nothing of me or my responsibilities." Seth kept walking until he passed out of sight behind
a stand of palms.

Anqet spent a while adjusting her thoughts. Then she
clambered out of the pool. Uni appeared. It was a mark of
Seth's power over her that she hadn't once considered
where her bodyguard might have been during the last few
minutes.

"I need to think," she said.

Uni bowed.

Leaving a trail of water droplets behind her, Anqet
retreated to her room. Her maid helped her change into
one of the simple gowns Rennut had given her. Her own
wardrobe was depleted by the adventures of the past few
weeks. As she pulled the wide straps of the sheath into
place to cover her breasts, Anqet pondered Seth's confession.

No wonder he'd been so reluctant to confess the
truth. He worked so hard at appearing evil and depraved.
Anqet shook her head in bewilderment. She'd never met
anyone who pursued a bad reputation.

"Ridiculous," she said aloud. She blinked. "It is ridiculous. That's why he's embarrassed."

Perhaps that curious pride of his made him prefer
that she succumb to his physical lures rather than admit
that he was in love with her.

"He loves me," Anqet said.

Her maid called from across the room.

"No, I don't want anything. You may go." Anqet
began to comb her hair, muttering to herself. "Do I
believe him? He could lie to the gods at judgment and get

away with it. How do I know he's telling the truth? How?"
She frowned.

"Think. Like Dega told you to," she said to her
reflection in a hand mirror. "Could he be so evil and yet
take such loving care of his little brother? What about
Dega? Could Seth command his loyalty and affection if he
were as despicable as you thought? Would he be so
embarrassed about the truth if he weren't too proud to ask
for your understanding and admiration? Whoever heard of
anyone refusing their claim to honor?"

The mirror slipped from Anqet's hand. A spy. He was
Pharaoh's agent. That meant he was engaged in a lethal
pastime, for Merab and his gang would kill Seth at the
least hint of betrayal. Merciful Isis, what was Seth up to?
He said something about urgent business. He expected to
catch the tomb robbers. If this was so, she hoped he
would send for Dega and his warriors.

Anqet twisted her hands together. It was knowing so
little that drove her to distraction. If Seth was going to risk
his life on some mysterious quest for the king, she wanted
to know about it. The high-handed wretch. He had no
right to make her love him and then run around taking
chances with his life. She'd lost too many loved ones
already.

She had talked herself into accepting Seth's innocence, and at the same time she was irritated with the
man for deceiving her. Anqet hopped from her chair and
charged out of the bedchamber. At the door, she snapped
at Uni.

"Where is he?"

"Gone, lady," the Nubian said.

"The coward. Where?"

"To the marshes. The master hunts with the little
lord, his brother."

Anqet fumed. Finally, she smiled a mischievous smile
that made Uni shuffle his feet.

"Come on, Uni. I want to speak with Lady Rennut
about my wardrobe."

8

Seth relinquished the reigns of the chariot to Khet. The boy gave an ecstatic whoop and urged the horses into a gallop. They raced down the avenue toward home, leaving the bearers and others of their party behind. Seth saw the deep rut long before they were upon it. He grasped one side of the chariot and braced his feet but said nothing to Khet. They hit the trough broadside. Khet hurtled over the front of the vehicle. His head nearly caught a blow from a rear hoof, but Seth seized his brother by the neck and pulled him back to safety. Pulling the horses to a walk, Seth let Khet lean back against him, his face pale, his eyes round.

"You will watch next time?" Seth asked sweetly.

"Y-yes. I don't feel well."

"Near-death has that effect. Breath deeply. I've got you. You aren't going to fall."

Khet clung to the chariot and inhaled.

"I said you had a great deal to learn about being a warrior."

Khet whipped around to face Seth. "You knew I'd hit that hole. I could have gotten killed!"

"Not with me to catch you. You needed a lesson. Perhaps now you'll admit it's too soon to give up on your scribe's lessons."

Seth paused to listen to an epithet concerning himself and a hippopotamus. Khet stared ahead and refused to speak to his brother for the rest of the journey.

Khet's stiff back and lifted chin filled Seth with remorse. He hadn't meant to frighten the boy so. It was Anqet's fault. She frustrated him so that his body and his heart screamed for relief from the tension. He had sought release by punishing his beloved Khet.

Back at the manor house, Seth had no chance to apologize. Khet jumped out of the chariot and charged inside. Seth followed at a slower pace but caught up with his brother in the entryway before the reception hall. Khet stood motionless with his arms stiff at his sides and his back to Seth. Voices came from the room beyond. Seth came up behind Khet and placed his hand on the boy's shoulder. Only one person evoked that expression of diffidence and anxiety. Seth gave his younger brother a quick hug of reassurance.

"Courage, Little Fire. He won't stay long."

Seth looked more closely at the boy. "It wasn't your doing. He's wrong to blame your mother's death on you."

Khet only hunched his shoulders. With the boy close at his side, Seth walked into the reception hall to greet his older brother. He paused after three steps into the room. Khet hesitated too. Sennefer, immaculate in pleats and gold-trimmed wig, stood beside a transformed Anqet.

The girl had worked devil's magic. She had become mist and flame. Transparent white froth drifted about her body. Her neck, arms, and ankles gleamed with the crimson hue from ornaments of red jasper. A band of thin sheet gold encircled her head like a diadem. Anqet lifted her head, and Seth took in the smooth, fragile slope of her forehead, the sinuous line of reddened lips.

She turned toward him. Seth managed a polite greeting and took a seat opposite Sennefer. Barely aware of the presence of Rennut, he pulled a stool next to him for Khet. He took a goblet that was handed to him but kept his eyes on Sennefer and Anqet.

The two were conversing as if they'd known each other for seasons. The jackals in Seth's head yowled at the sight. Their clamor rose to a virulent scream when Sennefer leaned close to Anqet, took her hand, and kissed it. First he had had to listen to how this adolescent Lord Menana was going to rescue her, and now Sennefer hovered over Anqet like a dragonfly.

Anqet inclined her head. Seth eyed her as she rose, took a harp from a table, and strummed a minor chord. Her voice trilled a sharp needle of excitement through him. She sang to his brother.

> Lost! Lost! Lost! O Lost my love to me!
> He passed by my house, nor turns his head;
> I deck myself with care; he does not see.
> He loves me not. Would God that I were dead!

He lost track of the words while he watched Anqet's mouth. Following the curved line of her lips, he lost himself in the memory of their feel and taste. Anqet's singing filled his heart until Seth felt as if his ka was lifted up and floated on her words.

> Sweet, sweet, sweet as honey in the mouth,
> His kisses on my lips, my breast, my hair;
> But now my heart is as the sun-scorched South,
> Where lie the fields deserted, gray and bare.

> Come! Come! Come! And kiss me when I die,
> For Life—compelling Life—is in thy breath;
> And at that kiss, though in the tomb I lie,
> I will arise and break the bands of Death.

The world reformed around Seth. Anqet's song had shattered it, so that only he and she existed in a bright and secret place away from everything.

Sennefer rose from his chair and bowed before Anqet, hands raised in submission. Seth wanted to kick him. His brother guided the singer to a place nearer his own chair. Seth glowered at Anqet. He didn't hear Sennefer when the older man addressed him.

"Seth, are you ill? You haven't heard anything I said."

"What?" Seth couldn't help the way he spat out the word.

"I asked how it was that Lady Anqet is with you when she told me over a week ago that she was going to sail for the North."

"She changed her mind. Have some melon."

Sennefer looked at Anqet. "Did you change your mind?"

Anqet remained silent.

"Sennefer, what are you doing here?" Seth glared at the man. "You're supposed to be in Thebes helping Ay plan the king's progress for the Feast of Opet."

"I came to take Khet back with me," Sennefer said with tranquillity. "He enjoys the holiday, and it would be a good opportunity for him to meet the high priest of Amun."

Seth felt Khet stir at his feet. Curse Sennefer for disturbing the boy's balance. It was time to end this gathering before his older brother could brew more trouble.

"It grows late, Little Fire," Seth said to Khet. He took his younger brother by the hand. "Go to my body servant. He knows a treatment for strained muscles. Tell him to rub your neck with mukha oil."

Khet smiled at him gratefully and left. Both Sennefer and Rennut started to talk at once. Seth ignored them and seared Anqet with his eyes. The girl gazed back at him, unaccountably at ease under his stare. As he looked at her, Anqet's eyes shifted to look past his shoulder. Her lips pressed together. Seth felt a hand settle on his bare arm.

"Will you not greet me after so long an absence, my lord Seth?"

Seth turned. Gasantra moved up to him, brushing her exposed chest against him as she touched her lips to his. Seth backed away. He caught Gasantra's hand as it roamed along his chest and led her to a seat next to Sennefer.

"What are you doing here?" he asked.

"I invited the lady Gasantra," Sennefer said. "I know how fond of her you are, and she hasn't paid us a visit in months."

Gasantra adjusted a fold of her gown where it tied below her breast. "I didn't know you'd hired this corrupt little asp, Seth. You can send her away. I had no idea you were so lonely, but I'm here now."

Everyone stared at Gasantra.

The woman rested her arms on her chair and smiled at Seth. "After all, my love, she is a poor substitute. You must admit it."

Seth cursed under his breath and rounded on Sennefer. But his words never left his mouth, for Anqet excused herself and glided from the room in silence. Seth's eyes followed her, admiration for the girl's dignity uppermost in his thoughts. He considered pursuing her, but Sennefer moved in on him. Rennut took Gasantra to the gardens, and Seth found himself at the mercy of his brother's quiet disapproval.

There were six spiritual aspects to a person: the ka, the external life-force; the ba soul; the yakhu, or shining one; the name; the shadow; and the heart, seat of intellect and emotions. Anqet was busy composing a curse that would damn each of the aspects that composed the woman named Gasantra. She had read an especially virulent one on a temple wall in Memphis.

"Burning be on you," Anqet said. "You shall have no soul thereby, nor spirit nor body nor shade nor magic nor bones nor hair nor utterance nor words. You shall have no grave thereby, nor house nor hole nor tomb."

Anqet looked around the pavilion where she'd taken refuge after Gasantra's insults. The words of the curse were powerful and evoked images she hadn't counted on. She was angry with Gasantra, but not that angry. Even the obscene and obnoxious Lady Gasantra didn't merit non-existence.

Anqet damned the woman in her thoughts anyway. Her plan to evoke an admission of love from Seth had been spoiled by that lady's presence. They were together at this moment, she was certain of it. Anqet wasn't fool enough to think Seth would resist his old lover's advances.

The idea of Seth and Gasantra together made Anqet clamp her teeth together in an effort to stop a yell of rage.

The words of her unfinished curse came back to her, but she waited for the rage to quiet. When she was confident that she could reenter the house with decorum, Anqet left the pavilion with Uni close behind. At the door to her room, Uni's night replacement waited. Anqet nodded to the two men and sailed inside.

Discarding her borrowed costume, she bathed and donned a loose, filmy shift. Two hours later, she sat on the bed, having lost the battle to throw off her anger and go to sleep. She wasn't staying in Annu-Rest with Gasantra. Why should she put up with the woman's insults and watch her paw Seth? Anqet's eye fell on the blocked door that connected her room with the count's suite. By the goddess Hathor, she would tell him she wasn't staying. She would tell him at once. He wasn't going to sleep peacefully when she couldn't.

Anqet shoved aside the furniture in front of the entrance. The door swung open to reveal shadows and moonlight that streamed in from the garden on her right. Before her, across the long chamber, stood the canopy that protected Seth's bed. A breeze stirred the curtains that shrouded the enclosure. Ephemeral beams played across the distance between Anqet and the canopy, but they cast too little light. She couldn't tell if the count lay within.

Anqet pulled her body erect and her shoulders back, and took a step toward the canopy. A soft thud of a door closing caused her to shrink back into the shadows.

Naked and entirely at ease, Lady Gasantra walked into the master's suite from the foyer to Anqet's left. Anqet's eyes widened. Gasantra reached the canopy and turned her back to Anqet. The woman shoved the curtains aside to reveal a sleeping Seth. He lay on his stomach amid the tousled sheets, unclothed, facing Gasantra.

Anqet crept closer, still in the shadows, and ran her eyes over the long, clean lines of Seth's legs and the curve of his buttocks. Even asleep, the man stirred her erotic urges.

Gasantra approached and sat beside the count on the

bed. Anqet turned away, intent on leaving as quickly as she could.

"Beautiful Seth, you refused my favors this night. I can't allow you to do that."

Anqet stopped and listened. She should have kept going, but it wasn't in her power to ignore the fact that Seth hadn't wanted the woman.

Gasantra was running her hands over Seth. He lay unaware while she caressed a line from neck to waist to hip. She eased him over on his back. Seth gave a sigh and tried to turn away, but Gasantra held him and kissed him. Anqet saw the woman's hand reach between his legs and gently stroke. She began to look around the room for one of Seth's throwing sticks. Seth's moan brought her eyes back to the lovers. Gasantra had straddled her victim, imprisoned his arms above his head, and was attacking his lips with her mouth.

Anqet reached for a bronze vase that rested in a stand beside her and was ready to hurl it at the woman when she heard Seth's voice.

"Gasantra!"

Seth's eyes were open and he lay staring at his lover. His next words were drowned beneath Gasantra's groping mouth. He tore his lips free and lifted her from his body. Before the woman could protest, he was out of the bed and standing.

"Get out," he said.

Anqet grinned foolishly. Her heart did a bouncing dance in her chest.

"No," Gasantra said. "I can please you. The evidence of that is plain." Her gaze fastened on his erection.

Seth shook his head. "Leave me."

"Leave you to that over-endowed whore, you mean. You would toss me aside for her? Ah, no, my stallion. I've waited for you too long. I don't give away my possessions."

Gasantra reached under the bed. Terror burst upon Anqet, for she knew what always lay beneath Seth's bed. Gasantra came up with a dagger and flew at Seth. He dodged her, but the blade caught him on the left biceps. Gasantra whirled around, ready to spring again.

Seth was never in great danger. If she hadn't been so angry and frightened, Anqet would have known this. At that moment, she only saw Seth in peril. As Gasantra raised her dagger arm, Anqet hurled the bronze vase like one of her own throwing sticks, and the vessel struck Gasantra's arm, forcing her to drop the dagger. Seth grabbed and held the cursing woman while she tried to kick and bite him. The count saw Anqet and laughed.

"No need to hide, sweet one. She can't get away."

Anqet stayed where she was, for three men burst into the room: Seth's body servant, Uni, and Anqet's night guard. Seth handed the subdued Gasantra to Uni with instructions that she be escorted back to Thebes early the next morning.

"Lascivious half-breed." Gasantra's breasts heaved in rage. "May you be cursed with impotence." She stalked to the door ahead of her escort, her breasts bouncing. "I warn you, Seth. You're mine. No one else will take my place, especially not that little harlot of yours. You belong to me."

"Then you shouldn't wish me impotent," Seth said to her.

The door shut. Anqet rushed to Seth and took his arm. Blood oozed from the cut. She took a kilt from a clothing chest, ripped it, and began to clean the wound. She was busy tying a bandage on the wound when she felt Seth's hand on her hair. Anqet looked up and found the count's eyes on her. His hand cupped her chin.

"What were you doing here?" he asked. He sounded uncertain, hesitant.

With the wound bound, Anqet had nothing to distract her from Seth's unclothed nearness. She edged away from him, but he put his arm around her shoulders.

"I was coming to tell you I was leaving," she said.

Anqet looked into Seth's eyes. They were made black by the night and the moonlight. He was still, with the stillness of a wild creature faced with the outbreak of a thunderstorm. Anqet held Seth's stare, absorbed by the candor and hurt she perceived.

"Why do you want to leave me?"

She heard the pain.

"I wasn't leaving you. I was leaving you and Gasantra."

Seth bent to whisper in her ear. "There is no 'me and Gasantra.' There hasn't been since the night I found you in her house."

Anqet put her hand on Seth's bare chest.

"Why?"

"Beloved, it has taken me many sleepless nights to find the answer to that question. I am obsessed."

Anqet smiled. Seth looked down at her, a wrinkle of perplexity furrowing his brow. On his chest she traced the hieroglyphs symbolizing love.

"I will have the truth from you, my lord count. I want no more burrowing under the cover of spurious iniquity." Anqet spread her hand wide over the count's heart and waited.

Seth dropped his arms from her. He stepped back a pace and cocked his head to one side. Anqet could see the spasm of tension that passed through the muscles of his stomach and thighs.

The quiet whispered to her of defeat. Through the silence came Seth's low whisper:

> Come through the garden, Love, to me.
> My love is like each flower that blows;
> Tall and straight as a young palm-tree,
> And in each cheek a sweet blush-rose.

Seth held out his hand to her. "Come, beloved."

He took her to the garden, to that secluded corner of wildness. There, upon a white cover from his bed, he knelt before Anqet and opened his arms. She knelt in front of him. Seth took her face in his hands and kissed her—slowly, with leisured expertise. After a while, the sounds of leaves brushing against each other, of the wind, of nocturnal insects, faded. Anqet fastened her arms about

Seth's neck. The heat of his body taunted her through the insubstantial protection of her shift. Without interrupting their kisses, Seth placed his hands so that they almost touched her and ran them over her shoulders, arms, and thighs, then settled them on her waist.

Anqet tightened her arms around Seth's neck. She pressed herself into his firmness. That familiar knot of tightness formed in her groin. Seth's kisses grew frenzied, and with impatient movements, he tore the shift. He leaned into her so that they collapsed on the ground with Seth above her.

Anqet twisted her legs around Seth's and heaved upward with her hips in an unthinking natural movement that evoked a sigh of pleasure from the count. He slithered down her body, spreading wet kisses on her neck, breasts, and stomach. His mouth reached the knot of sensation between her legs and caressed it.

Anqet shuddered. Her hands twisted in Seth's hair. A volcano erupted within her. And still Seth touched her.

A desperate frenzy made her writhe under Seth's lips and hands. Anqet caught him under his arms and pulled Seth up until he was between her legs He loomed over her.

"Beloved," he said. "There will be pain."

Anqet said nothing. Instead she reached out hesitantly and clasped his penis. That gesture ended Seth's doubts. He nestled between Anqet's legs and plunged within her. She felt a lance of pain that gradually eased as Seth guided himself in and out of her.

A new avenue of delight opened as he journeyed inside her body. Anqet clamped her hands on Seth's buttocks and directed the rhythm and force of his movements until he lost all restraint. Anqet felt him pulsate inside her. He trembled with pleasure and cried out, a startled, shaken moan that filled her with triumph and called forth a burning explosion of her own body. Seth arched his back, then collapsed into her arms. Anqet cradled him and kissed his hot cheek It was as wet as her own. She heard Seth's broken whisper.

"I don't understand."

Anqet didn't have to ask what he meant.

"You gave your love. For once, you gave your love, along with your body"

Somehow they ended up back in Seth's bedchamber. Anqet woke on her side, Seth's body curled around her, his arm draped over her. She drew his hand to her breast and lay thinking. No Egyptian girl grew up in ignorance of sexual matters. Her mother had spoken to her of sexuality and love when Anqet was still a little girl. Now she understood why Taia took such care that her daughter understand the physical act. Sex was a powerful force. Making love with Seth was like taking a journey in the sun-boat of Ra.

Often Anqet had come upon her parents in each other's arms. Oblivious of her presence, they appeared suffused with the light of the solar orb.

Anqet kissed Seth's palm. He nuzzled the back of her neck and yawned. The count sat up abruptly and stared down at her. His auburn hair was tousled, and he grinned a charming, lecherous grin.

"Beloved," he said. "What a marvelous bottle and stopper we make."

He lunged at her. They shared passion. Afterward, Anqet rested her head on Seth's chest and listened to his heart beat. She whispered to him.

"My love."

"Mmmm."

"There's something I have to know, now that I can think clearly."

She paused, searching for words that would fit her dilemma. She'd made a mistake before with Seth.

"I have to know," she said. "I can't believe you burned your mother's body and deprived her of eternal life."

Seth's heartbeat fluttered, quickened. Anqet raised her head and looked at him. As before, on the galley, his face was emotionless. He was as distant as the northern homeland of his mother, but Anqet refused to let him shut her out.

"Let me share the pain. My father and mother always told me that sharing each other's pain made their love a fortress."

Seth grimaced. Anqet pressed her hands against his cheeks.

"I love you, Seth. Don't shut me out of our fortress."

Her lover took a deep breath, his eyes closed. He took her hands in his. Anqet watched the color fade from his lips.

"Our gods were not her gods," he said. "Father would send me to the priests for instruction, and she would scoff at the teachings and tell me the stories of her own gods—the gods of the forests and mountains." Seth licked his lips and cast an apprehensive glance at Anqet. "She said she belonged with her own gods, not these 'foreign monstrosities.'"

Anqet squeezed Seth's hand. "Go on."

"Father wanted her with him in his tomb, and in the afterlife. She believed that her ka had to return to the forests of her tribe."

"They brought you into this fight?"

"Yes."

Anqet put her arms around him.

"She died," Seth said. "Father put her in their tomb to wait for him." He pulled away from Anqet, sat up, and hugged his knees. "She made me promise to—to set her soul free to return home, but I couldn't. Father would have . . . So I waited. Sometimes at night I would dream that her ka screamed at me to fulfill my promise, but I waited until Father was gone. And now his soul screams at me."

Seth lowered his head. Anqet put her hand on his shoulder; it trembled, and she pulled him back into her arms.

"This setting free," she said. "You did it by fire."

Seth nodded. "At night. In the desert, where none could interfere." He rested his head on Anqet's shoulder.

"I had to do it. I promised. She didn't belong in the Two
Lands, so I set her free to go home."

"And now you fear to meet your father in the afterlife,
knowing he will blame you."

Lifting his head, Seth whispered to her. "Yes."

"But Seth, in the afterlife there is only contentment.
I'm sure Osiris has given your father the wisdom to
understand what you did."

His voice low and breathless, Seth asked her, "Are
you sure? In truth?"

"Of course. Besides, your father loved and married
Rennut after he lost your mother. They will be together
with the gods." Anqet kissed Seth's cheek and whispered
in his ear. "You tried to do what was right. In that you are
no different than any good man faced with such a choice.
Seth, you are good. You put another's happiness above
your own."

Auburn hair swung forward as Seth lowered his head.
When he raised his eyes, they brimmed with gratitude
and humor.

"I thank you, but don't let anyone else know of my
virtues. I've spent much time collecting opinions to the
contrary."

Anqet grinned at him. "Then show me more of your
corrupt and evil talents, my lord count."

It was midmorning when they emerged from his
rooms freshly bathed and attired. Gasantra was gone, but
Rennut waited for them. With Anqet looking on, Seth's
stepmother managed to whine long enough to get Seth to
make the daily tour of the estate in her place. Taking
Anqet's hand, the count headed for the service buildings
to the rear of the house. Seth scowled at Anqet when she
sniggered at him.

"I can't help it," he said. "I want to be alone with
you, but she'd find us wherever we were. I'd rather do her
chores myself than listen to her complain about how
wrinkled her skin will get if she has to go out."

"Poor Seth." Anqet looked up at him innocently. "You
could ask Gasantra to run the place for you."

He chased her all the way to the brewery. They arrived at the low adobe building, breathless and laughing. Seth scandalized the master brewer by kissing her at length in the middle of the room where workers ground wheat, crumbled dough into water jars, and sieved brew into vats. The kiss ended any thoughts of work. Ignoring the smiles of the men and women around them, Seth and Anqet wandered through the stables, past the granary and bakery, and back to the gardens.

They stopped under the shade of a sycamore. Seth pushed Anqet against the trunk of the tree. Placing his hands to either side of her head, he pressed his body to hers and kissed her. Anqet smiled under his kiss. She could feel Seth's erection.

"Curse you," he said. "I come near you and swell near to bursting."

"I suffer a like malady."

Seth smiled. "I know, but I was beginning to think you had inhuman control over it."

"That's not fair," Anqet said. She pushed him back so that she could see her lover's face clearly. "I thought you evil, and you did your best to encourage that belief."

"I'm sorry."

"Why, Seth?"

The count pulled her down beside him to sit beneath the tree. His eyes grew unfocused while he pondered his answer.

"Out of habit, I suppose." Seth took Anqet's hand. "For as long as I can remember, people have treated me as if I were tainted, like a good wine with impurities that made it not quite acceptable. After a while, I learned that it can be convenient to be thought evil." Seth's old malicious grin made an appearance. "You'd be surprised at the rewards vice brings."

"Since we are speaking of evil," Anqet said, frowning, "you may as well tell me who the dupe is."

Seth gave her a blank look. "What dupe?"

"Remember the night you tried to seduce me at the palace, and Lord Sennefer interrupted? I listened to your conversation with Merab later on. Seth! Let go. You're hurting me."

Seth slackened his hold on her arms, but could barely contain his excitement. "I never saw Merab that night. What are you saying? Merab met someone else? Who? What did they say? Bareka! You've known this for days and didn't tell me."

"Calm yourself."

Anqet removed herself from Seth's grasp since he was unable to resist shaking her.

"If it wasn't you, who was it?" she asked. "It was so dark. Merab was talking to someone, but I couldn't see him clearly. I assumed it was you." Anqet thought furiously while Seth watched her. "I could only hear a few words. Something about 'old heretic.'"

"Akhenaten, the king's brother, the old pharaoh," Seth said. "They were probably talking about the royal tomb."

Anqet nodded. "Then they mentioned the 'dupe.' I think Merab was talking about a place to store the royal furnishings." Anqet slammed a fist into her hand. "I couldn't hear. The only words I caught were the ones the stranger said to Merab. He said 'change' and 'further,' or something like that."

Seth pondered her news but eventually gave up trying to make sense of such vague information.

"If only you'd seen who it was," he said. "I'm sure it was Merab's leader." The count shrugged. "There's nothing to be done about it."

Anqet moved closer to Seth, once again afraid for him. "You court danger, my love."

"If I don't, I get bored."

"Great Amun-Ra! Don't sat that."

Anqet could see that any attempt to dissuade Seth from peril was useless. She would have to live with anxiety.

"You don't understand the excitement of the hunt," Seth said. His eyes brightened to a gleam of sunlit metal.

Anqet quelled this enthusiasm with a stern look. "I'm

afraid I do, having been the quarry of one of your hunts."
She held up a hand. "I don't want to hear it. Tell me how
beautiful I am instead."

Seth chuckled at her and began to chant lines from a
bridal song.

Fair are her arms in the softly swaying dance,
  Fairer by far is her bosom's rounded swell!
The hearts of men are as water at her glance,
  Fairer is her beauty than mortal tongue can tell.

"Beware, my lady."

They both jumped. Khet stood nearby, grinning at
them.

"Beware. Sweet words in my brother's mouth often
signify danger."

Seth groaned. Anqet laughed.

"Go away, Little Fire," Seth said.

Khet hesitated, then came forward. He stood in the
shadow cast by the sycamore. He carried a bookroll, and
his hands slid back and forth over its surface.

"Seth?" the youth said.

Seth dragged his eyes away from Anqet. "Mmmm."

"I want to be a priest."

"No you don't."

Anqet saw Khet swallow. She felt admiration as the
boy lifted his chin and braved the count's wrath.

"I want to be a priest of Amun-Ra."

Seth dropped Anqet's hand. "It's Sennefer, isn't it?
He's been filling your ears with godly prattle. Blast his
name. I told him no. I'm telling you no."

Khet flashed defiance at his brother. "Sennefer says I
can aid the Two Lands best by serving the Hidden One. I
can help the poor. Pharaoh needs honest priests."

Anqet watched the two with growing dismay but did
nothing to interfere.

Seth faced his younger brother and griped him firmly
by the shoulders. "It's wrong for you, Little Fire. You
don't belong in a temple chanting to a statue, counting

tithes, scrambling for place among a pack of vicious place-seekers."

"I belong with Sennefer." Khet searched his brother's face. "Don't I?"

Glancing down at Anqet and back at Khet, Seth shook his head. "You belong with the one who makes you happy, with the one to whom you give happiness." Seth released Khet. "I forbid you to become a priest."

"No! He wants me to work with him. I have to." Khet dodged his brother and raced away.

Seth started to follow, but Anqet restrained him.

"Wait," she said. "Let me talk to him."

"You?"

Anqet got up. She placed her hand on Seth's cheek. "He and I have become friends while you've been conducting your mysterious meetings and doing Rennut's chores."

Anqet sped after Khet. She found him beside one of the garden pools. The bookroll lay discarded on the ground, and Khet sat facing the water. One of his hands was buried in the fur of the hound Meki. The dog had been brought to Annu-Rest at Seth's order, and boy and dog had become each other's shadows.

At Anqet's approach, Meki lifted his head and glanced her way, then rested it back on Khet's knee. Anqet sat beside the dog. Khet's hand glided over the soft fur as it had over the surface of the bookroll. Anqet looked at the flushed face with its high, delicate cheekbones and murky eyes.

"He loves you," she said.

Khet nodded, still subjecting the water to an intense examination.

"He doesn't give his heart to many."

"I have to be a priest," Khet said.

"Why?"

Meki groaned. Khet stopped twisting his fur. He avoided Anqet's eyes.

"I don't know," he said.

Anqet leaned over the dog and spoke in a conspiratorial tone: "Seth and I are in love."

"I know." Khet sighed. "I had to listen to an inventory of your virtues and physical attributes from the moment you arrived. It was almost as boring as composition."

Anqet ignored this comment. "You know what I have discovered about love? It's something my parents taught me without my knowing it." Anqet paused. Khet frowned at her, but she had his attention. "The best kind of love is the kind that is given freely. Did you ever feel that you had to earn Seth's love?"

"No," said Khet. A smile brightened his face. "He liked me even after I ruined the bow Pharaoh gave him three years ago."

They grinned at each other.

"Priests have to be extremely educated," Anqet said casually. She stroked Meki. "You'd have to study at least another six years before you'd even become a libation priest, and then study another four years."

"That's ten years," Khet said.

"And then there's the copy work. I hope you like hymns and *The Book of the Dead*. How many chapters are there in it?"

"Hundreds." Khet groaned.

Anqet looked at the boy sideways. "Priests are also celibate during sacred times. They're supposed to be anyway."

"I forgot." Khet shuddered. "I don't think I want to give up pleasure; I only found it a few weeks ago."

"If you're anything like your brother, it would drive you mad."

Meki stood up. Khet stood up. He held out his hand to Anqet.

"Seth says we are as like as two blocks of a pyramid," the boy said. He straightened his wrinkled kilt. "I think I'd rather be a warrior."

"Then why don't you find Seth and tell him?"

With a word of thanks, the boy charged off, trailed by a loping Meki.

Anqet decided to wait for Seth in the shelter of the pavilion. Someone had left a basket of flowers and greenery inside, so she amused herself by making a bouquet. There were daisies, red poppies, and flowering rushes. Roses and woody nightshade were also in the basket, along with those most Egyptian of all flowers, the blue and rose lotuses. She buried her nose in the blood-red softness of a poppy.

A tall form shaded her from the sun's light. Anqet looked up to see Lord Sennefer framed in the entry of the pavilion. Quietly elegant in a long robe that tied at neck and hips, Sennefer regarded her with sorrow-blackened eyes.

"So," he said. "Once again my ungovernable brother has taken purity in his hands and soiled it."

9

"You don't understand," Anqet said to Lord Sennefer. "We're in love." It wasn't possible that she sounded like one of the lovesick friends she always teased.

Sennefer didn't answer her at once. He tapped the book he was carrying against his thigh for a few moments and then threw it to the floor.

"Mighty Amun-Ra!"

Anqet started and dropped her bouquet, and Sennefer picked it up. His calm restored, he took a seat beside her.

"Forgive me, my lady." Seth's brother touched the petal of a rose lotus. "It's just that you're so innocent. Even now. And so good. I can't stand the thought of what will happen."

Beginning to feel like a ruined work of art, Anqet hastened to reassure Sennefer. "Don't worry, my lord. Seth has changed. He loves me."

"Do you know how many women have thought my brother was in love with them?" Sennefer handed Anqet the flowers. "I should have warned you. I blame myself for what has happened. I thought he'd be distracted by Gasantra, so when she asked to come along . . ."

"You're wrong," Anqet said. The man was starting to annoy her.

Sennefer shook his head wearily. "Has he pledged to make you his wife?"

"I hadn't thought about it," Anqet said.

Sennefer's anxiety was making her nervous. Why did she have to think about these things? She wanted to be

163

happy without having to worry about the future. Unfortunately, Sennefer had stirred up the flames of her conscience. No woman could afford not to worry about the future when it might bring a fatherless child.

Sennefer was looking at her as if she were a wounded duckling.

"He loves me," she said again in defiance.

Sennefer stood and glanced over her head at the entrance to the pavilion. Anqet turned to see Seth bounding up the steps. When he saw Sennefer, the joyous smile faded from his lips, and he hurried up to Anqet, slipping an arm around her waist.

"Don't speak to Khet of the priesthood again, Sennefer. He knows my decision and will obey."

"It is for him to decide—and me," Sennefer said.

"You gave up your rights to him long ago when you blamed him for killing your mother with his birth. Father bound him to me as my ward."

Sennefer's quiet voice cut through the silence that followed. "And will you be so responsible toward this innocent whom you have defiled?"

"You'd do well to follow the advice of the sage Ptahhotep; *Concentrate on excellence. Your silence is better than chatter.*" Seth cocked his head to the side and surveyed his brother. "I'll take care of Anqet."

Sennefer's move was so sudden that it caught Anqet and Seth by surprise. The older man gripped the count's wrist. He jerked Seth to him, away from Anqet.

"Then, my dissolute sibling, you will marry the lady Anqet."

Seth tried to free his wrist, but Sennefer held it fast.

Anqet stood where she was, mute and wretched. She wanted Seth to shout his willingness to claim her. Instead, the count glared at his brother, his wrist caught in Sennefer's grip.

"I give you warning," Seth said. "Keep your sanctimonious qualms to yourself."

Anqet put her hand on Sennefer's fist that still imprisoned Seth's wrist. She stared into her lover's eyes.

"Seth, I must know the truth. Don't you want to marry me?"

The count made no answer. His jaw was clamped shut, rigid. Sennefer yanked Seth's wrist as Anqet dropped her hand. The venom in the older man's face made her step back, although the wrath was directed at Seth.

Sennefer snapped out a command. "Tell her." He locked Seth's eyes in a merciless stare. "Tell her of your betrothed."

"*Gods*, Sennefer." Seth's head dropped, and he leaned on his brother's arms.

Anqet sat down. Coldness seeped into her skin, her muscles, and her bones. Her lips moved.

"Your betrothed," she managed to say.

"No!" From his position in Sennefer's grasp, Seth reached out to her with his free hand. "Not anymore." The count glared at his implacable brother. "Curse you, Sennefer. There was no need." He turned back to Anqet. "I was fifteen. Father arranged a match with the daughter of Prince Tjekerma of Memphis. There was a betrothal agreement by proxy. She came to Annu-Rest." Seth closed his eyes.

"And you cast her aside," Sennefer said.

Anqet shook her head. The pain in Seth's face told her that Sennefer's words did not hold the truth.

Seth lifted his head and spoke in a quiet, level tone.

"She was lovely, and devout, and her family had debts. Our marriage was to pay for those debts. One night after a game of senet, she told me of her sacrifice. That was the word she used. 'Sacrifice.'"

"Sacrifice!" Sennefer said. "She dared to speak of sacrifice?"

Seth nodded and smiled at Anqet. "She was willing to sacrifice herself to a half-breed barbarian for the sake of her family. She said the words as if somehow my impurity would stain her like dung. Her greatest comfort was knowing that the gods would reward her in the netherworld for the happiness of which she was deprived in this life."

"She was a fool," Anqet said.

Seth glanced at his brother. "There were already enough people in my family who hated me. I wanted no others."

Sennefer gave a long sigh. Anqet thought she could see regret in his face.

"None of that matters," Sennefer said. "What matters is that you've refused to marry anyone at all. You take your pleasure and leave; you don't even have concubines."

Seth ignored his brother. He stared at Anqet as she rose and faced him.

"We can't have love without respect," she said. "Am I not worthy of your honor?"

Seth could only repeat, "I'll take care of you. Beloved, marriage puts love in prison, encases it in stone. We would cast ourselves against its granite walls until we were bloody and bruised."

Anqet backed away from Seth. She heard none of the hurt-child fear. She heard the man she loved tell her only that he didn't care enough to guard her integrity. Seth was speaking to her, but she couldn't seem to hear him. Her lips trembled, and she pressed them together.

"It's my fault," she said. "I knew you; I knew the risks. It's my fault."

Anqet walked out of the pavilion. At the bottom of the steps, Seth's distraught voice came to her. She stopped, but didn't turn around. Her voice rang out.

"No, my lord count. I don't want the honor of becoming your concubine."

Anqet walked down the path to the house without answering Seth's call. The scuffle that took place in the pavilion failed to catch her attention, as did the inquiries of the guard Uni.

She reached her bedchamber. With unthinking, jerky movements Anqet replaced the furniture in front of the door to Seth's suite. She cast distracted looks about the room, then settled on a stool with her harp. Her fingers lay flat and immobile on the strings.

He didn't love her enough to marry her. Seth wanted

her. He loved her. Didn't he? Could she have been wrong? Was his affection an elaborate ruse of seduction? Oh, what made her think such a glamorous and beautiful man would love her—an ordinary country rustic?

Very well. She wasn't a grand court lady, but she was a noblewoman with honor and property, and could accept nothing less than marriage. If Seth loved her, he should understand that she needed to know that he honored her. But what if great noblemen didn't love? Nonsense. Only last week Pharaoh canceled an arranged marriage for one of his cousins because the young man had fallen in love with a girl from the Hare nome. Noblemen loved as deeply as commoners. It was her fate to want the only one in Egypt who feared love as one feared an evil spell.

Like crocodile after prey Anqet's thoughts slithered and slipped through her mind. Shaken by having so quickly found and doubted love, she found herself losing the ability to judge the truth. Love had struck and fled as quickly as a duck is felled by a throwing stick.

Sennefer was wrong. That disastrous betrothal was only part of the reason Seth fled from marriage. Born into a family of permanent enemies, he had no experience of selfless love. Perhaps Seth wasn't capable of such love. He was afraid. Her savage, brave warrior was afraid.

Anqet leaned her head on the harp, and sobbed.

The tears were dry on her face and neck and it was dark when she heard a whisper.

"My lady."

A dark head came into view, and wide shoulders. She scrambled away, certain that Seth had come for her. Strong hands grasped her.

"My lady, it is Sennefer."

"My lord?"

"Quietly," Sennefer said. "Dear Lady Anqet, I can't stand by and let my brother abuse you. I have come to offer my protection once again. Come with me tonight, away from here."

It was the only way. There was nothing for her in the house of the count of the Falcon nome.

"How will we get away?" Anqet asked.

"I have prepared. Uni has been given a sleeping draft."

"And Seth?"

There was a pause.

"Seth is recovering from our fight."

Anqet stood up and moved closer to Sennefer. "Is he hurt?" She was annoyed at herself for asking.

"He hit his head," Sennefer said in a puzzled tone. "Not hard, but it appears that he already had an injury."

"Oh. Um, yes."

Anqet didn't pursue the topic. Taking only a small sack of possessions, she crept through the house at Sennefer's side. They went boldly out the front doors and through the gate where a groom waited with a chariot. Sennefer walked the horses down the avenue until they were out of earshot, then slapped them into a trot.

She dared not look back. There was a tether from her heart to the ruler of Annu-Rest, and it stretched endlessly with the distance. It wouldn't break. It hurt so much that she hadn't even asked Sennefer where they were going.

Their destination turned out to be a mosquito-infested hamlet by the Nile. Sennefer informed Anqet that his galley would come for them at daybreak. He conducted her to a one-room house at the edge of the settlement. A servant was waiting to take the chariot.

A bowl of oil lit the interior of the abode. A crack ran through the mud bricks on one wall. The only furnishings were a low table on which the lamp rested and a pallet. Anqet sank down on it to wait for Sennefer to finish instructing his servant. He appeared shortly. Outside she could hear the chariot being driven away. A memory stirred. Something like this had happened before.

Sennefer shut the door of the hut. Holding a flask, he stood looking down at her, a faint smile on his lips. His heavy, disheveled black locks and flushed face reminded Anqet of a statue of a conquering pharaoh. Lord Sennefer dropped down beside her and offered her water from the earthenware canteen. Anqet drank while he watched.

"I had not thought that such beauty could be a burden," Sennefer said.

"I don't think my appearance remarkable." Anqet stared glumly at the crack in the wall. Sennefer turned her face and gazed at her.

"Surely men have told you how magnificent your eyes are. Has no one ever commented on the softness of your skin?" Sennefer's eyes roamed over her breasts. "I can't believe my brother was the first to hunger for the feel of those curves beneath his hands."

"Please." Anqet looked away from Sennefer's glittering eyes.

"I would set aside my wife and marry you," Seth's brother said.

Anqet hung her head, unable to meet his gaze. "I am honored." She moved away from him. "No."

"You still want him."

"I will have no one."

Lord Sennefer laid his hand on her cheek and turned her face to him. "You will have my brother, who is wicked, but you will not have me."

Alarmed by the man's intensity, not wanting to hurt him, Anqet could think of nothing to say. She had never suspected that Sennefer even thought much about her. He was a good man. He was kind, and almost as handsome as Seth in his own way. Yet when she looked at him, she felt no rush of blood, no heat in her loins, no urge to run her hands over his bare flesh.

"I am grateful for your kindness, Lord Sennefer. I am fond of you."

"Fond!"

Sennefer's hand slipped to her neck. Anqet shrank back at the wrath in his voice and face.

"I offer you something my own mother never had—a position as wife. I offer you love, and riches." Sennefer's voice dropped low. "I'll protect you from him. He will never touch you again. I'll see to it. Give to me what you gave to my despoiling brother."

Anqet had always thought Sennefer more concerned with gods than with women. So when he brushed his lips across her own, she gawked at him stupidly. But when he slipped his tongue inside her mouth and cupped her breast in his hand, she exploded. Like a dizzy scorpion, she scrambled backward. Sennefer let her go immediately. He rested his weight on one arm and regarded her calmly while she stuttered a refusal.

"No," he said, as though admonishing a child. "No, little marsh-cat, he has corrupted you with his lust and his impure seed." Sennefer took Anqet by the shoulders and pulled her to him, slowly, with unhurried tranquillity. "I'll make you pure again. That witch's spawn will not defile my beautiful rose lotus."

What frightened Anqet most was the contrast between Sennefer's absolute serenity and the twisted strangeness of his words. She tried to free herself, but Sennefer's strength was as great as his brother's. She shouted. Sennefer paid no attention. He turned her around and laid her on her back on the pallet. Anqet cried out and writhed as he lowered his body on hers.

Sennefer paused. "Please, my lady. Don't shout so. No one here interferes with me. They know better."

Holding Anqet's wrists behind her back with one hand, Sennefer pushed her skirt above her waist. Anqet let her body go limp. She couldn't afford to panic. She would have only one chance to escape. She watched Sennefer loosen his kilt. When he was exposed, she aimed her knee at his crotch and shoved, but he anticipated her, and her knee was met by an arm that slammed her leg aside. When he lunged again, Anqet fastened her mouth on his neck and bit. Sennefer bellowed, cuffed her lightly on the temple, and raised up over her.

"Very well," Lord Sennefer said, his chest heaving. "We will begin with force and end with pleasure."

Pinned beneath Seth's brother, Anqet watched the man draw back his hand for a blow that would end her resistance. A scream of panic welled in her throat, and she struggled to free her arms. The crushing weight lifted from her body, and at the same time she heard a bellow of rage.

Sennefer flew back, given wings by having been lifted and thrown by Seth. Anqet scrambled out of the way as Sennefer landed on his side. He leapt to his feet. He barely had time to cover himself before Seth regained his breath and charged him. The two collided. Seth's momentum sent them to the wall where they wrestled until Sennefer got his foot between their bodies and shoved his brother away.

Seth came at him again, his fury renewed by Anqet's distress. Sennefer pounded at Seth's head with joined fists. The brothers careened around the small space in a bloody and violent dance. Sennefer tossed the count onto the table and Anqet clutched at the lamp as men and furniture collapsed.

Sennefer gained the upper hand on the ground and fastened his hands around the count's neck. Terrified, Anqet sprang at Sennefer, clawing at his hands as they squeezed Seth's neck. The attacker swatted her aside. Anqet landed against a wall, the air knocked out of her, but Seth took advantage of the distraction, twisted sideways, and cuffed his brother on the side of the head. Sennefer crashed to the ground. Seth latched onto him, grabbing the older man's neck and digging his fingers into the vulnerable windpipe. Sennefer gagged.

Anqet struggled to her feet in time to see the count take hold of his brother's head and twist. She didn't know much about fighting, but she knew a death grip. Once more, she flew at the combatants, tugging at Seth's arm. She might as well have been a moth, so little attention did he pay her. Sennefer cried out. Seth winced, but kept twisting. Anqet balled her fist and slammed it into Seth's arm. He started and looked at her.

"Seth, he's your brother," Anqet said. "Let him go." Seth shifted his gaze to Sennefer's tormented body. "Seth, let him go."

The count obeyed her. Sennefer moaned and lay half conscious.

Without taking his eyes from Sennefer, Seth asked Anqet, "Did he hurt you?"

"No."

"Then I won't kill him."

She couldn't help the near hysterical laugh that burst out of her. "You certainly won't."

Seth gave her a worried smile. "No, I won't. You're right, beloved."

Moving off Sennefer, Seth knelt beside his brother. He brushed aside the black hair that covered the man's eyes. Anqet handed the count the water flask, and he sprinkled Sennefer's bloody face. The older man's eyes fluttered open. Seth drew Anqet into the circle of his arm as they gazed at his brother.

"I'll send someone to help you," the count said. "If I stay, we'll fight, and the lady forbids it. Don't come home, precious brother. It won't be safe."

They left by chariot at once. As they drove back down the avenue toward Annu-Rest, Seth held Anqet to him. His skin was damp and covered with a fine film of dust. There was a bruise at the base of his throat.

"I thought I'd lost you," Seth said. "Then I realized Sennefer was gone too. Bareka! He's always been jealous, but I never realized how much until tonight." Seth hugged her.

Anqet gave herself time to shelter in the safety of the count's arm, time to recover a little from this most recent shock before she said anything. Somewhere in the hidden reaches of her ka she knew there was a frightened little girl ready to scream. She didn't want that little girl to escape.

"I'm so tired," she said. Her whole body ached from Sennefer's rough handling. "I wish I could go home."

"We're almost there."

Anqet looked up at Seth. In the gray light she could see the tense set of his jaw. "You're wrong. I'm very far from home."

They arrived at a house in turmoil. Rennut met them at the door and fired questions at Anqet. Seth answered impatiently, hiding the truth. He sent the house servants and the groggy Uni back to bed and conducted Anqet to her room. Khet met them outside the chamber, chattering anxious inquiries, but the count soothed his brother with promises of a talk in the morning. Anqet smiled at Khet and took refuge in her bedchamber. Seth followed.

Anqet splashed water on her face from a basin and let it dribble down her neck. It felt so good that she began splashing it on her shoulders. Seth watched her in silence. Anqet padded to the bed and slumped forward with her arms on her knees. Her thoughts and emotions seemed buried in hot, stifling sand.

"I love you," Seth said. He took a step toward her.

"And I love you. I'll write to Lord Menana tomorrow."

Seth knelt in front of her and took her face in his hands. "You aren't asking that adolescent for help. I'm going to take care of you." He kissed her with autocratic thoroughness.

Anqet allowed the kiss, but did not respond. Seth pulled her head back and stared at her. Anqet met that soft green perusal.

"You will force me to remain here as your concubine. Perhaps Sennefer was right about you. Certainly you can't pretend to be any different than the man who just tried to rape me."

Anqet walked to the door and jerked it open to reveal an alert bodyguard. "Good evening, my lord count."

The door to Anqet's room slammed in Seth's face. His eyes opened wide. He touched the wooden surface as if he couldn't quite believe Anqet had thrown him out. Aware of the guard standing by, Seth gathered his wits and stalked into his own rooms.

He bathed in silence. As water ran over him, he was scourged by images of Sennefer's body on Anqet's. By the innumerable gods! He'd almost been too late.

And the rage. Seth shivered in the warm air. Only

174   S U Z A N N E   R O B I N S O N

once before had he experienced such mindless wrath and hurt at once. Sennefer had been the cause of that too.

She's all right. Sennefer didn't injure her. She said so. But she's suffering. I know it. And she won't let me comfort her. Bareka! I must surely have gray hairs now, with the fright she gave me.

Awakening to find the girl gone had made him panic as no encounter with a rampaging nomad could. He had felt as if some essential part had been ripped out of his ka, leaving him with only a partial, lost soul.

Seth dismissed the servants who attended his bath and lay down on the bed. She had thrown him out. She'd ordered him out of a room in his own house. What was worse, he had obeyed. He dared not stay in the face of her rejection.

She had accused him of being no different than Sennefer, of expecting her to sacrifice her own peace and integrity to his convenience. The look in her eyes when she spoke of his betrayal still haunted him. But what made him cringe with remorse was the gallant way she accepted her own responsibility for their love. Her words came back to him: "I decided to make love to you. I could have said no. I should have. A woman knows the risks of mating without marriage or contract. I let my emotions rule. You see, I've never loved anyone before."

"Never loved anyone before." He remembered her in the garden beneath him. She had responded to him with a natural, spontaneous eroticism that drove him to a burning frenzy. "Never loved anyone before." She had given herself, despite her fears, despite the risk. And he had thought so little of her gift that he put his own fears above Anqet's feelings.

Seth laid his arm across his eyes and tried to sleep. Anqet's face kept appearing in his mind. He saw her as she had been after lovemaking: flushed, lazily content, her nipples erect, a fine sheen of perspiration covering her thighs.

He was so intent on this image that he failed to hear the footsteps that came in from his private garden.

"Well met, my lord count."

Seth was up and pointing his dagger at Merab as the words died in the air. The thief stood before him, flanked by two henchmen. Merab held up a placating hand. His face was as expressionless as a mud brick. A bag fat with cubelike morsels hung from his belt. Merab fished out a piece of coconut and popped it in his mouth.

"No need (*crunch*) to upset (*crunch*) yourself." Merab swallowed. "It's only your old ally."

Seth lowered his dagger. He strolled away from Merab to a clothes chest and took his time donning a kilt. When he returned to the intruders, his face was a smooth mask.

"How did you get past my guards?"

"I didn't get past them. I killed them. Don't worry; there were only three of them."

Seth indulged in a long yawn, stretching his arms wide. Merab scowled at him.

"You weren't supposed to be here for days," Seth said. "You forgot we were to meet in the village?" Merab wasn't supposed to be in the house at all.

"I was ready, so I came," Merab said. "No sense in waiting around for Pharaoh's agents to find my cargo. Besides, I hadn't seen you for too long a time. Your retirement to the country took me by surprise. "Merab stuffed three chunks of coconut into his mouth. "I mished you."

Seth draped his body across a chair. "I'm flattered." He traced the slick ebony of the chair arm. "This yearning for my company is new. One might think you don't trust me."

"One would be correct."

"Where's the loot?" Seth asked.

Merab wandered over to a table and picked up a dagger sheath of reddened gold. "It will arrive tonight."

"Fool," Seth said in a sweet voice. "You could have warned me. That's barely enough time to get rid of my stepmother and my pestilence of a little brother. Stay here while I make arrangements for their departure." He got up. "I assume you're staying here."

"Of course," Merab said. "As I told you, I missed you."

Seth shut the door behind him and motioned for Anqet's bodyguard.

"There are three men inside. Watch them. They mustn't see Lady Anqet, but don't interfere with them."

He slipped into Anqet's room. Taking up one of her gowns, Seth crept to the bed and put his hand over her mouth. Her face was damp with tears. She fought him briefly before she recognized him. After he spoke to her, she lay still, dread in her eyes. At first, Seth rushed into an explanation of his intrusion, but Anqet wasn't listening. Seth stopped in midsentence.

"It's me," he said. Incredulous, he took in the girl's rigidity, the trembling that shook her body. "You think I've come to force you. Gods! What have I done?"

Seth took his hands from Anqet's bare shoulders. He put them over his face and collected his thoughts.

"I have made you fear me. Sweet, beloved Anqet, I could never hurt you. No more could I rape you, or any woman, than I could rape my own ka." Seth stood up and put his heart in his voice, for he knew that his happiness depended on regaining Anqet's trust. "I would sooner die than lose your regard. What touches you touches my soul."

His answer didn't come in words. He watched Anqet come to him, a dark curved shadow. She stopped before him, placed a hand in his own, and laid her head on his chest. Seth let out the breath he'd been holding. Almost disoriented with relief, grateful, he wrapped his arms around this soft creature who governed his happiness.

They remained entwined for as long as he could risk it. Too soon he was forced to steal out of the main house and into the building beside it with Anqet at his side. Once inside the servants' quarters, they found Uni, and the three of them went into a storeroom off the kitchen. Lined with shelves that held oil, beer, and wine, the place was a cubicle. Uni brought in a pallet. At Seth's orders, he went to clear out Anqet's room.

"Remember," Seth cautioned the man, "the lady Anqet does not exist. Tell the others. And tell them to keep out of our visitors' way. I want no confrontations."

He settled Anqet on the pallet. She hugged her knees to her chest and grinned at him.

"Plans go wrong?"

"Yes, and don't smirk at me. If Merab finds you, we're both in danger. Curse him. He was supposed to meet me in the village in three days' time." Seth nuzzled Anqet's cheek. "It's my own fault. I should have sent everyone away, but I lost interest in everything but you."

"How long will Merab stay?"

"Only a day or two," Seth said. "You'll be safe here. This is a spare storeroom, and Uni will see to it that no one wanders in."

Seth pulled a large chest close to the entry. "Keep this against the door. Can you move it? Good. Rest now, and I'll return soon. Uni will bring food." He kissed her but pulled away quickly. It wouldn't do to face Merab with his penis as stiff as a spear.

He rushed back to the house and roused his stepmother. Cutting through her protests, he ordered her to Memphis in a military tone that left her no option but to obey.

Khet was less amenable to being ordered about. The boy sensed his brother's tension and demanded an explanation. They stood outside the stables arguing in the early morning sunlight while grooms prepared a chariot for Rennut.

"Anqet isn't going. Where is she? Why should I go if she doesn't?"

"Quiet!" Seth hauled Khet into the tack room. "I told you. Anqet must remain hidden until my guests leave."

Khet pulled his arm out of Seth's hold. "Something's wrong. I can tell. Your tongue becomes a whip when you're uneasy. Does this have anything to do with Sennefer? Where is he? And by the way, what happened last night?" When Seth glared at him, the boy folded his arms and narrowed his eyes. "I could always ask Anqet. Seth, let go!"

Seth lowered his brother to the floor and sought to control his temper. Khet was looking at him with the pained eyes of a gazelle. He cursed and hugged the boy to him.

"Little Fire, I'm sorry. I forget that you're growing up." Seth fixed Khet with an intense stare. "These men are dangerous. I never planned to have them in the house, but they came. I must deal with them for Pharaoh. I can't tell you why."

"For Pharaoh?"

Seth nodded.

"How can you deal with them alone?"

Khet was too observant sometimes. "I won't. I'll send for Dega. He's waiting upriver at the village of Crooked Palm."

"But I can help."

Seth shook his head. "A good warrior obeys his commander. I'm engaged in a campaign. Obey my command and go to Memphis. I can't attack the enemy as long as you are here. I fear for you."

"Can I take Meki?"

Seth smiled and tousled Khet's hair.

"Take Meki. I promise to send for you soon. When this is over, you can come with Anqet and me to Thebes."

Khet nodded. Seth could see that the boy was dissatisfied but resigned. He sent Khet to hurry Rennut and went to find his ally in crime.

Merab was in the garden with his two assistants watching fish in one of the ponds. The man was amusing himself by attempting to stab a large perch.

"Come inside," Seth said. "We have to discuss the route my ships will take, and then I want to see the cargo."

He managed to keep Merab entertained with business, food, and wine until dusk. There had been a frightening moment that morning when Khet and Meki charged through the reception hall and collided with Merab. The thief took a swipe at the hound, but Khet grabbed the dog and pulled him to safety. The boy crouched at Merab's feet and wrapped his arms around Meki's neck. No words were exchanged as Seth left his chair and strode to his brother.

The thief stared down at Khet with a smile on his lips and a grimace in his eyes. "So this is Khet. Greetings, small warrior. I've been curious about you, most curious." Merab stretched out a hand to Khet. Meki snarled, and Seth pulled his brother to him, out of Merab's reach. The man took a step toward Khet but stopped when Meki bristled and growled at him. Merab backed up, giving Seth a chance to slide his body between the thief and the dog. Ordering Meki and Khet out of the house, Seth moved away with his brother.

"Don't bundle the child off on my account," Merab said. He held the boy's eyes with his own and tried to detain Khet with a hearty purr. "I like children. Let's visit awhile, young one. I'm sure you and I can tell each other fascinating stories about your brother."

The boy shook his head, but his eyes were still drawn into Merab's imprisoning stare.

"Khet's in a hurry," Seth said. "He's going to Memphis." He swept the boy across the room.

When they were near the door and out of earshot, Khet hissed at him.

"I don't like that man."

"Nobody does. Now go."

Khet glared at Merab. The man had taken a seat and was stuffing his cheeks with roast pigeon while he kept his eyes on Khet. An apprehensive look settled over the youth's face. He ignored Seth's drag at his arm and studied the intruder intently. He jerked Seth down so that he could whisper in his ear.

"Seth, that man is evil. Make him go away, or something terrible is going to happen."

"I'm trying to make him go away. What's wrong with you? You're acting like you've seen a monster from the desert."

Khet started to pull Seth toward the front portico,

suddenly more eager to leave than Seth could have wished. He joined Rennut and the party of servants that would accompany them to Memphis. Seth's last sight of the boy convinced him that Khet had experienced an intuitive loathing for Merab. The boy stood beside his tutor in a chariot, his body rigid and his face blank. Meki growled nervously and crouched beside the boy on the ground. Puzzled, Seth watched Khet's figure until it was lost around a bend in the avenue that led to the village of Annu-Rest at the northern edge of the estate.

With the family on their way and Merab satiated with an afternoon's gorging, Seth felt free to go with the thief to the town of Annu-Rest. There, moored at the water's edge, were two innocuous cargo vessels, ostensibly loaded with sacks of grain, jars of oil, beer and wine, and crates of linen. With peeling paint and cluttered decks, the two ships looked like any of the thousands of such craft that plied the Nile.

Seth stepped after Merab onto the deck of the largest freighter and joined him and the captain of the ship. While Merab conversed with the man, Seth observed this newest thief. Paheri was a tall man of muscular build whose most distinctive feature was a shaved head. It wasn't the fact that he shaved his head that was unique, for this was a common practice. What made Paheri's head noticeable was the white scar that ran in a straight line from the middle of his forehead down the center of his skull in a wide, shining band. To Seth it looked as if someone had taken a wood plane to Paheri's scalp.

He decided it was time to sow the first seeds of doubt and fear among his allies. He yawned elaborately and stretched, arching backward and taking quick glances around the ship. He cut through Merab's rumble.

"I want to see the cargo," he said.

Merab and Paheri exchanged looks.

"It's still daylight," Merab said.

Seth looked purposely at the unkempt and brutal-looking oarsmen scattered about. "I see no one here who shouldn't be. Show me."

They took him to an enclosure formed by stacks of grain and linen. Paheri stuck his hand between two bales and dragged out a cloth-wrapped bundle. He knelt and spread the packet out at Seth's feet. From the folds of the material tumbled a mass of glitter.

Seth's heart pounded. Ear studs, pectorals, an Osiris pendant, rings—all bearing royal symbols. He picked up a massive earring of gold. From the stud hung a large gold ring, the interior of which was filled with two uraei, royal snakes. The two serpents flanked a tiny figure of Tutankhamun's brother, the heretic pharaoh Akhenaten. From the ring were suspended strands of miniature beads of gold, malachite, carnelian, and lapis.

Seth trailed the beads across his palm. He remembered these earrings. He'd last seen them worn by the old pharaoh when Tutankhamun was a babe. He remembered standing by, a youth bored with his new duty as honor guard-nursemaid-companion to the royal child, while Akhenaten played with his brother. He saw Pharaoh toss the youngster in the air and catch him. A minister sought words with the king. Deep in conversation, Pharaoh gave the child the earpiece but failed to notice what Tutankhanum was doing with it until Seth leapt forward to snatch the earring before the prince could swallow it whole.

"Seth," Pharaoh had said, laughing, "your sharp eyes have saved my brother. Horemheb tells me he's in need of alert men. We shall have those falcon's eyes trained by one who can put them to use."

Now he closed his hand over the earring. Tossing it back on the pile of jewelry, Seth kicked at it. "You stuck to portable things, I take it."

Paheri grunted. He removed several bales from a crate and opened the container. Inside lay two alabaster vases, each the size of a ten-year-old child. Inlaid with gold and turquoise, they were worth more than a year's labor to a farmer.

Seth lifted an eyebrow. "You had enough time to cart away quite a bit, Paheri. Tell me. Who among the necropolis police did you bribe?"

"You don't need to know that," Merab said.

"You must have talked some mortuary priests into joining you too," Seth continued brightly. "I must say, you fellows have an intense loyalty. I myself wouldn't be able to trust a priest gone bad, or a policeman. Or have you killed them?"

"Shhh!"

Merab hustled Seth out of the enclosure, Paheri close behind.

Paheri stuck his face close to Merab's. "I told you we should have killed the priests," the captain said.

"Shut up," said Merab.

Seth was standing in the middle of the deck with a perplexed look on his face. Several crewmen were busy coiling a rope in front of him.

"You know"—Seth rubbed his chin, deep in meditation—"I remember the funeral." Furtive glances were cast at him. "There was this relief in the tomb. I had to stand still a lot, and that's always tedious when you're young, you understand. Anyway, there was this relief and an inscription. A curse, actually. A curse on anyone who violated the king's tomb. Oh, it was a fine curse."

Seth grinned and raised his voice: *"Amun shall deliver them to the flaming wrath of the King on the day of his anger; his serpent-crown shall spit fire on their heads, and shall consume their limbs, and shall devour their bodies. . . . They shall be engulfed in the sea, it shall hide their corpses. . . . Their sons shall not succeed them; their wives shall be violated before their eyes. . . . They shall belong to the sword on the day of destruction."*

Seth chuckled and flung an arm about Merab's shoulders. The man swore at him as he noticed sickened looks on some of his men's faces.

"Yes indeed," Seth said. "I'm glad we're all barbarians here. It wouldn't do to take the curse too seriously. Why, I do believe my sleep would be disturbed with pictures of my head on fire or my bloated corpse floating in the sea. And then there's the fact that without proper burial, one is damned." He slammed Merab on the back. "But I'm a half-breed. I don't take much stock in the power of dead kings or Amun-Ra. Do you Merab?"

"Will you be quiet!"

"Get him out of here," Paheri said. "Before he has my crew puking on the deck."

When they got to the manor house, Merab was still fuming at Seth over a pitcher of beer in the feasting hall.

He growled his ire: "You did that deliberately."

"What?" Seth asked.

"Don't cast that stick at me, my lord. You were trying to stir up trouble. I'll have no more of it."

"You won't?"

The count hooked a leg over the arm of his chair and sipped his beer. He stared at Merab. The older man squirmed under that cold surveillance and sought a way to put Seth on the defensive.

"I won't. And another thing. You never told me what happened after you caught that spy of a singer. What did you do with her? Who did she serve?"

"I told you. She was waiting for her lover."

"And you believed her?"

"After the way I asked that question? Of course. Besides, it doesn't matter now. She's dead."

Merab pounded his fist on a table. "You should have let me question her."

Seth toyed with the midnight-blue beads in his belt. "My dear Lord Merab, I was having too much fun to share my entertainment with anyone. I used her until I got tired of her, and then I slit her throat. She made a pretty corpse."

Merab examined him. Seth met his gaze openly.

"Sorry you missed the game, my friend. I tell you what. After this is all over, you and I will amuse ourselves if that's what you want. I have two slaves back in Thebes— twins. Bareka! They're good together. Long fingers and wide mouths that can swallow you entirely."

Merab was distracted from the topic of dead singers.

10

In the darkness of the storeroom, Anqet glided back and forth on top of Seth. She heard him murmur words of surprise and pleasure, and she swooped down and located his mouth while maintaining her slow pumping movement. She felt Seth's hips rise to meet her own. Anqet stopped her movements and sucked at Seth's mouth. He tried to speak again, but she smothered the words. When he would have grasped her buttocks and moved her up and down his penis, she caught his hands and pinned them beside his head. She waited, feeling him pulsate within her.

Seth tore his mouth from hers. "You're killing me" He was pleading.

Anqet laughed and stayed still. She stroked his ribs and thighs. With agonizing slowness, she resumed her pumping motions so that each stroke was glutted with sensation. Seth heaved and tried to reverse their positions.

"No," Anqet said. She shoved him back beneath her. "I am master."

To prove her words, she sat up with him still inside her. She tensed her leg muscles and began to move up and down. She felt Seth tense under her. His body trembled. A helpless moan escaped his lips. Anqet toppled forward.

In a growing frenzy she slithered over the wet surface of Seth's body, stroking faster and faster. She could feel her lover's hardness reach deep within her. In a delirium

184

of pleasure, she sought to thrust him to the very center of her body. She groaned and writhed as climax exploded through her. Seth cried out in response. His hands clenched on her buttocks, and a hot stream of his seed filled her. Collapsing on top of him, she rested on the muscled couch as Seth stroked her hair and back with shaking fingers.

"Thoth, lord of magic, concocted a love potion and gave it life," he said. "It's name is Anqet."

"And Seth, lord of carnal pleasure, sent to earth a love-charm bearing his name to tempt her beyond forbearance."

"I only came to talk with you and see that you fared well. I didn't think you wanted me."

"I want you," Anqet said. "It's my permanent state. I was worried, and time passes slowly when you're locked up. I thought Merab had surely killed you. If you hadn't come when you did, I was going to take Uni and search for you."

"I'm sorry. Merab will be gone tomorrow."

Anqet lifted herself from Seth. "And then I'll leave." She put her hand over Seth's mouth. "I have decided. Now tell me. Have you sent for Dega?"

"Yes, but the messenger hasn't returned from Crooked Palm. Neither has the man I sent to take care of Sennefer. About your leaving."

"I don't want to speak of it."

"But—"

"No," Anqet said.

Seth sat up. "If I didn't have to check on those messengers, I'd argue with you. May the gods damn Merab." He kissed Anqet and began putting on his clothes. "I must go."

When he was gone Anqet washed, replaced her gown, and lay down again.

It's no use. If I see him, I have to have him. If only he weren't so cursedly tempting. Even his walk is carnal. And his hips. Anqet drifted off to sleep with visions of Seth's naked body.

There was a knock at the storeroom door. Three taps—silence—four taps. Seth's signal. Anqet roused at the first sound. She dragged her barricade from the threshold and opened the door. An arm shot inside and grabbed her, giving Anqet no chance to run. Merab hauled her out into the yard with the aid of an assistant with yellow teeth and bad breath.

They dragged her to a lump on the ground that turned out to be a bound and gagged Uni. The Nubian stared a mute apology at her. In the predawn darkness it was hard to make out much beyond the patch of light cast by a torch in the hand of another of Merab's men.

Merab grabbed a handful of Anqet's hair. "I knew he was lying. Thinks he's dealing with a fool. My man saw him leave the storeroom. Where is he?" Merab yanked on her hair. "Where is the count?"

"To the Boiling Lake with you." Anqet spat on the ground. "I don't know where he is."

Merab let her go. "Hold her."

Yellow Teeth and another man took Anqet's arms. Merab drew back his arm. A loud snap accompanied by a scream and leap from Merab made Anqet jump. Merab yowled, rubbing his posterior. From the darkness she heard Seth's voice.

"You wanted to know where I was, so I thought I'd let you know. Release the lady Anqet at once."

Still rubbing his injured anatomy, Merab pulled a dagger and pointed it at Anqet's throat. Anqet's mouth went dry. She stared down the blade at the red face of the thief.

Merab searched the blackness. "You are a difficult man to follow, Count Seth. Thank you for coming back. Show yourself or the girl dies."

Silence. Anqet closed her eyes and counted. One. Two. Three. Four. Five. She opened her eyes. Holding his favorite whip, Seth stepped into view ten paces from the group.

Merab pointed to a spot in front of him. "Come here."

Seth let the lash of the whip drop in preparation for a second attack. Merab delicately jabbed his dagger. Anqet stopped her cry, but she couldn't stop the trickle of blood that ran down her neck.

"No!" Seth shouted.

"Come here," Merab said. "And drop that whip."

"Don't—" said Anqet.

Merab increased the pressure of the dagger, and Anqet thought better of finishing her sentence. Seth walked up to Merab. The thief held Anqet at daggerpoint while two of his men bound the count's hands behind him with leather thongs. Once Seth was immobilized, Merab turned on him. Before he could do anything, a high-pitched whistle cut through the air. Merab grunted and let out an answering call.

From all directions came the sound of pounding feet. Seth cursed and exploded into action.

"Run, Anqet!"

The count kicked Merab in the stomach. He bowled Yellow Teeth over with his shoulder. Anqet dodged the remaining thief and headed for Seth. Men came running from every direction, strangers with daggers, clubs, and spears. One hit Seth in the stomach. Anqet charged him from behind. The three of them ended up in a pile on the ground. When Anqet rolled to her knees beside Seth, she found herself and the count in the middle of a ring of spearpoints.

"Get them up," Merab said.

Merab shouldered his way to them. At a gesture from him, Anqet was dragged away from Seth. Merab rubbed his stomach. Standing in front of Seth, he growled an order. Four men held the count's legs and arms.

"Half-breed cur," Merab said. He slammed his fist into Seth's stomach.

Anqet cried out and struggled with her captors, but they held her fast. Rage flooded her as she watched the thief batter Seth.

Merab hit his victim twice more. The two men holding Seth's legs fell back, for they weren't needed anymore;

the count hung between the two thieves holding his bound arms.

Merab gathered a fistful of auburn hair and pulled Seth up to face him. "Look at me."

Seth's metal-green eyes opened.

"Not so proud and haughty now, are you. Think you can treat me like a stupid peasant?"

Merab backhanded Seth across the face. Blood streamed down the count's cheek from a cut made by a ring on Merab's hand. Anqet watched in horror. She saw Merab nurse the hand with the ring on it.

The ring. She leaned forward to get a closer look at the object that had injured Seth. Merab's ring had a flat bezel inscribed with that isolated feather of truth. It was a duplicate of the one she'd seen on Lord Sennefer's hand the night he had offered her protection from Seth.

Merab's ring; Sennefer's ring. With a feather on each. A feather. Anqet's thoughts raced back to the conversation between Merab and his leader. She had thought they were saying "further," and all along it was "feather." No doubt the ring was used by the thieves to identify themselves to one another.

"Oh no," she said aloud.

No one heard her. The count sagged between his captors. Merab was puffing away, exhausted by beating the defenseless man.

Slowly, with defiant grace, Seth pulled himself erect. "Tired already? I suppose that's what comes of forever stuffing one's mouth with sweets. You're puffing like an overheated cow."

"*Argh!*" Merab charged at Seth.

Anqet cried a warning, but Merab was halted by a man with a shaved and scarred head.

"Paheri, let go."

"Lord Merab," Paheri said. "Remember the master."

Merab calmed down at once. He jerked free of Paheri and stood opposite his battered but insolent captive. Anqet could see the hunger in Merab's face. This man wanted to hurt Seth. She grew cold when a sly, pleased smile joined that look of hunger.

"Yes," Merab said. With elaborate care, he grasped Seth by the shoulders and helped him stand more erect. "I forgot. The master's orders were that you and the lady not be harmed."

Seth tried unsuccessfully to pull away from Merab's solicitous hands. He glanced uneasily at Anqet, who tried to speak. Merab interrupted.

"Yes, my dear Count Seth, the master has decided to pay you a visit." Merab's voice dripped with date-wine sweetness. He tenderly smoothed Seth's hair back from his forehead. "You are honored, my young savage. Few know of the master, and fewer still have ever met him. Of those, only Paheri and I are alive."

Merab giggled. Paheri snorted while his men shuffled nervously. Anqet let out the breath she was holding as Merab took his hands from her lover. She'd seen the mingled triumph and apprehension on Seth's face at the mention of the master. Thoth alone knew how the count planned to get them out of Merab's clutches. She knew only that they'd better escape before the master arrived.

"A parting warning against any escape attempts," Merab said.

The thief threw his whole body into the punch he directed at Seth. The count's head snapped back and he crumpled, his limp body sinking to the ground.

Anqet tore loose from the men who restrained her and flung herself down beside Seth. She cradled him in her arms. The cut from Merab's ring still bled. The last blow had already raised a livid bruise on his temple. Anqet could see that Merab had narrowly missed doing permanent damage to his victim's eye.

"You might have killed him," Paheri said after a quick examination of Seth's body. He cut the bonds at the count's wrists.

"Take them to the chapel," Merab said.

Surrounded by armed men, Anqet followed the one who bore Seth through the service yard and across the

gardens to the opposite side of the manor grounds. Beside
the house lay formal grounds with a stone-paved avenue
flanked by four tall poles from which flew red and white
streamers.

The party entered the temple through an open outer
court with a roofed colonnade round the sides.

They trooped into the inner court with its rows of
pillars. Paheri directed his man to lay Seth beneath the
column nearest the entrance to the sanctuary. They lit
the candles mounted in stands at the vestibule and filed
out. Anqet rushed to Seth's side. She heard Paheri
deploying his men around the outer court, which was
the only exit.

Touching her fingers to Seth's throat, she could feel
the voice of his heart throb steadily. She tore the bottom
of her shift and dabbed at the cut on his face. She needed
water. She hesitated to enter the sanctuary itself, but
finally snatched up a candle and went in. As she expected,
there was libation water in a storage room beside the altar.
She muttered a brief prayer. On her way back with a bowl,
Anqet saw a gilt-wood statue of Amun-Ra standing beside
the falcon-headed sun-god. Other silent figures were
shrouded in darkness.

Seth was lying as she had left him. Anqet unfastened
the heavy falcon pectoral of gold and turquoise that hung
to his chest. She loosened the matching beaded belt.
Working first on his injured face, she sponged the count
clean. While she worked, Anqet prayed that Seth would
rouse quickly. She had to talk to him before the master of
the tomb robbers arrived.

It seemed as though time slowed on purpose. The
solar orb refused to show itself. Anqet sat beside Seth and
studied the angular line of his jaw. She took his hand and
sheltered it at her breast. The long fingers were cold.
Anqet heard him take a deep breath. Seth moved his
head. He grimaced and moaned. She studied him
with one hand on his cheek. He opened his eyes and
shut them.

"Where?" he asked.

"In the chapel."

His chuckle turned into a cry of pain. Anqet allowed him a few moments to recover. She had to say it.

"Oh Seth, why could you not keep that clever tongue of yours still?"

The count fixed her with a blurry stare. "Because I didn't want them to turn their attention to you. Those men are executioner's meat. They'd think nothing of passing you around for sport, and I didn't think Merab would stop them. Ah!"

"Don't try to sit up yet," Anqet said. She shifted Seth's head to her lap. "Can you concentrate? There's something I have to tell you, and it can't wait."

"I'll be all right in a few minutes. I've had worse done to me." Seth managed a smile.

Anqet didn't return the smile. "My love, do you remember the words I overheard between Merab and the master? I said one of them might be 'further.'" Anqet broke off. The double doors at the other end of the court swung open. "Seth, listen to me."

"Not now. Help me." The count hauled himself upright, using her and the column for support. He swayed on his feet until he put his hand on the column. He tried to draw Anqet around behind him. She stood close so that she could support him, but refused to hide at his back.

Three men approached through the dark court. One led the way flanked by two shorter figures. The leader had a sedate, graceful walk, the kind of walk Anqet would expect of royalty or a high priest. As the leader neared the pool of light given off by the candles, she clutched Seth's arm.

"I must warn you," she said.

Seth held up his hand. She watched his eyes widen in shock, the color draining from his face, and knew it was too late.

"Gods help me," Seth whispered. "*No.*" He lowered his head.

Anqet squeezed Seth's arm. "This isn't your doing. Don't let him destroy you. Don't let him destroy us."

Only she heard Seth draw a long, shuddering breath. Anqet watched her lover draw a mask of contempt over his mortal pain.

"I love you," she said. Seth nodded but kept his eyes on the intruders.

The visitors stopped five paces away from them. The leader took two steps that brought him into the candlelight.

Seth lifted his chin. "Welcome, master."

"I thank thee, beloved brother."

Seth's older brother stood before them as Anqet had never seen him. Discarding his semipriestly robes, he now wore the short kilt and battle armor of a warrior. A leather corselet overlaid with gold bound his chest, its crossed straps forming the protective wings of a bird of prey. The master's wrists were also guarded by bands of gold-encrusted leather. He wore a long, braided wig and gold headband, and on his shoulders lay a broad collar entirely of gold and lapis lazuli.

"Going to a feast?" Seth asked.

Sennefer ignored his brother. He held out his hand to Anqet.

"Rose lotus, I tried to spare you this unpleasantness."

"Hypocrite," Anqet said. "Spare me? You wanted me for yourself. You're everything you accused Seth of being. And worse."

Sennefer gave an impatient sigh and motioned to Paheri and Merab. As the two headed for Anqet, Seth stepped between her and them. The thieves paused.

"Falcon," Sennefer said. Seth didn't take his eyes from the assailants. "Falcon, you don't want her caught between us, do you?"

Seth shook his head but remained where he was.

Sennefer appealed to Anqet. "Come. You must leave for your own sake."

"I'm not leaving Seth," Anqet said.

"Yes you will," Sennefer replied. "You will be my wife."

Anqet took her place beside Seth. She slipped her hand in the count's.

"You're a criminal," she said. "How could you desecrate houses of eternity?"

Sennefer waved his hand at Paheri and Merab. The two resumed their places behind him.

"Very well. I can see that the witch's spawn has afflicted you with his vile magic."

"Magic?" Seth shook his head. "What are you talking about?"

"You bewitched her." Sennefer's eyes lit with anger. "Look at her. Look at those full lips and that body. She is the embodiment of desire and breeding. How could such a woman be so enslaved to a tainted seed if not by witchcraft?"

Seth's voice rose. "I used no magic. She loves me. Is that so hard to believe?"

Sennefer regarded his brother quietly.

"No," the master said. "No, it's not hard to believe, little brother." Sennefer spoke with genuine affection. As he came closer to Seth, the older man drew a dagger from a gold-and-lapis sheath. He smoothed the flat of the blade against his palm. "I didn't expect it to be this hard," he said, as if resuming a conversation already in progress. He smiled lovingly at Seth.

"After all these years of working to gain power," Sennefer said, "all these years of waiting for the right opportunity to destroy you and take back what is mine, I didn't expect to feel any regret about killing you. It seems you've winnowed your exasperating self into my ka. It will be difficult."

Anqet shivered. Sennefer spoke as if they were all sitting in the garden discussing a servant problem.

"Sennefer," she said. She made her tone gentle. "You don't want to do this. You're brothers. I know you love each other, in spite of all the pain. Don't you see? How can you be so devout and do this?"

"Why, it's because of my faith, of course." Sennefer made a sudden movement that brought the point of the dagger to the base of Seth's throat. The count stood relaxed, his arms at his sides. "God of sin and evil," Sennefer said to his brother, "I have come to end your reign in the Two Lands. Mighty Amun-Ra has given me this task, and now I have succeeded. I shall rescue the flower of Egypt and make her pure."

Seth mimicked his brother. "Might Amun-Ra. Flower of Egypt. Spare me. If you're going to kill me, at least admit it's because you hate me. For once admit the truth. You've always hated me, no matter how much I tried to earn your love. You've always wanted what I had, and that includes Anqet."

Anqet watched the two men. For the moment they'd forgotten her. She was afraid. They looked like two lions in a pit.

Seth slapped the dagger away from his throat and raised his voice. "What I don't understand is why you waited so long after you tried to kill me the first time."

"I didn't mean it that first time!" Sennefer glared at his younger brother. "You fell out of the chariot, and the bull charged."

"You left me to face it. You waited for it to charge. You waited."

Sennefer shouted back. "You stole my father. You stole my future. I'm taking back what's mine."

Sennefer lunged at Anqet and tossed her to Merab and Paheri. "Hold her, and let no one interfere. How much longer will the men be in the house? No, Seth."

Sennefer pointed the dagger at his brother as the younger man headed for Anqet. Seth stopped out of reach of the blade.

"You see," the master said, "my men are busy planting Akhenaten's stolen tomb furnishings in your chambers and around the house. Pharaoh will at last be faced with proof of your depravity. I and the high priest of Amun-Ra will be there to comfort him, and to urge him to put his trust where it belongs—in the wisdom of the servants of Amun-Ra."

Seth edged carefully toward his brother. "At last we get to the truth. The truth is that you and your priestly cohorts want to own Pharaoh, but you've made a mistake.

I never ruled Tutankhamun. He accepts my guidance, if he wishes. Pharaoh is young, but he is truly Pharaoh."

"Stay back," the master said.

Sennefer placed himself between Anqet and his brother, his dagger pointed at Seth. "I helped teach you to fight, brother, and know better than to let you approach. Merab, take the lady Anqet to the count's chambers."

Anqet had no intention of being herded like a she-goat. The sun was finally showing itself. In the meager light she took aim, stomped hard on Paheri's foot, and bit Merab's arm. Sennefer and Seth both cursed, but the noise produced by the two was nothing to the war cry that shrieked at them from the grounds outside. Everyone stopped. One of the Paheri's men, Yellow Teeth, stumbled through the double doors from the outer court, a spear embedded in his gut. Several others rushed past him in panic. Yellow Teeth was trampled as his eyes went vacant in death.

Tomb robbers stampeded into the inner court under a hail of spears and arrows. A second great war cry echoed just beyond the doors. This time Seth shouted a reply.

Anqet was dragged to the protection of a column near the sanctuary by her two captors while they shouted orders at their men. Neither man showed any sign of joining the battle. Anqet had to watch helplessly as Seth's warriors engaged the thieves in a bloody, hand-to-hand contest. Frantically she searched the wrestling figures for Seth. She saw Lord Dega. The young commander dashed inside the entrance at the head of a group of warriors.

A flash of red-black hair told Anqet Seth's location. She saw him swerve to avoid a club, only to go down beneath Sennefer's charge. The two rolled over and over in a cruel embrace, and Sennefer's face contorted with rage. He shouted Seth's name. The count fastened his hands on the arm that sought to plunge a dagger into his heart.

Unlike Sennefer's, Seth's face was devoid of emotion. The count ignored the vituperative stream of phrases his brother spat at him. Suddenly Sennefer pulled his weapon back. Seth, who had been pushing against the force of the master's arms, went off-balance and slipped toward his brother. Sennefer grabbed the count and pulled, adding to Seth's momentum.

Anqet screamed as Seth was forced onto the point of Sennefer's dagger. Her view was obscured by the flow of combat. When she could see again, Seth lay beneath his brother, blood streaming from a wound in his left arm. His muscles strained with the effort to keep Sennefer from plunging the dagger into his heart The injured arm gave way. Anqet watched unbelieving as Sennefer touched the point of the blade to the flesh between the count's ribs.

"Sennefer, no!" Anqet screamed.

Seth's brother must have heard her, though he never took his eyes from the man beneath him. He paused, and Anqet saw the rage drain from him. Anqet prayed to all the gods while Sennefer held her lover's life at daggerpoint. She could see the blade make a dent in Seth's flesh; then it pulled back. Sennefer said something to the count. Seth grinned at his brother even as his hands gripped Sennefer's wrist below the weapon. Anqet heard Sennefer utter a growl of mingled exasperation and amusement. The dagger sought its target, but the force behind it had dissipated with the exchange of words.

A high shriek came to Anqet's ears, followed by a growl. A war-ax hurtled into Sennefer's dagger arm. The handle slammed the master's forearm. Sennefer cried out and dropped the dagger. Seth rolled from under his brother and to his feet. A black streak flashed across the court. The dog Meki raced to Seth and took up a stance in front of his owner.

Anqet and Seth shouted at the same time: "Khet!"

Anqet traced the path of the war-ax back to the double doors where the slim youth craned his neck to see over the broad shoulders of two of Seth's lieutenants. At their shout, Sennefer turned to glare at his younger brother before being forced to retreat from a fresh assault led by Dega.

Paheri and Lord Merab held Anqet and dodged spears

and knives. Occasionally one of them would kick at an enemy as the fighting drew close. Otherwise, both seemed content to let their men and Sennefer take all the risks.

Without warning, Anqet found herself the object of a combined effort by Dega and Seth. The two men worked their way toward her from opposite directions, with Meki clearing a path for Seth with his snarling jaws. Seeing them, Merab pulled Anqet close in front of him as a shield. Paheri tugged at her, trying to hide his bulk behind her as well.

Dega reached the column and swiped at Paheri with his scimitar. Anqet took advantage of the distraction and smashed at the scarred head with her foot when the man ducked. Paheri scrambled out of range on all fours.

Dega turned to the two approaching thieves just as Seth pounced at Merab, and the head thief squealed in panic. Seth reached for the man's neck, but Sennefer appeared behind him, lifted him bodily, and threw him against a pillar.

Anqet was squirming and biting at Merab when the man let out a yelp. Khet had crouched, a club in his hand, and was pounding the man's feet. Anqet joined him, snatching the club and beating Merab about the shoulders. Like a crazed beetle, Merab scurried toward the exit without a thought for his compatriots.

Anqet took Khet's arm and dragged the boy after her. She dodged a scuffle between a charioteer and a bloody sailor. With Khet in tow, she headed for the men who had been assigned to protect this adventuresome youth, but Sennefer curled his arm around her waist and lifted her in the air.

Lunging for Khet, Sennefer caught an ankle and brought him slamming to the stone floor. Anqet saw Khet's head crack against a flagstone. The boy went limp. Sennefer dragged at his brother's leg, but Seth broke through the fighting with Meki as a vanguard and snatched the boy away. Anqet couldn't see what happened to the count and the unconscious boy, for Sennefer lifted her in his arms and plunged into the dark sanctuary.

The sounds of warfare faded as they crossed the vestibule and entered the home of the gods. Sennefer set Anqet on her feet, keeping one arm around her shoulders to prevent her from running. He muttered a prayer to the holy ones in apology for violating their sanctity.

Filtered light from the vestibule showed Seth's men in a final roundup of thieves. A scream made Anqet shudder, and she watched a tomb robber fall to his death, a scimitar piercing his abdomen. Abrupt silence followed, and she listened for Seth's voice.

In the stillness, she felt Sennefer's hard, armored body tremble. He held Anqet from behind, clasping both her arms so that they were pinned to her body. Together they stood listening and waiting at the sanctuary entrance. Anqet felt Sennefer's cheek resting against her head.

> *Assault the foe, slay ye him in his lair,*
> *slaughter ye him in his destined moment,*
> *here and now! Plunge your knives into him*
> *again and again!*

Sennefer broke off the quotation. Anqet had recognized the lines from the play *Horus and Seth*.

The master sighed. "I'm afraid it is I and not the evil Seth who may be slaughtered. In this performance, the wicked one will triumph. Unless..." Sennefer shifted his hold on Anqet. He drew a dagger from the sheath at his belt. "Unless my captive serves as safe conduct."

Anqet could hardly believe him. Safe conduct to where?

"Sennefer," she said, "Sennefer, he was trying to warn you before Dega attacked." Anqet twisted her head around to look up at the master's face. "Don't you understand? Seth has been Pharaoh's agent all along."

There was a long pause. Anqet could barely make out the deceptively pleasing outline of Sennefer's face.

"He was always a clever child, my Falcon."

The dagger angled toward Anqet's throat; she cringed

against Sennefer as he rested the edge of the blade on her neck.

Sennefer's voice sounded as empty and dead as the shell of a locust. "There is another escape for me, and for you."

Light violated the sacred darkness of the temple. Sennefer dragged Anqet toward the altar. He stopped with his back to the golden effigy of Amun-Ra on its pedestal. Seth stood inside the doorway between two men holding torches.

"Sennefer, it's over. Come out now."

"It isn't over, wicked one. Others will fight you after me."

The master pulled Anqet's head back. She felt the sharp edge of the dagger begin to move across her throat. She dared not move.

"I'll have one small victory," Sennefer said. "My rose lotus will be beyond the reach of your defiling hands. I only wish I could have saved Khet as well."

The dagger stung Anqet's throat. Amidst the roar of panic in her mind, she heard a calm voice.

"Wait," Seth said. "Don't be stupid. "It's me you want dead, not Anqet."

The master lowered his weapon. Anqet's legs trembled. She knew they would give way if Sennefer let her go. She looked at Seth. He hadn't moved. She could see the sheen of perspiration on his brown shoulders and the ugly red gash on his biceps. The count's next words filled her with terror.

"Release Anqet. I will come to you in her place."

"No!" she cried.

Sennefer clamped a hand over her mouth. He tightened his grip on her as she struggled. The master paused, then placed his hand on the back of Anqet's neck and reversed the dagger so that he held it ready to throw.

"Come die with me, beautiful and sinful brother."

"I won't go," Anqet said. "Stay back, Seth."

"Silence," the master said. "You will go, or I'll kill him now. See. He stands unprotected. Go." Sennefer pushed Anqet toward the door. "Come, Seth. If you betray me, the blade will end up in Anqet's back."

They met halfway. Anqet dared not endanger Seth's life, nor he hers.

"This is a terrible idea," Anqet said. "If you get yourself killed, I'll be mad at you throughout eternity."

Seth smiled down at her. "You frighten me more than Sennefer."

"Good."

At Sennefer's impatient demand, they moved away from each other. Anqet reached the safety of the doorway where Dega was waiting for her. Pale and frightened, Khet joined them there, leaving the shelter of his guardians and attaching himself to her side. They stood, helpless, watching the two men in the sanctuary.

When Seth was an arm's length away, Sennefer stopped him.

"Hold your arms out from your body."

Seth complied, and the master brought his dagger to rest beneath his brother's chin. Sennefer drew the count closer. "I'll be much happier in the next world knowing that you will suffer in the Lake of Fire for your sins. You may lower your arms. I can kill you at the slightest move."

"Then why aren't you doing it?" Seth asked.

"You want to die?"

"No. I'm curious." Seth stared into his brother's eyes. "You could have killed me when I was wounded. You had this blade poised above my heart." Seth frowned at his brother. "Come to think of it, you could have done away with me any time. You had no need to wait. A chance snakebite. An attack by robbers. A sudden illness. Any excuse would suffice."

"Hold your tongue."

"Panther, admit it. All the planning, the riches, the power—they weren't necessary for my death. They were necessary for your quest for ascendancy."

"Your death would make little difference to my other plans. You die for other reasons."

"Reasons that should have died with our parents," Seth said.

Sennefer looked over the count's shoulder at Anqet and the others crowded in the doorway. "Anqet is looking at me as if she wants to rend me with her own hands."

Beyond Anqet were charioteers, spearmen, and archers—Seth's men—watching, silent. Sennefer let out a long sigh. His body relaxed from its tense, watchful stance.

"You've ruined everything, Falcon," Sennefer said "We would have restored Amun-Ra to his rightful place in Pharaoh's life."

"We?"

Seth moved a little closer to his gold-clad brother.

"Who is we? You're talking about that old lecher of a high priest, aren't you?"

Sennefer nodded dreamily. "The first prophet of Amun-Ra. Yes. You see, I promised him Khet in return for his support in becoming vizier."

"You promised that perverted old man my Little Fire?"

Sennefer glared at the count. "It was necessary."

"Don't you care about what would happen to him?" Seth balled his fists and cursed. "Don't you care about any of us? Or are we all mere grains of wheat to be crushed between the mortar and pestle of your jealous ambitions? You hurt Anqet, and you hurt me. And you were going to throw your own brother into a pit of debauchery."

For the second time, Seth lost control. He knocked the dagger aside with a blow so hard that it flew out of Sennefer's hand. It slid across the stone floor. Sennefer dove for it with Seth in pursuit.

At the door, Anqet started for the two men, but Lord Dega held her back.

"The commander must deal with his brother alone. It is his wish."

Seth caught his brother's leg as the master reached for the dagger, tackling Sennefer as he struggled to his knees. The count reached around and grabbed the arm that held the dagger. Sennefer jabbed his elbow into the count's ribs. Seth doubled over. Sennefer twisted around and stabbed but Seth knocked the dagger aside. He fastened his hands on Sennefer's arm once more. Kneeling face to face, gasping for air, neither could move the other.

Sennefer smiled. "Falcon, you're bleeding like a sacrificial bull."

Seth laughed and increased the force of his grip.

"Remember the time we put all those sacrificial pigs in our tutor's room while he was bedding that peasant girl?" Seth asked. "The sow nearly gored me, but you stabbed her with a walking stick and plucked me out of the way." Seth looked into his brother's eyes, perplexed.

"I spent much time extricating you from disasters. Father would have thrashed you at least a dozen times for sneaking out of the house at night." Sennefer sighed and then said one bewildered word, "Falcon?"

"I'll let go if you will," Seth whispered. He looked from Sennefer's griefstricken face to the dagger between them.

The tension in Sennefer's arms relaxed. Seth slackened his hold, stood, and slowly backed away from the older man. Sennefer let him go without objection, but remained kneeling. He looked up at Seth, a quizzical smile on his lips.

Seth burst out: "Oh, Panther, I can't think of a way to get you out of this swamp you've sailed into."

Sennefer lowered his basalt-black eyes.

"You can't," he said. "I must navigate this sea alone it seems."

The master reversed his hold on the dagger and plunged it swiftly into his chest. The blade slid between the folds of the gold and leather armor.

Seth cried out his brother's name as he swooped down at the dying man. To the accompaniment of the horrified screams of their youngest brother, Seth gathered Sennefer in his arms

Sennefer stared up at his brother. "Little barbarian, you will see that I make the last journey as I should?"

"Of course. Everything will be correct—the embalming,

the mourners, the tomb. Just as you want. I pledge my
ka."

Sennefer nodded once. His eyes closed, and his
hand slackened its hold on Seth's. His face contorted with
pain.

"I should have taken you with me, Falcon. I fear to
make this journey alone."

"Horus will take you by the hand," Seth said. "Listen,
Panther. Don't be afraid. I know the words."

Steer to the west, to the land of the justified.
The women of the boat weep much, very much.
In peace, in peace to the west, thou praised one,
come in peace....

Seth felt his brother squeeze his hand and then relax.
His vision blurred with tears, Seth drew the dead man to
his chest and finished his chant.

When time has become eternity then shall we see
thee again, For behold, thou goest away to that
country in which all are equal.

Seth laid Sennefer's body gently before the image of
his god. As he knelt before the two golden forms, soft
arms encircled him.

"There was no other way, my love," Anqet said. "He
knew that."

Seth made no reply. He stayed on his knees with
Anqet at his side, feeling numb, and listened to Khet's
sobs.

Long after the chapel was deserted of warriors, his
wits finally drew themselves together from the splinters of
his senses. He wasn't sure which god had given him the
strength to survive the last few hours.

As if from a great distance, he was aware of Anqet's
silent companionship. An unwelcome thought passed through
his mind. Marriage had caused Sennefer's death as surely
as Pharaoh was shepherd of his people, marriage and

broken promises. Could he risk Anqet's love by marrying her? He had lost so much already.

Seth withdrew from Anqet's embrace.

"Come, beloved. I must comfort the brother I have left."

11

On the portico at dusk of the day following Lord Sennefer's death, Anqet knelt before an ebony-and-cedar chest. Bearing the hieroglyphs of the heretic king's name, the sepia panels of the box were surrounded by carved gilt symbols of life and fortune. Sennefer's men had spilled the contents when attacked, and Anqet was restoring them. She folded an intricately pleated robe with quivering fingers. Heretic or not, Akhenaten had been a god on earth, the Living Horus, and this was his raiment. As she closed the lid of the box, she caught a whiff of old funerary incense and dead flowers. She rubbed her hands on her skirt but stopped when she saw a crumpled papyrus beneath one leg of the box.

The contents of the roll were written in the cursive version of hieroglyphs used for everyday purposes. It was a hymn to the heretic's sun-god, the Aten:

August God who fashioned himself,
Who made every land, created what is in it,
All peoples, herds, and flocks,
All trees that grow from soil;
They live when you dawn for them,
You are mother and father of all that you made.

Anqet rolled the papyrus up hastily and thrust it in the cedar chest. She snapped the lid closed and eyed it warily. A hymn to the Aten in the Pharaoh's own hand.

"Amun-Ra, protect me."

Anqet stood up and wiped her palms on her skirt. She now realized the full implications of Sennefer's actions. Sennefer and his allies among the priesthood and nobility had dared to touch the sacred possessions of a god-king. How far did the intrigue extend?

Two servants filed past carrying more royal furniture. Anqet shook herself out of her reflection and searched the grounds for Seth. Members of one of the royal spear squadrons filed past with a line of prisoners. Servants went back and forth from the house carrying tomb furnishings, which were being gathered for shipment to Thebes. One of Seth's officers supervised the packing of chairs, stools, weapons, games, and walking sticks. The tomb robbers had been thorough. All around the manor house stood armed guards who allowed no strangers in the high-walled compound.

In the shadows cast by a row of palms, Anqet saw the count. A white bandage on his biceps, Seth stood with his arm around Khet's shoulders and spoke with a priest from the local temple of the god Monthu. The man would escort Sennefer's body to Thebes and the embalmers. Seth had told her he wasn't sure Pharaoh would allow Sennefer's burial after the count told him the truth about his brother. Tutankhamun might avenge himself on Sennefer by depriving him of life after death. Anqet understood; she might want to do the same thing if Hauron destroyed the souls of her mother and father.

Another group of prisoners shuffled by on their way to temporary incarceration in one of the cattle pens. Paheri was among them, but Merab had not been found. Lord Dega had sent patrols in search of the man and other escapees. Seth's young second-in-command led this latest group of thieves. Anqet smiled at him as he passed, and Dega raised his arm in salute.

When she looked back to Seth, the count had finished his business with the priest. He and Khet walked toward her. Khet's head drooped as though it were the too-heavy blossom of a plant. Seeing his two brothers in mortal combat and witnessing Sennefer's suicide had shocked the boy. He clung to Seth in desperation, uncertain of how to grieve for the brother he had loved so unconditionally.

Anqet inspected Khet's blue-shadowed eyes. She'd stayed awake with him for several hours last night while the boy stared into nothing and shed silent tears. Seth had finally ordered a mild sleeping draft for both of them. Khet was smiling at her now. It made Anqet's spirits lighten to know that the youth liked and trusted her. She smiled back at him.

"I still don't understand how you got here," she said to the boy.

"He recognized one of Merab's men talking to a gang of thugs in the village and decided to play spy," Seth said. "He bullied his tutor into a detour to Crooked Palm, where he met Dega."

Khet squirmed under his brother's annoyed look. "I was right, wasn't I? You needed help."

"You can't deny that," Anqet said.

"I'm not denying it," Seth said. "But he should have stayed with his guards."

"If I had, you might be dead," Khet said.

"Ah, forgive me, Little Fire. You risked your life for me, and I rail at you. This raising of children is not an easy thing."

As the two males exchanged solemn nods of commiseration, Anqet giggled at the spectacle of this aristocratic warrior and sparkling youth complaining like her old nurse. Her laughter made them grin back at her.

Seth's smile melted. "We leave for Thebes in the morning. Pharaoh must be told of what has passed."

Anqet's spirits plunged. She'd forgotten her own troubles. "I'll stay here and write Lord Menana."

"No."

"I did not ask permission."

Seth put his hands on his hips and looked down at her. "I didn't give it. Merab is still free. You can't stay here alone, and you're not writing anyone."

"Merab be damned to serpent's poison! I'm in no danger here." Anqet glared at Seth. "You may own everything within these walls, my lord count, including Khet, but you don't own me. You will never own me. I am Anqet of Nefer. I must live within the honor of my house and family, just as you must live in this house of ancient lineage."

He didn't want the responsibility, only the pleasure, of loving her. It galled Anqet to acknowledge this fact, but it was true.

Seth looked out at the busy servants, warriors, and slaves. He cast a sideways glance at Anqet, one she knew meant his devious wits were at work.

"I have word of your home from the man I sent there," he said.

Anqet stared at Seth. "You have word? What word?"

"All appears normal at your estate. On the surface." Seth leaned against a column in the shade of the portico. Khet moved beside him. Seth put a protective arm around his shoulders and looked at her with the eyes of innocence. "My agent asked about Nefer in the hamlet downriver. The estate runs as it always has, except that the mistress has been stolen to the sorrow of her loving uncle. Some scribe of the uncle's is steward in her place. Do you know a man named Thanasa, son of Thuty-hotpe?"

"Who?"

"I didn't think so. This Thanasa is the man your uncle left in charge of Nefer. My agent says he's increased the lord's share demanded of the tenant farmers by tenfold, and everything goes to Hauron. Harvest will see your people hungry, beloved."

"I told you! I must get help and rid Nefer of Thanasa." Anqet gritted her teeth.

"I'll help you, Anqet," Khet said from his place beside Seth. "We'll run this man off the way we did Lord Merab."

Seth threw up his hands. "Bareka! Will you two consider what you're saying? A woman and a boy intend to ally themselves with a rustic lordling to take over an estate guarded by men as brutal as any we've got in the cattle pens. You didn't think of that, did you? Thanasa is a skinny, hip-swashing viper, but he rules through the squadron of cutthroats Hauron left with him. They'd feed you to the crocodiles—if you were lucky."

Khet stirred and made a small sound of distress.

"So I'm to stay with you where it's safe," Anqet said.

"Only until I can think of the best way to deal with Hauron. The man is dangerous. He has control of you by law, and he's clever."

"I know that," Anqet said. "That's why I can't wait. I've been gone over a month, and there's no telling what he's done to my people. I'm worried about Bastis and Nebre."

"They've been exiled from Nefer. They have taken refuge with your precious Lord Menana. My agent says they are well."

"How can I be sure without seeing for myself?" Anqet asked.

Seth tossed his auburn head. "Don't you trust this heroic suitor you crave?"

"Don't be nasty," Anqet said.

Seth shoved away from the column. He faced Anqet. The two locked eyes.

"You can't go now," Seth said.

"I'll go to Thebes and hire warriors myself."

"Stubborn little witch. Hauron is in Thebes looking for you."

All thoughts of saving Nefer fled, and Anqet wrapped her arms around her upper body. Goose bumps raised on her flesh. Her heart pounded, and she felt light-headed. She almost expected to see Hauron behind her.

Warm, firm arms enclosed her, and she started. Seth pulled her head to his shoulder.

"Forgive me. I shouldn't have told you, but I was angry and worried."

From behind her, Anqet heard Khet's voice. "How do you know this man is in Thebes?"

"I told my men and a few of my friends to watch for him. One of my drinking companions is a servitor in the temple of Amun-Ra. Hauron came there searching for a girl, a girl who from the description could only be Anqet."

"Drinking companion?" Anqet lifted her head from Seth's shoulder. "You spoke my name in a tavern? Why?"

Seth grinned down at her. "Remember the night I had you brought to my ship and I got drunk? I was with my friend, and much bedeviled by you and your distaste for me. He helped me drink my pain away and gave me advice on how to seduce you."

"You are walking on the edge of a cliff, my love."

"I told you I liked danger," Seth said. "In any case, no matter how angry you become, you're not leaving my sight."

Anqet wriggled out of Seth's arms. "How many times must I repeat that you aren't my master? By the Nile, I hate the way you assume I'll do what you say, just because I like the way you—" Anqet remembered Khet. "You'd think you were Pharaoh."

"And you might as well be an addled quail-chick for all the wits you seem to have."

A hot flush of wrath spread over Anqet's fact. "I'm not stupid. Send Dega and some warriors north with me."

Both Anqet and Khet winced at the obscene and sacrilegious phrases Seth hurled at her. The count grabbed her wrist.

"Now it's Dega you choose as your protector."

Anqet was about to inform Seth that it was his fault she needed a protector when Khet shoved between them. Anqet glanced down at the boy; she had forgotten he was there. His eyes were bright with unshed tears, and she realized Khet was more upset by their arguing than she would have thought. Determined not to increase his distress, she settled for a glower at the count.

"Your pardon, Commander," Lord Dega said.

"I was passing by and heard Lady Anqet mention leaving for home. I must tell you that is not possible."

"I know," the count said.

"No, Commander. Before I left Thebes, the Living Horus said to me that not only were you to report personally when this business was finished, but that you were to bring the lady Anqet."

Seth stared at his equerry. Anqet stared at him too.

"Did Pharaoh say why he wished to see her?" Seth asked.

"No, my lord."

"But I have nothing to do with Lord Merab or any robberies," Anqet said.

Dega answered her. "Pharaoh has spoken."

Those three words overruled everyone's wishes. Anqet turned on Seth.

"I don't want to be in the same city as Hauron." She eyed Seth. "I have a feeling you're behind my being ordered to Thebes."

"Me?"

She caught Seth's brother by the arm. "Let's find Meki. It's time to feed him, and you should eat too."

"I'm not hungry," Khet said.

"Meki is."

They sailed for Thebes the next day at sunrise. Anqet was an unwilling member of the party that accompanied the count of the Falcon nome on his return to Pharaoh. But she was calm again. She was no longer prey to the fear that Hauron would pounce on her the moment they docked, not with Seth and his warriors surrounding her.

On board Seth's galley, Anqet kept her distance from the count. Certain that he had somehow persuaded Pharaoh to delay her, she kept busy with the self-appointed task of continuing Khet's lessons in composition.

They sat on the deck beneath the shelter of the pavilion in front of the main cabin. Anqet corrected the boy's script, ignoring Seth. After a few spurned attempts at conversation, the count became engrossed in the running of the ship. Wanting to make as much speed as possible, he ordered all oars in the water and the sail hoisted. The galley zigzagged downstream, beating into the wind with port and starboard tacks.

Out of the corner of her eye, Anqet watched Seth. Joining Lord Dega and several men, he and they positioned themselves about the deck and began to exercise. Stripped to a skimpy loincloth, the count stretched his arms wide

and leaned backward in an attempt to work out the
soreness that was a legacy of the battle with Sennefer.
Anqet stopped her instruction in midsentence when the
muscles in his arms and shoulders bunched and his hips
thrust. The sun played over the taut brown skin at his belly.

"Merciful Isis," Anqet said.

He was parading around like that on purpose. The
harlot. With a supreme effort, Anqet dragged her gaze
from her lover's glistening, spread legs.

"Khet, you've forgotten the determinatives on half
your words. Look, you've got fifty jars of wine rejoicing at
the storage yard."

Anqet tried to keep her eyes on the used papyrus
they employed for the lesson. Seth had stopped his exer-
cising to help two sailors secure a line to the mast. His
bare body twisted and stretched, and Anqet felt a tingling
between her legs.

"He's doing it on purpose."

"Who's doing what?" Khet asked.

"Nothing. I have an idea. You'd probably be more
interested in lessons if they were about something besides
accounts and religious instruction. Why don't you try
copying this triumph song. It's about the pharaoh Khamose
and his campaign to drive the Hyksos invaders from the
Two Lands."

Seth took a break. He had Dega pour water over his
heated body, the liquid drenching his loincloth. Anqet
turned back to Khet.

"Anqet, you've spilled ink all over your skirt."

For Anqet, it was a long journey downriver to the
capital. When the galley docked, a party of officials was
waiting with chariots and orders to attend Pharaoh at
once. After putting on court dress, Anqet found herself,
Seth, and Dega in the royal palace before she had time to
realize she was actually going to see the living god.

She and Dega waited in a long corridor friezed with
blue faience tiles and watched a Syrian vassal prince leave
Pharaoh's presence. In his gaudy red wool skirt, the man

padded past them at the head of a retinue of oiled and simpering courtiers.

The overseer of the audience hall, one Minhetep, stepped out of the reception chamber, bearing a gold staff. Minhetep saw Count Seth speaking to General Horemheb, turned, and disappeared behind the great doors of the hall. A stream of dignitaries burst from the room, making rapid strides. Anqet pressed her back to the wall as a priest in leopard skins pushed by her with several army officers. She stayed there while the king's favorite panther was escorted from the chamber by its keeper.

The overseer beckoned to Seth and Horemheb. Through the closing doors Anqet caught a glimpse of a vacant throne high on a dais and beside it, a slender figure in a double crown. Pharaoh waved a dismissing hand at the royal bodyguard. The corridor cleared of everyone but guards and the overseer.

Anqet's hands and feet grew cold with apprehension. What if Pharaoh blamed Seth for his brother's actions? What if the Living Horus desired revenge for the atrocity committed on the sacred body of his dead brother? Holy Amun-Ra, were they all to be executed? With growing trepidation she remembered a curse: *There is no tomb for one who is hostile to His Majesty; but his body shall be thrown into the water.* Anqet leaned back against the cold faience wall tiles. The punishment for the enemies of Pharaoh was total extinction—no tombs, no prayers or offerings to keep their kas alive.

Dega put his hand on her shoulder. "Is something wrong, lady?"

"What if Pharaoh blames Seth for . . . for . . ."

"Do not worry, my lady. The king has known Count Seth since the king was a babe. Pharaoh bears him great affection. I have seen the Living Horus defy even Divine Father Ay for Seth. The commander is in no danger."

Anqet was only partially reassured by Dega's words. The king loved Seth. Would he still love the brother of the man who desecrated tombs?

It was over an hour before the audience-hall doors parted. Minhetep stalked over to Dega and Anqet.

"The Living God, The King of the North and the South, the Golden One, Son of the Sun, sayeth thus: 'Lord Dega will bring unto my justice the one called Paheri and the other foes of Ra. The Lady Anqet will attend my majesty.'"

It took Anqet a while to understand that Dega was to see to their prisoners, who had followed in a separate ship, and she was to go into the presence of Pharaoh. Casting a fearful glance at Dega, Anqet trailed the tall, stiff-jointed overseer into the audience hall. It was empty. Feeling insignificant, shrinking beneath the pillars that supported the roof far overhead, Anqet was relieved when her guide conducted her through a door behind the throne. They went down a corridor, through two formal antechambers, and into a foyer guarded by a squad of men bearing spears and battle-axes.

The overseer vanished behind a door overlaid with sheet gold and engraved with the images of Pharaoh and the god Amun-Ra. The man reappeared. He held the door open, and motioned for Anqet to enter. Slipping inside, Anqet paused to take in the beauty of the room before her.

It was a chamber of light. Numerous high, narrow windows made the whole place bright yet let in little heat. Like Seth's room at Annu-Rest, it was adjoined by a terrace and a private garden filled with sycamores, palms, and willows. Papyrus plants, cornflowers, and poppies bordered the terrace. On one wall of the room was a line of shelves filled with bookrolls and writing utensils. Another wall bore armor, weapons, and walking sticks. On a table near the door Anqet saw a box. It held the double crown of Egypt. She examined this hallowed object discreetly before daring to step further into the room in search of Pharaoh.

From almost every object in the chamber, the gleam of gold and electrum struck her eyes. A gilt couch with lion-head finials stood on the terrace. Its rumpled cushions gave evidence of recent occupation. Where was Pharaoh? And Seth?

Anqet stepped further into the king's study and saw two people beside a pond brimming with blue lotus. Count Seth knelt before the young king. General Horemheb was absent. Anqet crept out to the terrace. Unsure of how to approach the pharaoh, she hoped one of the men would notice her. Tutankhamun was glaring at Seth. Anqet's heart started to vibrate in fear. The king was furious.

"No, I tell you," Tutankhamun said. His voice was raised in anger. "I forbid it."

"Please, Majesty."

"No." Tutankhamun whipped away from the count, saw Anqet, and beckoned to her. Anqet fell on her knees before the king and touched her head to the ground.

"Get up," the king told her. "Both of you get up. By the twelve gates of the netherworld, I refuse to allow it. Seth, you may not resign your command."

Anqet edged as close to Seth as she dared. She heard the cause of Pharaoh's anger with relief. Tutankhamun sat on the stone ledge of the pool and regarded them silently. Anqet glanced at Pharaoh. There was strain in his face. The smooth skin was pulled tight about the mouth, and there was a haunted sadness in his eyes. The king was looking at Seth, his full lips pursed in annoyance.

"You taught me to draw a bow. You showed me how to hold a javelin. You were with me when I heard that my brother was dead and that I would be king. Do you think me so ungrateful or so foolish as to blame you for something Sennefer did? You insult me, my lord."

"Majesty," Seth said, "your advisers, the princes of the kingdom and the empire, they will demand that I—"

"They will demand nothing," Tutankhamun said. He spoke calmly. The youth uttered the words that ended all protest. "It is my word."

"Pharaoh's word is performed," Seth replied.

Tutankhamun nodded. He stood up and came toward them. To Anqet's utter consternation, the boy linked arms with Seth and herself and directed their steps to the shade of the covered terrace.

Pharaoh was touching her, talking to her.

"And Seth told me how you fought as bravely as any warrior."

Tutankhamun settled back on the lion couch. He indicated a chair for Anqet and a place for Seth. The count sank to the floor. Tutankhamun laid a hand on the count's shoulder, as if to ensure that Seth would stay put. The king smiled at Anqet. She held still and tried to accustom herself to being looked at by the living god. It didn't help that the young man obviously enjoyed looking at her. She had seen that gleam in the eyes of another. Anqet flushed and studied her hands. The king addressed her.

"This is the second time I have come under obligation to you, Lady Anqet."

Anqet attempted to say something, but the sight of Pharaoh half reclining opposite her took the words from her head as fast as chaff flew in the wind. She cast a glance of appeal at Seth. The count smiled at her.

"Lady Anqet is in awe of thee, Majesty. Believe me, she isn't normally so quiet."

Tutankhamun's laughter came spilling out at Anqet. She blinked, and a timid smile graced her lips.

"At least say something," Tutankhamun said to her. "You will make me feel like a monstrous demon if I frighten ladies in private as well as in public."

"Majesty," Anqet said. She cleared her throat. "Majesty, thy words honor me. I regret to say that I fought out of terror, not bravery."

"Seth always tells me my fear only means I'm wise enough to recognize danger."

"I recognized it at once, Majesty," Anqet said.

This time both Seth and the king grinned at her. Anqet perceived a new direction in the king's thoughts. The boy let heavy lashes conceal his eyes as he spoke to Seth.

"So, my friend, you've made an enemy of the lady Gasantra. She returned from Annu-Rest bleating of some well-endowed tavern girl who has you enthralled. I assume she means our glorious Lady Anqet."

Seth frowned at one of the lion heads on the couch.

"Who prattles of such things to thee, Majesty? Such foolish gossip is unfit for the ears of Pharaoh."

"My ears have a great liking for gossip, thank you."

Seth turned toward the king. "Pharaoh, the lady Anqet is the most honorable, the most gentle and loving woman I've ever met. Gasantra is a jealous, whining hippopotamus."

Anqet lowered her head to conceal a blush.

"Oh?" Tutankhamun said.

"She tried to bed me after I told her I could no longer accept her favors," Seth said. He pounded a fist into his thigh. "Then she tried to knife me when I refused her advances."

Pharaoh's eyes lifted from Seth's thundercloud countenance to Anqet's distressed crimson face.

"Ah," the king said. He leaned down to Seth's ear. "But your interest lies elsewhere and has for quite a while."

Seth appeared to come out of his rage and remember to whom he was speaking. "Forgive me, Majesty. The events of the past few days have robbed me of sense."

Anqet felt her cheeks cool. What was wrong with Seth? He had almost declared their lovemaking to the divine pharaoh.

"Come, Seth," Tutankhamun said. "My curiosity has been burning for too long. Admit your love for Lady Anqet, and we'll arrange a contracting ceremony. It is feast season, the perfect time for it."

Lifting her head, Anqet met Tutankhamun's wide grave eyes. He knew! Anqet controlled her shock and tried to comprehend the unspoken message Pharaoh was sending her. He remained on the couch, his jeweled hand resting on Seth's shoulder, and sent a look of reassurance at her. What did the king intend?

It occurred to Anqet that Seth had said nothing. The count sat as if transformed into an obelisk.

"The lady Anqet and I are not betrothed, my king."

"Why not?" Tutankhamun asked. He sat up. "Do you mean you've kept this noble lady in your house under questionable circumstances, and have made no offer? Seth,

Gasantra has seen to it that every artisan and peasant farmer in the Two Lands knows of your conquest."

Anqet covered her face with her hands. In all her nightmares she had never dreamed of a humiliation so devastating as having her foolish love affair come to the notice of the divine pharaoh.

Tutankhamun's anger increased. "This lady will not suffer further at your hands, my lord commander." He stood up.

Seth and Anqet rose hastily. Tutankhamun glowered at his commander of chariots.

"I won't force you to marry. As I warned you, the lady Anqet has engaged more than my gratitude." The king clapped his hands.

The overseer of the audience hall slid into view.

"Take Lady Anqet to the women's quarters. Tell the countess Ta-usert that this girl will become a royal concubine."

"Majesty!" Seth roared.

"Be silent, my lord."

Anqet stood in a daze while Minhetep approached. It was absurd. She? Become the concubine of the living god? It was incredible. The overseer herded her toward the door. So stunned she could hardly navigate, she went with Minhetep. One did not question the decision of Pharaoh, even if Pharaoh was a boy two years younger than oneself. At the door she looked back. On the terrace, Seth was kneeling at Tutankhamun's feet, furious and supplicatory at the same time. Pharaoh shook his head.

The count's voice rose to a snarl. "You can't."

Tutankhamun dealt the count a hard, backhanded blow across the face. Seth tottered to one side but recovered. Anqet couldn't hear what he said. His face was hidden by the shining blackness of a court wig. Whatever passed between the two was over quickly. Pharaoh raised the count with his own hands, and indicated the chair opposite his golden couch. Seth sat down, his eyes veiled, his hands shaking as they rested on the arms of the chair.

"Lady Anqet," Minhetep said. He held the door open.

Anqet went out. As she passed the man, she caught his look of amusement. That expression did little to reassure her. She directed a cold stare at Minhetep and preceded him through the royal apartments.

Meeting Countess Ta-usert turned out to be one of the few cheerful experiences of the succeeding days. From the ruling family of the Hare nome, Ta-usert governed the concubines attached to Pharaoh's household. Nearly of an age to be Anqet's mother, the woman possessed the imperturbable good spirits and strong will needed to keep the large number of females and their offspring under control. The top of her head was even with Anqet's nose, but Anqet could tell that there was more strength in that spare body than in some men's.

Ta-usert received her in a chamber overflowing with blossoms and stocked with jars, vials, and pots containing eyepaint, lip color, and henna for tinting the hands and feet. The countess bid Anqet sit beside her on a couch.

"Amazing," Ta-usert said. "Pharaoh sent you to me personally?"

"Yes."

"Amazing."

"I don't understand," Anqet said.

Ta-usert looked her up and down. "Amazing. He knows how to choose, does our young pharaoh. The first time he selects a girl, he chooses as fine an example of beauty as any since the old heretic's queen. *Anqet*. Where have I heard that name? Anqet. Oh. Crocodile's teeth! Lady Anqet."

Anqet squirmed. Gasantra must have chattered herself hoarse spreading slander.

"I know what you've heard, Countess. Believe me. None of it is true."

"Child, it doesn't matter. The king has chosen you."

Ta-usert hopped to her feet and paced back and forth in front of Anqet.

"Finally," the woman said. "I told that old prude Ay

three years ago it was time the king learned to take his pleasure. But he refused, did Father Ay."

"Well, twelve is a bit young." Anqet felt foolish and irreverent discussing the sexual habits of the god-king.

"Young? I was younger." Ta-usert stopped in front of Anqet and folded her arms across her breast. "Do you have any notion of how difficult it is to rule almost one hundred young women when the king they are supposed to serve is a child? For years there's been nothing to do. Nothing. And then when the boy comes into his manhood, that fool of a regent Ay puts it into his head that his first duty is to the Great Wife Ankhsenamun. What a waste."

Anqet giggled. Ta-usert snorted, then burst into laughter along with Anqet. Holding her stomach, tears streaming down her face, Anqet tried to make the countess understand.

"This is terrible," she said.

"What's terrible?"

"I don't want to be one of Pharaoh's concubines."

Ta-usert stopped laughing. "Amazing."

"I know," Anqet said. She wiped her moist cheeks.

"You're mad. You could be the first woman to bear a child to the living god. The charms of your Count Seth can't compare to that honor."

Ta-usert grasped Anqet by the arm and pulled her to her feet.

"Don't be upset, girl. You haven't a choice anyway. And it isn't as if the king were ill favored. The beauty of the gods is in that one. Come along. You need a wash and food. We'll talk. You can tell me about Count Seth, and I'll tell you about His Majesty." Ta-usert clapped her hands. "Things are going to happen at last. It's obvious Pharaoh isn't going to pine after the Great Wife anymore. My dear Anqet, you and I will introduce our beloved young Majesty to the realm of pleasure."

"Oh no."

The countess grinned at her and patted Anqet's cheek. "Amazing."

After being washed, oiled, scented, and painted,

Anqet was taken to a wardrobe chamber stacked with
see-through garments of every fashion. Ta-usert swept
through the piles and snatched gowns. She threw them at
Anqet as the girl padded after her.

"We'll try these. There'll be no problem trying to
hide a fat belly on you. Oh, this is exciting. I haven't had a
new trainee in years."

"Countess, please. I don't want to be Pharaoh's
concubine."

"Don't say that," Ta-usert warned. "You know better.
Pharaoh has spoken."

Anqet nodded. A black vulture of misery settled on
her shoulder. The only man she'd ever wanted had been
such a stubborn fool that he'd gotten her into this mess.
Seth loved her. She knew that now. He loved her enough
to die in her place. Anqet cringed at the memory of
Sennefer's dagger at her neck.

Somehow, Seth had the idea that if they were husband and wife, their easy friendship would shatter. He had
fastened on marriage as the catalyst for disaster, when she
knew that a man and woman were like two gods in an
unformed world. They could create or destroy their own
realm. Her parents had built their own world, although
Anqet realized that Rahotep and Taia had dwelt too much
in their private kingdom. She needed no isolation in
which to grow her love for Seth. Neither could she feed it
on the barren ground of a less-than-honorable relationship.

Anqet pulled at the gossamer folds of a robe while
Ta-usert fastened the drapes of the garment beneath her
breast. The woman's hands adjusted the pleats across her
chest. A maid brought golden sandals.

Anqet moaned. "What am I going to do?"

"I'll tell you what to do later," Ta-usert said. "Right
now, I want to get an idea of which stones look best on
you. Thank Hathor your skin doesn't have a yellow tint.
Nothing seems to flatter yellow skin, and especially not
gold. Here, try this."

From a casket borne by two wardrobe girls, the
countess produced a heavy broad collar of alternating

turquoise and malachite beads mounted in gold. A matching pair of bracelets went on Anqet's wrist. A gold leather belt wrapped twice around her waist, then cascaded to her feet. A veil of sheet gold draped over the shoulder-length wig Ta-usert mounted on her head. Anqet held her head still. Her neck already strained with the effort to support the artificial tresses, the extra weight of the veil made her want to tear the whole edifice off her head. She reached up and started to lift the wig.

"Don't touch," Ta-usert said. She stepped back for a look. "Turn around, child. Don't hold your head so stiffly. Let your muscles relax. Lift your chin. Oh, I was right. Look at those eyes. Blue reflects into them. And you can wear the court linen to perfection. Maybe a little henna on the breasts."

"No," Anqet said.

"It would make them show up more."

"You've already got the gown pleated perfectly," Anqet said. "It will ruin all your work."

"True, true."

The following days were spent in Ta-usert's company. Anqet learned cosmetic formulas, court manners, the names of every royal official attached to the women's quarters and of those who served Pharaoh. Through all the lessons, the countess spread tidbits of gossip. Prominent in the lady's stories was the notorious and desirable Count Seth.

"Ah, I don't blame you for succumbing to that one. Were I ten years younger—no, I wouldn't have to be any younger. I remember, last year Pharaoh asked to be taken to one of the fertility rites of the god Hap, and Seth agreed. They went in disguise, you see. Nearly tore the palace down to its foundations, did Vizier Ay. He didn't like the idea of our pharaoh being initiated into the mysteries of the flesh by quite such a master as our count."

In a repeat of the boredom of her days as a royal singer, Anqet endured her incarceration. She learned to dance. Not the free-flowing country dances of her home, but sensuous dances involving muscles she seldom used. While she enjoyed the exercise, she dreaded the idea of performing such an exhibition for the young king. What was worse, during the long nights, she lay awake wondering if she was going to spend the rest of her life buried in this female, jewel-encrusted tomb. Only six days had passed, but Anqet felt as if she'd been dropped down a well and forgotten.

Staying with the concubines wouldn't have been so bad if she hadn't been heartsick and damnably frustrated. She longed for the sight of her lover's eyes, reed-green with passion as they looked at her. She craved the feel of his body pressed against hers. The ladies of Pharaoh's palace made her yearnings worse with their constant talk of men. Lord so-and-so was renowned for his virility. The overseer of the king's architects kept five concubines incessantly with child. Prince Bakenkhonsu, whom Seth had exiled to Sile, had discarded his wife.

Sometimes it was hard for Anqet not to fall asleep. There were no books to read, no letters to write, no accounts to be done, no tenants to supervise. Nothing substantial to do. She could dance. She could sing and play instruments. She could talk to the other women. She could go for chariot drives or boat rides. She could scream.

On the afternoon of the sixth day of captivity, Anqet was again being outfitted by the countess Ta-usert. The woman had produced a floor-length shawl with a border of crimson gold and was adjusting the garment over Anqet's gown.

"Yes, yes, I was right. Red-gold and the amethysts are perfect on you. If only your ankles weren't so small. Those anklets wobble when you take a step."

Anqet yawned. A maid came in and whispered to Ta-usert. The countess spun around like a desert wind and clapped her hands.

"It's time. What luck that you're dressed. Pharaoh commands your presence. Don't gawk at me, child. Come along, and remember what I've taught you. Eagerness and innovation are all-important." Ta-usert shoved Anqet through a door behind which the overseer of the audience hall was waiting. The woman grinned at her. "Amazing."

Minhetep stuttered a greeting at her and stared. Anqet fidgeted with her collar. She patted the gold-wrapped strands of her wig.

"Is something wrong?" she asked.

Minhetep started. "No, my lady. No indeed. No. No."

Too soon for Anqet's liking, she waited on the same terrace where only a few days ago she had become a royal concubine.

"Amun-Ra, protect thy servant," she prayed. "I beseech thee. Help me."

A great tramping sounded outside the king's study. Pharaoh entered, bringing with him the overseer of the audience hall, Divine Father Ay, Treasurer Maya, several chief prophets, priests, assorted fanbearers, bodyguards, generals, and orderlies. Anqet dropped to the ground while Minhetep whispered to the king. Tutankhamen waved his hand, and the flood of courtiers receded in silence. Anqet heard the youth approach. A slim brown hand wearing signet rings of the god-king grasped her arm and raised her.

"Greetings, Lady Anqet It's warm; come inside."

Tutankhamun placed her on a cushion opposite his lion couch. Slaves wafted tall ostrich-feather fans over the king. Goblets of cool beer were brought.

Tutankhamun took a long drink, then swept off the white-and-blue headcloth and accompanying serpent headband. He rubbed his temples. Anqet could see red lines where the heavy royal diadem had pressed at his temples. The youth winced when his fingers touched the pressure points. Forgetting her own anxiety, Anqet watched the boy try to alleviate the pain.

Finally she could stand it no longer. She got up and stretched out a faltering hand. Tutankhamun's eyes widened in surprise, but he allowed her to stand at his back, place her fingers on his temple, and smooth them over the mistreated skin. She traced delicate paths over the king's forehead. Anqet kept her own breathing steady and asked the king to do the same. She sensed a release of tension in the boy's shoulders and arms.

They remained in this position for some time. The only sounds in the chamber were their breathing and the rhythmic creak of the wooden staffs of the fans. Anqet waited for Pharaoh to speak. Tutankhamun sighed and looked up at her.

"Thank you. I just spent seven hours at the temple of Amun-Ra. Festival of Opet is near, and the high priest wants a completely new sacred boat for the god, the greedy old—no, if I think of him I shall fall into a rage. Mmmm. That spot is tender."

Anqet kept silent at the reference to the high priest of Amun-Ra. She was sure Pharaoh referred to the man's part in the defilement of his brother's tomb.

"Majesty, I have a recipe for a healing balm that will help the soreness. I will make some."

"That is good of you."

"It is my honor to serve Pharaoh," Anqet said.

The king tilted his head up and smiled at her. Anqet gave him a nervous smile.

"I'm sorry I haven't been able to see you until today," the youth said. A shadow came over his face. "I had to deal with the thieves Count Seth brought to me. Which reminds me—" The king took Anqet's hands from his forehead. He guided her to sit beside him. "There will be no talk of what happened or who led the villains. The priests of Amun-Ra are powerful and have many spies. Do you understand, lady?" Tutankhamun held her eyes with his.

Anqet murmured her assent. The temple of Amun-Ra owned more land than any in Egypt except Pharaoh. Its vast wealth and influence rivaled that of the king.

"Seth told me you could be trusted."

Trapped in the gaze of her god-king, Anqet pledged upon her ka that the secrets of Pharaoh could be entrusted to her. At last the king released her from his soul-exposing gaze. Anqet shivered.

"The vizier Ay judged the prisoners in the temple of Amun-Ra," Pharaoh said with an ironic sneer. "I insisted on that location. Paheri and the other enemies of the gods have been punished. They—are not."

A wave of cold washed over Anqet. She had known the punishment of the murderers would come swiftly. She listened to the king's firm voice. They had been impaled on stakes, according to Ay's decree.

The king rubbed his forehead again. His hands curled into fists. He had forgotten Anqet.

"They made me leave him alone—the high priest of Amun-Ra. Seth and the others, they say I must wait. He's too powerful."

It took a while for Anqet to notice that the king was staring at her. Dark, soft curls strayed over his brow, displaced by the breeze stirred by the fans moving overhead. Without warning, he left the couch. Anqet stood up and watched him down the contents of his goblet.

"Brave Lady Anqet, I shall be tempted to cast aside my good intentions if you keep getting more and more beautiful. No wonder Seth defied me."

"Majesty, I don't understand."

"No? Well, it's my fault. I intended to explain after I sent you to Ta-usert, but Ay thought the prisoners should be judged. Seth is miserable."

Anqet's stomach turned over. "Majesty, you wish to punish Count Seth for the atrocity by separating us?"

"By the Two Lands! What an idea." Tutankhamun collapsed on the lion couch. "Come here, Lady Anqet. Sit down. This matchmaking is much harder than bribing ambassadors or subduing a Libyan revolt."

"Matchmaking?"

Tutankhamun sat up and grinned at her. "Yes. I'm sure it's plain to you that Seth fears marriage. He is in love and in terror at the same time. I can't have that. Seth is dear to me, and I need him, with his wits intact. So I decided that he needed to know what his life would be like without the woman he loves."

"Oh," Anqet breathed. Relief spread through her.

"You do want him, don't you? I haven't misjudged?"
Tutankhamun looked at her with an open, grave expression. "I am not well versed in love matters. If you don't
want Seth, you may stay with me. I want you."

"I want Count Seth, Majesty. I want him, but he
doesn't understand that I have responsibilities and honor."

The king took her hand and squeezed it. "He understands, but he's unable to think clearly at the moment.
After I sent you away, he actually defied me." Tutankhamen
studied Anqet's face. "I think I would have dared such a
thing for you, were I in his place."

"Pharaoh is generous."

"I'm beginning to regret being so generous," the king
said. "But let me continue. Seth is too powerful for you to
resist. In fact, I can think of no one who could successfully
thwart him." Tutankhamun chuckled. "Except my sacred
majesty."

Anqet's spirits began to lift. Her lips curled in
amusement.

"And how long does Pharaoh think it will take to
destroy the battlements of isolation of which his commander of chariots is so enamored?"

Tutankhamun laughed. "Not long. For three days he
was in such a rage that he dared not appear before me.
Dega says he wrecked two taverns and a stable trying to
drink away his wrath. It took him another two days to
recover. Yesterday and today our count spent on patrol
with his men."

"He is a stubborn man, my Pharaoh."

"That's why I ordered him to attend me at the
evening meal. You will be there, and we'll give Seth a
look, but not a taste, of the delicious wine he craves."

Anqet couldn't stop the tears that came to her eyes.
"Majesty, thy gift is unsurpassed."

"I am Pharaoh. Pharaoh cares for his people, especially for two to whom he owes so much."

12

The wind stirred the garlands that hung about the neck of a winejar on the veranda of Count Seth's town house. At a prudent distance from this jar sat the count. He regarded the wine container with a malevolence born of another night of drinking. Dressed for his mandatory appearance at Pharaoh's table, he was spending a few quiet moments with Khet before he left. The boy sat at his feet and polished one of Seth's ceremonial daggers. Seth pressed his fingers into his closed eyes. Fire burst into life in his head at the touch.

"I miss Anqet," Khet said in a lost voice.

Seth removed his hands from his eyes. "You do?"

"Yes. She made composition bearable, and everyone was happy when she was with us." Khet held the bronze blade up to the lamplight and examined it. He let it fall to his lap and gazed out at the tree-crowded courtyard. "Something is missing now that she's gone. I don't know what it is, even though I've tried to understand." The boy glanced up at Seth. "She's so unlike Rennut. Anqet knows things, and she talks to me."

"I will spend more time with you, Little Fire."

"That's good." Khet nodded. "That's part of what's wrong. Anqet disappeared into Pharaoh's house, and now you are removed from me, as if part of you is gone too."

Seth put a hand on Khet's arm. "I'm sorry." He watched Khet grip the dagger until the flesh of his hand was white.

"I'm afraid," said Khet.

Leaving his chair, Seth crouched in front of his brother. "I won't leave you."

"Why did he hate us?" Khet bit his trembling lower lip.

"Sennefer didn't hate us He was jealous of me, and it's true that he couldn't love you as he should have, but he didn't hate either of us." Seth gave Khet a bitter smile. "He tried hard to hate us, I admit But in the end, he gave up and let his love rule. That's why you and I are alive."

Seth released Khet and watched the boy. Khet gazed back at him with eyes full of questions and pain.

"I know you've been hurt, Khet. I tried to prevent it."

"But I disobeyed orders," the boy said. "I know. Orders should be obeyed."

Seth rumpled his brother's hair and stood up. "Most of the time. Now I must go. Promise not to harry your tutor into letting you stay up late. If you're to begin training under Lord Dega in the morning, you'll need rest."

"I promise."

Seth left Khet busy with a manuscript Anqet had found in the study at Annu-Rest. It was the first time Seth had known the boy to read anything voluntarily. Anqet located an eyewitness account by one of their ancestors of a decisive battle in the defeat of the Hyksos invaders. They had begun reading it together before Sennefer's death.

He was continually discovering acts of kindness the girl had shown to Khet, to Rennut, to Uni, and others. She drew the members of his family together in a way he would never have thought possible. Rennut sent a message asking after Anqet, even wanting to know if the girl could come to Memphis.

"Probably to serve as her steward and scribe," Seth said to himself.

The journey to the palace was spent sinking into a depression fed by his loss of Anqet, Sennefer's suicide, and what he considered Pharaoh's betrayal of his trust. On top of this mountain of ill fate rested his inability to search out that foul worm Hauron. The man wasn't on his yacht, which was docked in the harbor, and none of the man's servants could be convinced to reveal his whereabouts.

Seth tried to fight off unhappiness with thoughts of
what he would do to persuade Hauron that he should never
see Anqet again. Unfortunately, that thought led to the idea
that since Anqet was Pharaoh's concubine, Seth might not
see her either. The Divine One had said he would give
Anqet time to adjust to her new, honored status. This remark
was the only thing that had prevented Seth from committing
suicide by trying to snatch Anqet from His Majesty's grasp.
Once the king touched her, there was no hope.

He was a fool. There wasn't any hope at all. Tutankhamun was the living god If he didn't love the king so
much, he would hate him—and surely be struck down by
the gods.

By the time he approached the entrance to the king's
private dining chamber, Seth knew a blackness of the soul
that equalled the darkness of a closed sarcophagous. It
suited his mood, therefore, that the room he entered was
shadowed. A few lamps were scattered about, but Seth
could tell that this was to be one of Pharaoh's more
intimate evenings. The semidarkness all but concealed the
enamel paneling that depicted wild gazelles, ibex, and
quiet lagoons filled with ducks and cranes.

Seth paused inside the door to let his eyes adjust to
the lack of light. Minhetep, at his post beside the door,
nodded a greeting. A small form jumped out from behind
the overseer of the audience hall.

"Count Seth, be welcome."

"Ta-usert," Seth said "May Amun-Ra bless thee." He
looked around for Anqet.

"Yes, my beauty. Pharaoh is waiting. Run along."

Ta-usert patted his arm and licked her lips at him as if
he were a freshly roasted oryx set on a tray for her
consumption.

Seth passed through the guests Tutankhamun had
favored with an invitation. He greeted Prince Khai and his
new consort. Prince Ahmose, distant cousin to the king,
murmured a welcome to Seth in his hushed, timid voice.
He could see several others lounging on cushions and

chairs. Next to the commander of the king's archers was Lady Gasantra.

She was watching him. Seth nodded to her curtly. Gasantra smiled and gave him one of her long, carnal inspections that ended at his groin. Seth swerved away from Gasantra's domain and headed for Pharaoh's customary place in a back corner of the room. In gold-spangled and pristine linen, the king lay on a couch, feet crossed at the ankles, arms behind his head. Seth went down on his knees beside the youth, his head bowed. Tutankhamun stared at the ceiling.

"How are the taverns of Thebes?"

Seth cursed silently. It was disconcerting how the young king found out the most embarrassing details of his life.

"Taverns can be repaired, Majesty. I'm not so sure about my head."

Tutankhamun chuckled and propped himself up on his elbows. He called for a pillow. Seth breathed more easily as he settled onto the cushion. He watched the clouds of ostrich feather sweep the air over Pharaoh's head while the king joked with Prince Khai and promised the commander of archers a place in the next expedition to quell the Rutenu people.

Flute and drum struck up a dreamy tune. Bare pale bodies glided in under the watchful eye of Ta-usert and began to dance. Under the cover of watching the performers, Seth searched the chamber for Anqet. She wasn't there, and he dared not ask Pharaoh where his newest concubine was.

"I'm going on that expedition, no matter how many advisers say I'm too young," Tutankhamun said when Khai and the archer moved away.

"Yes, Majesty."

"No arguments from you? How odd."

Seth glanced up at the king. "Pharaoh is ready to lead his armies, and I have no wish to argue with the Living Horus and provoke another punishment."

"What punishment? Are you angry with me? You're lucky you have my affection. My father would have banished you for defying him."

"I know. Pharaoh is—kind." Seth lowered his eyes.

Tutankhamun shooed off the line of dancers as it wove around his couch. The girls snaked away to the blushing Prince Ahmose. The king turned on his side, rested on a forearm, and lowered his voice.

"I've never seen you this way, Seth. Your eyes hold the grief of Isis. Your brother's death weighs upon your ka."

"And I have lost my beloved Anqet," Seth said.

"You wouldn't have lost her if you had cared enough to make her your wife."

"She asked too much." Seth gripped the edge of the couch and pinned his king with his gaze. "My Pharaoh, Majesty, can you say to me that having a wife is a good thing?"

Seth saw the color drain from Tutankhamun's face. Briefly the king failed to meet Seth's eyes, but the youth soon raised his head and smiled.

"Anqet is not the Great Royal Wife, thank the mighty Amun-Ra. Anqet, if I remember your words, is the most gentle and loving woman in the Two Lands." Tutankhamun lifted his eyes to look over Seth's head. "And I think you will agree that the lady is also a gift from the gods."

Seth turned in the direction of the king's gaze. She had come in when his back was turned, and he was unprepared. Anqet stood at a side door and directed a line of servants bearing food. A reverent obscenity escaped him. Tutankhamun lifted a brow, but made no comment as Seth stared at the girl.

Anqet wore white. A rare white wig cascaded to her waist and blended with the ivory hue of her gown. A blue lotus was fastened to her headband, and a heavy broad collar of gold, lapis lazuli, and red jasper lay on her shoulders. Seth drank in the sight of the breasts that swelled just below that costly necklace. He swore again, silently, as he felt his loins begin to burn. He wanted to snatch her away and burrow deep inside her body.

"Seth," Pharaoh said. "Go talk with Prince Ahmose for a while. You look as if you could use the calming influence."

"Majesty," Seth said.

Tutankhamun sat up and laid a hand on Seth's shoulder. "No defiance, my lord count. I will not have it."

"Yes, Majesty."

He wanted to punch the living god. Seth left the king and passed Anqet on her way to Pharaoh with a tray of food. He brushed by her and let his arm graze hers. She looked at him with those luminous, earth-dark eyes. She gave him a sad smile and joined the king on his couch. Seth exercised military discipline, walking over to Prince Ahmose without turning around. His vicious scowl sent teasing naked dancers bouncing in all directions, and the prince thanked him. Seth bowed in silence and took the winecup Ahmose offered.

"Our delinquent count has returned."

Seth drained his cup. "Lady Gasantra. Have you been practicing your arts of emasculation on more willing victims?"

Ahmose stuttered an excuse and melted into the shadows. Seth didn't hear Gasantra's reply, for he was spying on Anqet where she sat beside the king. He failed to notice Gasantra sidling up beside him and worming her body against his side.

He watched Anqet offer Pharaoh a tray of seasoned pigeon legs. Tutankhamun lifted one and gave it to her. He whispered something. Anqet threw back her head and laughed softly. The king drew her close, and the two engaged in an intimate dialogue. Seth looked at the king's hand. It rested familiarly on the girl's arm. He felt as if the lid of a granite sarcophagus had slammed shut and imprisoned him in hopelessness. Something tugged at his arm.

"Seth, listen to me. Now do you see what she is? She practices evil magic." Gasantra spit her words out. "She would spread her legs on Pharaoh's couch in front of us if he commanded it. No doubt she's been on her back most of the time since she seduced our glorious Pharaoh."

Seth dragged his eyes from the pair across the room.

"What? What did you say?"

"It wasn't important," Gasantra said. She spread her hand over Seth's bare chest and moved it along his ribs.

"Where is your pride, count of the Falcon nome? You're acting like a heartbroken pet. Has she taken your manhood along with your heart?"

"Of what use is the kind of pride you're talking about, woman?"

"At least cease this pathetic gawking," Gasantra said. She grasped Seth around the waist and pulled him into the darkness behind a table of refreshments.

Afraid that he would lose control and rend the two lovers apart, Seth let Gasantra guide him. It was strange that he could hardly feel her hands on his thighs or her mouth at his throat. Desperate to expunge the pain in his ka, he gave Gasantra an impatient shove, leaned against the wall, and tried to master himself. Gasantra pursued him. To his disgust, she slipped her hand inside his kilt, clasped his penis, and stroked. He sucked in his breath. Reaching for her hand, he removed it from his body and shoved the woman away.

Gasantra moved back to him. She ran her tongue along the smooth skin of his neck. "Come, lover. You've engaged in far more lurid behavior, and with the king present."

"Leave me."

Gasantra lifted her face from his chest and glanced over her shoulder. "Pharaoh saves you from ravishment, it seems."

There was no mistaking that firm, quiet voice. It was heard over music and talk because all listened for it, whatever else might be going on. Seth arranged the folds of his kilt and emerged from seclusion. Pharaoh was alone. Seth searched the room for Anqet.

There she was, next to Prince Ahmose.

Seth reclaimed his seat below the king. He propped his back against the couch so that he could see Anqet without appearing to look for her.

"Have something to eat." Tutankhamun waved his hand at a tray.

"I'm not hungry, my Pharaoh."

"Then have this. It's black wine from Ahmose's estate

near Memphis. Memphis. I must have someone look into the question of Lady Anqet's estate."

"I'm already doing that, Majesty." Seth narrowed his eyes. Prince Khai was kneeling before Anqet. "Her uncle is in the city, Golden One, and he has control of the girl's fortune." Seth's fingers grew white as they strangled his goblet. Prince Khai risked a broken neck if he didn't stop rubbing Anqet's arm with his cheek.

Tutankhamun sat up and reached for a triangular pastry covered with honey and nuts. "I want Anqet to have what is hers. I've already promised to remove Hauron. After all, she is mine, and he has no rights over her. What's wrong? Oh. Don't worry about Khai. He means no harm. I was saying that since Anqet is mine, I will cause this Hauron to remove his people from her home at once."

Anqet is mine. The words ripped through Seth's ka. He turned away from the sight of Anqet so obviously content in her new status. If his rival had been anyone else in the Two Lands, he would have fought to death for her. He squeezed his eyes shut and bent his head so that his face was screened by his hair.

"Majesty, may I go? I have no appetite."

"Stay."

Seth turned to the youth he had thought his friend. "Send me to Kush, or to Babylon. I'll take Khet with me. I can't stay here."

The king touched Seth's arm. "You can stay here."

Strained laughter escaped Seth. He couldn't hold it back. He gave Tutankhamun a grief-stricken smile and whispered:

> *...Beware of approaching the women! ...*
> *A thousand men are turned away from their good:*
> *A short moment like a dream,*
> *Then death comes for having known them.*

The laughter came again. It carried pain, an offering born of his soul and given to his god-king. "Divine Pharaoh, knowing Anqet and losing her is indeed a good way to attain death."

"Then perhaps you should reconsider your distaste for marriage."

Seth gave a tired sigh. "I want no other woman. I can't bear anyone else. I begin to see why marriage is necessary. How else can one keep a lover from the hands of—"

"Pharaohs?"

"And others."

The king dropped down beside Seth and clapped him on the back. "I think you wouldn't refuse Anqet if she were free."

"I would ask her if she wanted me still. Please, Majesty, I don't want to stay here."

"Then go ask Lady Anqet if she will have you."

Seth made no move. He gaped at the king.

"Did you hear me?" Tutankhamun asked. "Take Lady Anqet to my garden and beg her to forgive you. Offer marriage." Tutankhamun stood up and pulled Seth with him. He turned the count around. Giving Seth a shove, he hissed in his friend's ear.

"For once, I've been the teacher and you the pupil. Go."

Unable to speak, Seth obeyed. His feet moved on their own. They moved faster as the meaning of Pharaoh's words reached his ka. He was so intent on the girl that he stumbled over Gasantra.

"Come home with me," she said. She made sure Anqet was watching and slipped her hand inside Seth's belt. "Show her how little she means to you."

Seth pulled the woman's hand from his stomach without bothering to look at her. He said something to her that he immediately forgot and left Gasantra standing alone in the middle of the room. He shoved past Khai, took Anqet's arm, and escorted her out of the room without a word. To his amazement, she went peacefully.

During the walk to the king's garden, Seth made

supplications to Hathor: *Goddess of love, let her forgive me. Let her still love me.*

Anqet sat opposite Seth in Pharaoh's garden and waited for her lover to speak. The evening had been long and harrowing. Without the king's admonishments she would have clawed Gasantra into jackal-meat. For a good part of the time, she'd been sure that Seth hadn't missed her, that he had adjusted to their separation and no longer cared. Then she caught him watching her while Prince Khai plied his silly gallantries. She had seen that same malevolence in those green eyes when Seth fought for her life with Lord Merab. After witnessing that look, she'd been hard-pressed to keep an absurd grin off her face.

He wasn't looking at her. Anqet peered at her lover. Seth was facing her, but he veiled his provocative eyes. There was a quiet tension about his face and body.

"Have I the right, still, to call you beloved?" Seth raised his eyes to hers.

"I know little of love, Seth, but mine doesn't evaporate like water in the desert."

Seth took her hand in both of his. "Beloved, Pharaoh says he will release you if you will have me. I—curse it! I feel as if I were being torn in two by a pair of lions. I know this marriage business will end in ruin."

Anqet snatched her hand away. Throwing the heavy strands of her wig over her shoulders, she stood up and looked down on Seth

" 'Ruin,' is it?"

"I don't want what happened to my parents to happen to us."

Boiling oil pumped through Anqet's veins. Her voice rose. "Oh, I see. Then you must repeat the mistakes of those who have come before you? You are your father? You learned nothing from your sorrows, or from Sennefer's tragedy? Your brother died for this—so that you could hide from love and life?"

Seth sprang up. He grabbed her roughly by the shoulders, then pushed her away. Taking long strides, he charged toward a myrrh tree.

Anqet stalked over to him. She wanted to punch his taut stomach. She had no chance to alleviate her wrath. Seth whirled on her and dropped to his knees.

"Beloved, are you willing to marry a fool and a coward?"

Anqet joined Seth on the ground. "If the fool will promise not to live in the shadows of his dead mother and father."

"I will try." Seth traced a finger along her cheek. "The shadow of the dead isn't a pleasant place to stay. Anqet, sweet passion, come home with me."

Anqet closed her eyes and let her whole being concentrate on Seth's mouth and body in the kiss that followed. After a while, Seth lifted his lips from hers and spoke in a hoarse whisper.

"If we don't leave, I'll take you here beneath Pharaoh's myrrh tree."

They walked together out of the king's apartments. In the corridor near the dining chamber, Gasantra blocked their way.

"I understand," the woman said. "You pass her between you. Or is this part of the lessons you teach the Living Horus? Did you train her so that Pharaoh would learn your own habits of pleasure?"

"Is she always so strident?" Anqet asked as they strolled past Gasantra.

"Not ordinarily," Seth answered. "But then, you know how loud a vulture can screech when deprived of a carcass."

Gasantra howled. Her voice chased them down the hall.

"I may not be a fearful opponent, love, but there are others more powerful than I who have cause to resent you. Enjoy the little piece of muck while you can. It won't be long before I have you at my feet."

"Better than in your bed," Seth said.

* * *

The sun wrapped Thebes in an embrace of hot stillness. Pampered foreign vegetation in gardens wilted, and
all who could sought refuge in workshop, tavern, house,
and temple. The molten heat within Hauron's mind far
surpassed the afternoon sun-storm. The liquid metal of
hate bubbled inside that living crucible. Like the metal-
smith who keeps his fire white-hot by blowing in it
through a hollow reed, Hauron fed his wrath. The past few
weeks of frustration had only made his torture worse. The
girl was in the city, but he couldn't find out where.

Hauron followed the servant to a house he'd never
been in before. As he stepped into the darkness from the
sunlight, he bumped into a priest. The man was burdened
with two caskets, an arm strung with clacking amulets and
several bags that smelled of herbs and dried dung. The
caskets rattled, for they held bottles. It wasn't his habit,
but Hauron excused himself. It was never wise to annoy a
magician priest. He continued on his way after a polite
nod in the man's direction.

He was ushered into the presence of a woman in a
room perfumed with flowers. She reminded him of a
basking lizard. It might have been the iridescent paint on
her eyes or the way she molded her body to the couch
where she lay; or perhaps it was the smooth coldness of
her face that gave the amphibian impression. She stirred,
and Hauron watched the somnolent slowness with which
she got to her feet. She said her name. At once, the anger
he'd been holding in check surfaced.

"Lady Gasantra, tell me why you sent for me as if I
were the boy who carries your fly whisk."

Gasantra cocked her head to one side and looked at
him without rancor. "My sister's husband is lay priest at
the temple of Amun-Ra. He told me you were looking for
a girl called Anqet."

"You know where she is? Please tell me. I've been so
worried. We were attacked—"

"I've heard," Gasantra said. She gestured toward a
seat and offered wine. "Before I tell you where your niece

is, can you tell me what will happen to her if you find her?"

Hauron stared into his winecup. He traced the fluted pattern in the bronze and prayed to Amun-Ra for the strength to keep his impatience and his wrath under control. He had lost the girl over a month ago, and in all that time, his suffering had grown like an animal being fattened for sacrifice. Even now, the wine failed to dull his appetite. He was never sated for long and wouldn't be until he had delved within the female demon who called herself his niece. Hauron downed his wine.

"I intend to take my niece home. Her father died recently, and I am her only family."

"And your home is near Memphis? I suppose that's far enough away." Gasantra took a chair beside Hauron and motioned for a slave to refill his winecup. "Drink deeply, my lord, for you won't enjoy what I have to say. Your niece has been here in Thebes, masquerading as a singer and playing whore to the commander of chariots."

Hauron lowered his drinking cup. It took him a few moments to understand, and when he did, all trace of the well-bred nobleman vanished. He wasn't aware of throwing the cup against the wall until wine splattered on the painted plaster. The cup bounced into a table leg. The slave attending them fled. Hauron grabbed Lady Gasantra by her arms. His fingers pressed into her flesh as he brought her face close to his.

"She has coupled with a man? Find your tongue, woman." Hauron shook Gasantra so hard that her wig began to slip back on her head. "Count Seth has touched her? By the loins of Ra, if he has touched her before me, I'll kill her and him. Speak, before I beat the words out of you."

Hauron threw Gasantra back in her chair and stood over her, his legs braced apart.

"Guards!"

Hauron whipped around to find two men with spears racing toward him. He threw up his hands and backed away from Gasantra. The woman sat up in her chair. She pushed her wig back into position and sent the men to stand on either side of the door. She drank from her own winecup before speaking.

Cursing himself, Hauron stepped away from the woman and began to make excuses for his behavior.

Gasantra waved a hand at him. "I am pleased."

Hauron shut his mouth, straightened his kilt, and said nothing.

"You want Anqet," Gasantra said. "I want Count Seth. To have him, I must get rid of your niece." Gasantra's eyes traveled over Hauron's body from head to foot. She smiled. "I was thinking of killing her, but giving her to you would be much more satisfying."

"Damn your ka. Where is she?" Hauron moved toward Gasantra, then stilled as one of the guards pounded his spear on the floor.

"With Seth of course. My porter questioned one of the count's grooms. You'll have to make haste if you don't want to see Anqet married to him."

"I'll get her from him," Hauron said.

"From Seth? A Hittite army couldn't pry her from him."

Hauron gazed at the woman's masklike features, assessing her. What he saw caused him to abandon his fatherly pretensions; he'd already revealed too much of himself anyway.

"Perhaps an army can't get her away, but Pharaoh's judgement can. I'll appeal to the vizier. If you can use your influence at court to gain me an audience."

Gasantra bowed from her sitting position. Hauron watched her breasts swinging forward and shifted his hips uncomfortably. The woman dismissed her guards. She poured more wine for him and invited him to the couch.

Hauron's temper cooled when he realized that Gasantra was going to be an ally. She plotted, and the more he listened to her plans, the calmer he became. At the conclusion of their discussion, he had enough wine in him and was so at ease that he made no objection to the way her hand slid across his shoulders and played with the muscles of his chest. She murmured something about his strength, but the voice he heard was Anqet's. Hauron turned on the couch. Keeping his eyes on hers, he grasped the woman's ankles and pulled them apart so that she straddled the cushions.

Gasantra's face went red, and her breasts rose and fell, but she allowed him to tear her robe aside. Wasting no time in unnecessary gallantries, Hauron slid his hands up Gasantra's thighs to her crotch. Still holding her gaze, he pressed his fingers into her flesh. The woman groaned. Hauron quickly knelt between her thighs. Tearing his own clothing askew, he lowered himself upon her.

"It won't be long now, Anqet." Hauron jabbed into the swollen flesh beneath him and ignored the whimper of pleasure from the owner of that flesh. "Not much longer."

Anqet woke from deep slumber. She lay unmoving. Something had disturbed her. The sound of a sharply drawn breath made her turn to Seth. He lay on his side with his bandaged arm uppermost. Anqet rested her hand on his bare hip and listened.

"N-no." Seth shoved her hand off as he tossed over on his back. Anqet jumped. He shouted an incoherent warning, then cried out: "Sennefer, no!"

At the first cry, Anqet started shaking him. "Seth, Seth wake up."

There was a groan; the count woke. He sat up and stared at her, his chest heaving and his hands reaching for her. He sank onto her breast.

"A dream, it was only a dream."

Anqet stroked his fine hair and spread kisses on it. "Tell me."

"I was at home in Annu-Rest. In the chapel." Seth's voice was a dry whisper.

"And it was so real, you could feel the hardness of the columns," Anqet said.

"Yes. The sanctuary was black, except where I was. Sennefer dragged me to the foot of the god's image. He tied my hands, and then bound them to the statue." Seth cringed into her embrace. "The dagger was still in his chest."

Seth lifted his head from her breast and stared into Anqet's face. "He bled and bled, all over his gold corselet. He went back into the darkness and returned holding Khet in his arms. My Little Fire. Khet's face was so white. Sennefer laid him on the floor before the god and started to pray. I thought Khet was dead, but while Sennefer was praying, the little one opened his eyes and tried to get up. I screamed at Sennefer, but he didn't hear me. He pulled the dagger out of his chest. The blade dripped with his blood. He shoved it into Khet's heart. I tried to stop him, but the ropes held me at the feet of the god.

"Sennefer put the dagger back in his own wound and picked Khet up." Seth shook his head. His hands gripped Anqet's fingers until it hurt. "Their blood mingled when he carried my Little Fire to the god. Sennefer lay Khet beside me. I couldn't move. It was as if my arms and legs were as heavy as pyramid stones. I couldn't even fight Sennefer when he pushed me on my back. He took the dagger from his chest again and stabbed me as he had Khet. Anqet, Anqet, the metal cut into my heart. I lay there bleeding. Sennefer was bleeding all over me, and I was in a pool of Khet's blood. I looked up past Sennefer and saw the face of the god. It was my father."

When the disjointed recitation ended, Anqet wrapped Seth in her arms.

"Do you suppose the gods are angry with me?" Seth asked. "I should consult a dream interpreter."

"Perhaps. My love, you grieve for your brother. He died tragically, and you blame yourself. There. I have interpreted your dream." Anqet kissed Seth. "After my mother died, I dreamed that she came back. But in the dreams, she always treats me as if I were a child." She smiled into the darkness. "She tells me what to wear and not to tease poor Lord Menana. I've become a woman, but Mother stays the same in the netherworld."

Seth relaxed.

"It was so real. There's an ache where Sennefer stabbed my chest." Seth squeezed his eyes shut. "I fear his ka seeks revenge."

Anqet rubbed the smooth flesh over Seth's heart. She caressed his ribs and traced the line of his hip and leg.

"Sennefer's ka is in the keeping of the gods, and they will teach him. You parted from him in love, Seth. His ka has no reason to persecute you."

Seth bit his lip and gave her an uncertain look.

"You won't be able to rest if you don't stop thinking about it," Anqet said.

She stroked Seth's back. Seth turned his face to her breast and nuzzled at her. In a quick movement, he was on top of her, hips worming between her legs. He delved into her mouth with his tongue.

"You must help me think of other things." He flexed his hips. "Help me."

Seth fastened his mouth on her breast. Anqet felt his warm tongue tease her nipple. She pressed his head to her, then caught him under his arms and pulled him up until he lay between her legs again. In an instant, he was inside her, making slow thrusts that built her excitement with each motion. Anqet felt her own hips gyrate in response. As their agitation spiraled, she grasped his buttocks and tried to pull him deeper inside. Her movements inflamed Seth beyond control. He stabbed himself inside her with a violence that brought Anqet to groaning madness. Their gasps of fulfillment mingled, and Seth dropped onto her shoulder.

Anqet gave a small exclamation of impatience.

Seth's head popped up.

"What's wrong?"

"It doesn't last long enough," Anqet said.

"What doesn't?"

"This lovemaking you've taught me. That final pleasure. It doesn't last nearly so long as it should."

Seth stared at her.

"When we are at that moment, I want us to stay there, bursting into flames, for hours. And then it's over too soon."

Seth shook his head. "I think that much pleasure would kill me. You already try my strength as it is. I'll be an old man in less than a year."

"Nonsense. You'll last at least long enough for me to find another strong and beautiful man to take your place. Seth, don't tickle!"

Seth had no more bad dreams that night. In the morning he exercised with Khet and Dega, but he was back at midmorning with a host of jewelers, weavers, wigmakers, and seamstresses in his wake. He burst in upon Anqet while she was tuning her harp. They spent the rest of the morning choosing materials and designs for her wardrobe.

"My countess must look like a countess," Seth said.

"Since when did you worry about how your family looks?"

"Since I acquired a betrothed who likes to run around dressed like a coppersmith's wife."

Anqet hurled a bolt of linen at Seth, but her dresser caught it. A warrior in leather and gold approached the count while Anqet was busy discussing the price of a set of obsidian cosmetic bottles. Seth rejoined her and dismissed the artisans.

"Pharaoh summons us, beloved."

"Why?"

"He wants to make arrangements for our marriage agreement. I promised to hold the witnessing immediately so that he could attend. He's rarely able to attend private celebrations. Pharaoh must eternally preserve the sacred majesty of his father, the god. Do you mind?"

"Do I mind having the lord of the Two Lands put his sacred name to our marriage agreement? You jest. There could be no greater magic to protect our love than the testament of the Golden One." Anqet gave Seth an oblique glance. "And with Pharaoh as a witness, you'd never dare put me aside."

She had to cajole Seth out of his offended mood all the way to the palace. Tutankhamun awaited them in an apartment off his bedchamber. The king paced down a row of columns and tapped a papyrus against his palm. He wasted no time on ceremony.

"There is trouble," the king said.

Anqet and Seth glanced at each other.

"I am always at thy service, my Pharaoh," Seth said.

"It isn't me who is in trouble. Lord Hauron has petitioned the vizier for the return of Lady Anqet."

Anqet's skin went to gooseflesh. She wrapped both hands around Seth's arm and forced herself to attend to Pharaoh's words.

"Ay will hear Hauron's plea this afternoon." Tutankhamun handed Seth the papyrus. "He claims dominion over her as head of her only remaining family. Such a claim cannot be put aside without offending the divine order."

Light-headed, numb, Anqet gripped Seth's hand. He squeezed it, glanced at the document in his hands, and hugged her.

"Don't worry, beloved. We'll marry, and Hauron will have no further power over you."

"You cannot marry," the king said. "Not until the plea is heard and Hauron gives permission for Anqet to take a man, which he will not."

Anqet lifted a hand to Pharaoh. "Majesty, Hauron wants revenge. He will take me away and—"

"No he won't," Seth said. His face took on the look of a hunting cat contemplating its prey. "I'll kill him first."

Tutankhamun squared his shoulders and frowned. "You will not kill him."

"May I cut off his hands?"

"Seth," the king said He noticed Anqet's stricken face. "Lady, I am sorry. Hauron has made a formal plea, and Ay tells me that unless you have a witness to prove your uncle unfit, he will be forced to decide in favor of Lord Hauron's claim."

Anqet nodded. She couldn't make her tongue move. Seth put his arm around her and radiated menace.

"I'll speak with Lord Hauron. He must be made to understand how quickly he will join the gods if he makes this claim."

"You will do nothing," Tutankhamun said. He fixed Seth with a royal glare. "I am the guardian of the sacred law of this kingdom. How can I punish corrupt judges and enforce justice if I allow you to subvert the decisions of my chief official? Be silent, my lord." The king quelled Seth with an economic gesture of his hand.

"Hauron will destroy me," Anqet said. She closed her eyes and leaned on Seth.

The count cursed and put his hand to the dagger in his belt.

The king began his pacing again. "Where is your much-renowned expertise in strategy, my friend? If you can employ it in battle, you can use it now."

"We need proof that Hauron means to do me harm," Anqet said. "But I have no witnesses. He made sure none could come to my defense when he tried to rape me." She fell silent. She couldn't speak of what Hauron had tried to do. Not to Pharaoh.

"We will let Hauron take Anqet," Seth said. "No, I haven't gone mad, my Pharaoh. Hauron will take Anqet. I'll follow. From what Anqet has told me, her uncle won't be long in attempting to force her. I'll be there to stop him, and bring a witness who will swear in a hundred courts as to his vileness."

Fear left Anqet. She blazed a smile at Seth. "We will set a trap. We'll drag him in our net, throw him on the bank, and let him suffocate in the clean air." She exchanged bloodthirsty grins with Seth and the king.

Tutankhamun laughed at her. "Lady Anqet, you are indeed a match for my greatest warrior. Let us sit. I want to hear the plan. I wish I could go along."

"Where is the king's sacred impartiality?" Seth asked.

Pharaoh opened his mouth but evidently could think of no response. Then a sly expression crept over his face. The king took Anqet's hand and let her to a chair.

"There is another way to protect you, lady," Tutankhamun said. He put her hand to his cheek. "I could always take you as my concubine again."

Seth strolled over to a winejar, nonchalant and amused.

"If you do, Golden One, I'll bring my stepmother to court."

Tutankhamun made a gesture to ward off evil.

"Please, my Pharaoh," Anqet said. "If Rennut comes to court, we'll all end up drunkards or deaf from listening to her complaints."

Anqet was pleased with the scheme they developed and so faced the prospect of meeting Hauron again with courage, and even a little glee. The next day, when she stood before the vizier in one of the king's audience halls, she was able to watch Hauron march in without flinching. Seth and Lord Dega waited beside Ay's chair. A scribe sat on the floor with a papyrus stretched across his lap, pen poised to write. Royal guards watched at intervals down the length of the hall. Several bureaucrats from Ay's staff muttered together in a corner. Anqet tried to look aside unobtrusively, for Pharaoh beheld the proceedings from an alcove screened by hangings.

Minhetep's staff tapped on the floor. Anqet turned toward the doors and observed Hauron walking toward her. For half a breath she was transported back to a dark country house; she held a jar over her head and brought it crashing down on the man's skull. Then she was back, standing beside Hauron while the vizier listened to her uncle's story. His success depended much upon his eloquence, and Hauron's tongue spewed forth believable lies as easily as a sailor slipped between the thighs of a whore.

"And so, my dear niece was stolen from me while we were on our way to my Delta estate. I searched for her for many weeks only to find that the criminals had sold her to Count Seth. The man seduced the poor child." Hauron spread his arms and lifted his voice in impassioned appeal. "What vile acts has this degenerate performed upon my ward? Please, my lord vizier, restore Lady Anqet to my protection. Though she has been soiled, I still love her as a daughter. My brother would have wanted me to care for her, and I've failed him. I will spend the rest of my life regretting how my carelessness caused her to be thrown into the clutches of this man." Hauron pointed at Seth. "Redress. I demand redress."

Anqet was watching Hauron. He might have been her father's twin soul, so much did he remind her of Rahotep. Like her father, he bore age well. His arms were knotted with muscles, and his body was suffused with a tight strength that spoke of constant exertion. His indulgences hadn't yet made his eyes weak or his skin flaccid. In his costly linen and electrum jewelry, he rivaled even Seth's brilliant elegance. Hauron's breath was free of the odor of wine or beer. He was being careful in the abode of Pharaoh. With his sincerity and demands for restitution, he would have convinced even her of his honesty had she not been the victim of his drunken madness. Within the courtly dove lurked the crocodile.

Vizier Ay called for her to speak. With a secret glance at her lover, Anqet fell on her knees before Ay and pleaded not to be given into Hauron's custody. She let her words become fevered. She trembled and began to sniffle. Poor Ay regarded her with alarm. He edged back in his chair as if to avoid contact with her. He asked for witnesses to support her claims. At this demand, Anqet burst into tears and wailed. The scribe covered his ears. Ay winced. Seth roared his anger at Hauron; he lunged at the man. Dega held his commander back with difficulty. Ay shot to his feet, delivering judgement in favor of Hauron. Anqet drove her wails to a high-pitched scream and collapsed on the floor.

Hauron slithered over to Anqet, and she allowed him to bundle her out of the reception chamber. Yelling obscenities at Hauron, Seth called after her.

Hauron hissed at her. "Be quiet. It won't do you any good to cry. No one believes you."

Hauron jerked Anqet along as he hurried out of the palace. She noticed that he kept glancing back over his shoulder. Out in the main courtyard, he threw her into a chariot, took the reins from a groom, and charged out of the palace grounds. There followed a mad dash through the streets of Thebes. Anqet could perceive no pattern to

Hauron's frenzied wanderings. He stopped once to bind
her hands in front of her.

Anqet howled tearfully, but Hauron slapped her twice
and finished the job She watched him look back the way
they had come, as if he expected to see something. The
long shadows of early evening were all that Anqet saw.
They were all she expected to see. Could her uncle
suspect that Seth was following them? From first-hand
experience, Anqet was aware of her lover's ability to stalk
an enemy. She attributed Hauron's uneasiness to the man's
cautious nature.

After another series of dashes through various en-
claves in the city, Anqet noticed that Hauron had slowed
his pace. He walked the horses through a section of town
where Anqet had never been. Light was fading, and she
was growing uneasy, for Anqet recognized the character of
the area they had entered. Short, muscular men with
oiled hair and beards, the scent of foreign spices and
herbs, the staccato patter of Babylonian. A foreign quarter.

In striped skirts of blue and yellow, a merchant
paused at the door of a tavern. His shoes were pointed and
curled at the toes. He yelled at someone inside. Raucous
laughter was the response. Anqet grew nervous, even
though she knew there was no reason to be frightened.
Seth was nearby. He watched them, ready to attack Hauron
the moment the man tried to hurt her. Anxiety curdled
through her stomach. Hauron stopped at the tavern where
the merchant had yelled. He muscled Anqet past the
Babylonian and into the establishment.

The air in the room was thick with incense, body
odor, and stale beer. Black forms jostled by them in the
dark, crowded space. Anqet took one look at the patrons
and jumped for the door. Hauron caught her by the hair
and yanked her back. He grasped her bonds and dragged
her behind him. They weaved through the chairs and
cushions, passing men slumped over stools or wallowing in
pools of liquor. Throughout the lower floor of the tavern
moved naked young women who served drinks, laughed,
and teased customers. Anqet's gaze slid away from a

corner where several men crowded around a girl, hands and bodies moving in an obvious rhythm.

Hauron stopped to speak to the owner of the tavern. Anqet's eyes burned from the heavy incense. She looked past him into another room. Children. Nude, painted children. A fat Egyptian went into the room and returned, leading a boy who couldn't have been more than ten. The child yawned through reddened lips. The fat man picked him up and disappeared up the stairs to the second floor. Anqet felt ill.

She prayed silently. *Holy Isis, strike these people dead for their abominations. Send them to the Boiling Lake, or let me do it for you, somehow.*

Hauron pulled her toward the stairs. On the second floor there was a hall with twelve closed doors. They went by three. From behind the fourth came a child's sleepy voice. Anqet heard the voice cry out. She stopped, but Hauron pulled her into a room farther down the hall and slammed the door shut.

Anqet faced her uncle. Hauron let his eyes roam over her.

"I knew I'd find you," he said. "I wanted revenge too badly not to find you. You're going to pay for what you did, and for what your mother did."

"We didn't do anything to you," Anqet said. She kept her eyes on Hauron and listened for Seth. He should be right outside the door.

"You both refused me. I'll have revenge for that. You nearly emasculated me. But don't worry, I'm fit to service you, and I will. I'll have you over and over until you beg for mercy." Hauron took up a wine goblet that lay ready on a tray and gulped down its contents. He refilled it and consumed the whole again.

As she watched him, Anqet's fear grew. The wine would peel away the fragile skin of the man and leave her at the mercy of a fiend. As if he knew her thoughts, Hauron spread his lips in a wine-dampened leer.

"I was going to wait until I got you away from Thebes,

but laying hands on you has made waiting impossible. What are you looking at?"

"Nothing."

"You think your warrior count will come for you?" Hauron put the goblet back on the tray. "It gives me much satisfaction to tell you that Count Seth has been detained."

Anqet's wits fled. Terror washed through her.

"What do you mean?"

"I'm not as stupid as you seem to think," Hauron said. "Someone warned me that Count Seth would take you from me by force, so I arranged an accident." Hauron chuckled, then shouted at her. "He's dead! I've had your young stallion killed. His corpse should be floating in the river about now."

Anqet's rage took Hauron by surprise. She gave a demon's howl and sprang at the man before he could react, her nails clawing at his eyes. Deep bloody furrows appeared on his cheeks and neck. Wrath gave her the strength to pound the man's stomach hard enough to make him double over. She leapt for the door, but Hauron stuck his foot out and tripped her.

Still gasping from her blow, he was on top of Anqet before she could get up. He slapped her. Anqet cried out and threw up her bound hands. Hauron dragged them away and hit her again and again with his open hand until she lay barely conscious.

Blood trickled from her mouth. Hauron propped her up. Something pressed to her lips. Wine flowed into her mouth, wine laced with something that made her lips and tongue numb. She sputtered and turned her head away, but Hauron forced the liquid down her throat. Anqet gulped it down by reflex. She opened her eyes. Hauron held her. His face was near, and it spun in circles. As darkness overtook her, she heard Lord Hauron chuckle.

"Ah, my fiery niece, what a marvelous whore you will make."

13

He was tangled in a spider's web. Thrashing his arms
and legs, Seth tried to escape the strands that held him.
Pain burst through his skull, so he stopped fighting. He
opened his eyes but shut them again because there was a
small sun in front of his face. Instead, he concentrated on
the spider web. Seth stretched his fingers. They clasped
taut leather bands that stretched from bonds around his
wrists to stakes driven into the ground. Since his legs
were also spread and immobile, he assumed they too were
tied down.

The pain in his head subsided a little. What had
happened? He and Dega had been tracking Anqet and
that piece of offal, Hauron. In spite of the adze pounding
in his skull, Seth forced himself to recall that secret chase.
The man almost lost him twice in crowded streets. Seth
took a back street to catch up, and then barreled down the
Road of Libyan Captives. They approached an intersection. Dega pointed to a chariot as it disappeared around a
corner farther up the road. Seth whipped his team into a
gallop. Donkeys shuffled into his path from an alley,
braying in fright. Seth hauled at the reins. His team
reared and spun on their back hooves. He and Dega flew
out of the chariot. His head plowed itself through the
earth. Five pairs of feet surrounded him. Seth remembered
a voice. It rasped out an order as Seth started to get up. A
club descended on his head, and here he was. He had no
idea what had happened to Dega.

Stupid, Seth said to himself. *Uncle Hauron made*

plans for you. You misjudged his cleverness as you did Anqet's.

Anqet! Anqet was in Hauron's grasp, and he had put her there. Seth tugged at his bonds. They only tightened. He risked opening his eyes again. The small sun turned out to be a translucent alabaster lamp on the floor near his head. It was the only light in the room. Again he strained at the lashes that held him. He sank back on the ground, as secure as before.

How long had he been here? There were no windows through which to judge the time. Seeking to quell his apprehension about Anqet's safety, he looked around his prison. He was in a room bare of furniture, yet well finished with plaster and paintings on the wall. Seth lifted his head. That frieze of papyrus clumps and herons—he'd seen that design before.

A door opened and closed behind Seth's head. Someone walked in and paused. There was a thud, like something being dropped, then footsteps. Even before his jailer came into view, the heavy, spiced perfume that wafted toward him announced her identity. He watched Gasantra come to kneel beside him. She wore only a filmy open drape and from one hand dangled an amulet in the form of the sacred eye of Horus. She carried a small vial in the other.

Gasantra crouched beside Seth and set the vial on the floor. "My men assured me you would be well."

Gasantra stroked his face. Seth jerked his head free of the woman's touch.

"Release me, Gasantra."

Gasantra shook her head. "There's something I have to do first, and anyway, I'm not letting you go until I'm sure that witch is far away from us."

Seth tried to pounce on Gasantra and fell back. "What have you done with her? Where is she? If she's hurt, I'll strangle you. I swear it. Where's Dega?"

"Shhh."

Seth tried again to toss off the hand that caressed his forehead. Gasantra held up the eye of Horus. Of white-

and-blue enamel, it was suspended from a gold chain. Gasantra clasped the object and recited obscure words.

His voice loud in the empty room, Seth cursed at the woman and asked, "What are you muttering about?"

"I'm going to break her power over you," Gasantra said. She resumed her chant.

"I love her, you goat."

Gasantra gave him a pitying look. "No, my sweet lord, you don't. I finally discovered why you've been acting so cruelly. She has bewitched you. I consulted a magician priest, and he agreed. He gave me this amulet. It was expensive, but he assured me that if I perform the spell correctly, you will love me again."

"I never loved you. Let me go."

Time was passing quickly. He had to get free.

"Gasantra—beautiful, sweet Gasantra, please release me. I promise I'll do anything you want. Only cut these straps."

Gasantra laughed at him. "Oh no. Not until I've performed the spell."

"This is ridiculous. Ugh!"

Seth choked on the noxious liquid Gasantra poured into his mouth without warning. He coughed and twisted his head away, but the woman forced the vial past his lips and pinched his nose so he couldn't keep his mouth closed. She followed the dose with a cup of water obtained somewhere beyond his view. Seth drank deeply and swore at her. Above him, Gasantra's face blurred, and darkness closed around him. Moments passed during which he could do nothing but listen to his own panting.

A liquid heat began to churn through his arms and legs. It spread to his loins and stayed there, roiling. Seth's eyes widened. Perspiration beaded his forehead. He could feel his genitals tingle. Unwanted stimulation made him pant, and he strained at his bonds in an effort to escape his own arousal. Gasantra removed the falcon pectoral he was wearing and replaced it with the eye amulet. It lay cold on his chest.

From the oven his body had become, Seth struggled to keep hold of reality. He had to get free.

Gasantra crouched over him. She fumbled at his belt, chattering incantations all the while.

"What are you doing?"

The woman paused with her hands on his kilt. "I'm going to break her hold over you. This is part of the counterspell." Gasantra tugged at the cloth and threw it away.

Seth strained away from his tormentor. "No!"

Gasantra paid no attention. She made strange signs with her hands, then got up and retrieved a bottle from a darkened corner. She knelt between Seth's legs and poured oil on his burning flesh.

"I will kill you." Seth jammed his teeth together as the cool oil ran over his penis.

He gasped. Gasantra's slick hands stroked him. Waves of unwanted pleasure traveled through his body. Desperately, Seth tried to think of escape while Gasantra teased him. Against his will, his hips flexed, and he drove himself back and forth between her hands.

Gasantra was insane. He would kill her. To kill her, he had to be free. He had to get free. Anqet needed him. Anqet.

Seth moaned and let his body relax under Gasantra's accomplished hands. He thought of Anqet. He pictured her round night-black eyes, her full breasts. He dwelt on the long, long legs of the girl he loved and tried not to let his hatred of Gasantra overwhelm the passion he needed for his purpose. When Gasantra lowered herself to enclose his penis inside her flesh, he deliberately imagined Anqet's warm softness. Feigning ensorcelled submission, he drove his tongue into the mouth of the woman on top of him. She pumped at him. He gave a massive thrust. Gasantra shouted and collapsed on top of him. Seth felt his own release pulse through his imprisoned phallus as his body arched upward. He let his arms and legs relax and went limp.

Gasantra lifted herself; she patted his face. "Seth? What's wrong? Seth?"

He waited a short time before he moaned and fluttered his eyes open. He spoke in a weak whisper.

"Gasantra?"

The woman examined him anxiously. Seth widened his eyes as if bewildered.

"Gasantra? My love? Why do I feel so odd?"

Gasantra gave a triumphant laugh. "Oh Seth, it worked. You're free of Anqet."

"Anqet?" Seth let his tone become querulous. "Who's Anqet? Why am I tied down like this? I feel so tired." Seth drew in his breath as Gasantra pulled free of him. He looked up at the woman and did his best to simulate innocence and trust.

"Are you truly cured, my love?" Gasantra asked.

"Have I been sick? I must have a fever. I'm so hot. I'm burning alive." Seth moved his head from side to side, his eyes closed. Tousled hair fell over his face. "Help me."

"Don't be afraid."

He watched her retrieve a knife from the shadows and begin to cut his bonds.

Gasantra crooned to him. "Don't worry. It's only a potion."

Seth let her cut his ankles free. He lurched to a sitting position and eyed the knife in Gasantra's hand. The woman was fool enough to come close. She set the knife down and kissed him. She rubbed her hand over his bare thigh. Her nails scraped his damp skin and sped up toward his groin. Seth submitted to the caress while he grasped for the knife. He found it in time to keep Gasantra from pulling him on top of her. He grabbed her by the neck and rested the knife below her left eye. He spoke sweetly and softly.

"Tell me where Hauron has taken Anqet, or I will peel your eyeballs out of your head."

"You tricked me!"

Gasantra squirmed and spat at him.

"You missed," Seth said. He pressed the point of the

knife into Gasantra's skin, but stopped before it broke the surface. Gasantra squawked.

"They're at the Inn of the Silver Fish!"

Seth hurled the woman from him. "He took her to that cavern of obscenity?" He grabbed up his kilt and dressed hastily. "What about Dega? Quickly, or I'll beat it out of you."

Gasantra cowered against the wall. "Gone. Escaped. I don't know where."

Seth found his dagger on a table. He thrust it into his belt and pointed a finger at Gasantra.

"Run. Find a mudhole and bury yourself in it, for if Anqet is harmed, I'll come back for you. You'll die slowly by my own hand."

Seth jerked his belt tight, made for the door, and opened it cautiously. Men rushed past. He ducked back inside until they were gone. He heard metal sing. A yell ended on a gurgle. Seth glanced back at Gasantra's groveling figure and eased out into the hall. One of the woman's hired thugs came racing at him from the direction of the noise. He saw Seth and raised a scimitar but stopped in midstride with a startled "*Uuuuugh.*" Seth hopped out of the way as the man fell on his face before him with a spear in his back. Seth stepped over the body to meet the spearman.

"Dega, my tranquil killer, you've saved me a fight."

Seth clapped his equerry on the back. Dega grinned and wiped the blood from a cut on his forehead.

"I followed you here, then went for help," Dega said as they rushed from the house. "I think we'll need your personal troop for this task after all, my lord."

Hopping aboard his chariot, Seth nodded agreement. "Where we're going, we'll need every warrior."

In the middle of the chamber at the Inn of the Silver Fish, Anqet sat on the floor. She rested elbows on knees and cradled her head in her hands. She'd been sick on one of Hauron's costly robes. With shaking hands, she made a quick examination of her body. She was unhurt, except for a few bruises, and untouched. Anqet looked at her hands and realized for the first time that they were unbound. What had prevented her molestation?

An exclamation came from behind a half-closed door to her right. She heard her uncle's voice.

"What do you mean he's still alive? You let a woman stop you? Go back and finish the work you were assigned." There was a rumble of protest. "I don't care if he's dangerous. Take as many men as you need. Find him, and kill him. Make it look like an accident. Go."

Seth was alive! Thank the gods. But he was in trouble, and he didn't know where she was. It was up to her to escape.

The room was equipped with a washbowl and waterjar. Anqet made sure Hauron was still talking. She crept to the bowl and poured out enough water to make the jar easy to lift. She drank from it as well, to cleanse her mouth. On the same table lay the remains of a meal. She stuffed a slice of melon in her mouth in an effort to settle her stomach.

Anqet tiptoed over to the side door, the waterjar in her hands. Hauron was still talking with the guards. She dashed quietly to the main entrance and cracked the door open. A man stood guard outside. She closed the door and returned to the other exit. Hauron was coming. She flattened herself on the wall beside the door and raised the jar over her head. Lord Hauron bustled past. Anqet brought the jar down, but he turned, saw her, and ducked out of the way. The jar shattered on the floor.

Hauron charged for her. Anqet sprang out the side door, slammed it closed, and dropped a bar into place. She raced to another door, but Hauron had anticipated her and leapt for her, tackling her. Anqet bit fiercely at his neck. Hauron screamed and flung her away. She landed on her feet and raced out of the chamber. In the hall she met the startled guard. Anqet spun in the opposite direction and fled.

At the stairs, she looked down on pandemonium. Chairs and tables sailed in the air. Naked women and children screamed and cowered against the walls. A man saw Anqet and came toward her. She fled back the way she'd come, only to meet Hauron running down the hall. Anqet ducked into the nearest room and barred the door. Hauron pounded at it. She looked for another way out. There was none.

"What's going on?" asked a sleepy voice.

Anqet spotted a mound of pale, flaccid skin on a pallet—the fat Egyptian.

"Lovely," the man said. He tried to get up but was hampered by his own corpulence.

Anqet walked over to a washstand, grasped the water jar, and cracked it over the man's head. He fell back, drenched and unconscious. A squeak came from beneath the flab. Anqet fished under it and pulled out the boy she had seen earlier.

"I'm sorry, little one," Anqet said. "I didn't know you were there."

While Hauron battered at the door, she took the child's hand. Hair disheveled, facepaint smudged, he planted small feet in the customer's belly and hopped to the floor. He came to her willingly, making no sound. The bar at the door splintered, and Hauron burst in. Behind him Anqet could see men fighting—royal troops and Hauron's thugs. Hauron was bleeding from a cut on his lip. The marks from her teeth and nails decorated his body. He bore a dagger and glared with a hate so violent that it erased all humanity from his eyes.

Anqet edged farther away with the boy at her back. Hauron came toward her slowly. Anqet looked around, frantic for a weapon. At her feet lay a potsherd from the broken water jar. Triangular and concave it had a jagged point. She grabbed the shard. Hauron was almost upon her. She wedged the boy securely between her body and the wall. She felt his hands grasp her skirt.

Hauron licked blood from his lip. "I'll have my revenge before I escape your lover."

"Anqet!" Seth's bellow reached them from below.

Anqet screamed back. "Seth!"

Hauron waved the dagger at her. Anqet blocked the attack with one arm and stabbed Hauron's throat with the pointed end of the shard. It sank into flesh and broke. Hauron snarled and backed away long enough to remove the point from his throat.

Anqet dropped the useless fragment. She'd missed hitting a vein. She shoved the boy more securely behind her as Hauron charged, roaring, the dagger poised for a deathstroke. Anqet braced her legs to kick at the man. She knew he would kill her this time.

The dagger came down at her. She kicked. Hauron moaned, then went still. The dagger fell from his hand as Anqet's uncle sank to the floor. Someone flew at her, and she was swept off her feet and crushed in Seth's arms. Outside, the sounds of battle quieted. Seth squeezed her and whispered endearments.

"I'm fine," she said. "Not hurt at all. N-not at all." Anqet burrowed her face into the count's neck.

"I never thought a few moments could age me like this," said Seth. "Fear has given me two hundred years." He rocked Anqet back and forth. He held still. "By all the gods."

Anqet looked up. Seth was staring over the bodies of the fat man and Hauron at the boy who stood against the wall. The child stared back at them, eyes wide and streaked with green paint.

"Put me down," Anqet said.

"No."

"I'm fine, Seth. The child needs me."

Seth called for Dega. The warrior appeared and took charge of the boy. He cajoled the child with gentle words, and the two left, hand in hand.

"This is a horrible place," Anqet said as she watched the child.

The count crushed her to him once more. "I know, beloved, but it won't be anymore. I have an excuse to raze this place; I'll see to it. Are you sure he didn't hurt you?"

Anqet looked down at Hauron's body. "He was going to, but he was interrupted. Oh Seth, let's go home."

Refusing to let her walk, Seth carried Anqet from the room that held her uncle's corpse.

It amused Anqet that her self-possessed count was as jittery as a maid at her first festival. After all, the signing of the marriage contract had been relatively private, as private as it could be with the Son of the Sun as chief witness. Admittedly, Ipet-esut, the temple of Amun-Ra, was an overwhelmingly grandiose place for such a ceremony, but she thought Seth would have relaxed once they reached the king's private chambers. Instead, he lurked at her side, exotic and desirable in gold and lapis lazuli, and fingered his gold dagger.

They had a moment alone while the high priest of Amun-Ra made his formal obeisance to the king.

"My love," Anqet said. "I haven't changed just because our names are written together in the House of Life." Anqet smoothed back an auburn curl and whispered in Seth's ear. "If we quarrel, I can divorce you, you know. But I don't think I'll be able to because I want you every time I look at you."

Seth turned his head. His gaze touched her lips and throat with green flames, then settled on her eyes.

"I'm no longer so worried about our marriage."

"Then why are you acting as if you expected a bandit attack?"

"I don't know." Seth tugged at his massive broad collar. "I keep expecting someone to hop out and try to take you away from me again."

"Why?"

Seth waved away a servant carrying a wine flagon.

"Think about it," he said. "Since we met you've slipped my grasp five or six times. My only hope is that marriage will act as glue and stick you to my side." Seth clenched his hand around the pommel of the dagger. "Until we signed the marriage agreement, I was even afraid Pharaoh would interfere."

Anqet smiled at Seth's stepmother as the woman passed by on her way to greet General Horemheb.

"You're not serious. The king doesn't want me. He was only trying to get you to realize what you wanted."

"I know, but—"

"Compose yourself. We must accept the good wishes of our friends."

Anqet moved with Seth among the people gathered in the royal dining chamber. She surveyed the guests and noted that General Horemheb was gesticulating wildly at Vizier Ay in front of a table laden with gold plates and wineflasks. Countess Ta-usert stood beside Lord Dega and ogled the young warrior. Anqet could see the woman's mouth form the word "amazing." Dega gave her a perplexed smile and offered a wine goblet. Rennut pattered across the room, grasped Khet, and steered the boy away from a pile of spiced and honeyed shat cakes. Khet wriggled away from his stepmother.

Anqet grinned as she saw Prince Khai and Dega both rescue the boy. At her suggestion, Khet would be in Dega's charge while she and the count spent a few days alone. Dega's peaceful authority would give the high-strung, mischievous Khet an anchor when Seth had to leave his brother. Seth returned to Anqet from his greeting of the high priest of Amun-Ra.

"Uni came to me," he said. "The galley is ready to sail for Nefer. We need only escape our friends." Seth cast a glance at a group of his warrior officers. "You're sure Nefer is far enough away?"

"Yes," Anqet said.

"We could go to Kush."

Seth's voice trailed away. Anqet looked in the direction of his gaze. Tutankhamun was still in quiet conversation with the high priest, who resembled a starving leopard in his animals skins and long kilt. The first servant of the god laid a wrinkled hand on the king's arm and muttered at the youth. Anqet watched Tutankhamun's nostrils flare. His black eyes widened and then went blank.

"Trouble," Anqet said.

Seth nodded. "After I told His Majesty of the high

priest's part in the desecration, it took all my influence to persuade him not to kill the old lecher. Let's go before Pharaoh feeds the high priest to his new lion cub." Seth took Anqet's hand, and they scooted toward the door.

"Seth."

General Horemheb's voice made Anqet jump. Seth groaned and turned back to his commander.

"Seth, how long did you say you'd be gone? Dear Countess, you are a vision fit for the gods. Seth, fifty Libyan prisoners escaped yesterday before they could be sent to the gold mines. I need a squadron to help chase them. And we need to talk about several new problems. The king's majesty is worried because the Hittite king is threatening Pharaoh's North Syrian vassals again, and we've also gotten word of an influx of refugees fleeing Bedouin raiders on the northeastern frontier."

Horemheb paused for breath, but not long enough for Anqet or Seth to say anything before he charged on with his list.

"And the king of Babylon is worried that his Assyrian vassals are snuggling up to Pharaoh while they plan a revolt. They are. Seth, you've been remiss these past weeks. We must speak of these happenings and take council with Pharaoh."

"My general, the king has spoken to me of these things. Pharaoh says Anqet and I have time before he needs us back in Thebes."

"I don't agree," Horemheb said.

Anqet could see herself sailing to Nefer alone. She slipped her arm around Seth's waist and pressed her body close to his. At once, Seth shook his head at the general. Horemheb grumbled at them.

"Don't pester my former concubine, general."

Pharaoh joined Anqet and Seth, and gave Horemheb a nod of dismissal. He pressed three fingers to his temple and smiled ruefully at Anqet.

"Lady, you must teach my body servant to get rid of headaches."

"I will, Majesty," Anqet said with a smile.

Tutankhamun beamed at them. "I've come to give you escort. You won't get away from Thebes without me to interfere with Horemheb, and Ay, and Rennut. I forbade your stepmother to join you on the galley. You are in my debt."

"The living god is a beneficent protector," Seth said as he bowed to the king.

Anqet nodded. Tutankhamun walked them to his own private door that led to a concealed exit from the palace. No one stopped them, not even the high priest of Amun-Ra. The old man aimed a look of malevolence at Seth and Anqet as they passed. When Tutankhamun pushed the door open, revealing a sentry, Seth closed it again. He glared in the direction of the retreating high priest.

"Majesty, you will be cautious?"

Tutankhamun sighed and played with a scarab bracelet on his wrist. "He and that pack of greedy temple bureaucrats were behind it all. Don't worry. I'm not a fool. I know the priesthood of Amun-Ra is too powerful for me to oppose openly. I want revenge, but not at the cost of civil war."

Seth nodded his approval.

"We'll speak of the ways of revenge when you return."

"Thy will is mine, Golden One."

The king and Seth looked at each other without speaking, and Anqet was suddenly glad she wasn't the high priest of Amun-Ra. She stirred uneasily, for the king transferred his attention to her.

"I envy you," the king said to the count. "You will have privacy and love. I rule the Two Lands, and I can have neither."

Those words, and the king's young, brooding face, made Anqet brave. "Divine Majesty, at my house you will always find both."

Seth smiled his concurrence. Anqet was rewarded with a brief glimpse of the king's surprise and unfettered joy before the living-god mask of gravity dropped into place.

"I think Seth has found a woman unsurpassed. Per-

haps in a few weeks I shall come to your haven of privacy
and love."

They slipped out the door while the king stood guard.
Seth grabbed Anqet's hand. She lifted her skirts and
dashed down the corridor with him. It led to an enclosed
courtyard. Seth sent a guard for their chariot, then took
advantage of their isolation.

"Little singer." Seth wedged her between his body
and a pillar and tried to swallow her mouth.

Anqet grinned beneath his lips. She slipped her
hands inside his robe to stroke his ribs. She felt his
erection prod at her thigh. Seth moved back from her and
glanced down at his hips.

"I hate waiting," he said.

Anqet pulled her robe back into place across her
breasts. "Cultivate patience. I've had to wait to go home
for months."

"By Pharaoh's mercy, I forgot my wedding gift."

"You've given me enough jewels to fill Pharaoh's
treasury."

Seth tapped her nose with his forefinger. "This is a
special gift. I sent my best squadron to Nefer. Thanasa,
son of Thuty-hotpe, and his band of leeches have fled your
home. Bastis will be there to greet us when we arrive—
and Nebre."

"Seth-Seth-Seth-Seth!"

Anqet threw herself into his arms. He spun around
with Anqet hanging from his neck, set her on her feet,
and grinned down at her. Anqet glanced over her shoulder. The gate to the outside was opening to reveal their
chariot.

"My love," she said.

"Yes, enticing wife."

"Before we leave Thebes, I must ask. What had the
king to say about Sennefer's burial?"

She expected tension and grief. She saw resigned
sadness and peace.

"At first he wanted to destroy my brother's ka. He
ordered it done, but—I don't know—he looked at me after

he said the words, and changed the order." Seth shook his head. "Osiris has given the Golden One unsurpassed mercy. Pharaoh decreed that Sennefer should lie at Annu-Rest. I will put him beneath the chapel."

"And Merab?"

"Vanished. Dega thinks he's fled to the land of the Hittites or to Babylon."

Anqet took Seth's hand. Noting the predatory look on his face, she pulled him toward the gate. "I suppose we could start at Annu-Rest and follow the trail of coconut to our wily Lord Merab."

Seth shook his head again.

"The only trail I intend to follow is the one that leads to your bed."

That night, Anqet lay with Seth in the cabin of the galley. She nestled in the count's arms and ran her hand along the burnished surface of a muscle in Seth's arm. The count opened his eyes.

"So, beloved, you go home at last."

"Bringing a mate with me," Anqet said. She smiled into Seth's water-green eyes. "When I first fled to Thebes, I wanted nothing more than to rid myself of Hauron and return to my ordered and predictable life, yet after all that has happened, I think staying at Nefer all my life would be boring. I was so young."

Seth nodded. He traced a line across her forehead. "And now you are old, aged, wrinkled. Ouch!"

They wrestled until Anqet toppled them to the floor. Seth twisted away from her. As she sat looking up at him, he moved back to the bed. Golden lamplight caressed sleek, strong legs and a bare abdomen. Seth stood before Anqet. He lifted his arms, beckoning, and chanted to her.

> *Come through the garden, Love, to me.*
> *My love is like each flower that blows;*
> *Tall and straight as a young palm tree,*
> *And in each cheek a sweet blush-rose.*

About the Author

SUZANNE ROBINSON has a doctoral degree in anthropology with a specialty in ancient Middle Eastern archaeology. She has now turned her attention to the creation of the fascinating fictional characters in her unforgettable historical romances.

Suzanne lives in San Antonio with her husband and her two English springer spaniels. She divides her time between writing historical romance and mystery under her first name, Lynda.

Printed in the United States
by Baker & Taylor Publisher Services